*Inspector Maigret
Omnibus 2*

GEORGES SIMENON

*Inspector Maigret
Omnibus 2*

PENGUIN BOOKS

PENGUIN CLASSICS

UK | USA | Canada | Ireland | Australia
India | New Zealand | South Africa

Penguin Books is part of the Penguin Random House group of companies whose addresses can be found at global.penguinrandomhouse.com.

The Saint-Fiacre Affair first published as *La Mese de Saint-Fiacre* by Fayard 1932
This translation first published in Penguin Classics 2014
The Misty Harbour first published as *Le port des brumes* by Fayard 1932
This translation first published in Penguin Classics 2015
Maigret first published, in instalments, in *Le Jour* from 20 February to 15 March 1934
This translation first published in Penguin Classics 2015
The Judge's House first published as *La Maison du juge* by Éditions Gallimard 1942
This translation first published in Penguin Classics 2015
This selection first published in Penguin Classics 2015
001

Copyright 1932, 1934 and 1942 by Georges Simenon Limited
Translation of *The Saint-Fiacre Affair* copyright © Shaun Whiteside, 2014
Translation of *The Misty Harbour* copyright © Linda Coverdale, 2015
Translation of *Maigret* copyright © Ros Schwartz, 2015
Translation of *The Judge's House* copyright © Howard Curtis, 2015
GEORGES SIMENON ® Simenon.tm
MAIGRET ® Georges Simenon Limited
All rights reserved

The moral rights of the author and the translators have been asserted

Set in 13 / 15.5pt
Typeset in Dante MT Std by Palimpsest Book Production Ltd, Falkirk, Stirlingshire
Printed in Great Britain by Clays Ltd, St Ives plc

A CIP catalogue record for this book is available from the British Library

ISBN: 978–0–241–24135–6

www.greenpenguin.co.uk

Penguin Random House is committed to a sustainable future for our business, our readers and our planet. This book is made from Forest Stewardship Council® certified paper.

Contents

The Saint-Fiacre Affair   1
The Misty Harbour   127
Maigret   285
The Judge's House   403

The Saint-Fiacre Affair

Translated by SHAUN WHITESIDE

HUG BLOCK

L'AFFAIRE SAINT-FIACRE

ROMAN
PAR
GEORGES SIMENON

A. FAYARD & Cⁱᵉ - PARIS   PRIX 6 FR.

1. The Little Cross-Eyed Girl

A timid knock at the door; the sound of something being set down on the floor; a furtive voice:

'It's half past five! The first bell has just rung for mass . . .'

Maigret propped himself on his elbows, and as he looked in amazement at the skylight that pierced the sloping roof the voice continued:

'Are you taking communion?'

Detective Chief Inspector Maigret was standing up now, barefoot on the freezing floor. He walked towards the door, held shut with a piece of string rolled around two nails. There was the sound of scurrying footsteps, and when he looked into the corridor he caught a glimpse of a woman in a camisole and a white skirt.

Then he picked up the jug of hot water that Marie Tatin had left him, closed his door and looked around for a mirror to shave in.

The candle only had a few minutes left to live. Outside the skylight it was still pitch dark, a cold night in early winter. A few dead leaves still clung to the branches of the poplars in the main square.

Because of the double slope of the ceiling, Maigret could only stand upright in the middle of the attic room. He was cold. All night a draught whose source he had not been able to identify had left him with a chill on the back of his neck.

But precisely that quality of cold unsettled him, plunging him into a mood that he thought was forgotten.

The first bell for mass . . . Chimes over the sleeping village . . . When he was a little boy, Maigret hadn't got up so early.

He used to wait for the second chime, at a quarter to six, because in those days he didn't need to shave. Had he only washed his face?

No one brought any hot water in those days. Sometimes the water was frozen in the jug. A little while later his shoes would echo on the metalled road.

Now, as he got dressed, he heard Marie Tatin coming and going in the front of the inn, shaking the grate of the stove, clattering the dishes, turning the coffee mill.

He put on his jacket and his coat. Before going out he took from his briefcase a piece of paper with an official label attached:

> Municipal Police of Moulins.
> Issued for any eventuality to the Police Judiciaire, Paris.

Then a squared sheet. Meticulous handwriting:

> I wish to inform you that a crime will be committed at the church of Saint-Fiacre during first mass on All Souls' Day.

The piece of paper had been hanging around the offices of the Quai des Orfèvres for several days. Maigret had noticed it by chance and been taken aback.

'Saint-Fiacre, near Matignon?'

'Probably, because it reached us via Moulins.'

And Maigret had put the paper in his pocket. Saint-Fiacre! Matignon! Moulins! Words more familiar to him than any others.

Saint-Fiacre was the place of his birth, where his father had been estate manager of the chateau for thirty years! The last time he had gone there had been, in fact, after the death of his father, who had been buried in the little cemetery, behind the church.

A crime will be committed . . . during first mass . . .

Maigret had arrived the previous day. He had put up at the only inn, the one that belonged to Marie Tatin.

She hadn't recognized him, but he had recognized her, from her eyes. The little cross-eyed girl, as she had been called back then. A skinny little girl who had become an even thinner old maid with an even worse squint, moving endlessly around in the front room, in the kitchen, in the farmyard where she raised rabbits and chickens.

The inspector went down the stairs. At the bottom, the inn was lit by paraffin lights. The table was laid in a corner. Some coarse grey bread. A smell of chicory coffee, boiling milk.

'You're wrong not to take communion on a day like today! Especially when you take the trouble to go to the first mass . . . Heavens! There's the second peal!'

The bells rang out faintly. There was a sound of footsteps in the road. Marie Tatin fled to her kitchen to put on her black dress, her lace gloves, the little hat which refused to sit straight on her bun.

'I'll let you finish eating. Will you lock the door behind you?'

'No need! I'm ready.'

How confused she was to find herself walking along the road with a man. A man who had come from Paris! She took tiny steps, leaning forwards in the cold morning. Dead leaves somersaulted on the ground. Their dry rustle suggested frost in the night.

Other shadows converged towards the faint light from the church door. The bells were still ringing. There were some lights in the windows of the single-storey houses: people hastily getting dressed for first mass.

And Maigret savoured the sensations of his youth again: the cold, stinging eyes, frozen fingertips, an aftertaste of coffee. Then, stepping inside the church, a blast of heat, soft light; the smell of candles and incense . . .

'Please excuse me. I've got my prie-dieu,' said his companion.

And Maigret recognized the black chair with the red velvet arm-rest, the one that had belonged to old Tatin, the cross-eyed girl's mother.

The rope that the bell-ringer had pulled a few moments before still quivered at the end of the church. The sacristan had just finished lighting the candles.

How many were they, in this ghostly gathering of bleary-eyed people? Fifteen at most. There were only three men: the sexton, the bell-ringer and Maigret.

. . . a crime will be committed . . .

In Moulins, the police had assumed it was a bad joke and hadn't been concerned about it. In Paris, they'd been amazed when the inspector followed it up.

He heard a noise coming from the door to the right of the altar and could guess, second by second, what was going on: the sacristy, the tardy altar boy, the priest silently putting on his chasuble, placing his hands together in prayer, heading towards the nave, followed by the little boy tottering in his robe.

The little boy had red hair. He rang the bell. The murmur of liturgical prayers began.

. . . during first mass . . .

Maigret had looked at all the shadows, one by one. Five old women, three with their own reserved prie-dieu. A fat farmer's wife. Some younger village girls and a child . . .

The noise of a car, outside. The creak of a door. Small, light steps and a woman in mourning dress walking all the way across the church.

In the chancel there was a row reserved for the people from the chateau: hard pews of polished old wood. And it was there that the woman sat down, without a sound, followed by the eyes of the village women.

'Requiem aeternam dona eis, Domine . . .'

Maigret could still have given the response. He smiled at the thought that he had once preferred requiem masses to the others, because the prayers are shorter. He could remember masses lasting only sixteen minutes!

But already his eyes were fixed on the occupant of the gothic pew. He could barely see her profile. He didn't at first recognize the Countess of Saint-Fiacre.

'*Dies irae, dies illa* . . .'

But it was, it was her! The last time he had seen her she had been twenty-five or twenty-six. She was a tall, thin, melancholic woman, only ever seen from a distance in the grounds of the chateau.

And now she must have been at least sixty. She prayed ardently. Her face was emaciated, her hands too long, too refined, clutching a rosary.

Maigret had stayed in the back row of straw chairs, the ones that cost five centimes at high mass but are free at low mass.

. . . a crime will be committed . . .

He stood up with the others for the first reading from the Gospel. Details crowded in from all directions, and memories flooded over him. He suddenly found himself thinking:

'On All Souls' Day, the same priest celebrates three masses . . .'

Back in his day, he had had lunch at the priest's house, between the second and the third. A boiled egg and goat's cheese!

The Moulins police were right after all. There could be no crime! The sacristan had taken his seat at the end of the pew, four seats away from the countess. The bell-ringer had walked flat-footedly away, like a theatre director who doesn't care to watch his play.

The only men left were Maigret and the priest, a young man with the passionate gaze of a mystic. He was in no hurry, unlike the old priest that the inspector had known. He didn't leave out half the verses.

The stained-glass windows paled. Day was breaking outside. A cow lowed in a farm.

And soon everyone bowed their heads for the Elevation of the Host. The altar boy's shrill bell rang out.

Maigret was the only one not to take communion. All the women stepped towards the communion rail, hands clasped, faces closed. The hosts had a pale, almost unreal gleam as the priest held them momentarily in his hand.

The service continued. The countess held her face in her hands.

'Pater Noster . . . Et ne nos inducas in tentationem . . .'

The old lady parted her fingers, revealing her tormented face, and opened her missal.

Four minutes to go! The prayers. The last reading. And that would be it. And there would have been no crime!

Because the warning said: *first mass* . . .

The proof that it was over was the sexton rising to his feet and stepping inside the sacristy.

The Countess of Saint-Fiacre had put her head in her hands again. She didn't move. Most of the other old women were as motionless as she was.

'Ite missa est.' . . . 'The mass has been said.'

It was only then that Maigret realized how anxious he had been. It had only now caught up with him. He gave an involuntary sigh. He couldn't wait for the end of the last reading and was looking forward to breathing the fresh outside air, seeing people moving about, talking about this and that.

The old women woke up all at the same time. Feet moved on the cold blue tiles of the church. First one village girl headed for the exit, then another. The sacristan appeared with a snuffer, and a thread of blue smoke replaced the candle-flames.

Day had broken. A grey light entered the nave along with the cold air.

There were still three people. Two. A chair moved. Then the only one left was the countess, and Maigret's nerves tightened with impatience.

The sacristan, who had finished his task, looked at Madame de Saint-Fiacre. A look of hesitation flickered across his face. At the same time the inspector stepped forwards.

They were both quite close to her, startled by her stillness, trying to see the face hidden by the clasped hands.

Worried, Maigret touched her shoulder. And the body tilted, as if nothing had been holding it upright, then rolled to the ground and lay there inert.

The Countess of Saint-Fiacre was dead.

They had carried the body to the sacristy and laid it on three chairs set side by side. The sacristan had run to fetch the village doctor.

And Maigret forgot how uncanny his presence was. He took a few minutes to understand the suspicious question in the priest's ardent gaze.

'Who are you?' he asked at last. 'What brings . . .'

'Detective Chief Inspector Maigret, Police Judiciaire.'

He looked the priest in the face. He was a man of thirty-five, with features that were regular but so serious that they suggested the unshakeable faith of monks from another age.

He was deeply troubled. His voice less firm, he murmured, 'You don't mean that? . . .'

They had not yet dared to undress the countess. They had put a mirror to her lips, to no avail. They had listened to her heart, which had stopped beating.

'I see no wounds,' was all Maigret said in reply.

And he looked around him at this setting, not a detail of which had changed in thirty years. The cruets were in the same place and the chasuble ready for the next mass, and the altar boy's cassock and surplice.

The gloomy daylight, entering through an ogive window, diluted the rays from an oil lamp.

It was hot and cold at once. The priest was clearly gripped by terrible thoughts.

'But you're not trying to say that . . .'

What a drama! At first Maigret didn't understand. But memories from his childhood rose up like bubbles.

A church where a crime has been committed has to be reconsecrated by the bishop . . .

How could there have been a crime? There had been no gunshot! No one had gone near the countess. Throughout the whole of the mass, Maigret hadn't taken his eyes off her.

And no blood had been spilled; there was no apparent wound!

'The second mass is at seven o'clock, isn't it?'

It was a relief to hear the heavy tread of the doctor, a red-faced chap who was struck by the atmosphere and who looked at the inspector and the priest in turn.

'Dead?' he asked.

But he had no hesitation in undoing her bodice, while the priest averted his eyes. Heavy footsteps in the church. Then the peal rung by the bell-ringer. The first chime of the seven o'clock mass.

'All I see is an embolism that would have . . . I wasn't the countess's regular doctor; she preferred to be treated by a colleague in Moulins. But I was called to the chateau two or three times. Her heart was in very poor shape.'

The sacristy was very cramped. There was hardly enough room for the three men and the body. Two altar boys arrived, because there was mass at seven.

'Her car must be outside,' said Maigret. 'We'll have to have her taken home.'

And he still felt the priest's anxious eyes on him. Had he guessed something? Either way, while the sacristan, with the help of the driver, guided the body towards the car, he approached the inspector.

'Are you sure that . . . I still have two masses to say. It's All Souls' Day. My congregation is . . .'

Since the countess had died of an embolism, couldn't Maigret find it in himself to reassure the priest?

'You heard what the doctor said . . .'

'And yet you've come here today, to this very mass . . .'

Maigret tried to stay calm.

'A coincidence, Father . . . My father is buried in your cemetery.'

And he hurried towards the car, an old-model coupé. The chauffeur was turning the crank. The doctor didn't know what to do. There were a few people in the square who had no idea what was happening.

'Come with us . . .'

But the corpse took up all the room inside the car. Maigret and the doctor crammed themselves in beside the driver's seat.

'You look surprised by what I said,' murmured the doctor, who hadn't yet regained all his confidence. 'If you knew the situation you might understand . . . The countess . . .'

He fell silent, glancing at the black-liveried chauffeur, who was absently driving his car. They crossed the sloping square, bounded on one side by the church built on the incline, on the other by the Notre-Dame pond, which was a poisonous grey that morning.

Marie Tatin's inn was on the right, the first house in the village. On the left there was an avenue lined with oaks and, at the end, the dark mass of the chateau.

A uniform sky, cold as a skating-rink.

'You know this is going to cause a fuss . . . That's why the priest is pulling such a face . . .'

Dr Bouchardon was a peasant, and the son of peasants. He wore a brown hunting suit and high rubber boots.

'I was going duck-hunting in the ponds . . .'

'You don't go to mass?'

The doctor glanced at him.

'It didn't stop me being friends with the old priest . . . But this one . . .'

They entered the grounds. The details of the chateau could be seen now: the ground-floor windows obscured by shutters, the two corner towers, the only old parts of the building.

When the car parked near the steps, Maigret peered through

the barred basement windows and saw kitchens full of steam, and a fat woman busy plucking partridges.

The driver didn't know what to do and didn't dare open the doors of the car.

'Monsieur Jean isn't up yet . . .'

'Call anyone . . . Are there any other servants in the house? . . .'

Maigret was sniffling. It was really cold. He stood in the courtyard with the doctor, who started stuffing a pipe.

'Who is Monsieur Jean?'

Bouchardon shrugged and gave a strange smile.

'You'll see.'

'No, tell me, who is he?'

'A young man . . . A charming young man . . .'

'A relative?'

'If you like! . . . In his own way! . . . Well, why don't I get it out of the way . . . He's the countess's lover . . . officially, he's her secretary . . .'

And Maigret looked the doctor in the eye, remembering that they had been to school together. Only, no one recognized him. He was forty-two! He had put on some weight.

He knew the chateau better than anyone. Especially the servants' quarters. He had to take only a few steps to see the estate manager's house, his birthplace.

And perhaps it was the memories that troubled him so much! Especially the memory of the Countess of Saint-Fiacre as he had known her: a young woman who had personified, to the working-class little boy that he was, femininity, grace, nobility . . .

And she was dead! She had been pushed, like an inert object, into the car, and they had had to fold her legs. They hadn't even buttoned up her blouse, and white underwear contrasted with the black of her mourning dress!

. . . a crime will be committed . . .

But the doctor claimed that she had died of an embolism. What supernatural creature had predicted such a thing? And why alert the police?

In the chateau people were running about. Doors were opening and closing. A butler, not yet in full livery, half-opened the main door and hesitated to come any further. A man appeared behind him, in pyjamas, his hair tousled and his eyes weary.

'What is it?' he shouted.

'The gigolo!' the doctor murmured cynically into Maigret's ear.

The cook had been alerted as well. She watched in silence from the basement window. Skylights opened in the roofs leading into the servants' bedrooms.

'Well! What are we waiting for? Let's carry the countess to her bed,' Maigret thundered indignantly.

It all struck him as sacrilegious, clashing as it did with his childhood memories. It made him uncomfortable, not just emotionally, but physically as well!

. . . a crime will be committed . . .

The second peal of bells rang for mass. People would be in a great hurry. There were farmers who came from far away, on carts. And they had brought flowers to put on the graves in the cemetery.

Jean didn't dare approach. The butler, who had opened the door, was shocked and stood there frozen.

'Your ladyship . . . Your lady . . .' he stammered.

'So? Are you going to leave her there? Well?'

Why on earth was the doctor wearing an ironic smile on his face?

Maigret took charge of the situation.

'Right! Two men . . . You!' (He pointed at the chauffeur.) 'And you!' (He pointed at the butler.) 'Carry her to her bedroom.'

And as they leaned towards the coupé, a bell rang out in the hall.

'The telephone! . . . That's strange, at this time of day! . . .' Bouchardon muttered.

Jean didn't dare go and answer it. He seemed in a daze. It was Maigret who hurried inside and picked up the receiver.

'Hello! . . . Yes, this is the chateau . . .'

And a clear voice said, 'Could I speak to my mother? She must have come back from mass . . .'

'Who's speaking? . . .'

'The Count of Saint-Fiacre . . . And in any case that's no concern of yours . . . Let me speak to my mother.'

'One moment. Will you tell me where you're calling from?'

'From Moulins! For heaven's sake, I told you . . .'

'It would be better for you to come here,' Maigret said, as he hung up.

And he was forced to press his back to the wall to let the two servants pass, carrying the corpse.

2. The Missal

'Are you coming in?' the doctor asked as soon as the countess was laid on her bed. 'I need someone to help me undress her.'

'We should find a maid!' Maigret exclaimed.

Jean went upstairs and came back down a short time later with a woman in her thirties, who darted frightened glances.

'Get out!' the inspector snapped at the servants, who wanted to do precisely that.

He held Jean back by the sleeve, looked him up and down and led him over to a window.

'What is the nature of your relations with the countess's son?'

'But . . . I . . .' The young man was gaunt, and his striped pyjamas, of dubious cleanliness, added nothing to his dignity. His eyes avoided Maigret's. He kept tugging on his fingers as if to stretch them.

'Wait!' the inspector interrupted. 'Let's be frank so as not to waste any more time.'

Behind the heavy oak door of the bedroom there was the sound of people coming and going, the squeak of bedsprings, muttered orders being given to the maid by Dr Bouchardon: they were undressing the corpse!

'What exactly is your situation at the chateau? How long have you been here?'

'Four years . . .'

'Did you know the Countess of Saint-Fiacre?'

'I . . . That is to say, I was introduced to her by some mutual friends . . . My parents had just been ruined by the collapse of a little bank in Lyon . . . I came here in a position of trust, to deal with the personal affairs of . . .'

'Excuse me! What did you do before?'

'I travelled . . . I wrote art reviews . . .'

Maigret didn't smile. And in any case the atmosphere wasn't conducive to irony.

The chateau was huge. From outside it had a certain charm. But the interior looked as seedy as the young man's pyjamas. Dust everywhere, ugly old objects, a pile of useless junk. The curtains were faded.

And on the walls there were lighter patches, indicating that furniture had been removed.

The best furniture, obviously! The pieces that had some value!

'You became the countess's lover . . .'

'Everyone is free to love whoever . . .'

'Idiot!' muttered Maigret, turning his back on the young man.

As if things weren't obvious enough already! You only had to look at Jean. You only had to breathe the air of the chateau for a few minutes! And catch the expressions on the servants' faces!

'Did you know her son was on his way?'

'No . . . What has that got to do with me?'

And his gaze was still evasive. With his right hand he tugged on the fingers of his left.

'I'd like to get dressed . . . It's cold . . . But why are the police concerned about? . . .'

'Yes, go and get dressed!'

Maigret pushed the door of the bedroom and avoided looking in the direction of the bed, on which the dead woman lay entirely naked.

The bedroom looked like the rest of the house. It was far too big, too cold, filled with mismatched old objects. As he went to lean against the marble mantelpiece, Maigret noticed that it was broken.

'Have you found anything?' the inspector asked Bouchardon. 'Just a moment . . . Would you leave us alone, please, mademoiselle?'

And he closed the door behind the maid, pressed his forehead against the window and let his eye wander across the grounds, carpeted with dead leaves and frost.

'I can only confirm what I told you a moment ago. Death is due to a sudden heart attack.'

'Caused by? . . .'

The doctor gestured vaguely, threw a blanket over the corpse, joined Maigret by the window and lit his pipe.

'Perhaps a shock . . . Perhaps the cold . . . Was it cold in the church?'

'On the contrary! Of course, you've found no trace of a wound?'

'Nothing!'

'Not the tiniest sign of an injection?'

'I thought of that. Nothing! And there's no poison in the countess's blood. So you understand that it would be hard to claim . . .'

Maigret's face was severe. On the left, under the trees, he could make out the red roof of the estate manager's house, his birthplace.

'In just a few words . . . life at the chateau?' he asked under his breath.

'You know as much as I do. One of those women who are models of good behaviour until the age of forty or forty-five . . . That was when the count died, and the son went to Paris to pursue his studies . . .'

'And here?'

'A series of secretaries came and stayed for various lengths of time . . . You saw the latest one . . .'

'The fortune?'

'The chateau is mortgaged . . . Three-quarters of the farms have been sold . . . Now and again an antique dealer comes for anything valuable that's left . . .'

'And what about the son?'

'I don't know him well. They say he's quite a character . . .'

'Thank you!'

Maigret went to leave, but Bouchardon came after him.

'Between ourselves, I'd be curious as to what coincidence it was that brought you to the church this morning of all mornings . . .'

'Yes! It's strange . . .'

'I have the feeling I've seen you somewhere before . . .'

'It's possible . . .'

And Maigret hurried along the corridor. He was finding it hard to concentrate, because he hadn't had enough sleep. He might also have caught a cold at Marie Tatin's inn. He spotted Jean coming down the stairs, wearing a grey suit but still in his slippers. At the same time a car without a silencer drove up in the chateau courtyard.

It was a little racing car, painted canary yellow, long, narrow, uncomfortable-looking. A moment later a man in a leather coat burst into the hall, took off his cap and yelled, 'Hello! Anyone there? Is everyone still asleep around here?'

But then he noticed Maigret looking at him curiously.

'What the? . . .'

'Shh! I need to talk to you . . .'

Standing beside the inspector, Jean was pale and anxious. As he stepped past him, the Count of Saint-Fiacre punched him lightly on the shoulder and joked, 'Still here, you rogue?'

He didn't seem to be angry with him. Just to hold him in complete contempt.

'At least there's nothing serious happening, is there?'

'Your mother died this morning, in church.'

Maurice de Saint-Fiacre was thirty, the same age as Jean. They were the same height, but the count was broad, slightly fat. And everything about him, particularly his leather outfit, hinted at a life of frivolity. His clear eyes were cheerful and mocking.

It took those words from Maigret to make him frown.

'What did you say?'

'Come in here.'

'Good heavens! When I've . . .'

'When you've what?'

'Nothing. Where is she? . . .'

He was stunned, beside himself. In the bedroom, he lifted the blanket just enough to see the dead woman's face.

No explosion of grief. No tears. No dramatic gestures.

Just three murmured words.

'Poor old thing!'

Jean had thought it was time for him to walk towards the door, and Maurice noticed and shouted at him, 'You, get out of here!'

He started getting nervous. He paced back and forth. He bumped into the doctor.

'What did she die of, Bouchardon?'

'A heart attack, Monsieur Maurice . . . But the inspector might know more than I do on the subject . . .'

The young man turned excitedly towards Maigret.

'Are you from the police? . . . What did? . . .'

'Could we talk for a few minutes? I'd like to take a quick stroll down the road. Will you be staying here, doctor?'

'I was about to go hunting and . . .'

'Well you can go hunting another day!'

Maurice de Saint-Fiacre followed Maigret, staring dreamily at the ground in front of him. When they reached the main avenue of the chateau, seven o'clock mass was coming to an end, and the congregation, larger than the one at first mass, was coming out and assembling in little groups in the square in front of the church. Some people had already gone into the graveyard, and only their heads could be seen over the top of the wall.

As the sun rose, the cold became more intense, probably because of the breeze that swept the dead leaves from one end of the square to the other, making them wheel like birds above the pond of Notre-Dame.

Maigret stuffed his pipe. Wasn't that the main reason why he had dragged his companion outside? And yet, even in the dead woman's bedroom the doctor had been smoking. Maigret was used to smoking anywhere at all.

But not at the chateau! It was a special place which, throughout the whole of his youth, had represented everything inaccessible in the world.

'The count called me into his library today, to work with him!' his father had said with a hint of pride.

And Maigret, a little boy in those days, watched respectfully the pram being pushed by a nanny in the park. The baby was Maurice de Saint-Fiacre.

'Would anyone stand to benefit from your mother's death?'

'I don't understand . . . The doctor just said . . .'

He was anxious and twitchy. He snatched the piece of paper that Maigret held out to him, the one that announced the crime.

'What does this mean? Bouchardon is talking about a heart attack and . . .'

'A heart attack that someone predicted a few days ago!'

A few villagers watched them from a distance. The two men approached the church, walking slowly, following their own trains of thought.

'What did you plan to do at the chateau this morning?'

'I'm wondering that very thing myself,' the young man said carefully. 'You asked me a moment ago whether . . . Well, then, yes! There is someone who stands to gain from my mother's death . . . I do!'

He wasn't joking. He looked concerned. A man passed on a bicycle, and he greeted him by name.

'Since you're from the police, you must have worked out the situation already . . . Besides, that animal Bouchardon will have had no compunction about spilling the beans. My mother was a poor old woman. My father is dead. I've gone away. Left all on her own, I think she went slightly deranged. At first she spent her time at church . . . Then . . .'

'The young secretaries!'

'I don't think it was what you believe, and what Bouchardon was trying to insinuate. Nothing untoward! Just a need for affection. The need to look after someone . . . which these young men took advantage of to take things further . . . There you are! That didn't mean she wasn't devout. She must have had terrible crises of conscience, torn as she was between her faith and this . . . this . . .'

'You were saying you stood to gain? . . .'

'You're aware that there isn't much left of our fortune . . . And people like the chap you saw a moment ago have high ambitions . . . Let's say that in three or four years there would have been nothing left at all . . .'

He was bare-headed. He ran his fingers through his hair. Then, looking Maigret straight in the eye and pausing for a moment, he added:

'It remains for me to tell you that I came here today to ask my mother for forty thousand francs . . . And I need those forty thousand francs to cover a cheque that will otherwise bounce . . . You see how everything links together!'

As they passed a hedge he pulled a twig from it. He seemed to be struggling not to let events get on top of him.

'And to think I brought Marie Vassiliev with me!'

'Marie Vassiliev?'

'My girlfriend! I left her in her bed, in Moulins . . . She's quite capable of hiring a car right now and running off. That's all I need!'

They were only now turning out the lights in Marie Tatin's, where some men were drinking rum. The Moulins bus was about to set off, half empty.

'She didn't deserve that!' Maurice said dreamily.

'Who?'

'My mother!'

And at that moment there was something childlike about him, in spite of his height and his developing paunch. Perhaps he was finally on the brink of crying?

The two men were walking up and down near the church, forever pacing out the same path, now facing the pond, now turning their backs on it.

'Look, inspector! It isn't at all possible that someone might have killed her . . . or at least I can't imagine . . .'

Maigret thought about it, so intensely that he forgot all about his companion. He was remembering the tiniest details of the first mass.

The countess in her pew . . . No one had gone near her . . . She had taken communion . . . She had knelt down with her face in her hands . . . Then she had opened her missal . . . A little later, she had her face in her hands again . . .

'Would you excuse me for a moment?'

Maigret climbed the steps and entered the church, where the sacristan was already preparing the altar for high mass. The bell-ringer, a clumsy peasant in heavy hobnail boots, was straightening the chairs.

The inspector walked straight towards the pews, bent down and called the sexton, who turned round.

'Who picked up the missal?'

'Which missal?'

'The countess's . . . It was left here.'

'Is that right?'

'You, come here!' Maigret said to the bell-ringer. 'Have you seen the missal that was here earlier?'

'What?'

Either he was stupid or he was pretending to be. Maigret was agitated. He noticed Maurice de Saint-Fiacre standing at the end of the nave.

'Who has been near this pew?'

'The doctor's wife was sitting there at seven o'clock mass . . .'

'I didn't think the doctor was a religious man.'

'Perhaps he isn't – but his wife . . .'

'Right! Tell the whole village that there's a big reward for anyone who brings me the missal.'

'To the chateau?'

'No! To Marie Tatin's.'

Outside, Maurice de Saint-Fiacre walked beside him again.

'I don't understand this matter about the missal.'

'Heart attack, isn't that right? . . . Maybe caused by some kind of shock . . . And it happened shortly after communion, in other words after the countess had opened her missal . . . Let's imagine that in that missal . . .'

But the young man shook his head.

'I can't imagine any sort of message that might have given my mother such a shock . . . Besides, it would be so . . . so hateful . . .'

He was having difficulty breathing. He looked grimly at the chateau.

'Let's go and get a drink!'

He headed not towards the chateau, but towards the inn, where his entry caused some awkwardness. The four farmers drinking were suddenly ill at ease. They greeted him with a mixture of respect and fear.

Marie Tatin ran from the kitchen, wiping her hands on her apron. She stammered:

'Monsieur Maurice . . . I'm so distraught at the news . . . Our poor countess . . .'

She was crying. She probably cried her heart out every time someone died in the village.

'You were at mass too, weren't you?' she said, calling Maigret as her witness. 'To think that nobody noticed anything. I was here when they came and told me . . .'

It is always embarrassing, in such cases, to show less grief than people who are uninvolved. Maurice tried to hide his impatience as he listened to these words of condolence and to grant himself some composure he fetched a bottle of rum from the shelf and filled two glasses.

A shiver ran down his back as he drained his glass in one, and he said to Maigret, 'I think I caught a cold on my way here this morning.'

'Everyone around here has a cold, Monsieur Maurice.'

And, to Maigret: 'You should take care too. I heard you coughing last night . . .'

The villagers left. The fire was blazing.

'A day like today!' said Marie Tatin.

And it was impossible to tell whether she was looking at Maigret or at the count, because her eyes went in different directions.

'Wouldn't you like a bite to eat? But look at me! I was so flabbergasted when I was told . . . that it didn't even occur to me to change my dress . . .'

She had just put an apron on over the black dress that she only ever wore to go to mass. Her hat was on the table.

Maurice de Saint-Fiacre drank a second glass of rum, and looked at Maigret as if asking him what to do.

'Let's go!' said the inspector.

'Will you have lunch here? I've killed a chicken and . . .'

But the two men were already outside. In front of the church there were four or five carts, their horses tethered to trees. Heads could be seen coming and going above the low wall of the cemetery. And, in the courtyard of the chateau, the only touch of vivid colour was the yellow car.

'The cheque was crossed?' Maigret asked.

'Yes! But it will be deposited tomorrow.'

'Do you do a lot of work?'

Silence. The sound of their footsteps on the paved road. The rustle of dead leaves carried by the wind. The horses snorting.

'I am the very definition of a good-for-nothing! I've done a bit of everything. You see! The forty thousand . . . I was going to set up a film club. Before that I ran a wireless business . . .'

A faint sound of gunshot, on their right, beyond the Notre-Dame pond. They saw a huntsman striding towards the bird he had killed, towards which his dog was hurrying.

'It's Gautier, the estate manager,' said Maurice. 'He must have gone hunting . . .'

Then all of a sudden he had a fit of annoyance, stamped his heel on the ground, pulled a face and nearly sobbed.

'Poor old thing!' he muttered, his lips pursed. 'It's . . . it's so wretched! . . . and that little swine Jean who . . .'

As if by magic, they saw Jean pacing the courtyard of the chateau, side by side with the doctor, who must have been engaged in a heated discussion with him, since he was waving his thin arms around.

They occasionally caught the smell of chrysanthemums in the wind.

3. The Altar Boy

There was no sun to distort the images, and no greyness either to blur the outlines of things. Everything stood out with sharp clarity: the trunks of the trees, the dead branches, the pebbles and especially the black clothes of the people who had come to the cemetery. The whites, on the other hand, gravestones or starched shirt-fronts, or the bonnets of the old women, looked unreal and perfidious: whites too shockingly white.

Had it not been for the crisp breeze cutting into people's cheeks, it was almost as if they were under a slightly dusty bell-jar.

'I'll see you in a minute!'

Maigret left the Count of Saint-Fiacre outside the cemetery gate. An old woman, sitting on a little bench that she had brought with her, was trying to sell oranges and chocolate.

Oranges! Fat ones! Unripe! And candied . . . They put your teeth on edge, they rasped your throat but, when he was ten years old, Maigret had devoured them anyway, because they were oranges.

He had turned up the velvet collar of his overcoat. He didn't look at anyone. He knew that he had to turn to the left, and that the grave he was looking for was the third one past the cypress tree.

All around, the cemetery was covered with flowers. The previous day, some women had washed certain gravestones with a brush and soap. The gates had been repainted.

HERE LIES ÉVARISTE MAIGRET . . .

'Excuse me! No smoking.'

The inspector barely noticed that anyone was talking to him. At last he stared at the bell-ringer, who was also the grave-digger, and put his pipe, still lit, in his pocket.

He couldn't think about one thing at a time. Memories came flooding in, memories of his father, a friend who had drowned in the Notre-Dame pond, the child of the chateau in his beautiful pram . . .

People looked at him. He looked at them. He had seen these faces before. But back then, that man holding a little boy in his arms, for example, the one walking behind a pregnant woman, had been a little boy of four or five.

Maigret had no flowers. The tombstone was blackened. He came out grumpily and muttered to himself, making a whole group of people turn round: 'We really need to find the missal!'

He didn't want to go back to the chateau. There was something about it that disgusted, even infuriated him.

Certainly, he was under no illusion about the men. But he was furious with them for sullying his childhood memories! Especially the countess, whom he had always considered as noble and lovely as a character in a picture-book . . .

And there she was, a batty old lady who kept gigolos!

Not even that! There was nothing honest or open about it! The famous Jean was just playing at being a secretary! He wasn't handsome, he wasn't even all that young!

And the poor old woman, as her son had said, was tormented, torn between the chateau and the church.

And the latest Count of Saint-Fiacre risked arrest for presenting a dud cheque!

Someone was walking in front of Maigret with his gun over his shoulder, and the inspector suddenly noticed that he was heading towards the estate manager's house. He thought he recognized the silhouette he had seen in the field from a distance.

A few metres separated the two men, who were about to enter the courtyard where a few hens were huddled against a wall, in the shelter of the wind, their feathers trembling.

'Hey! . . .'

The man with the rifle turned round.

'Are you the Saint-Fiacre estate manager?'

'And you are?'

'Detective Chief Inspector Maigret, Police Judiciaire.'

'Maigret?'

The estate manager was struck by the name, but couldn't remember exactly why.

'Have you been told what's going on?'

'I've just been informed . . . I was hunting . . . But what do the police? . . .'

He was a small, squat man, grey-haired, his skin criss-crossed with fine, deep wrinkles, and pupils that looked as if they were lying in ambush behind thick eyebrows.

'I was told her heart . . .'

'Where are you going?'

'I'm hardly going to go into the chateau with my boots covered in mud and my rifle . . .'

The head of a rabbit hung from his game-bag. Maigret looked at the house they were walking towards.

'Wait a moment! They've changed the kitchen . . .'

He felt a suspicious glance upon him.

'Fifteen years ago!' murmured the estate manager.

'What's your name?'

'Gautier . . . Is it true that the count arrived without . . .'

His whole attitude was hesitant, reticent. And Gautier didn't even invite Maigret inside. He pushed open his door.

The inspector came in anyway and turned right, towards the dining room, which smelled of biscuits and brandy.

'If you have a moment, Monsieur Gautier . . . You're not needed at the house . . . But I have a few questions to ask you . . .'

'Hurry up!' said a woman's voice in the kitchen. 'Apparently it's horrible . . .'

And Maigret ran his fingers along the oak table, its corners decorated with carved lions. It was the one from his childhood! It had been sold on to the new estate manager after his father's death.

'Can I offer you something?'

Gautier chose a bottle from the sideboard, perhaps as a way of gaining some time.

'What do you think about Monsieur Jean? . . . And by the way, what's his surname? . . .'

'Métayer . . . A respectable family from Bourges . . .'

'Did he cost the countess a lot of money?'

Gautier filled the glasses with brandy, but remained stubbornly silent.

'What business did he have at the chateau? As estate manager I assume you look after everything . . .'

'Everything!'

'So?'

'He didn't do anything . . . A few private letters . . . At first he claimed to be making the countess some money, thanks to his knowledge of finance . . . He bought some shares that collapsed in a few months . . . But he insisted that he would make it all back and more thanks to a new photographic process that one of his friends had invented . . . It cost the countess about a hundred thousand francs, and the friend disappeared . . . And last of all there was some story about photographic printing . . . I don't know a thing about it. Something like photoengraving or heliogravure, but cheaper . . .'

'Jean Métayer was a busy man!'

'A lot of effort for not much result . . . He wrote articles in the *Journal de Moulins*, and they had to take them because of the countess . . . That was where he did his printing experiments, and the editor didn't dare throw him out . . . Cheers! . . .'

And, suddenly uneasy:

'There were no rows between him and the count.'

'Nothing at all?'

'I assume you're just here by chance . . . Since it was a heart attack, there's no reason to . . .'

What annoyed Maigret most was that he couldn't catch the estate manager's eye. He wiped his moustache and moved into the other room.

'Do you mind if I get changed? . . . I was supposed to be going to high mass and now . . .'

'I'll see you later!' said Maigret as he left.

And he was just closing the door when he heard the still invisible woman asking, 'Who was that?'

They had put sandstone paving stones down in the courtyard, where he had once played marbles on the beaten earth.

The square was filled with groups of people in their Sunday best, and the sound of organ music filtered from the church. The children, in their new suits, didn't dare to play. And handkerchiefs protruded from everyone's pockets. They all had red noses, which they blew noisily.

Scraps of phrases reached Maigret's ears:

'He's a policeman from Paris . . .'

'. . . Apparently he's come about the cow that died at Mathieu's the other week . . .'

A cocky young man with a red flower in the buttonhole of his navy-blue serge waistcoat, his face well scrubbed and his hair shiny with brilliantine, dared to call out to the inspector:

'They're waiting for you at Tatin's, it's about that guy who stole . . .'

And he nudged his friends in the ribs, holding in a laugh that exploded in any case as soon as Maigret turned his head away.

He hadn't been making it up. At Marie Tatin's the atmosphere was hotter now, and thick with pipe smoke. At one table a family of villagers were eating food they had brought from the farm and drinking big bowls of coffee. The father was cutting a dried sausage with his penknife.

The young people were drinking lemonade, the old ones brandy. And Marie Tatin trotted ceaselessly about.

In one corner a woman got up as the inspector came in and took a step towards him, fearful and hesitant, her lips moist. Her hand rested on the shoulder of a little boy; Maigret recognized his red hair.

'Are you the inspector, sir?'

Everyone looked in his direction.

'First of all I want to tell you, sir, that we've always been honest people in our family! But we're poor . . . You understand? . . . And when I saw that Ernest . . .'

The boy, extremely pale, stared straight ahead without showing the slightest emotion.

'Are you the one who took the missal?' Maigret asked him, bending towards him.

No answer. A keen, shy glance.

'Answer the inspector . . .'

But the little boy didn't open his mouth. His mother swiftly gave him a slap that left a red mark on his left cheek. The boy's head rocked for a moment. His eyes moistened slightly, his lips trembled, but he didn't move.

'Are you going to give him an answer, you little wretch?'

And to Maigret:

'Children today! For months he's been pleading with me to buy him a missal! A big one like the one the priest has! Can you imagine that? . . . So, when I was told about the countess's missal, I immediately thought . . . And besides! I'd been surprised to see him coming back between second and third mass, because he usually eats at the presbytery . . . I went into his room and found it under the mattress . . .'

Again the mother's hand struck the child's cheek. He did nothing to defend himself.

'I couldn't even read at his age! But I was never bad enough to steal a book . . .'

There was a respectful silence in the inn. Maigret held the missal in his hands.

'Thank you.'

He was in a hurry to examine it. He walked to the back of the room.

'Inspector, sir . . .'

The woman was calling to him. She was puzzled.

'I was told there was a reward . . . Not because Ernest . . .'

Maigret held out twenty francs, which she put carefully in her purse, before dragging her son towards the door, saying crossly, 'As for you, you young delinquent, just you wait till I get you home . . .'

Maigret's eye met the boy's. The glance lasted a matter of seconds. But they both knew that they were friends.

Perhaps because Maigret himself had once wanted – without ever owning one! – a gilt-edged missal, containing not only the ordinary of the mass but all the liturgical texts in two columns, in Latin and French.

'What time will you be back for lunch?'

'I don't know.'

Maigret was about to go to his room to examine the missal, but when he remembered the draughts from the roof he chose instead to take the main road.

It was as he walked slowly towards the chateau that he opened the bound book with the Saint-Fiacre coat of arms. Or rather he didn't open it. The missal opened all by itself, at a page where a piece of paper had been slipped between two pages.

Page 221: 'Prayer after communion.'

The piece of paper was a roughly cut scrap of newspaper which, at first glance, looked odd, as if it had been badly printed.

> Paris, 1 November. A dramatic suicide occurred this morning in a flat on Rue de Miromesnil occupied for several years by the Count of Saint-Fiacre and his Russian girlfriend, a certain Marie V...
>
> After informing his girlfriend that he was ashamed of the scandal provoked by a member of the family, the count fired a bullet into his head from a Browning and died a few minutes later without regaining consciousness.
>
> We have reason to believe that this was a particularly painful family drama, and that the person in question is none other than the mother of the unfortunate man.

A goose that had wandered into the path furiously stretched its gaping beak towards Maigret. Bells rang, and the crowd shuffled slowly out of the little church accompanied by the smells of incense and snuffed candles.

Maigret had shoved the missal into his pocket, making it bulge, and had stopped to examine the terrible piece of paper.

The crime weapon! A newspaper cutting, seven centimetres by five!

The Countess of Saint-Fiacre went to first mass, knelt down in the pew reserved for the members of her family for two centuries.

She took communion. It was planned. She opened her missal to read the 'prayer after communion'.

There was the weapon! And Maigret turned the bit of paper in all directions. He found something not quite right about it. He looked among other things at the alignment of the letters, and was convinced that it had not been produced by a rotary press as a real newspaper would have been.

It was a simple galley, hand-printed. And in fact the sheet bore exactly the same text on the other side.

The murderer hadn't taken the trouble to refine it, or perhaps he hadn't had time. Would it have occurred to the countess to turn the page over? Would she not have died first, from shock, indignation, shame or anguish?

There was a frightening expression on Maigret's face: because he had never before seen a crime at once so cowardly and so skilful.

And whoever had committed the crime had also called the police!

Assuming that the missal wouldn't have been found . . .

Yes! That was it! No one was supposed to find the missal! In which case it would have been impossible to speak of a crime, to accuse anyone at all! The countess had died of a sudden heart attack!

He suddenly turned on his heel. He reached Marie Tatin's while everyone was talking about him and the missal.

'Do you know where little Ernest lives?'

'Three houses past the grocer's, on the main street . . .'

He ran off in that direction. A single-storey cottage. Enlarged photographs of the father and mother hung on either side of the dresser. The woman, already in her house clothes, was in the kitchen, which smelled of roast beef.

'Is your son here?'

'He's changing. There's no point in him dirtying his Sunday clothes . . . You saw how I shook him! . . . And to think that he's only ever had good examples in front of his eyes and who . . .'

She opened a door and shouted, 'Come here, you scoundrel!'

And the boy could be seen in his underpants, trying to hide himself.

'Let him get dressed,' said Maigret. 'I'll talk to him later . . .'

The woman went on preparing lunch. Her husband was probably at Marie Tatin's, having an early drink.

At last the door opened, and Ernest came shiftily in, wearing his weekday suit, the trousers of which were too long.

'Come for a walk with me . . .'

'Really?' the woman exclaimed. 'In that case, Ernest . . . Hurry up and put on your good suit . . .'

'There's no need! . . . Come on then, my little man . . .'

The street was deserted. The life of the village was concentrated on the square, the cemetery and Marie Tatin's.

'Tomorrow I'll give you an even bigger missal, with the first letters of each verse in red . . .'

The little boy was amazed. So the inspector knew that there was such a thing as missals with red letters, like the one on the altar?

'Only, you're going to tell me quite honestly where you got this one! I'm not going to tell you off . . .'

It was odd to see the old peasant suspicion appearing on the boy's face. His mouth was shut. He was already on the defensive.

'Did you find it on the prie-dieu?'

Silence! His cheeks and the top of his nose were scattered with freckles. His fleshy lips were tight as he tried not to show any emotion.

'Don't you realize that I'm your great friend?'

'Yes . . . You gave my mum twenty francs.'

'So?'

The boy savoured his revenge.

'On the way back my mum said she'd only slapped me for show, and gave me fifty centimes.'

Bull's-eye! The boy knew his stuff! What thoughts was he rolling about in that head, too big for his thin body?

'And the sacristan?'

'He didn't say anything to me . . .'

'Who took the missal from the prie-dieu?'

'I don't know . . .'

'And where did you find it?'

'Under my surplice, in the sacristy . . . I was supposed to go and eat in the presbytery. I'd forgotten my handkerchief . . . When I moved my surplice I felt something hard . . .'

'Was the sacristan there too?'

'He was in church, putting the candles out . . . You know the ones with the red letters are very expensive . . .'

So someone had taken the missal from the prie-dieu and hidden it momentarily in the sacristy, under the altar boy's surplice, with the clear intention of coming to get it later!

'Did you open it?'

'I didn't have time . . . I wanted my boiled egg . . . Because on Sunday . . .'

'I know.'

And Ernest wondered how this man from the city could know that there was an egg and bread and jam at the priest's house on Sunday.

'You can go.'

'Is it true that I'll have . . . ?'

'A missal, yes . . . Tomorrow . . . Goodbye, son.'

Maigret held out his hand, and the boy hesitated for a moment before holding out his own.

'I know it's just a joke!' he said none the less as he walked away.

A crime in three stages, then: someone had set the article, or had it set, using a linotype machine, the kind that you only find in a newspaper office or a very big printworks.

Someone had slipped the piece of paper into the missal, carefully choosing the page.

And someone had taken the missal back, had hidden it momentarily under the surplice, in the sacristy.

Had the same man done everything? Had each action been performed by a different person? Had two of the actions been performed by the same person?

As he was passing in front of the church, Maigret saw the

priest coming out and heading towards him. He waited for him under the poplar trees, beside the woman selling oranges and chocolate.

'I'm going to the chateau . . .' he said as he joined the inspector. 'It's the first time I've celebrated mass without even knowing what I'm doing . . . The idea that a crime . . .'

'It really was a crime,' Maigret murmured.

They walked in silence. Without a word, the inspector held out the piece of paper to his companion, who read it and gave it back.

And they walked another hundred yards without uttering a word.

'Chaos creates chaos . . . But she was an unhappy creature . . .'

They both had to hold on to their hats as the wind grew stronger.

'I didn't have the energy . . .' the priest added in a grim voice.

'You?'

'She came to see me every day . . . She was ready to return to the ways of the Lord . . . But every day, in there . . .'

There was a hint of harshness in his voice.

'I didn't want to go there! And yet it was my duty . . .'

They nearly stopped, because two men were walking along the big avenue of the chateau and they were about to meet them. They recognized the doctor, with his brown beard and, beside him, Jean Métayer, who was talking feverishly to him. The yellow car was in the courtyard. They guessed that Métayer didn't dare go back to the chateau while the Count of Saint-Fiacre was there.

The village was wrapped in an ambiguous light. An ambiguous situation! With all those dark comings and goings!

'Come on!' said Maigret.

And the doctor must have said the same thing to Métayer, then dragged him along until the moment when he could say, 'Hello, Father! You know, I can reassure you at last . . . It's true that I'm a non-believer, but I can guess your horror at the idea that a crime might have been committed in your church . . . Well, it hasn't! . . . Science is clear on the matter . . . *Our* countess died of a heart attack . . .'

Maigret had walked over to Jean Métayer.

'One question . . .'

He was aware of the tension in the young man, who was panting with anxiety.

'When was the last time that you went to the *Journal de Moulins*?'

'I . . . wait . . .'

He was about to speak, but his unease made him cautious. He darted a suspicious glance at the inspector.

'Why are you asking me that?'

'Doesn't matter!'

'Am I obliged to answer?'

'You are free to remain silent!'

Not the face of a degenerate, perhaps, but a face that was worried, tormented. Nervousness far beyond the average, capable of interesting Dr Bouchardon, who was talking to the priest.

'I know I'll be the one tormented! . . . But I will defend myself . . .'

'Of course! You will defend yourself!'

'First I want to see a lawyer. It's my right . . . And besides, what right do you have? . . .'

'Just a moment. Have you studied law?'

'For two years.'

He tried to regain his composure and smile.

'No charges have been brought, nobody's been caught in flagrante . . . So you have no right to . . .'

'Very good! Ten out of ten!'

'The doctor maintains that . . .'

'And I claim that the countess was killed by the most revolting sort of swine. Read this!'

And Maigret held out the piece of printed paper. Suddenly quite stiff, Jean Métayer looked at his companion as if he was going to spit in his face.

'By the . . . What did you say? . . . I can't allow you to . . .'

And the inspector, gently resting his hand on his shoulder, said:

'But my dear boy, I haven't said anything to *you* at all! Where's the count? Go on reading. You can give me the paper later on . . .'

A flame of triumph flared in Métayer's eyes.

'The count is talking cheques with the estate manager! . . . You'll find them in the library! . . .'

The priest and the doctor walked ahead, and Maigret heard the doctor's voice saying, 'No, Father! It's human! It's more than human! If only you had studied a little physiology rather than poring over the writings of Saint Augustine . . .'

And the gravel crunched under the feet of the four men who slowly climbed the steps, turned even harder and whiter by the cold.

4. Marie Vassiliev

Maigret couldn't be everywhere at once. The chateau was huge. That was why he could only have the most approximate idea of the morning's events.

It was the time of day when, on Sundays and holidays, country folk delay going home, savouring the pleasure of being in a group, in their best clothes, in the village square or at the café. Some of them were already drunk. Others were talking too loudly. And the children in their stiff clothes looked admiringly at their fathers.

At the Château de Saint-Fiacre, Jean Métayer, looking sallow in the face, had gone all alone to the first floor, where he could be heard pacing back and forth in one of the rooms.

'If you'd like to come with me . . .' the doctor said to the priest.

And he led him towards the countess's bedroom.

On the ground floor, a wide corridor ran the length of the building, pierced by a row of doors. Maigret could hear the hum of voices. He had been told that the Count of Saint-Fiacre and the estate manager were in the library.

He tried to go in, got the wrong door and found himself in the drawing room. The communicating door with the library was open. In a gilt-framed mirror he caught the image of a young man sitting on a corner of the desk, looking overwhelmed, and the estate manager, standing foursquare on his short legs.

'You should have worked out that there was no point in pushing the matter!' Gautier was saying. 'Especially when forty thousand francs were involved!'

'Who answered my phone call?'

'Monsieur Jean, of course!'

'And he didn't pass the message on to my mother!'

Maigret coughed and stepped into the library.

'Which phone call are you talking about?'

And Maurice de Saint-Fiacre replied, unabashed, 'My call to the chateau the day before yesterday. As I've already told you, I needed money. I wanted to ask my mother for the necessary sum, but that . . . that . . . well, that Monsieur Jean, as they call him here, was the one I got through to . . .'

'And he told you there was nothing to be done? And you came anyway . . .'

The estate manager observed the two men. Maurice had stepped away from the desk he was perched on.

'I didn't take Gautier aside to talk about this, by the way!' he said agitatedly. 'I didn't hide the situation from you, inspector. Tomorrow, a complaint will be lodged against me. Obviously, with my mother dead, I'm the sole natural heir. So I asked Gautier to find the forty thousand francs for tomorrow morning . . . And well! Apparently it's impossible.'

'Completely impossible!' repeated the estate manager.

'Naturally we can't do anything before the notary gets involved, and he won't bring the interested parties together until after the funeral. And Gautier adds that even without that it would be hard to find forty thousand francs to borrow on what's left of the estate . . .'

He had started pacing back and forth.

'It's obvious, isn't it? It's staring us in the face! And there's even a chance that they won't let me walk at the head of the cortège . . . But incidentally . . . One more question . . . You mentioned a crime . . . Is it possible that? . . .'

'No complaint has been brought, and probably none will be,' said Maigret. 'So the courts will not be involved in the affair . . .'

'Leave us on our own, Gautier!'

And as soon as the estate manager had left, he said sadly, 'A crime, really?'

'A crime that doesn't officially concern the police!'

'Explain yourself . . . I'm beginning to . . .'

But a woman's voice was heard in the hall, accompanied by the more serious voice of the estate manager. Maurice frowned and walked towards the door, opening it abruptly.

'Marie? What are? . . .'

'Maurice! Why won't they let me in? . . . It's intolerable! I've been waiting at the hotel for an hour . . .'

She spoke with a very marked foreign accent. This was Marie Vassiliev, who had arrived from Moulins in an old taxi that could be seen in the courtyard.

She was tall and very beautiful, with blonde hair, probably dyed. Seeing that Maigret was looking at her carefully, she started talking rapidly in English, and Maurice replied in the same language.

She asked him if he had any money. He replied that it was out of the question, that his mother was dead, that she had to go back to Paris, where he would join her soon.

Then she laughed sarcastically:

'With what? I don't even have enough money to pay for the taxi!'

Maurice de Saint-Fiacre started to lose his composure. His mistress's shrill voice echoed around the chateau, lending a note of scandal to the scene.

The estate manager was still in the corridor.

'If you stay here, I'll stay with you!' announced Marie Vassiliev.

And Maigret said to Gautier: 'Send the car away and pay the driver.'

The chaos mounted. Not material, reparable chaos, but a moral chaos that seemed to be contagious. Gautier himself was losing his footing.

'And yet we need to talk, inspector,' the young man said.

'Not now!'

And he pointed at the aggressively elegant woman who was pacing up and down in the library and the drawing room as if drawing up an inventory.

'Who is this stupid portrait of, Maurice?' she exclaimed with a laugh.

Footsteps on the stairs. Maigret saw Jean Métayer walking past, now wearing a big overcoat and carrying a suitcase. Métayer must have suspected that he wouldn't be allowed to leave, because he stopped by the library door and waited.

'Where are you going?'

'To the inn! I think it would be more dignified of me to . . .'

Maurice de Saint-Fiacre, to get rid of his mistress, led her towards a bedroom in the right wing of the chateau. They went on talking in English.

'Is it true that forty thousand francs couldn't be borrowed on the chateau?' Maigret asked the estate manager.

'It would be difficult.'

'Well do the impossible, by tomorrow morning!'

The inspector hesitated to leave. At the last minute he decided to go to the first floor, where a surprise awaited him. While downstairs everyone seemed to be milling around aimlessly, upstairs someone had made the Countess of Saint-Fiacre's bedroom neat and tidy.

The doctor, with the assistance of the maid, had washed the corpse.

The atmosphere was no longer sordid and ambiguous, as it had been that morning! And the body wasn't the same either.

The dead woman, wearing a white nightdress, lay on her four-poster bed in a peaceful and dignified pose, with her hands folded over a crucifix.

Everything was already in place: lit candles, holy water and a sprig of olive-wood in a cup.

43

Bouchardon looked at Maigret as he came in and seemed to be saying: 'Well! What do you think? Isn't this a good piece of work?'

The priest prayed, soundlessly moving his lips. He remained alone with the dead woman while the other two left.

In the square in front of the church the groups had thinned out. Through the curtains of the houses, families could be seen sitting down at the table for lunch.

For a few seconds, the sun tried to pierce the clouds, but then a moment later the sky turned dreary again, and the rustling of the trees grew louder.

Sitting in the corner by the window, Jean Métayer was eating mechanically as he gazed out on the empty road. Maigret was sitting at the far end of the dining room of the inn. Between them was a family from a nearby village that had arrived in a van, bringing groceries from home, and Marie Tatin was serving them drinks.

Poor Marie Tatin was in a state. She no longer had any idea what was going on. Usually she only let out an attic room from time to time, to a workman who had come to do some repairs at the chateau or one of the farms.

And here she had not only Maigret, but another lodger too: the countess's secretary.

She didn't dare to ask any questions. All morning she had heard her customers saying terrible things. She had heard them talking, among other things, about the police!

'I'm worried that the chicken may be overcooked . . .' she said as she served Maigret.

And her tone was the one in which she might have said, for example: 'I'm afraid of everything! I don't know what's going on. Holy Virgin, protect me!'

The inspector looked at her affectionately. She had always looked as fearful and sickly as she did now.

'Marie, do you remember . . .'

Her eyes widened. She was already making a defensive movement.

'. . . the thing that happened with the frogs?'

'But . . . who . . .'

'Your mother had sent you to pick mushrooms in the field behind the Notre-Dame pond . . . Three boys were playing there . . . They took advantage of a moment when you were thinking about something else to swap the mushrooms in your basket for frogs . . . And all the way home you were worried because the things were croaking . . .'

She had been studying him attentively for a few moments, and at last she stammered: 'Maigret?'

'Look! Monsieur Jean has finished his chicken and is ready for his next course.'

And all of a sudden Marie Tatin seemed completely transformed: she was more troubled than before, but also, increasingly, more trusting.

How odd life was! Years and years without the slightest incident, with nothing to break the monotony of the days. And then, all of a sudden, incomprehensible events, dramas, things you don't even read in the newspapers!

As she served Jean Métayer and the villagers, she sometimes gave Maigret a look of complicity. When he had finished, she asked shyly:

'Will you take a little glass of brandy, sir?'

'You used to call me by my first name, Marie!'

She laughed. No, she didn't dare!

'But you haven't had lunch yourself!'

'No, I have! I always eat in the kitchen, without stopping. A mouthful now . . . A mouthful later . . .'

A motorbike passed along the road. They could just make out a more elegant young man than most of the inhabitants of Saint-Fiacre.

'Who was that?'

'Didn't you see him this morning? Émile Gautier, the estate manager's son.'

'Where's he going?'

'Probably Moulins! He's practically a city-dweller. He works in a bank.'

People could be seen coming out of their houses, walking along the road or heading towards the cemetery.

Strangely, Maigret was sleepy. He felt exhausted, as if he had been over-exerting himself. And it wasn't because he had got up at half past five in the morning, or because he had caught a cold.

It was the atmosphere that was oppressing him. He felt personally affected by events, and filled with disgust.

Yes, disgust! That was the word! He had never imagined that he would find his village in this state. Even his father's grave, the stone quite blackened, where he had been told he couldn't smoke!

Opposite him, Jean Métayer emanated self-confidence. He knew he was being watched. As he ate, he forced himself to remain calm and even affected a vaguely contemptuous smile.

'A little glass?' Marie Tatin suggested to him as well.

'No, thank you! I never drink alcohol . . .'

He was polite. He liked to display good manners on all occasions. At the inn he ate with the same precious gestures as he would have done at the chateau.

Once his meal was finished, he asked: 'Do you have a telephone?'

'No, but there's one opposite, in the kiosk . . .'

He crossed the road and went into the grocery shop run by the sacristan, where the kiosk was situated. He must have been asking for a long-distance call, because he was seen waiting in the shop for a long time, smoking cigarette after cigarette.

When he came back, the villagers had left the inn. Marie Tatin washed the glasses in anticipation of Vespers, which would bring in new customers.

'Who were you calling? Remember that I can find out by going to the telephone . . .'

'My father, in Bourges.'

His voice was brusque, aggressive.

'I asked him to send me a lawyer straight away.'

He was like one of those yappy little dogs who show their teeth even before you go to touch them.

'Are you so sure that they're going to bother you?'

'I will ask you not to speak to me before my lawyer arrives. Believe me, I'm sorry there's only one inn around here.'

Did he hear the words that the inspector muttered as he left?

'Idiot! . . . Stupid little idiot . . .'

And Marie Tatin, although she didn't know why, was afraid to be left on her own with him.

The whole day would be marked by chaos, by indecision, probably because no one felt qualified to take control of events.

Maigret, wrapped up in his heavy overcoat, was wandering about the village. He was seen now in the church square, now around the chateau, whose windows were lighting up one by one.

For night was falling quickly. The church was illuminated and echoed with the sound of organ music. The bell-ringer closed the cemetery gate.

And groups of people, barely visible in the darkness, had gathered to ask each other whether they should visit the bedside of the deceased. Two men set off first, and were received by the butler, who didn't know what was supposed to happen either. No tray had been prepared for visiting cards. They tried to find Maurice de Saint-Fiacre to ask his advice, and the Russian girl replied that he had gone for a walk.

She was lying down, fully clothed, smoking cigarettes with a cardboard filter.

Then the maid ushered the people in with a shrug of indifference.

That was the signal. There were hurried confabs at the end of Vespers.

'No, they are! Old Martin and young Bonnet have been already!'

Everyone went, in procession. The chateau was dimly lit. The villagers walked along the corridor, and silhouettes stood out at each window in turn. They held their children by the hand, shaking them to stop them making any noise.

The stairs. The first-floor corridor. And at last the bedroom, which the people entered for the first time.

The only person there was the countess's maid, who witnessed the invasion with horror. People crossed themselves with a sprig of boxwood dipped in holy water. The more audacious of them murmured beneath their breath: 'She looks as if she's sleeping!'

And others, in an echo:

'She didn't suffer . . .'

Then footsteps rang out on the uneven parquet floor. The stairs creaked. People were heard saying:

'Shh! . . . Hold on tightly to the banister . . .'

The cook, in her kitchen in the basement, saw only the legs of the people passing.

Maurice de Saint-Fiacre came back just as the house was being invaded. He looked wide-eyed at the villagers. The visitors wondered whether they were supposed to talk to him or not. But he just nodded to them and went into Marie Vassiliev's room, where they heard English being spoken.

Maigret was in the church. The sacristan, snuffer in hand, was walking from candle to candle. The priest was taking off his sacerdotal garments in the sacristy.

On each side, the confessionals with their little green curtains designed to shield the penitents from view. Maigret remembered when his face didn't come up high enough to be hidden by the curtain.

Behind him the bell-ringer, who hadn't seen him, was closing the main door and drawing the bolts.

Then all of a sudden the inspector crossed the nave and stepped into the sacristy, where the priest was startled to see him appear.

'I'm sorry, Father! Before I do anything else I'd like to ask you a question . . .'

In front of him, the priest's regular features were serious, but it seemed to Maigret that his eyes blazed with fever.

'This morning, a disturbing event took place. The countess's missal, which was on her prie-dieu, suddenly disappeared and was found hidden under the altar boy's surplice, in this very room . . .'

Silence. The sound of the sacristan's footsteps on the church carpet. The louder footsteps of the bell-ringer leaving by a side door.

'Only four people could have . . . I must ask you to excuse me . . . The altar boy, the sacristan, the bell-ringer and . . .'

'Me!'

His voice was calm. The priest's face was lit only on one side by the flickering flame of a candle. From a censer, a thin thread of white smoke rose in spirals towards the ceiling.

'Was it . . . ?'

'I was the one who took the missal and put it here, while waiting for . . .'

The box of communion wafers, the cruets, the two-note bell were in their place, as they had been when little Maigret was an altar boy.

'Did you know what the missal contained?'

'No.'

'In that case . . .'

'I must ask you not to question me further, Monsieur Maigret. It's the secret of the confessional . . .'

An involuntary association of ideas. The inspector remembered the catechism, in the dining room at the presbytery. And

49

the edifying image that had formed in his mind when the old priest had told the story of a medieval priest who had had his tongue ripped out rather than betray the secret of the confessional.

He found it preserved intact on his retina, after thirty-five years.

'You know the murderer . . .' he murmured none the less.

'God knows him . . . Excuse me . . . I have to attend to a sick person . . .'

They left via the presbytery garden. A little fence separated it from the road, where people leaving the chateau stayed in groups a short distance away to talk about what had happened.

'Do you think, Father, that it might not be your place . . .'

But they bumped into the doctor, who was muttering into his beard:

'Listen, Father! Do you not think that this is starting to turn into a fairground? . . . Perhaps someone should go down there and restore some order, if only to calm the villagers down! . . . Oh! You're here, inspector! . . . Well, you're making a fine mess of things . . . As we speak, half the village is accusing the young count of . . . Especially since that woman got here! . . . The estate manager is going to see the farmers to get together the forty thousand francs which, it seems, are necessary for . . .'

'Dammit!'

Maigret walked away. He was too upset. And wasn't he being accused of being the cause of the chaos? What blunder had he committed? What had he done? He would have given anything to see events play out in a dignified atmosphere!

He strode towards the inn, which was half full. He heard only the scrap of a sentence:

'Apparently if they can't be found he will go to prison . . .'

Marie Tatin was the very image of distress. She was pacing back and forth, alert, trotting like an old woman even though she wasn't more than forty.

'Is the lemonade for you? . . . Who ordered two beers? . . .'

In his corner, Jean Métayer was writing, sometimes raising his head to listen in on the conversations.

Maigret walked over to him and couldn't read his scribbles, but saw that the lines were clearly divided, with only a few crossings-out, each one preceded by a number:

1 . . .
2 . . .
3 . . .

The secretary was preparing his defence as he waited for his lawyer!

A woman a few metres away said, 'There weren't even any clean sheets, and they had to go to the estate manager's wife to ask for them . . .'

Pale, with drawn features but a determined expression, Jean Métayer wrote:

4 . . .

5. The Second Day

Maigret slept the sleep, at once troubled and sensual, that one only ever has in a cold country room that smells of stables, winter apples and hay. Draughts circulated all around him. And his sheets were frozen, except in the exact spot, the soft, intimate hollow that he had warmed with his body. Consequently, rolled up in a ball, he avoided making the slightest movement.

Several times he had heard the dry cough of Jean Métayer in the neighbouring attic room. Then came the furtive footsteps of Marie Tatin getting up.

He stayed in bed for another few minutes. When he had lit the candle, he couldn't face washing with the icy water from the jug and, deferring the task till later, went downstairs in his slippers, without putting on a detachable collar.

Down below, Marie Tatin was pouring paraffin on a fire that wouldn't light. Her hair was rolled up in hairpins, and she blushed as she saw the inspector appear.

'It isn't yet seven o'clock . . . The coffee isn't ready . . .'

Maigret had one slight worry. In his half-sleep, half an hour before, he had thought he heard a car passing. And yet Saint-Fiacre isn't on the main road, and there was hardly any traffic apart from the bus that passed through once a day.

'Has the bus left, Marie?'

'Never before half past eight! And more often nine o'clock . . .'

'Is that the bell ringing for mass already?'

'Yes! In winter, it's at seven o'clock, six in the summer . . . If you want to warm yourself up, sir . . .'

She showed him the fire, which was blazing at last.

'Can't you bring yourself to call me by my first name?'

Maigret was cross with himself as he caught a flirtatious smile on the poor spinster's face.

'The coffee will be ready in five minutes . . .'

It wouldn't be light before eight o'clock. The cold was even keener than on the previous day. Maigret, coat collar turned up and hat down over his eyes, walked slowly towards the patch of light emanating from the church.

It wasn't a feast day any more. There were only three women in the nave. And there was something slapdash, something furtive about the mass. The priest walked too quickly from one corner of the altar to the other. He turned round too quickly, arms outspread, to murmur, swallowing syllables: *'Dominus vobiscum!'*

The altar boy, who was struggling to follow him, said *'Amen'* out of time, and hurried to ring his bell.

Was the panic going to begin again? The murmur of the liturgical prayers could be heard, and sometimes the sound of the priest taking a breath between two words.

'Ite missa est . . .'

Had this mass lasted twelve minutes? The three women got to their feet. The priest recited the last passage from the Gospel. A car stopped in front of the church, and a moment later hesitant footsteps were heard in the square.

Maigret had stayed at the end of the nave, standing right next to the door. So when it opened, the new arrival was literally face to face with him.

It was Maurice de Saint-Fiacre. He was so surprised that he nearly beat a retreat, murmuring, 'Sorry . . . I . . .'

But he stepped forwards and made an effort to regain his composure.

'Is mass over?'

He was clearly in a state of nerves. There were circles under his eyes as if he hadn't slept that night. And when he opened the door he had brought the cold in with him.

'Have you come from Moulins?'

The two men whispered to one another as the priest recited the prayer after the Gospel, and the women closed their mass-books and picked up their umbrellas and handbags.

'How did you know? . . . Yes . . . I . . .'

'Shall we go outside?'

The priest and the altar boy had gone into the sacristy, and the sacristan was snuffing the two candles which were all that had been required for the low mass.

Outside, the horizon was slightly brighter. The white of the nearby houses stood out against the gloom. The yellow car was there, between the trees in the square.

Saint-Fiacre's unease was obvious. He looked at Maigret with some astonishment, perhaps surprised to see him unshaven, and without a detachable collar under his coat.

'You got up early! . . .' murmured the inspector.

'The first train, an express, leaves Moulins at three minutes past seven . . .'

'I don't understand! You didn't take the train because . . .'

'You're forgetting Marie Vassiliev . . .'

It was perfectly simple! And natural! The presence of Maurice's mistress could only be an embarrassment at the chateau. So he drove her to Moulins by car, put her on the Paris train, came back and, in passing, entered the illuminated church.

And yet Maigret wasn't satisfied. He tried to follow the anxious glances of the count, who seemed to be waiting for something, or to fear something.

'She doesn't seem easy!' the inspector said meaningfully.

'She's known better days. And she's very touchy . . . The idea that I might want to hide our relationship . . .'

'Which has lasted for how long?'

'A little less than a year . . . Marie isn't interested . . . There have been embarrassing moments . . .'

His eye fixed at last on a single point. Maigret followed it and noticed, behind him, the priest, who had just come out of the church. He had a sense that those two glances had met, that the priest was just as embarrassed as the Count of Saint-Fiacre.

The inspector was about to call out to him. But with awkward haste the priest had already addressed a brief word of greeting to the two men and gone inside the presbytery, as if escaping.

'He doesn't look like a country priest . . .'

Maurice didn't reply. Through the lit window the priest could be seen sitting over his breakfast, and the housekeeper bringing him a steaming pot of coffee.

Some children, with bags on their backs, were starting to make their way towards the school. The surface of the Notre-Dame pond was assuming the colours of a looking-glass.

'What arrangements have you made for . . .' Maigret began.

And the other man replied, far too quickly:

'For what?'

'For the funeral . . . Did someone sit vigil in the room of the departed?'

'No! It was briefly discussed . . . Gautier said people didn't do that any more . . .'

The sound of a two-stroke engine was heard coming from the chateau courtyard. A few moments later a motorbike passed along the road, heading towards Moulins. Maigret recognized Gautier's son, whom he had seen the previous day. He was wearing a beige mackintosh and a checked cap.

Maurice de Saint-Fiacre didn't know what attitude to assume. He didn't dare get back into his car. And he had nothing to say to the inspector.

'Did Gautier find the forty thousand francs?'

'No . . . Yes . . . that is . . .'

Maigret looked at him curiously, surprised to see him so agitated.

'Did he find them, yes or no? I had a sense, yesterday, that he wasn't happy about the idea. Because in spite of everything,

55

in spite of the debts and mortgages, you'll be able to raise much more money than that . . .'

But no! Maurice didn't reply! He looked distraught, for no apparent reason. And the words he uttered bore no relation to what had gone before.

'Tell me honestly, inspector . . . Do you suspect me?'

'Of what?'

'You know . . . I need to know . . .'

'I have no more reason to suspect you than anyone else . . .' Maigret replied evasively.

And his companion pounced on the assertion.

'Thank you! . . . Well, that's what you have to tell people . . . You understand? . . . Otherwise my position isn't tenable . . .'

'Which bank does your cheque have to be presented at?'

'The Comptoir d'Escompte . . .'

A woman was walking towards the public laundry, pushing a barrow that carried two baskets of linen. The priest, in his house, paced back and forth, reading his breviary, but the inspector had a sense that he was darting anxious glances at the two men.

'I'll join you at the chateau.'

'Now?'

'In a moment, yes.'

It was quite plain: Maurice de Saint-Fiacre wasn't at all happy with that. He got into his car like a condemned man. And behind the windows of the presbytery the priest could be seen watching him leave.

At the very least Maigret wanted to go and put on a collar. Just as he arrived outside the inn, Jean Métayer was coming out of the grocer's shop. He had merely put a coat on over his pyjamas. He looked triumphantly at the inspector.

'Phone call?'

And the young man replied sharply, 'My lawyer will be here at ten to nine.'

He was sure of himself. He sent back some boiled eggs which hadn't been cooked for long enough and tapped out a march on the table with his fingertips.

From the skylight of his room, where he had gone to get dressed, Maigret could see the courtyard of the chateau, the racing car and Maurice de Saint-Fiacre, who looked as if he didn't know what to do. Was he preparing to walk towards the village?

The inspector got a move on. A few minutes later he himself was on his way to the chateau. They met about a hundred metres from the church.

'Where were you going?' Maigret asked.

'Nowhere! I don't know . . .'

'Maybe to pray at the church?'

And those words were enough to turn his companion pale, as if they had a terrible, mysterious significance.

Maurice de Saint-Fiacre was not built for stress. Superficially, he was a tall, strong young man, athletic and perfectly healthy.

But looking closer you saw that he was soft. His muscles, beneath a layer of fat, seemed to have hardly any energy. He had probably spent a sleepless night, and he looked thoroughly deflated.

'I assume you've had the announcements printed?'

'No.'

'But . . . the family . . . the local aristocrats . . .'

The young man lost his temper.

'They wouldn't come! You know that very well! Once they would have done! When my father was still alive . . . During the hunting season, there would be up to thirty guests at the chateau at once, for weeks . . .'

Nobody knew that better than Maigret, who, during the hunting season had, without his parents' knowledge, loved to wear the white shirt of a beater!

'Since . . .'

And Maurice waved a hand to suggest: 'Insolvency . . . junk . . .'

The whole of Berry must have been talking about the mad old woman who was frittering away the last years of her life with so-called secretaries! And farms being sold one after the other! And sons behaving like idiots in Paris!

'Do you think the funeral might happen tomorrow? . . . You understand? . . . It would be better to get this business over and done with as soon as possible . . .'

A dung cart passed slowly along, and its wide wheels seemed to crush the pebbles in the road. Day had broken, a day greyer than the previous one, but not as windy. In the distance Maigret saw Gautier, who was crossing the courtyard and about to head in his direction.

And it was then that a strange thing happened.

'Will you excuse me? . . .' the inspector said to his companion, setting off in the direction of the chateau.

He had barely walked a hundred metres when he turned round. Maurice de Saint-Fiacre was on the steps of the presbytery. He must have rung the doorbell. And yet, when he saw he had been spotted, he walked away quickly without waiting for a reply.

He didn't know where to go. His whole bearing proved that he was terribly ill at ease. The inspector caught up with the estate manager, whom he had seen coming towards him and who was waiting for him with an arrogant look.

'What can I do for you?'

'I'd like a simple piece of information. Have you found the forty thousand francs the count needs?'

'No! And I defy anyone to find it around here! Everyone knows what his signature is worth.'

'And so? . . .'

'He will manage as best he can! It has nothing to do with me!'

Saint-Fiacre turned on his heels. It looked as if he had a desperate urge to do something and that, for one reason or another, he couldn't. Making up his mind, he strode towards the chateau and stopped near the two men.

'Gautier! Come to the library so that I can issue you with instructions!'

He began to set off, then said, evidently with some considerable effort:

'See you shortly, inspector.'

Passing in front of the presbytery, Maigret had the distinct sensation of being watched through the curtains. But he wasn't sure because, since it was day, the lights were turned out.

A taxi was parked outside Marie Tatin's inn. In the dining room, a man of about fifty, dressed to the nines, pinstriped trousers and a black silk-lined jacket, was sitting at Jean Métayer's table.

When he saw the inspector come in, he rose eagerly to his feet, extending a hand.

'I am told that you are a member of the Police Judiciaire . . . Allow me to introduce myself . . . Tallier, barrister-at-law, from the court at Bourges . . . Will you join us? . . .'

Jean Métayer had got to his feet, but his attitude demonstrated that he didn't approve of his lawyer's conviviality.

'Innkeeper! . . . We'd like to order, please . . .'

And, in a conciliatory voice:

'What would you like? Given how cold it is, I'd suggest hot rum for everybody? . . . Three hot rums, my girl . . .'

The girl in question was poor Marie Tatin, who wasn't used to such manners.

'I hope, detective chief inspector, that you will forgive my client. If I understand correctly, he has treated you with a degree of suspicion . . . But don't forget that he is a boy from a good family, who is of good character, and who is outraged by the suspicions directed towards him . . . His bad mood yesterday, if I may say so, is the best proof of his absolute innocence . . .'

With a man such as this, there was no need to say a word. He answered his own questions, while performing suave hand gestures.

'Of course, I'm still not au fait with all the details . . . If I understand correctly, the Countess of Saint-Fiacre died yesterday, during first mass, of a heart attack . . . On the other hand, a piece of paper has been found in her missal which suggests that her death was caused by a violent shock . . . Did the son of the victim – who happened to be nearby – register a complaint? . . . No! . . . And such a complaint would, in my opinion, be rejected . . . The criminal act – if we may speak of a criminal act – is not in fact sufficiently clear for legal proceedings to be instigated . . .

'We are agreed, are we not? . . . No complaint! And hence no legal action.

'Which is not to say that I don't understand the inquiry that you are pursuing on a personal, unofficial basis . . .

'My client will not tolerate being hounded in this way. He must be cleared of all suspicion . . .

'Listen to me carefully . . . What, in the end, was his situation at the chateau? . . . That of an adopted child . . . The countess, left on her own, separated from a son who had left her with nothing but problems, was comforted by the devotion and uprightness of her secretary . . .

'My client is no idler . . . He did not, as he might easily have done, lead a carefree life at the chateau . . . He worked . . . He looked for investments . . . He even looked into the latest inventions . . .

'Would he have derived any benefit from the death of his benefactress? . . . Need I say anything more? . . . No! Am I not correct? . . .

'And that, inspector, is what I want to help you establish . . .

'I should add that I will be putting some necessary measures in place in tandem with the notary . . . Jean Métayer is a trusting young man . . . Never in his life would he have imagined such events taking place . . .

'His belongings are at the chateau, along with the belongings of the late countess . . .

'And yet, as of now, other people have turned up there, with the clear intention of getting their hands on . . .'

'A few pairs of pyjamas and some old slippers!' groaned Maigret as he got up from his chair.

'Excuse me?'

Throughout the whole of the conversation, Jean Métayer had been writing things down in a little notebook. And it was he who calmed down his lawyer, who had in turn leaped to his feet.

'Leave it! I knew straight away that the inspector would be against me! And I have since learned that he belonged indirectly to the chateau, where he was born in the days when his father was the estate manager of the Saint-Fiacres. I warned you . . . You were the one who wanted . . .'

The clock struck ten. Maigret calculated that Marie Vassiliev's train would have arrived at the Gare de Lyon half an hour earlier.

'You will excuse me!' he said. 'I will see you again in due course.'

'But . . .'

He in turn stepped into the grocery opposite, whose bell rang. He waited a quarter of an hour for a call to be connected to Paris.

'Is it true that you're the son of the old estate manager?'

Maigret was exhausted, more than he would have been after ten normal investigations. He ached, both emotionally and physically.

'Paris speaking . . .'

'Hello! . . . The Comptoir d'Escompte? . . . This is the Police Judiciaire . . . A piece of information please . . . Has a cheque signed Saint-Fiacre been presented this morning? . . . You say it was presented at nine o'clock? . . . So, insufficient funds . . . Hello! . . . Please don't hang up, madam . . . You asked the bearer to present it a second time? . . . Excellent! . . . Ah! That's what I wanted to know . . . A young woman, is that right? . . . A quarter of an hour ago? . . . And she paid in the forty thousand francs? . . . Thank you . . . Of course you can pay! . . . No! No! Nothing in particular . . . Given that the deposit has been made . . .'

And Maigret left the cabin with a weary sigh.

Maurice de Saint-Fiacre, during the night, had found the forty thousand francs and sent his mistress to Paris to deposit them at the bank!

Just as the inspector was leaving the grocer's shop, he saw the priest leaving his house, clutching his breviary and heading towards the chateau.

Then he speeded up and almost ran to get to the door at the same time as the priest.

He missed him by less than a minute. By the time he reached the main courtyard the door was closing behind the priest. And when he rang the doorbell there were footsteps at the end of the corridor, near the library.

6. The Two Camps

'Let me go and see if the count can . . .'

But the inspector didn't give the butler time to finish his sentence. He stepped into the corridor and headed for the library. The butler heaved a sigh of resignation. There wasn't even a way of keeping up appearances any more! People were treating the place like a hotel! It was chaos!

Maigret paused before opening the library door, but to no end, because he didn't hear a sound. It was, in fact, what gave his entrance an impressive quality.

He knocked, thinking that the priest might be somewhere else. But a voice immediately rang out, clearly and firmly, in the absolute silence of the room:

'Come in!'

Maigret pushed the door, which happened to catch on an air vent. The Count of Saint-Fiacre, who stood leaning against the gothic table, was looking at him.

Beside him, the priest was staring at the carpet, frozen, as if a single movement would have given him away.

What were they doing there, the two of them, not talking, not moving? It would have been less embarrassing to interrupt an emotional scene than to plunge into that silence, so deep that his voice seemed to trace concentric circles in it like a pebble in water.

Once again Maigret sensed Saint-Fiacre's weariness. The priest looked ill at ease, and his fingers drummed against his breviary.

'Forgive me for disturbing you . . .'

It sounded ironic, but it wasn't deliberate. Does one disturb people when they are as inert as inanimate objects?

'I have some news from the bank . . .'

The count's eyes settled on the priest, and his gaze was harsh, almost furious.

The whole scene would play out in that rhythm. They were like chess-players thinking, foreheads resting on their hands, sitting in silence for a few minutes before moving a pawn and then relapsing into stillness.

But it wasn't concentration that held them frozen like that. Maigret was certain that it was the fear of making a false move, or some kind of clumsy manoeuvre. The situation between them was ambiguous. And each of them advanced his pawn regretfully, always ready to move it back again.

'I've come for the funeral instructions!' the priest felt the need to say.

It wasn't true! A bad move. So bad that the Count of Saint-Fiacre smiled.

'I knew you would call the bank!' he said. 'And I will confess to you why I decided to take that course of action: it was to get rid of Marie Vassiliev, who didn't want to leave the chateau . . . I let her believe that it was of vital importance . . .'

And in the eyes of the priest Maigret now read anxiety and reproach.

'Poor wretch!' he was doubtless thinking. 'He's tying himself up in knots! He's falling into the trap. He's lost . . .'

Silence. The scrape of a match and puffs of tobacco smoke that the inspector exhaled one by one as he questioned the count:

'Did Gautier find the money?'

A brief moment's hesitation.

'No, inspector . . . I'm going to tell you that . . .'

The drama was being played out not on Saint-Fiacre's face, but on the priest's. The man was pale, his lips taut. He opted not to intervene.

'Inspector, I . . .'

He couldn't help it.

'I would like you to suspend this conversation until we have had a private discussion on the matter . . .'

Maurice smiled as he had done a few moments before. It was cold in the room, too vast now that the fine books of the library had been removed from it. A fire had been prepared in the hearth. All that was needed was a match to be thrown on it.

'Do you have a lighter or . . .'

And as he bent over the fireplace the priest gave Maigret a desolate, pleading look.

'Now,' the count said as he turned back towards the two men, 'I'm going to explain the situation in a few words. For a reason that I do not know, the parish priest, with the best of intentions, is sure that it was I who . . . why mince words? . . . who killed my mother! . . . Because it is a crime, isn't it? Even if it isn't one that falls within the scope of the law . . .'

The priest didn't move, but stood quivering and still as an animal that is aware of an imminent danger, a danger for which it is no match.

'He must have been very devoted to my mother . . . He probably wanted to ensure that the chateau didn't find itself at the centre of any kind of scandal . . . Yesterday evening, via the sacristan, he sent me forty thousand francs and a little note . . .'

And the priest's expression said, beyond any possible doubt:

'Wretch! You are destroying yourself with your own hands!'

'Here is the note!' Saint-Fiacre continued.

Maigret read under his breath: 'Be careful. I am praying for you . . .'

At last! It was like a breath of fresh air. All of a sudden Maurice de Saint-Fiacre no longer felt rooted to the ground, condemned to stillness. And he also stripped away the mask of seriousness, which didn't match his character.

He started pacing back and forth, a sense of relief apparent in his voice.

'So, inspector, now you know why you saw me roaming around the church and the presbytery this morning . . . I accepted the forty thousand francs, which must obviously be considered a loan, first of all, as I have told you, to get rid of my mistress – forgive me, Father! . . . – and also because it would have been particularly disagreeable to be arrested at that moment . . . But we are all still standing as if . . . Please, do sit down . . .'

He went and opened the door and heard a noise on the floor above.

'The procession is starting up again!' he murmured. 'I think I'll have to call Moulins and ask them to set up a chapel of rest . . .'

Then, abruptly:

'I suppose you understand now! Once I had accepted the money, I had to swear to the priest that I wasn't guilty. It was hard to do that in front of you, inspector, without increasing your suspicions . . . That's all! . . . As if you'd guessed my thoughts, you haven't left me alone for a moment this morning, near the church . . . The priest turned up here, I still don't know why, because as soon as you came in he was reluctant to speak . . .'

His gaze darkened. To dispel the rancour that assailed him he laughed, an awkward laugh.

'It's simple, isn't it? A man who has lived a riotous life, and who has signed bad cheques . . . Old Gautier avoids me! . . . He too must be sure that—'

He suddenly looked in amazement at the priest.

'Well, Father . . . What did you? . . .'

The priest had in fact assumed a funereal appearance. His gaze avoided the young man's, and tried to avoid Maigret's as well.

Maurice de Saint-Fiacre understood and exclaimed more bitterly:

'There we are! People still don't believe me . . . And the one who wants to save me is the very one convinced of my guilt . . .'

He went and opened the door again and called out, forgetting the presence of the dead woman in the house:

'Albert! . . . Albert! . . . Faster than that, damn it all! . . . Bring us something to drink . . .'

And the butler came in and walked to a cupboard from which he took whisky and glasses. They watched him in silence. Then Maurice de Saint-Fiacre said with a strange smile:

'In my day there was no whisky in the chateau.'

'It was Monsieur Jean . . .'

'Ah!'

He took a great swig and locked the door behind the manservant.

'Many such things have changed . . .' he murmured to himself.

But he didn't take his eyes off the priest, who stammered, with mounting unease:

'You will forgive me . . . I have to go and do the catechism . . .'

'Just one moment . . . You are still convinced of my guilt, Father . . . No, don't deny it . . . Priests don't know how to lie . . . But there are a few points I'd like to explain to you . . . Because you don't know me . . . You weren't at Saint-Fiacre in my day . . . You've just heard people talking about me . . . There are no material clues . . . The inspector, who witnessed the events, knows something about that . . .'

'Please . . .' stammered the priest.

'No! . . . You're not drinking? . . . To your health, inspector . . .'

And his face was grim. He was furiously following the train of his thoughts.

'There are lots of people who might fall under suspicion . . . And yet your suspicions rest entirely on me . . . And I wonder why that is . . . It kept me awake last night . . . I thought about all the possible reasons, and in the end I think I've found . . . What did my mother say to you?'

This time the priest's face drained of blood.

'I don't know anything . . .' he stammered.

'Please, Father . . . You've helped me, certainly! . . . You let me have those forty thousand francs that give me time to breathe and bury my mother in a decent way . . . I thank you with all my heart . . . Except at the same time, you are letting all your suspicions weigh upon me . . . You pray for me . . . It's too much, or not enough . . .'

And a hint of anger, or menace, began to appear in his voice.

'At first I thought I might be able to have an explanation from you, without Detective Chief Inspector Maigret being present . . . Well, I won't conceal the fact that I'm glad he's here too! . . . The more I think about it, the more I have a sense that there's something murky . . .'

'Monsieur, please don't torture me any more . . .'

'And for my part, Father, I warn you that you will not leave here before you have told me the truth!'

He was a different man. He had reached his limit. And like all weak, meek people, his ferocity was excessive.

His voice was now so loud that it must have been audible in the mortuary chamber, just above the library.

'You saw my mother often . . . And I imagine that Jean Métayer attended your church as well . . . Which of the two told you something? . . . It was my mother, wasn't it? . . .'

Maigret remembered what he had heard the day before:

The secret of the confessional . . .

It was then that he understood the priest's torment, his anxiety, his martyred expression as Saint-Fiacre's torrent of words crashed down on him.

'What could she have told you? . . . I know her, after all . . . You might say that I was present when things began to slip . . . We are among people who know all about life . . .'

He looked around, with silent rage:

'There was a time when people only came into this room holding their breath, because my father, the *boss*, was working there . . . There was no whisky in the cupboards . . . But the shelves were full of books as the combs of a beehive are saturated with honey . . .'

And Maigret remembered too!

The count is working . . .

And those words were enough to keep the tenant farmers waiting in the hall for two hours!

The count let me into the library . . .

And Maigret's father was worried, because it was beginning to sound like an important event.

'He didn't like to waste logs, but instead settled for a paraffin heater that he put right next to him, to supplement the boiler . . .' said Maurice de Saint-Fiacre.

And, to the distraught priest:

'You never knew that . . . You only ever knew the chateau in a state of chaos . . . My mother after she lost her husband . . . My mother whose only son got up to all sorts of nonsense in Paris and only ever came home to ask for money . . . And then, the secretaries . . .'

His eyes were so glistening that Maigret expected to see a tear fall from them at any moment.

'What did she say to you? . . . She was afraid to see me turning up, wasn't she? . . . She knew there would be yet another hole to fill, something she'd have to sell to put me back on my feet once again . . .'

'You should calm down!' the priest said in a flat voice.

'Not before knowing . . . whether you've suspected me without knowing me from the very first moment . . .'

Maigret broke in.

'The priest made the missal disappear . . .' he said slowly.

He had already worked it out! He was coming to the aid of Saint-Fiacre. He imagined the countess, torn between sin and remorse . . . Didn't she fear punishment? . . . Didn't she feel a little ashamed before her son? . . .

She was a sick and troubled soul! And why, in the secret of

the confessional, might she not one day have said, 'I'm afraid of my son . . .'

Because she must have been afraid of him. The money that passed to people like Jean Métayer was Saint-Fiacre money, meant for Maurice. Was he not bound to come sooner or later and ask for an explanation? Would he not . . .

And Maigret felt that these ideas were dawning, still confused, in the young man's brain. He helped him to set them out more clearly.

'The priest can't say anything if the countess's words were spoken under the secret of the confessional . . .'

It was quite clear. Maurice de Saint-Fiacre broke off the conversation.

'You will forgive me, Father . . . I forgot your catechism . . . Please don't be angry with me for . . .'

He turned the key in the lock and opened the door.

'Thank you . . . As soon as . . . as soon as possible I'll give you back the forty thousand francs . . . Because I assume they don't belong to you . . .'

'I approached Madame Ruinard, the widow of the old notary . . .'

'Thank you . . . Goodbye . . .'

He nearly slammed the door but restrained himself and looked Maigret in the eyes, snapping:

'What rubbish!'

'He wanted . . .'

'He wanted to save me, I know! . . . He was trying to avoid a scandal, somehow to glue the pieces of the Château de Saint-Fiacre back together . . . That's not the point! . . .'

He poured himself some whisky.

'It's that poor woman I'm thinking about! . . . Take Marie Vassiliev, for example . . . And all the others, in Paris . . . They have no pangs of conscience . . . While she, on the other hand! . . . And bear in mind that what she wanted above all from that fellow Métayer was affection . . . Then she hurried to the confessional . . . She must have seen herself as a monster . . . And from there to fearing my revenge . . . Ha! Ha! . . .'

His laugh was terrifying.

'You see me raging furiously at my mother because . . . And the priest hasn't understood a thing! . . . He sees life purely in terms of the scriptures! . . . In my mother's lifetime, he must have tried to save her from herself . . . Now that my mother is dead, he thought it was his duty to save me . . . But right now, I'm willing to bet, he's convinced that I was the one who . . .'

And he looked the inspector straight in the eye and said:

'And what about you?'

And when Maigret didn't reply:

'Because there has been a crime . . . A crime that only the worst kind of wretch could commit . . . A revolting coward! . . . Is the law really powerless to deal with him? . . . That's what you said . . . But there's something I want to tell you, inspector, and I grant you permission to use it against me . . . When I get hold of that little scoundrel, I'm the one he'll have to deal with . . . And I won't need a gun! No, no weapons . . . These hands will be quite enough! . . .'

He was clearly fired up by alcohol. He must have been aware of it, because he ran his hand over his brow, looked at his reflection in the mirror and addressed a mocking grimace to himself.

'However it's also true that without the priest I would have been arrested even before the funeral! I haven't been very nice to him . . . The old notary's wife who's paying my debts . . . Who is she? . . . I don't even remember her . . .'

'The lady who always dresses in white . . . The house with the gate with gold arrows, on the Matignon road . . .'

Maurice de Saint-Fiacre calmed down. His fever had only been a flash in the pan. He began to pour himself a drink, hesitated, drained the contents of his glass in one go, with a pout of revulsion.

'Do you hear that?'

'What?'

'The locals filing past upstairs! I should be up there, in mourning, red-eyed, shaking hands and looking grief-stricken! Once they're outside they'll start talking . . .'

And, in a suspicious voice:

'But in fact if, as you say, the law can do nothing about the affair, why are you staying in Saint-Fiacre?'

'Something else might happen . . .'

'And if I discovered the guilty party, would you stop me from . . .'

His clenched fingers were more eloquent than any speech.

'I will leave you now,' Maigret said abruptly. 'I must go and keep an eye on the other front . . .'

'The other front?'

'The one at the inn! Jean Métayer and his lawyer, who arrived this morning . . .'

'He's got a lawyer?'

'He's a far-sighted young man . . . This morning, people were organized like this: at the chateau, you and the priest; at the inn, the young man and his counsel . . .'

'Do you think he was capable of . . .'

'Please excuse me if I serve myself?'

And Maigret drank a glass, wiped his lips and stuffed one last pipe before leaving.

'I assume you don't know how to use a linotype machine?'

A shrug.

'I don't know how to use anything at all . . . That's precisely the problem! . . .'

'And you're not going to leave the village without telling me under any circumstances, are you?'

A serious, deep expression. And a serious, deep voice:

'I promise you!'

★

Maigret went outside. He was about to walk down the steps when suddenly, out of nowhere, there was a man standing next to him.

'Excuse me, inspector . . . I wonder if you might give me a few moments of your time . . . I've heard . . .'

'What?'

'That you were almost part of the household . . . Your father was in the trade . . . Please do me the honour of coming to my house and joining me for a drink . . .'

And the grey-bearded estate manager led his companion across the courtyards. Everything was ready at his house. A bottle of brandy whose label announced its venerable age. Some biscuits. A smell of cabbage and bacon came from the kitchen.

'From what I've heard, you knew the chateau in different circumstances . . . When I arrived there, the chaos was just beginning . . . There was a young man from Paris who . . . This brandy is from the days of the old count . . . No sugar, I assume?'

Maigret stared at the table with the carved lions holding brass rings in their mouths. And once again he felt his physical and emotional exhaustion. In the old days, he had only been allowed to come into this room in his slippers, because of the waxed parquet.

'I'm very embarrassed . . . And you're the one whose advice I want to ask . . . We are poor people. You are familiar with the estate manager's trade, which doesn't make a man rich . . .

'Some Saturdays when there was no money in the cash box, I paid the farm workers myself . . .

'And sometimes I even paid for the livestock that the tenant farmers said they needed . . .'

'In other words, to cut a long story short, the countess owed you money!'

'The countess didn't know anything about business . . . The money disappeared in all directions . . . It was only for indispensable matters that none could be found.'

'And it was you who . . .'

'Your father would have done the same, wouldn't he? There are times when you mustn't let the local people know that the coffers are empty . . . I took money from my savings . . .'

'How much?'

'Another little glass? . . . I didn't do the sums. At least seventy thousand . . . And now once again, for the funeral, I'm the one who . . .'

Maigret saw it vividly: his father's little office, near the stables, at five o'clock on Saturday. All the people who worked at the chateau, from linen maids to day labourers, waited outside. And old Maigret, sitting in the office lined with green baize, made little piles of silver coins. They all passed by in turn and wrote their signature or a cross in the accounts book.

'Now I wonder how I'm going to recover the . . . For people like us it's . . .'

'Yes, I understand! You've had the fireplace changed!'

'Well, it was made of wood . . . The marble looks better . . .'

'A lot better!' muttered Maigret.

'You understand! All the creditors will pounce on us! We'll have to sell up! And with all these mortgages . . .'

The armchair Maigret was sitting in was new, like the mantelpiece, and must have come from a shop on Boulevard Barbès. There was a phonograph on the sideboard.

'If I had no sons I wouldn't mind, but Émile has his career to think of . . . I don't want to rush things . . .'

A girl crossed the corridor.

'Do you have a daughter as well?'

'No! She's a local girl who comes and helps out.'

'Well! We'll talk again, Monsieur Gautier. Excuse me, but I've still got lots of things to do . . .'

'One last little glass?'

'No, thank you . . . You said around seventy-five thousand, didn't you?' And he left, hands in his pockets, passed through the flock of geese, walked along the Notre-Dame pond, which was no longer lapping at the shore. The church clock rang on the stroke of noon.

At Marie Tatin's, Jean Métayer and the lawyer were having lunch. Sardines, herring fillets and garlic sausage for starters. On the nearby table were the glasses that had held the aperitifs.

The two men were in a cheerful mood. They welcomed Maigret with ironic glances. They winked at each other. The lawyer's briefcase was closed.

'Did you find any truffles for the chicken, at least?' he asked.

Poor Marie Tatin! She had found a very small tin in the grocer's, but she couldn't get it open. She didn't dare admit it.

'I found some, monsieur!'

'Then hurry up! This country air gives you a terrific appetite!'

It was Maigret who went to the kitchen and who used his knife to cut into the metal of the tin while the cross-eyed woman stammered in a low voice:

'I'm confused . . . I . . .'

'Shut up, Marie!' he muttered.

One camp . . . Two camps . . . Three camps?

He felt a need to joke to escape reality.

'By the way! The priest asked me to bring you three hundred indulgences! To make up for your sins!'

And Marie Tatin, who didn't get the joke, looked up at her companion with a mixture of fear and respectful affection.

7. Appointments in Moulins

Maigret had phoned Moulins to order a taxi. At first he was surprised to see one arriving about ten minutes after his call, but, as he was heading for the door, the lawyer, who had been finishing his coffee, cut in.

'Sorry! That's ours . . . But if you want to join us . . .'

'Thank you, but . . .'

Jean Métayer and the lawyer left first, in a big car that still bore the family crest of its former owner. A quarter of an hour later Maigret left in turn and as he travelled along, chatting to the driver, he observed the landscape.

The setting was monotonous: two rows of poplars along the road, ploughed fields as far as the eye could see, with the occasional rectangle of copse, and the blue-green eye of a pond.

Most of the houses were little shacks. This made sense, because there were no small landowners.

Nothing but large estates, one of which, the one that belonged to the Duke of T— included three villages.

The Saint-Fiacre estate had covered two thousand hectares before the sequence of sales.

The sole means of transport was an old Paris bus bought by a farmer, which travelled between Moulins and Saint-Fiacre once a day.

'We're in the middle of the countryside here,' said the driver. 'You haven't seen anything yet. But in the depths of winter . . .'

As they drove along the main Moulins road the clock on the church of Saint-Pierre struck half past two. Maigret stopped the cab outside the Comptoir d'Escompte and paid the fare. Just as he turned away from the taxi to head towards the bank, a woman came out of it, holding a little boy by the hand.

And the inspector quickly immersed himself in the contemplation of a shop window so as not to be noticed. She was a countrywoman in her Sunday best, her hat balanced on her hair, her waist constrained by a corset. She held herself upright, dragging the child along behind her, paying him no more heed than she would have done to a parcel.

It was the mother of Ernest, the Saint-Fiacre altar boy.

The street was busy. Ernest would have liked to stop and look at the window displays, but he was caught up in the wake of the black skirt. Nevertheless, his mother bent down to say something to him. And, as if it had been decided in advance, she stepped inside a toyshop with him.

Maigret didn't dare to get too close. And yet he received the information he needed in the form of some whistle-blasts that emanated from the shop a moment later. They were trying out every imaginable whistle, and in the end the altar boy had to opt for a two-note boy-scout model.

When he came out he was wearing it around his neck, but his mother continued to drag him along and wouldn't let him use the instrument in the street.

A bank branch like any other in the provinces. A long oak counter. Five clerks leaning on desks. Maigret made for the counter marked 'Current Accounts', and a clerk rose to his feet and waited to serve him.

Maigret wanted to find out about the exact state of the Saint-Fiacre fortune, and particularly about the transactions of the previous few weeks, or indeed the previous few days, which he thought might provide him with a clue.

But he paused in silence for a moment, studying the young man who stood there politely, without a hint of impatience.

'Émile Gautier, I assume?'

He had seen him pass by twice on his motorbike, although hadn't been able to make out his features. But it was the striking resemblance to the estate manager of the chateau that left no doubt.

Not so much a resemblance in terms of detail as a resemblance in terms of breeding. The same peasant origins: marked features, robust bones.

His degree of social advancement was more or less the same, his skin better groomed than that of the farmers, his expression intelligent, his assurance that of an 'educated' man.

But Émile wasn't yet a city type. His hair, although brilliantined, was still rebellious and stood up in a tuft on the top of his head. His cheeks were pink, like those of village toughs, scrubbed clean on Sunday mornings.

'That's me.'

He wasn't troubled. Maigret was sure that he must be a model employee, in whom his manager had every confidence and who would soon be due for promotion.

A black suit, made to measure but by a local tailor, in indestructible serge. His father wore celluloid collars. He, on the other hand, wore soft ones, but his tie was still elastic.

'Do you recognize me?'

'No! I assume you're the policeman . . .'

'And I would like some information about the state of the Saint-Fiacre account.

'That's easy! I've been put in charge of that account, as I have of many others.'

He was polite, well brought up. At school he must have been the teacher's pet.

'Let me have a look at the Saint-Fiacre account!' he said to a clerk sitting behind him.

And his eye skimmed a big sheet of yellow paper.

'Would you like a statement, the balance or general information?'

At least he was precise!

'Would general information be all right?'

'Would you mind coming over here? . . . People might hear us . . .'

And they reached the end of the room but were still separated by the oak counter.

'My father must have told you the countess was very chaotic . . . I was constantly having to stop cheques that would otherwise have bounced . . . In fact she wasn't aware of it . . . She drew cheques without worrying about the state of her account . . . And then, when I phoned her to let her know, she lost her head . . . Even this morning, three dud cheques were presented, and I was forced to turn them down . . . I've been given an order not to pay anything before . . .'

'Is she completely ruined?'

'Not exactly . . . Three farms out of five have been sold . . . The two others have been mortgaged, along with the chateau . . . The countess had a block of flats in Paris that brought her in a small income . . . But when all of a sudden she paid forty or fifty thousand francs into her son's account, it threw everything out of kilter . . . I always tried to do what I could . . . I delayed payments two or three times . . . My father . . .'

'Lent some money, I know.'

'That's all I can tell you . . . Right now, the balance is exactly seven hundred and seventy-five francs . . . Bear in mind that property tax hasn't been paid for last year, and that the bailiff issued a first warning last week . . .'

'Is Jean Métayer aware of this?'

'He's aware of everything! And perhaps more than aware.'

'What do you mean?'

'Nothing!'

'Do you think he has his feet on the ground?'

But Émile Gautier, the soul of discretion, did not reply.

'Is that all you want to know?'

'Do any other residents of Saint-Fiacre have their accounts at your branch?'

'No!'

'No one came today to make a transaction? To cash a cheque, for example?'

'No one.'

'And you were at your counter all the time?'

'I never left it!'

He wasn't concerned. Ever the model employee, he replied as one must to an important person.

'Would you like to see the manager? Although he won't be able to tell you more than I can . . .'

The streetlights were coming on. The main street was so busy it was almost like a big city, and there were long queues of cars outside the cafés.

A procession was passing by: two camels and a baby elephant bearing advertising streamers for a circus set up in Place de la Victoire. In a grocer's shop, Maigret noticed the altar boy's mother, still holding him by the hand and buying tins of food.

A little further on he nearly bumped into Métayer and his lawyer, who were walking busily along, talking. The lawyer was saying:

'. . . they'll have to block it . . .'

They didn't see the inspector and carried on towards the Comptoir d'Escompte.

You inevitably meet everyone ten times an afternoon, in a town that consists entirely of a street five hundred metres long.

Maigret was on his way to the printworks of the *Journal de Moulins*. The offices were at the front of the building: modern shop windows, with a large display of press photographs and the latest news, handwritten in blue pencil, on long strips of paper.

Mondchourie. The Havas Press Agency informs us that . . .

But, to get to the printworks, one had first to turn down a dark alley, guided by the noise of the rotary press. In a desolate studio, men in overalls worked at tall marble tables. In a glazed cage at the end were the two linotypes, rattling away like machine guns.

'The foreman, please . . .'

He literally had to shout, because of the thundering noise of the machines. The smell of ink caught his throat. A little man in blue overalls who was setting the type in a press form cupped a hand to his ear.

'Are you the foreman?'

'I'm the page setter!'

Maigret took from his wallet the piece of paper that had killed the Countess of Saint-Fiacre. The man put on steel-rimmed glasses, looked at it and wondered what it might mean.

'Is this one of yours?'

'What? . . .'

People ran past, carrying piles of newspapers.

'I'm asking you if this was printed here.'

'Come with me!'

It was easier in the courtyard. It was cold, but at least they could talk in an almost normal voice.

'What did you ask me?'

'Do you recognize the type?'

'It's 9-point Cheltenham.'

'From here?'

'Almost all linotypes use Cheltenham.'

'Are there other linotypes in Moulins?'

'Not in Moulins . . . But in Nevers, in Bourges, in Chatcauroux, in Autun, in . . .'

'Is there anything special about this particular document?'

'It's been printed using a planer . . . They wanted to make it look like a newspaper cutting, didn't they? . . . I was once asked to do the same thing, for a joke . . .'

81

'Aha!'

'At least fifteen years ago . . . When we still set the newspaper by hand . . .'

'And the paper doesn't give you a clue?'

'Almost all provincial newspapers use the same supplier. It's German paper . . . Excuse me . . . I have to finish setting the type . . . It's for the Nièvre edition . . .'

'Do you know Jean Métayer?'

The man shrugged.

'What do you think of him?'

'To listen to him you'd think he knew the trade better than we do. He's got a screw loose . . . We let him fiddle about in the workshop, because of the countess, who's a friend of the boss . . .'

'Can he use a linotype machine?'

'Hmm! . . . Well, he says he can! . . .'

'Well, could he have set this paragraph?'

'If he had a good two hours to spare . . . Starting the same line ten times over again . . .'

'Did he have access to a linotype machine any time recently?'

'What do I know? He comes! He goes! He irritates us all with his photographic techniques . . . You'll forgive me . . . The train won't wait . . . And my form isn't finished yet . . .'

There was no point pressing the matter. Maigret was about to go into the studio again, but the bustling activity in there put him off. These people didn't have much time on their hands. Everyone was running. The porters jostled him as they hurried to the exit.

But he did manage to take aside an apprentice who was rolling a cigarette.

'What do you do with the lines of lead type once they've been used?'

'They're melted down again.'

'How often?'

'Every two days . . . Look! The foundry's over there, in the corner . . . Careful! It's hot . . .'

Maigret went outside, a little weary, perhaps slightly discouraged. Night had fallen completely now. The pavement gleamed more brightly than usual because of the cold. Outside a draper's shop, a salesman with a head cold was pacing back and forth, accosting passers-by.

'A winter coat? . . . Lovely bit of English fabric from only two hundred francs . . . Come in! No obligation to buy . . .'

A little further along, outside the Café de Paris, where the click of billiard balls could be heard, Maigret spotted the Count of Saint-Fiacre's yellow car.

He went inside, looked around for the man and, not finding him, sat down at a table. This was the town's smartest café. On a raised platform, three musicians were tuning up and sorting out the sequence of their set with three cards, each one bearing a number.

A sound came from the phone cabin.

'A beer!' Maigret said to the waiter.

'Light or dark?'

But the inspector was struggling to hear the voice in the cabin. He couldn't quite make it out. Saint-Fiacre came out, and the cashier asked him:

'How many calls?'

'Three.'

'To Paris, yes? . . . Three times eight eighty . . .'

The count spotted Maigret and came towards him quite casually and sat down beside him.

'You didn't tell me you were coming to Moulins! I would have given you a lift . . . Admittedly it's a coupé, and in this weather . . .'

'Were you calling Marie Vassiliev?'

'No! I don't know why I would hide the truth from you . . . I'll have a beer too, waiter . . . No, in fact! Something hot . . . a hot rum . . . I was calling a certain Monsieur Wolf . . . If you don't know him, others are bound to, Quai des Orfèvres . . . A money-lender, if you like . . . I've resorted to his services several times . . . I've just been trying to . . .'

Maigret gave him a quizzical look.

'Were you asking him for money?'

'On any terms! And he refused anyway. Don't look at me like that! This afternoon I called in at the bank . . .'

'At what time?'

'Around three . . . The young man you know and his lawyer were coming out . . .'

'Were you trying to withdraw money?'

'I tried! Don't think for a moment that I'm trying to make you feel sorry for me! Some people are embarrassed when it comes to money. Not me . . . So! Once the forty thousand francs had been sent to Paris and Marie Vassiliev's train ticket bought, I've got about three hundred francs in my pocket. When I came here I hadn't foreseen any of this . . . I've just got the suit on my back . . . In Paris I owe several thousand francs to the landlady of my flat, who won't let me have my belongings . . .'

As he spoke, he watched the balls rolling on the green baize of the billiard table. The billiard-players were some young men from the town, of modest origins, who cast the occasional envious glance at the count's elegant outfit.

'That's all! I would have liked at the very least to be in mourning for the funeral. There isn't a tailor in the country who would give me two days of credit . . . At the bank, they told me my mother's account was blocked, and also that the balance came to just over seven hundred francs . . . And do you know who gave me this pleasant information?'

'The son of your estate manager!'

'The very same!'

He took a swig of the steaming rum and fell silent, still watching the billiards. The band struck up a Viennese waltz which seemed to be oddly in time with the sound of the billiard balls.

It was hot. The café was plunged in greyish murk, in spite of the electric lights. It was an old-fashioned provincial café, with only one concession to modernity in the form of a poster which announced: 'Cocktails 6 francs.'

Maigret smoked slowly. He too stared at the billiard table, lit harshly by lamps in green cardboard shades. From time to time the door opened, and after a few seconds a gust of frosty air caught them by surprise.

'Let's go and sit at the back . . .'

It was the voice of the lawyer from Bourges. He passed by the table at which the two men were sitting, followed by Jean Métayer, who was wearing white woollen gloves.

But they both looked straight ahead. They didn't see the others until they had sat down.

The two tables were almost facing one another. Métayer blushed slightly and ordered firmly:

'A hot chocolate!'

And Saint-Fiacre joked under his breath:

'Poor love!'

A woman sat down an equal distance from the two tables and, giving the waiter a familiar smile, murmured:

'The usual!'

He brought her a cherry brandy. She powdered her face and put on some lipstick. And she fluttered her eyelashes, unsure which table to focus her gaze upon.

Was Maigret, tall and comfortable, the one she should target? Was it the more elegant lawyer, already looking her up and down with a half smile?

'And there you have it! I'll be attending the funeral in grey!' murmured the Count of Saint-Fiacre. 'I can hardly borrow a black suit from the butler! Or wear one of my late father's morning coats!'

Apart from the lawyer, whose interest was focused on the woman, everyone was looking at the nearest billiard table.

There were three of them. Two were occupied. Cries of 'bravo!' erupted as the musicians concluded their piece. And all of a sudden, the sound of glasses and saucers could be heard again.

'Three ports, three!'

The door opened and closed again. The cold came in and was gradually absorbed by the warmth of the room.

The lamps above the third billiard table came on when the cashier turned to flick the electric switches, which were behind her back.

'Thirty points!' said a voice.

And, to the waiter:

'A glass of Vichy . . . No! A Vittel with strawberry syrup . . .'

It was Émile Gautier, who was carefully coating the tip of his cue with blue chalk. Then he set the marker to zero. His companion was the sub-manager of the bank, ten years his senior, with a pointed brown moustache.

It was only on his third stroke – which he missed – that he spotted Maigret. He greeted him slightly awkwardly. From that point on he was so engrossed in the game that he no longer had time to see anybody at all.

'Of course, if you're not scared of the cold there's room in my car . . .' said Maurice de Saint-Fiacre. 'Can I get you something? I'm sure one drink isn't going to finish me off . . .'

'Waiter!' said Jean Métayer loudly. 'Put a call through to Bourges 17!'

His father's number! A few moments later he closed himself in the cabin.

Maigret was still smoking. He had ordered a second beer. And the woman had finally focused her attention on him, perhaps because he was the largest person present. Every time he turned towards her she smiled at him as if they were old acquaintances.

She probably had little idea that he was thinking about the

old woman, as the son himself called her, who was laid out on the first floor of the chateau, with the locals processing past her and nudging one another.

But that was not how he saw her. He imagined her at a time when there had not yet been any cars outside the Café de Paris, and when no one drank cocktails.

In the grounds of the chateau, tall and lithe, elegant as the heroine of a popular novel, beside the pram being pushed by the nanny . . .

Maigret was only a little boy whose hair, like the hair of Émile Gautier and the altar boy, insisted on standing up in a tuft on the top of his head.

Was he not jealous of the count on the morning when the couple had left for Aix-les-Bains, in a car (one of the first in the area) full of furs and perfume? Her face was hidden behind her veil. The count was wearing big goggles. It looked like a heroic abduction. And the nanny was holding the baby's hand, waving goodbye . . .

Now, the old woman was being sprinkled with holy water, and the bedroom smelled of candle-wax.

Preoccupied, Émile walked around the billiard table, playing like a dream, counting under his breath, importantly:

'Seven . . .'

He lined up his shot again. He was winning. His boss with the pointed moustache said in a thin voice:

'Terrific!'

Two men studied each other across the green baize: Jean Métayer, to whom the lawyer was speaking incessantly with a smile on his face, and the Count of Saint-Fiacre, who stopped the waiter with a languid gesture.

'Same again!'

As to Maigret, he was now thinking about a boy-scout whistle. A two-note whistle, in bronze, of the kind he himself had never owned.

8. An Invitation to Dinner

'Another phone call!' sighed Maigret as he saw Métayer getting up yet again.

He watched after him and noted that he didn't go into either the cabin or the lavatory. The podgy lawyer, meanwhile, was no longer perched on the edge of his chair like someone hesitating to get up. He was looking at the Count of Saint-Fiacre. He looked almost as if he was about to smile.

Was it Maigret who was superfluous? The scene, at any rate, reminded the inspector of certain situations from his youth: three or four friends, in a bar like this; two women at the other end of the room. Discussions, hesitation, calling the waiter, to pass him a note . . .

The lawyer was in the same state of nerves. And the woman sitting two tables away from Maigret mistakenly thought that she was the source of the agitation. She smiled, opened her handbag and put a little powder on her face.

'I'll be back in a moment!' said the inspector to his companion.

He crossed the bar in the direction that Métayer had taken and saw a door that he hadn't noticed, which opened on to a wide corridor with a red carpet. At the end of the corridor was a counter with a big book and a telephone switchboard, a receptionist. Métayer was there, finishing a conversation with the girl. He left her just as Maigret stepped forwards.

'Thank you, mademoiselle . . . The first on the left, you say?'

He didn't hide from the inspector. He didn't seem bothered by his presence. On the contrary! And a little flame of joy flickered in his eyes.

'I didn't know it was a hotel . . .' Maigret said to the girl.

'Are you staying somewhere else? . . . You've made a mistake . . . This is the best hotel in Moulins . . .'

'Didn't you have the Count of Saint-Fiacre staying here?'

She nearly laughed. Then all of a sudden she turned serious.

'What has he done?' she asked with some concern. 'This is the second time in five minutes that . . .'

'Where did you send my predecessor?'

'He wants to know if the Count of Saint-Fiacre went out during the night from Saturday to Sunday . . . I can't answer now, because the night watchman hasn't turned up . . . So this gentleman asked me if we had a garage and he went there . . .'

Good heavens! Maigret had only to follow Métayer!

'And the garage is in the first street on the left!' he said, slightly irritated.

'Exactly! It's open all night.'

Jean Métayer had obviously been quick, because when Maigret stepped into the street in question, he emerged from it, whistling. The watchman was having a snack in a corner.

'I want to know the same thing as the gentleman who just left . . . The yellow car . . . Did someone come and get it during the night between Saturday and Sunday? . . .'

There was already a ten-franc note on the table. Maigret set down a second one.

'At about midnight, yes!'

'And they brought it back?'

'Perhaps at three o'clock in the morning . . .'

'Was it dirty?'

'A little bit, perhaps . . . You know, the weather's dry at the moment . . .'

'There were two of them, weren't there? A man and a woman . . .'

'No! Just a man on his own.'

'Small and thin?'

'No! On the contrary, very tall and athletic.'

The Count of Saint-Fiacre, of course!

When Maigret entered the café, the band was in full swing once more, and the first thing he noticed was that the corner where Métayer and his companion had been sitting was empty.

But a few seconds later he found the lawyer sitting in his own seat, beside the Count of Saint-Fiacre.

When Maigret appeared, he rose to his feet.

'Please excuse me . . . No, really! Sit where you were, please . . .'

He had no intention of leaving. He sat down on the chair facing him. He was very animated, his cheeks flushed, like someone in a hurry to finish a delicate job. He seemed to be looking around for Jean Métayer, but there was no sign of him.

'You will understand, inspector . . . I wouldn't have dared to go to the chateau. That's normal . . . But since chance will have it that we meet on neutral terrain, if I might put it that way . . .'

And he forced a smile. After each phrase he looked as if he was greeting the two others, thanking them for their approval.

'In a situation as awkward as this there's no point, as I have told my client, in complicating things further by being overly touchy . . . Jean Métayer has understood very clearly . . . And, when you turned up, inspector, I was just telling the Count of Saint-Fiacre that we asked only to reach an agreement . . .'

Maigret murmured:

'Good heavens!'

And he thought very precisely: *You, young fellow, will be lucky if the fist of the man you're talking to so smoothly doesn't make contact with your face . . .*

The billiard-players went on walking around the green baize. The woman got up, left her handbag on the table and went to the end of the room.

Someone else who's making a big mistake. She's just had a bright idea. Didn't Métayer go outside to talk to her without a witness? . . . So, she's going off to find him . . .

And Maigret wasn't mistaken. Hand on hip, the woman was pacing back and forth, looking for the young man.

The lawyer was still talking.

'There are very complex interests involved, and we for our part are willing . . .'

'To do what?' Saint-Fiacre cut in.

'Well . . . to . . .'

He forgot that the glass within reach wasn't his and drank from Maigret's in order to maintain his composure.

'I realize it may not have been the best choice of place . . . Or of time . . . But we do know better than anyone else about the financial situation of . . .'

'Of my mother! So?'

'My client, with a delicacy that does him credit, preferred to stay at the inn . . .'

That poor lawyer! The words, now that Maurice de Saint-Fiacre was staring at him, issued from his throat one by one as if he'd had to tear them out.

'You understand me, don't you, inspector? We know there is a will deposited with the notary . . . Don't worry! The rights of the count will be respected . . . But Jean Métayer is mentioned none the less. The financial affairs are confused. My client is the only one who knows them . . .'

Maigret admired Saint-Fiacre, who managed to remain almost angelically calm. There was even a faint smile playing on his lips!

'Yes! He was a model secretary!' he said without a hint of irony.

'Bear in mind that he is a boy from an excellent family, who has had a solid upbringing. I know his parents . . . his father . . .'

'Can we get back to the fortune?'

It was too good to be true. The lawyer could hardly believe his ears.

'Will you let me buy a round? Waiter! The same again, gentlemen? I'll have a St Raphaël and lemon . . .'

Two tables away the woman came back with a gloomy expression because she hadn't been able to find anything, and was resigning herself to launching an assault on the billiard-players.

'I was saying that my client is willing to help you. There are people he doesn't trust. He'll tell you himself that some shady operations have been carried out by people not over-burdened with scruples . . . So . . .'

Now came the hard part! In spite of everything, the lawyer had to swallow his saliva before he was able to continue:

'You found the chateau coffers empty . . . And yet it is indispensable that your mother, her ladyship . . .'

'Your mother, her ladyship!' Maigret repeated admiringly.

'Your mother, her ladyship . . .' the lawyer continued without blinking. 'Where was I? Yes! That the funeral should be worthy of Saint-Fiacre . . . As we wait for everything to be sorted out in everyone's best interests, my client will set about . . .'

'In other words, he will advance the funds necessary for the funeral . . . Is that it?'

Maigret didn't dare to look at the count. He stared at Émile Gautier, who had just played another long break, and waited, nerves on edge, for a row to break out next to him.

Not a bit of it! Saint-Fiacre had risen to his feet and was talking to someone who had approached their table.

'Please, come and join us!'

It was Métayer. Seeing him come in, the lawyer must have waved to him to tell him everything was going well.

'A St Raphaël and lemon for you too? Waiter!'

A round of applause rang out in the hall, because the band had finished its piece. And once the background noise had stopped it was more awkward, because the voices rang out more clearly. Now the silence was broken only by the click of the ivory billiard balls.

'I told his lordship, who understood very well . . .'

'Who's having the Raphaël?'

'Did you come from Saint-Fiacre by taxi, gentlemen? In that case I will put my car at your disposal to drive you back . . . You'll be a bit cramped. I'm already bringing the inspector . . . How much was that? No, I insist, it's my round . . .'

But the lawyer had got to his feet and was putting a hundred-franc note into the hand of the waiter, who asked him, 'All together?'

'Of course! Of course!'

And the count said with his most gracious smile, 'Too charming of you, too charming.'

Émile Gautier watched the four men leaving and politely standing aside to let one another pass in the doorway and forgot to get on with his game.

The lawyer sat in the front, beside Saint-Fiacre, who was driving. Behind him, Maigret made just enough room for Jean Métayer.

It was cold. The headlights weren't bright enough. The car had no silencer, which made it impossible to talk.

Was Maurice de Saint-Fiacre used to driving at such speed? Was he taking a little revenge? Either way, he covered the twenty-five kilometres from Moulins to the chateau in less than a quarter of an hour, braking through the corners, hurtling through the dark, once only just avoiding a cart that was taking up the middle of the road, which forced him to climb up the slope.

Their faces were whipped by the breeze. Maigret had to clutch the collar of his overcoat with both hands. They passed through the village without slowing down. They could just make out the light of the inn, then the pointed spire of the church.

The car stopped abruptly, throwing the passengers against one another. They were at the bottom of the steps. Servants could be seen eating in the basement kitchen. Someone laughed loudly.

'You'll allow me, gentlemen, to invite you to dinner . . .'

Métayer and the lawyer looked hesitantly at one another. The count pushed them inside with a friendly pat on the shoulder.

'Please . . . It's my turn, isn't it?'

And, in the hall:

'I'm afraid it won't be very cheerful . . .'

Maigret would have liked to say a few words in particular, but the count wouldn't give him time and opened the door to the smoking room.

'Will you wait for me for a few moments and have an aperitif? I need to give some instructions. Do you know where the bottles are, Monsieur Métayer? Do we have anything drinkable? . . .'

He pressed an electric switch. The butler was a long time coming and arrived with his mouth full and a napkin in his hand.

Saint-Fiacre briskly took it from him.

'Call the estate manager . . . Then please call the presbytery for me, then the doctor's house . . .'

And to the others:

'Will you excuse me?'

The telephone was in the hall, which, like the rest of the chateau, was badly lit. In fact, since there was no electricity supply in Saint-Fiacre, the chateau had to make its own power, and the generator wasn't powerful enough. The lightbulbs, rather than giving off a white light, revealed reddish filaments, as some trams do when they stop.

There were lots of deep shadows, in which it was barely possible to make out objects.

'Hello . . . Yes, I'd love to . . . Thank you, doctor . . .'

Maigret and the lawyer were worried, but they didn't yet dare admit their concern. It was Métayer who broke the silence by asking the inspector:

'What can I offer you? I don't think there's any port left. But there are some spirits . . .'

All the ground-floor rooms were in a row, separated by big

open doors. First the dining room. Then the drawing room. Then the smoking room, where the three men were sitting. And then the library, where the young man went to get some bottles.

'Hello! . . . Yes . . . Can I count on it? . . . Straight away . . .'

The count spoke on the phone a little longer, then walked down the corridor that ran alongside all the rooms, climbed the stairs, and his footsteps stopped in the dead woman's bedroom.

Other, heavier footsteps in the hall. There was a knock at the door, which opened immediately. It was the estate manager.

'You asked to see me?'

But he realized that the count wasn't there, looked in bafflement at the three people sitting together, retreated and asked the butler what was going on.

'Some mineral water?' Jean Métayer asked, concerned.

And the lawyer, full of goodwill, cleared his throat:

'We both have very strange professions, inspector . . . Have you been with the police for a long time? . . . I have been at the bar for nearly fifteen years . . . That is to say that I have been involved in the most troubling events you can imagine . . . Cheers! . . . Your good health, Monsieur Métayer. I'm happy for you about the turn things are taking . . .'

The count's voice, in the corridor:

'Well! You'll find some! Call your son, who's playing billiards at the Café de Paris, in Moulins . . . He'll bring whatever you need . . .'

The door opened. The count came in.

'Do you all have something to drink? . . . Are there no cigars here?'

And he gave Métayer an inquisitorial look.

'Cigarettes . . . I only smoke . . .'

The young man didn't finish his sentence, but turned his head away, embarrassed.

'I'll bring you some.'

'Gentlemen, please forgive me for the very basic meal that

you are about to have . . . We're a long way from the town and . . .'

'Come! Come!' interrupted the lawyer, who was beginning to show the effects of alcohol. 'I'm sure it'll be fine . . . Is that a portrait of one of your relatives? . . .'

He pointed to the wall of the big drawing room, at the portrait of a man in a stiff frock coat, his neck trapped in a heavy false collar.

'That's my father.'

'So it is! You look like him.'

The maid ushered in Dr Bouchardon, who looked suspiciously around, as if he expected trouble. But Saint-Fiacre welcomed him cheerfully.

'Come in, doctor . . . I expect you know Jean Métayer . . . His lawyer . . . A charming man, as you will see . . . As for the inspector . . .'

The two men shook hands, and a few moments later the doctor murmured in Maigret's ear: 'What have you been up to here?'

'Not me . . . Him!'

The lawyer, affecting composure, kept walking towards the little round table on which his glass was standing and didn't notice that he was drinking more than was sensible.

'How wonderful it is, this old chateau! . . . And what a setting it would be for a film! . . . That was what I said recently to the state prosecutor in Bourges, who can't stand the cinema . . . People film in all sorts of . . .'

He was growing animated and trying to draw someone into conversation.

The count, meanwhile, had approached Métayer and was being unnervingly friendly towards him.

'What's saddest about this place is the long winter evenings, isn't that so? . . . *In my day*, I remember that my father too used to invite the doctor and priest . . . They weren't the same as the ones we have today . . . But even then the doctor was a non-believer, and discussions always turned to philosophical issues . . . And sure enough, here is the . . .'

It was the priest, with circles around his eyes, his posture stiff, who didn't know what to say and hesitated in the doorway.

'I'm sorry I'm late but . . .'

Through the open doors two servants could be seen setting out the cutlery in the dining room.

'Give Father something to drink . . .'

The count was addressing Métayer. Maigret noticed that he himself was not drinking. But the lawyer would soon be drunk. He was explaining to the doctor, who was looking with bafflement at the inspector:

'A little diplomacy, that's all! Or, if you prefer, knowledge of the human soul . . . They are about the same age, both of good family . . . Tell me why they should be glaring at each other like a pair of china dogs? . . . Don't they have common interests? . . . The most curious thing . . .'

He laughed. He took a swig from his glass.

'. . . And to think that it happened by chance, in a café . . . So those dear old provincial cafés, where you could be in your own home, have their good side . . .'

The sound of an engine had been heard outside. A little later the count went into the dining room, where the estate manager was sitting, and they caught the end of a sentence:

'Both of them, yes! . . . If you like! . . . It's an order! . . .'

The ringing of a telephone. The count had rejoined his guests. The butler came into the smoking room.

'What is it?'

'The undertaker . . . He's asking what time they can bring the coffin . . .'

'Whenever he likes.'

'Certainly, Monsieur.'

And the count replied, almost gaily:

'Would you like to take your seats? . . . I've had the last

bottles brought up from the cellar . . . Pass me the first of them, Father . . . We're a bit short of ladies, but . . .'

Maigret wanted to hold him back by his sleeve for a moment. The other man looked him in the eyes, with a hint of impatience, pulled abruptly away and went into the dining room.

'I have invited Monsieur Gautier, our estate manager, and his son, who is a boy with a future ahead of him, to share our meal . . .'

Maigret looked at the bank clerk's hair and, in spite of his unease, couldn't help smiling. His hair was damp. Before coming into the chateau, the young man had straightened his parting, washed his face and hands and changed his tie.

'Take your seats, gentlemen!'

And the inspector was certain that Saint-Fiacre's throat was swollen with a sob. It went unnoticed, because the doctor involuntarily distracted everyone's attention by picking up a dusty bottle and murmuring:

'You've still got some 1896 Hospice de Beaune? . . . I thought the last bottles had been bought by the Larue Restaurant, and that . . .'

The rest was lost in the noise of scraping chairs. The priest, hands folded on the tablecloth, head lowered and lips moving, said grace.

Maigret noticed that Saint-Fiacre was staring at him intently.

9. In the Spirit of Walter Scott

The dining room was the room in the chateau that had lost least of its character, thanks to the carved wooden panels that covered the walls all the way up to the ceiling. The room was also higher than it was wide, which made it not only solemn but gloomy, because one felt as if one were eating at the bottom of a well.

On each panel there were two electric lamps, those elongated lamps that imitate candles, complete with fake wax drips.

In the middle of the table, a real seven-branched candelabra with seven real candles.

The Count of Saint-Fiacre and Maigret sat facing one another but could only see each other if they stiffened their backs to look above the flames.

On the right of the count, the priest. On his left, Dr Bouchardon. Chance had placed Jean Métayer at one end of the table, the lawyer at the other. And sitting next to the inspector were the estate manager on one side and Émile Gautier on the other.

From time to time the butler stepped forward into the light to serve the guests, but as soon as he stepped two metres back he was immersed in shadow, and his white-gloved hands were all that could be seen.

'Don't you think we could be in a novel by Walter Scott?'

It was the count who spoke, in an indifferent tone, and yet Maigret pricked up his ears, because he had heard an undercurrent, and had a sense that something was about to start.

They were only on their starters. On the table there was a random collection of bottles of white and red wine, claret and burgundy, and everyone was filling his glass as he felt like it.

'There's only one detail that doesn't fit . . .' Maurice de Saint-Fiacre continued. 'In Walter Scott the poor old woman upstairs would suddenly start screaming . . .'

Within a few seconds, everyone stopped chewing, and they felt as if an icy draught has entered the room.

'By the way, Gautier, has she been left all on her own?'

The estate manager swallowed hastily and stammered:

'She . . . Yes . . . There is no one in the countess's room . . .'

'That can't be very cheerful!'

At that moment a foot brushed insistently against Maigret's, but the inspector couldn't guess who it belonged to. The table was round. Anyone could have reached the middle. And Maigret's uncertainty was destined to continue, because in the course of the evening the little kicks would become increasingly frequent.

'Did she receive a lot of people today?'

It was embarrassing to hear him talking about his mother as if she were a living person, and the inspector noted that Jean Métayer was so struck by this that he stopped eating and looked straight ahead, his eyes becoming increasingly sunken.

'Almost all the local farmers!' the estate manager's serious voice replied.

When the butler noticed a hand reaching out towards a bottle he approached in silence. His black arm, ending in a white glove, was seen suddenly emerging from the darkness. The liquid flowed. And it was done in such silence, with such skill, that the lawyer, by now more than tipsy, wonderingly repeated the experiment three or four times.

He delightedly followed this arm which didn't even brush his shoulder. In the end he could restrain himself no longer.

'Incredible! You are a marvel, sir, and if I could afford a chateau I would take you on straight away . . .'

'Bah! The chateau will soon be for sale at a bargain price . . .'

This time even Maigret frowned as he watched Saint-Fiacre

talking like that, in a voice that was curiously indifferent but also rather unnatural. In spite of everything, there was something strident about his words. Were his nerves on edge? Was it a grim sort of joke?

'Chicken in half-mourning,' he announced as the butler brought in some chickens with truffles.

And a moment later, in the same light tone:

'The murderer will be eating chicken in half-mourning, like everyone else!'

The butler slipped his arm between the guests.

'But your lordship! . . .'

'Of course! What's so strange about that? The murderer is among us, of that there is no doubt! But don't let it take your appetite away, Father! The corpse is in the house too, and that hasn't taken away your appetite. Albert, a drop of wine for Father!'

Once again the foot brushed Maigret's ankle; he dropped his napkin and bent to look under the table, but it was too late. When he straightened up again, the count, still eating his chicken, was saying:

'I mentioned Walter Scott just now, because of the atmosphere that reigns in this room, but also and particularly because of the murderer . . . After all, we are at a funeral wake, are we not? . . . The funeral will take place tomorrow morning, and in all likelihood we will not be parted before then . . . Monsieur Métayer can at least claim to have supplied the bar with excellent whisky . . .'

Maigret tried to remember how much Saint-Fiacre had drunk. Less, at any rate, than the doctor, who exclaimed:

'Excellent! Yes indeed! But my client is also the grandson of wine-growers and . . .'

'I was saying . . . What was I saying? . . . Oh, yes! . . . Fill the priest's glass, Albert . . .

'I was saying that since the murderer is here, the others are to some extent acting as upholders of the law . . . That's why our gathering is like a chapter of Walter Scott . . .

'Let's be clear that our murderer is in no danger. Isn't that so, inspector? . . . It isn't a crime to slip a sheet of paper into a missal . . .

'By the way, doctor . . . When did my mother suffer her last attack? . . .'

The doctor wiped his lips and looked gloomily around:

'Three months ago, when you sent a telegram from Berlin to say that you were ill in a hotel room and that . . .'

'I was after some cash! That was it!'

'I said at the time that any further emotional turmoil would be fatal.'

'So . . . Let's see . . . Who knew? Jean Métayer, of course . . . And me, obviously! . . . Old Gautier, who's practically family . . . And last of all you and Father here . . .'

He gulped down a glass of white wine and pulled a face:

'So, logically speaking, almost all of us can be seen as potential suspects . . . If it amuses you . . .'

It was almost as if he were deliberately choosing the most shocking words he could find.

'. . . If it amuses you, we will examine each of our individual cases, one at a time . . . Let's start with Father . . . Would it have been in his interest to kill my mother? . . . You will see that the answer is not as simple as it seems . . . I shall leave aside the question of money . . .'

The priest was choking, but he didn't get up from his chair.

'Father had nothing to gain . . . But he is a mystic, an apostle, practically a saint . . . He has an eccentric parishioner whose behaviour is causing a scandal . . . One moment she's hurrying to church like the most fervent of believers, the next she's bringing scandal down upon Saint-Fiacre . . . No! Don't pull that face, Métayer . . . We're all men here . . . We are, if you wish, performing a psychological experiment.

'Father has a faith so ardent that it might drive him to extremes. Remember the days when sinners were purified by being burned at the stake . . . So, my mother is at mass . . . She has just taken communion. She is in a state of grace. But soon she will succumb to sin once more, and again she will be the subject of a scandal . . . If she dies there, in her pew, in a state of holiness . . .'

'But . . .' began the priest, whose eyes were filled with fat tears and who was gripping the table to keep himself calm.

'Please, Father . . . As I said, we are carrying out a psychological experiment . . . I just want to show you that even the most austere individuals can be suspected of the worst atrocities. Now, if we move on to the doctor, I find myself more perplexed. He isn't a saint. And what saves him is that he isn't a scientist either. Because if he were, he could have put the piece of paper in the missal to test the resilience of a sickly heart . . .'

The clatter of forks had faded away almost to nothing. And the faces were frozen, anxious, almost frantic. There was only the butler filling glasses in silence, with the regularity of a metronome.

'You are gloomy, gentlemen . . . Are there really subjects that one cannot discuss, even among intelligent people?

'The next course, please, Albert . . . So, let's leave the doctor aside, since we cannot consider him as a scientist or a researcher. He is saved by his mediocrity.'

He chuckled and turned towards the estate manager.

'Your turn! . . . A more complex case. We are still adopting the viewpoint of a Martian, aren't we? Two possibilities . . . First, you are the model estate manager, the honest man who devotes his life to his masters, to the chateau where he was born . . . In fact he wasn't born here, but no matter . . . In that case his position isn't clear. The Saint-Fiacre family has only a single male heir . . . And there is the legacy melting away in front of his nose . . . The countess is behaving like a madwoman . . . And perhaps the moment has come to save what is left . . .

'A noble gesture, worthy of Walter Scott, and not unlike that of the priest . . .

'But there is also the opposite possibility! You are no longer the model estate manager born at the chateau . . . You are a rogue who has for years been taking advantage of and abusing the weakness of your masters . . . When we are forced to sell farms, you buy them up on the sly . . . And when we are forced to raise mortgages, you are the one who takes them. Don't get angry, Gautier . . . Did the priest get angry? And besides, I haven't quite finished . . .

'You are almost the real owner of the chateau . . .'

'Your lorship!'

'Don't you know how to play the game? We're playing a game, I repeat! We're playing, if you like, at being police inspectors like your neighbour. The time has come when the countess has reached the end, when everything will have to be sold, and it will be observed that you are the one who has profited from the situation . . . Wouldn't it be better if the countess happened to die conveniently, thus at the same time sparing herself the need to acquaint herself with poverty? . . .'

And, turning towards the butler, a shadow in shadow, a demon with chalk-white hands:

'Albert! Go and fetch my father's revolver. If it's still there . . .'

He poured a drink for himself and both his neighbours, then held out the bottle to Maigret.

'Would you be so kind as to do the honours on your side of the table? Well! Here we are, about halfway through our game . . . But let's wait for Albert. Monsieur Métayer, you're not drinking . . .'

A strangled 'No, thank you' was heard.

'And you, sir?'

And the lawyer, with his mouth full and his tongue coated:

'No, thank you! No, thank you! I have all that I need. You know that you would make an excellent attorney general?'

He was the only one who laughed, and who ate with indecent appetite, who drank down one glass after another, of burgundy or claret, without even noticing the difference.

The shrill church bell struck ten. Albert handed the count a big revolver, and the count checked to see if it was loaded.

'Perfect! . . . I'll set it down here, in the middle of the table, which is round . . . You will notice, gentlemen, that it is an equal distance from each of you. We have looked at three cases. We will examine three more. Will you let me make a prediction first of all? Well, then! To stay in the tradition and the spirit of Scott, I must tell you that before midnight my mother's murderer will be dead! . . .'

Maigret looked at him keenly across the table and saw that Saint-Fiacre's eyes were too bright, as if he were drunk. At that very moment a foot again touched his.

'And now I shall go on – but do eat your salads. I am moving on to your neighbour on your left, inspector, to Émile Gautier . . . A serious boy, a hard worker who, as one says at prize-giving, has advanced entirely by merit and by stubborn hard work . . .

'Could he have killed?

'One initial hypothesis: he worked for his father, and in agreement with him.

'He goes to Moulins every day. He better than anyone else knows the family's financial state . . . He has every opportunity to see a printer or a typographer . . .

'Let us move on! Second hypothesis . . . You will forgive me, Métayer, for telling you, if you didn't know it already, that you have a rival. Émile Gautier is certainly no beauty. But he still filled the position that you filled so tactfully, before you did . . .

'Some years ago. Did he have certain hopes? Has he, since then, succeeded in stirring my mother's over-sensitive heart?

'Be that as it may, he was her official protégé and he was allowed to nurture all kinds of ambitions . . .

'Then you came . . . You conquered . . .

'Killing the countess while at the same time casting suspicion on yourself . . .'

Maigret's toes were uncomfortable in his shoes. It was all hateful, sacrilegious! Saint-Fiacre was speaking with the elation of a drunkard. And the others were wondering whether they would make it to the end, whether they should stay and endure this scene or get up and leave.

'You will realize that we are completely adrift on a sea of the imagination. Please note that even if the countess up there could speak, she could not give us the key to the mystery. The murderer alone knows how his crime was committed. Eat, Émile Gautier . . . Whatever you do, don't get upset like your father, who looks as if he is about to be sick . . .

'Albert! . . . There must be some bottles of wine left in a rack somewhere . . .

'Your turn, young man!'

And he turned with a smile towards Métayer, who leaped to his feet.

'My lawyer will be—'

'Sit down, for heaven's sake! And don't try to tell us that you can't take a joke at your age . . .'

Maigret looked at him as he uttered those words and he noted that the count's forehead was covered with big droplets of sweat.

'None of us is trying to look better than we are, isn't that so? Well, then! I see that you are trying to understand. Take a fruit! They're excellent for the digestion . . .'

The heat was unbearable, and Maigret wondered who had turned the electric lights out, leaving only the candles on the table lit.

'Your case is so simple as to be entirely without interest . . . You were playing a disagreeable part, and one that you would not play for long . . . In the end you were mentioned in the will . . . A will, however, that could be changed at any moment . . .

A sudden death and it would all be over! . . . You would pick the fruit of your . . . of your sacrifice . . . And, no doubt, you would marry a local girl whom you had had your eye on . . .'

'I beg your pardon!' the lawyer broke in, so comically that Maigret couldn't suppress a smile.

'Shut your mouth, you! Drink!'

Saint-Fiacre was adamant! He was drunk, there was no longer any doubt about it! He had that eloquence that drunks so often have, a mixture of roughness and refinement, of clear diction and slyly evasive words.

'Which leaves only me!'

He called for Albert.

'Listen, old man, go upstairs . . . It must be gloomy for my mother, being left all on her own . . .'

Maigret saw the servant's quizzical eye settling on the estate manager, who blinked assent.

'One moment! First put some bottles on the table . . . Whisky too . . . I shouldn't imagine anyone is concerned with protocol . . .'

He consulted his watch.

'Ten past eleven . . . I have been talking so much that I didn't hear the bells of your church, Father . . .'

And, as the butler nudged the revolver slightly as he put the whisky bottles down on the table, the count intervened.

'Careful, Albert! . . . It must be an equal distance from each of them . . .'

He waited for the door to close again.

'And there we are!' he concluded. 'That leaves only me! I won't be telling you anything you don't know if I say that I have never done anything good! Except perhaps while my father was alive . . . But since I was only seventeen when he died . . .

'I'm broke! Everyone knows that! The little weekly newspapers mention it in barely concealed terms . . .

'Dud cheques . . . I scrounge money from my mother as often as I possibly can . . . I invented that illness in Berlin to get hold of a few thousand francs . . .

'Bear in mind that that is the same as the missal trick, although on a smaller scale . . .

'And yet, what happens? The money that is my due is spent by little bastards like Métayer . . . I'm sorry, old man . . . We're still doing transcendental psychology . . .

'Soon there will be nothing left . . . I call my mother, when a dud cheque could mean jail for me . . . She refuses to pay . . . There are witnesses to back that one up . . .

'So, if it goes on, in a few weeks there will be nothing left of my inheritance . . .

'Two hypotheses, as for Émile Gautier. The first . . .'

Never in his career had Maigret felt so uneasy. And it was probably the first time that he had a very clear sense that he was not a match for the situation. Events were out of his control. Sometimes he thought he was starting to understand, and a moment later a phrase from Saint-Fiacre called everything into question again!

And there was still that insistent foot pressing against his own.

'Why don't we talk about something else!' the intoxicated lawyer exclaimed.

'Gentlemen . . .' the priest began.

'Excuse me! You owe me your time until midnight at least! I was saying that the first hypothesis . . .

'Oh, marvellous! You've made me lose my thread . . .'

And as if to find it again, he poured himself a full glass of whisky.

'I know that my mother is very sensitive. I slip the piece of paper into her missal, to frighten her and, in the process, move her to pity, planning to come back the next day to ask her for the necessary funds, and hope to find her more accommodating . . .

'But then you have the second hypothesis! Why wouldn't I want to kill too?

'Not all the money of the Saint-Fiacre family has been used up. There's a bit left. And, in my situation, a bit of money, however little, could be my salvation!

'I am vaguely aware that Métayer is mentioned in the will. But a murderer cannot inherit . . .

'Wouldn't he be suspected of the crime? He who spends part of his time in a printing works in Moulins! He who, living in the chateau, could slip the piece of paper in the missal as and when he wanted to?

'Did I not arrive in Moulins in the afternoon? And didn't I wait down there, with my mistress, to see the result of this manoeuvre? . . .'

He got to his feet, with his glass in his hand.

'Your health, gentlemen . . . You are gloomy . . . I am sorry to see that . . . My mother's whole life was gloomy during those last years . . . Isn't that so, Father? . . . It's only right that her last night should be accompanied by a little gaiety . . .'

He looked the inspector in the eye:

'Your health, Monsieur Maigret!'

Who was he making fun of? Of him? Of everyone?

Maigret felt he was in the presence of an irresistible force. Some individuals, at a given point in their lives, experience a moment of plenitude, a moment in which they are somehow elevated above the rest of humanity and themselves.

Sometimes, like a gambler in Monte Carlo, who one evening keeps winning, whatever he does. It is true of the opposition MP, unknown until that moment, whose speech shakes and topples the government, and who is more surprised than anyone, because all he wanted was a few lines in the parliamentary gazette.

Maurice de Saint-Fiacre was experiencing his moment. He was filled with a strength that he hadn't suspected himself of having, and the others could only lower their heads.

But wasn't it drunkenness that was sweeping him along like that?

'Let's return to the start of our discussion, gentlemen, since it isn't yet midnight . . . I said that my mother's murderer was among us . . . I have proved that it could be me or one of you, except perhaps the inspector and the doctor!'

'I'm still not sure . . .'

'And I prophesied his death . . .'

'Will you let me continue with my hypothetical game? He knows that the law can do nothing about him. But he also knows that there are several of us, or rather that there will be several people left, six at least, who know his crime . . .

'There again, we are confronted with several solutions . . .

'The first is the most Romantic, the most in tune with Walter Scott . . .

'But I have to introduce a new parenthesis . . . What characterizes this crime? . . . It's the fact that there are at least five individuals who gravitated around the countess . . . Five individuals who stood to gain from her death and who might, each in his own way, have thought of how to bring it about . . .

'Only one of them dared to do it . . . Only one committed the crime! . . .

'And yet I wouldn't be surprised if he took advantage of this evening to avenge himself on the others . . . He is lost! . . . Why not blow up the lot of us? . . .'

And Maurice de Saint-Fiacre, with a disarming smile, looked at each of them in turn.

'Is it exciting enough? The old dining room in the old chateau, the candles, the table covered with bottles . . . Then, at midnight, death . . . You will note that the scandal will be suppressed at the same time . . . Tomorrow people will come running, and won't understand a thing . . . They will put it down to accident, or an anarchist attack . . .'

The lawyer fidgeted in his chair and glanced anxiously around, towards the gloom that had fallen less than a metre from the table.

'If I might remind you that I am a doctor,' murmured Bouchardon, 'I would advise each of you to have a good strong cup of black coffee . . .'

'And I,' the priest said slowly, 'would remind you that there is a dead person in the house . . .'

Saint-Fiacre hesitated for a second. A foot brushed Maigret's ankle, and he quickly bent down, too late once again.

'I asked you to wait until midnight . . . I have examined only the first hypothesis . . . There is a second . . . The murderer, crazed and cornered, fires a bullet into his head . . . *But I don't believe he'll do it . . .*'

'I request that we move to the smoking room!' the lawyer squealed, getting to his feet and clinging to the back of his chair to keep from falling.

'And last of all there is a third hypothesis . . . Someone who cares about the honour of the family comes to the murderer's assistance . . . Wait . . . The question is more complex . . . Shouldn't scandal be avoided? . . . Shouldn't the guilty man be *helped* to kill himself? . . .

'The revolver is there, gentlemen, an equal distance from all our hands . . . It is ten to midnight . . . I say again that at midnight the murderer will die . . .'

And this time his voice was so firm that everyone remained silent. No one breathed.

'The victim is up there, with a servant sitting vigil . . . The murderer is here, surrounded by seven people . . .'

Saint-Fiacre drained his glass in one go. And the anonymous foot was still brushing Maigret's.

'Six minutes to midnight . . . Is that enough, Walter Scott? . . . Tremble, murderer . . .'

He was drunk! And he was still drinking!

'At least five people to steal from an old woman deprived of her husband, of affection . . . Only one who dared . . . It will be bomb or revolver, gentlemen . . . The bomb, which will blow all of us up, or the revolver, which will hit only the guilty man . . . Four minutes to midnight . . .'

And, brusquely:

'Don't forget that no one knows! . . .'

He grabbed the bottle of whisky and served everyone, starting with Maigret's glass and finishing with Émile Gautier's.

He didn't fill his own. Hadn't he drunk enough? A candle went out. The others would follow.

'I said midnight . . . Three minutes to midnight . . .'

He was affecting the airs of an auctioneer.

'Three minutes to midnight . . . two minutes . . . The murderer is about to die . . . You can begin a prayer, Father . . . And you, doctor, do you at least have your medical bag? . . . Two minutes . . . One and a half . . .'

And still that insistent foot against Maigret's. He didn't dare to bend down, for fear of missing another spectacle.

'I'm off!' shouted the lawyer, rising to his feet.

All eyes turned towards him. He was standing up. He gripped the back of his chair. He hesitated to take the three dangerous steps that would lead him to the door. He hiccupped.

And at that moment there was a great bang. Everyone was motionless for a second, maybe two.

A second candle went out, and at the same time Maurice de Saint-Fiacre toppled over, his shoulders struck the back of the gothic chair, he tilted to the left, lurched back to the right, but then fell back inertly, his head resting on the priest's arm.

10. The Wake

What followed was mayhem. Things were happening all over the place, and afterwards each of them could only have related a small part of the events that they had witnessed in person.

The dining room was now lit by only five candles. Huge areas were still in darkness, and agitated people came and went as if from the wings of a stage.

The gun had been fired by one of Maigret's neighbours: Émile Gautier. And as soon as the shot had gone off, he held out both wrists to the inspector in a slightly theatrical gesture.

Maigret was on his feet. Gautier stood up. So did his father, and all three formed a group on one side of the table, while another group gathered around the victim.

The Count of Saint-Fiacre's forehead still rested against the priest's arm. The doctor, leaning forwards, looked grimly around.

'Dead? . . .' asked the podgy lawyer.

No reply. The scene on that side of the table was sluggish, as if being played out by bad actors.

Only Jean Métayer belonged to neither one group nor the other. He had stayed beside his chair, anxious, shivering, not knowing where to look.

In the minutes leading up to his action, Émile Gautier had plainly prepared his demeanour, because as soon as he had set the gun back down on the table he literally made a declaration, looking Maigret in the eyes.

'He was the one who said it was going to happen, wasn't he? . . . The murderer had to die . . . And, because he was too much of a coward to take the law into his own hands . . .'

His self-confidence was extraordinary.

'I did what I saw as my duty . . .'

Could the others hear him from the other side of the table? There were footsteps in the corridor. It was the servants. The doctor went to the door to stop them from coming in. Maigret didn't hear what he said to get rid of them.

'I saw Saint-Fiacre prowling around the chateau on the night of the crime . . . That was how I worked out . . .'

The whole scene was badly directed. And Gautier was hamming it up to the rafters when he announced:

'The judges will decide whether . . .'

The doctor spoke.

'Are you sure it was Saint-Fiacre who killed his mother?'

'Absolutely certain! Would I have acted as I did if . . .'

'So you saw him prowling around the chateau the night before the crime?'

'I saw him as I see you now. He had left his car on the edge of the village . . .'

'You have no other proof?'

'I do, in fact! This afternoon, the altar boy came to see me at the bank, with his mother . . . It was his mother who made him speak . . . Shortly after the crime, the count asked the child to give him the missal and promised him a sum of money . . .'

Maigret was running out of patience and felt as if he had been left out of the play.

And yes, it was a play! Why else was the doctor smirking into his beard? And why was the priest gently pushing Saint-Fiacre's head away?

A play, moreover, that was being performed simultaneously as farce and drama.

For the Count of Saint-Fiacre rose to his feet like a man who had just been enjoying a snooze. His face was hard, with an ironic but threatening wrinkle in the corners of his lips.

'Come over here and say that again! . . .' he said.

And an unearthly cry rang out, as Émile Gautier screamed in fear and gripped Maigret's arm for protection. But the inspector stepped back, leaving the field open to the two men.

There was someone who didn't understand: Jean Métayer. And he was almost as frightened as the bank clerk. To top it all, one of the candlesticks was knocked over, and the tablecloth caught fire, spreading a smell of burning.

It was the lawyer who doused the incipient flames with the contents of a bottle of wine.

'Come here!'

It was an order! And the tone was such that disobedience was clearly out of the question.

Maigret had picked up the revolver. A glance was enough to show him that it was loaded with blanks.

He guessed the rest. Maurice de Saint-Fiacre letting his head rest on the priest's arm . . . A few whispered words to make his death seem believable for a moment . . .

Now he wasn't the same man. He looked bigger, more solid. He didn't take his eyes off young Gautier, and it was the estate manager who suddenly ran towards a window, opened it and shouted to his son:

'Over here . . .'

It was a good idea. Emotions were so heightened, and there was such confusion, that Gautier had a chance to get away at that moment.

Did the little lawyer do it on purpose? Probably not! Or else his drunkenness filled him with a kind of heroism. As the fleeing man made for the window, he stuck out his leg, and Gautier fell head first.

He didn't get to his feet unaided. A hand had grabbed him by the neck, lifted him up and set him on his feet, and he yelled again as he realized that it was Saint-Fiacre who was forcing him to stand upright.

'Don't move! . . . Someone shut the window . . .'

Saint-Fiacre started with a punch in the face of the young bank clerk, which turned purple. He did it quite coldly.

'Speak, now! Tell me . . .'

No one intervened. It didn't even occur to anyone, since they all felt that only one man had the right to raise his voice.

Only the boy's father murmured in Maigret's ear: 'Are you going to let him get away with that?'

He certainly was! Maurice de Saint-Fiacre was master of the situation, and he was up to the task.

'You saw me on the night in question, it's true!'

Then, to the others:

'You know where? . . . On the lawn . . . I was about to go in . . . He was coming out . . . I wanted to pick up some family jewels to sell them on . . . We found ourselves face to face, in the night . . . He was shivering . . . And this scoundrel told me he was coming from . . . Can you guess? From my mother's bedroom, that's right! . . .'

Then in a low voice, casually:

'I abandoned my plan. I went back to Moulins.'

Jean Métayer's eyes widened. The lawyer stroked his chin to maintain his composure and peered at his glass, which he didn't dare to pick up.

'It wasn't proof enough . . . Because there were two of them in the house, and Gautier might have been telling the truth . . . As I told you a moment ago, he was the first to take advantage of an old woman's confusion . . . Métayer only turned up later . . . Had Métayer, feeling that his position was under threat, not tried to take revenge? . . . I wanted to know . . . They were both suspicious of each other . . . It was almost as if they were challenging me . . .

'Isn't that right, Gautier? . . . The gentleman with the dud cheques who prowls around the chateau at night and wouldn't dare accuse anyone for fear of being arrested himself . . .'

And, in another voice: 'You will excuse me, Father, and you

too, doctor, for making you witness such a foul spectacle . . . But we've said it already: true justice, the justice of the courts, has no business here . . . Isn't that so, Monsieur Maigret? . . . Did you at least work out that I was the one kicking you a few moments ago? . . .'

He paced back and forth, leaving the light for the shadow and then the shadow for the light. He gave the impression of a man containing himself, who can remain calm only at the cost of a terrible effort.

Sometimes he came so close to Gautier that he could have touched him.

'How tempting it was to pick up the revolver and fire! Yes! I had said it myself: the guilty man would die at midnight! And you became the defender of the honour of the Saint-Fiacre family.'

This time his fist struck the young man so hard, right in the middle of the face, that blood spurted from his nose.

Émile Gautier had the eyes of a dying animal. He staggered under the blow and was on the point of bursting into tears of pain, of fear, of confusion.

The lawyer tried to intervene, but Saint-Fiacre pushed him away.

'I beg your pardon, monsieur!'

And his formality marked the distance that lay between them. Maurice de Saint-Fiacre was firmly in charge.

'You will forgive me, gentlemen, but I have only one small formality to carry out.'

He opened the door wide and turned towards Gautier.

'Come with me! . . .'

The young man's feet were riveted to the ground. The corridor was unlit. He didn't want to be alone there with his adversary.

It didn't take long. Saint-Fiacre walked over to him and hit him again, sending Gautier tumbling into the hall.

'Up you go!'

And he pointed to the stairs leading to the first floor.

'Inspector! I should warn you that . . .' the estate manager panted.

The priest had averted his head. He was suffering, but didn't have the strength to intervene. Everyone was exhausted, and Métayer poured himself a drink, anything at all, his throat was so dry.

'Where are they going?' the lawyer asked.

They could be heard walking along the corridor, whose tiles rang out under their footsteps. And Gautier's heavy breathing could be heard as well.

'You knew everything!' Maigret said to the estate manager slowly, in a very low voice. 'You agreed, you and your son! You already had the farms, the mortgages . . . But Jean Métayer was still dangerous . . . Getting the countess out of the way . . . And at the same time getting rid of the gigolo who was under suspicion . . .'

A cry of pain. The doctor went into the corridor to see what was happening.

'Nothing!' he said. 'That rogue doesn't want to go upstairs, so he's being helped along . . .'

'It's revolting! . . . It's a crime! . . . What's he going to do? . . .' cried the young man's father, dashing to the door.

Maigret followed him, along with the doctor. They reached the bottom of the stairs just as the two others got to the door of the room where the body was laid out.

And Saint-Fiacre's voice was heard:

'Go in!'

'I can't . . . I . . .'

'Go in!'

A dull thud. Another punch.

Old Gautier ran up the stairs, followed by Maigret and Bouchardon. All three of them reached the top just as the door closed again, and no one moved.

At first not a sound came from behind the heavy oak door. Gautier held his breath and pulled a face in the darkness.

A simple ray of light, under the door.

'On your knees!'

A pause. Hoarse breathing.

'Faster! . . . On your knees! . . . And now, ask forgiveness! . . .'

Another very long silence. A cry of pain. This time it was not a punch that the murderer was dealt, but a kick right in the face.

'Sor . . . sorry . . .'

'Is that all? . . . Is that all you can find to say? . . . Remember that she was the one who paid for your studies . . .'

'Sorry!'

'Remember that she was still alive three days ago.'

'Sorry!'

'Remember, you utter little scoundrel, that you used to climb into her bed . . .'

'Sorry! . . . Sorry! . . .'

'Better than that! . . . Come on, then! . . . Tell her you're a wretched insect . . . Repeat . . .'

'I am . . .'

'On your knees, I said! . . . Do you need a rug?'

'Ow! . . . I . . .'

'Plead for forgiveness . . .'

And suddenly these replies, separated by long silences, were followed by a series of loud noises. Saint-Fiacre could contain himself no longer. There were a number of thuds against the parquet floor.

Maigret opened the door a chink. Maurice de Saint-Fiacre was holding the back of Gautier's neck and banging his head against the floor.

At the sight of the inspector he let go, dabbed his forehead and stood up to his full height.

'It's done! . . .' he panted.

He noticed the estate manager and frowned.

'Don't you feel the need to plead for forgiveness as well?'

And the old man was so frightened that he fell to his knees.

In the faint light from the two candles, all that could be seen of the dead woman was her nose, which looked larger than usual, and her joined hands, clutching a rosary.

'Get out!'

The count pushed Émile Gautier outside and closed the door. And the group went back downstairs.

Émile Gautier was bleeding. He couldn't find his handkerchief. The doctor passed him his own.

For it was a horrible sight: a tormented, bloodstained face; a nose that was little more than a tumour, the upper lip split.

And yet the ugliest, the most odious thing about it was the eyes, with their evasive gaze.

Maurice de Saint-Fiacre, standing very straight like a master of the house who knows what he has to do, strode across the long ground-floor corridor and opened the door, receiving a gust of icy air.

'Clear off! . . .' he growled, turning towards the father and the son.

But just as Émile was leaving, he instinctively grabbed him.

Maigret was sure that he heard a sob issuing from the count's throat. He struck out again, convulsively, and shouted:

'Scoundrel! . . . Scoundrel! . . .'

The inspector had only to touch his shoulder. Saint-Fiacre regained control of himself, literally threw the body down the steps and closed the door.

Not so fast that they couldn't hear the old man's voice:

'Émile . . . Where are you? . . .'

The priest was praying, elbows on the sideboard. In a corner, Métayer and his lawyer stood motionless, their eyes fixed on the door.

Maurice de Saint-Fiacre came in, head held high.

'Gentlemen . . .' he began.

But he couldn't speak, choked as he was by emotion. He was utterly exhausted.

He shook the doctor's hand, and Maigret's, as if to indicate that it was time for them to leave. Then, turning towards Métayer and his companion, he waited.

The two men seemed not to understand. Or else they were paralysed by terror.

To show them the way he nodded his head and snapped his fingers.

Nothing else!

But in fact there was something! The lawyer looked for his hat, and Saint-Fiacre groaned:

'Faster! . . .'

Behind a door, Maigret heard a murmur, and he guessed that it must be the servants, trying to guess what was happening in the chateau.

He put on his heavy overcoat. He felt the need to shake Saint-Fiacre's hand once more.

The door was open. Outside, the night was clear, cold and cloudless. The poplars stood out against a sky bathed in moonlight. Footsteps echoed somewhere far away, and there was light in the windows of the estate manager's house.

'No, Father, you can stay . . .'

And Maurice de Saint-Fiacre's voice continued in the echoing corridor:

'Now, if you aren't too tired, let us go and sit vigil for my mother . . .'

11. The Two-Note Whistle

'Please don't think ill of me for paying you so little attention, Monsieur Maigret . . . But with the funeral and everything . . .'

And poor Marie Tatin busied herself, getting whole cases of bottles of beer and lemonade ready.

'Especially when people who have come a long way are going to want their lunch . . .'

All the fields were white with frost, and the blades of grass broke under their feet. Every quarter of an hour the bells of the little church sounded the death knell.

The hearse had arrived at dawn, and the undertakers had settled themselves at the inn, in a semi-circle around the fireplace.

'I'm surprised the estate manager isn't at home!' Marie Tatin had said to them. 'He must be at the chateau, with Monsieur Maurice . . .'

And already the first villagers were arriving in their Sunday best.

Maigret was finishing his breakfast when he looked out the window and saw the altar boy arriving, his mother holding him by the hand. But his mother didn't walk him all the way to the inn. She stopped on the corner, where she thought no one could see her, and pushed her son on ahead, as if to give him the necessary propulsion to reach Marie Tatin's inn.

When Ernest stepped inside, he looked very confident. As confident as a child at a prize-giving ceremony, reciting a poem he has been rehearsing for three months.

'Is the inspector here?'

Just as he was asking Marie Tatin that question, he spotted Maigret and walked towards him, both hands in his pockets, one of them fiddling with something.

'I came to . . .'

'Show me your whistle.'

Ernest immediately stepped back, looked away and muttered, 'What whistle?'

'The one you've got in your pocket . . . Have you wanted a boy-scout whistle for a long time? . . .'

The boy took it mechanically from his pocket and set it down on the table.

'And now tell me your little story.'

A suspicious glance, then a faint shrug. Because Ernest was already crafty. His eyes clearly said: 'Too bad! I've got the whistle! I'm going to tell you what I was ordered to say . . .'

And he recited:

'It's about the missal . . . I didn't tell you everything the other day because you scared me . . . But Mum wants me to tell the truth . . . They came and asked me for the missal just before high mass . . .'

But he was red in the face and suddenly picked the whistle up as if he was afraid of seeing it confiscated because of his lie.

'And who came to find you?'

'Monsieur Métayer . . . The secretary at the chateau . . .'

'Come and sit next to me . . . Would you like some grenadine?'

'Yes . . . With fizzy water . . .'

'A grenadine with sparkling mineral water, please, Marie . . . And are you happy with your whistle? . . . Make it work . . .'

The undertakers turned round at the sound of the whistle.

'Your mother bought it for you, yesterday afternoon, isn't that right?'

'How do you know?'

'How much did they give your mother at the bank yesterday?'

The little boy looked him in the eye. He wasn't blushing any more, he was quite pale now. He glanced at the door to measure how far away from it he was.

'Drink your grenadine . . . So it was Émile Gautier who saw you . . . He made you repeat your lesson . . .'

'Yes!'

'He told you to accuse Jean Métayer?'

'Yes.'

And, after a moment's reflection:

'What are you going to do to me?'

Maigret forgot to reply. He was thinking. He was thinking that his role in this matter had consisted solely in supplying the last link, a tiny link that perfectly completed the circle.

It was Jean Métayer that Gautier had wanted to incriminate. But the previous evening's events had scuppered his plans. He had worked out that the dangerous man was not the secretary, but the Count of Saint-Fiacre.

If everything had gone according to plan, he would have had to visit the little boy early in the morning to teach him a new lesson.

You will say that it was the count who asked you for the missal . . .

And now the boy repeated again:

'What are you going to do to me?'

Maigret didn't have time to reply. The lawyer came downstairs and into the dining room, approached Maigret with his hand outstretched, with a hint of hesitation.

'Did you sleep well, inspector? . . . Excuse me . . . I want to ask your advice, on behalf of my client . . . I have the most appalling headache . . .'

He sat down, or rather slumped, on the bench.

'The funeral's fixed for ten o'clock . . .'

He looked at the undertakers, then at the people passing in the road, waiting for the funeral to begin.

'Between ourselves, do you believe that it's Métayer's duty to . . . Don't get me wrong . . . We understand the situation, and it's purely out of delicacy that . . .'

'Please can I go now?'

Maigret didn't hear the boy. He was addressing the lawyer.

'Haven't you worked it out yet?'

'Meaning that if we examine . . .'

'A piece of advice: don't examine anything at all!'

'So in your view we'd be better off leaving without? . . .'

Too late! Ernest, who had grabbed his whistle, was opening the door and making off as fast as his legs would carry him.

'Legally we're all in an excel—'

'An excellent situation, yes!'

'Isn't that so? . . . It's what I was just saying to . . .'

'Did he sleep well?'

'He didn't even take his clothes off . . . He's a very nervous boy, very sensitive, like lots of people of good family and . . .'

But the undertakers pricked up their ears, got to their feet and paid for their drinks. Maigret got up too, unhooked his overcoat with the velvet collar and wiped his bowler hat with his sleeve.

'You both have a chance to slip away during . . .'

'During the funeral? . . . In that case, I'll have to phone for a taxi.'

'That's right.'

The priest in his surplice. Ernest and two other altar boys in their black robes. The cross carried by a priest from a neighbouring village, walking quickly because of the cold. And the liturgical chants that they delivered as they ran along the road.

The villagers were grouped at the foot of the steps. It was impossible to see inside. At last the door opened, and the coffin appeared, carried by four men.

Behind them, a tall silhouette. Maurice de Saint-Fiacre, standing very straight, his eyes red.

He wasn't wearing black. He was the only one not in mourning.

And yet, when his eye drifted across the crowd from the top of the steps, there was a moment's awkwardness.

As he came out of the chateau there was no one beside him. And he followed the coffin all by himself . . .

From his vantage point, Maigret noticed the estate manager's house, which had been his, its doors and windows closed.

The shutters of the chateau were closed as well. It was only in the kitchen that servants pressed their faces to the windows.

A murmur of sacred chants, almost drowned by the sound of footsteps on the gravel.

Bells pealing out.

Two pairs of eyes met: the count's and Maigret's.

Was the inspector mistaken? It seemed to him that the shadow of a smile hovered on Maurice de Saint-Fiacre's lips. Not the smile of a sceptical Parisian, or the smile of a ruined family.

A serene, confident smile . . .

During mass, everyone could hear the blaring horn of a taxi: a little scoundrel fleeing with a lawyer whose brain was dulled by a hangover.

The Misty Harbour

Translated by LINDA COVERDALE

LE PORT DES BRUMES

ROMAN
PAR
GEORGES SIMENON

A. FAYARD & Cⁱᵉ - PARIS   PRIX 6 FR.

1. The Cat in the House

When they had left Paris at around three o'clock, the streets were still bustling in the chilly late-autumn sunshine. Shortly afterwards, near Mantes, the lights had come on in the train compartment. Darkness had fallen outside by the time they reached Évreux, and now, through windows streaming with droplets, they saw a thick mist gleaming in soft haloes around the track lights.

Snug in his corner, resting his head against the back of the banquette, Detective Chief Inspector Maigret had not taken his half-closed eyes from the unlikely couple across from him.

Captain Joris was asleep. His clothes were wrinkled, his wig askew on his gleaming pate.

And Julie, clutching her imitation crocodile handbag, stared off into space while endeavouring, despite her fatigue, to look thoughtful.

Joris! Julie!

Inspector Maigret of the Police Judiciaire was used to having people suddenly take over his life like this, monopolize him for days, weeks, months, and then sink back into the anonymous crowd.

The rhythmic sound of the wheels carried his thoughts along, and they were always the same at the beginning of each case: would this investigation be challenging or dull? Thankless and demoralizing, or painfully tragic?

As Maigret considered Joris, a faint smile touched his lips. A strange fellow! And for five days back at Quai des Orfèvres, everyone had called him That Man, because they couldn't find out who he was.

A man picked up for wandering in obvious distress among

the cars and buses on the Grands Boulevards. Questioned in French, he remains mute. They try seven or eight languages. Nothing. Sign language proves fruitless as well.

A madman? In Maigret's office, he is searched. His suit is new, his underwear is new, his shoes are new. All identifying labels have been removed. No identification papers. No wallet. Five crisp thousand-franc bills have been slipped into one of his pockets.

The inquiry could not be more aggravating! Criminal records and case files are searched. Telegrams are sent at home and abroad. And although subjected to exhausting interrogation, That Man smiles affably all day long! A stocky fellow of about fifty, broad-shouldered, who neither protests nor gets upset, who smiles and sometimes seems to try to remember, but gives up almost immediately . . .

Amnesia? When the wig slides off his head they discover that a bullet has pierced his skull not more than two months earlier. The doctors marvel: whoever operated on him displayed superb surgical skill.

Fresh telegrams go out to hospitals and nursing homes in France, Belgium, Germany, Holland . . .

Five whole days of these painstaking investigations. The absurd results obtained by analysing some stains on his clothing and fine debris from his pockets: traces of salted cod's roe, dried and pulverized on the far shores of Norway for sardine bait.

Does That Man come from up there? Is he Scandinavian? There are indications that he has travelled a long way by train. But how can he have done this on his own, without speaking, with the befuddled appearance that makes him so conspicuous?

His picture appears in the newspapers. A telegram arrives from Ouistreham: *Unknown man identified!*

The telegram is followed by a woman – more of a girl, really – who shows up in Maigret's office, her haggard face inexpertly rouged and powdered: Julie Legrand, the mystery man's maid.

He is no longer That Man: he has a name and a profession. He is Yves Joris, formerly a captain in the merchant navy, now the harbourmaster at Ouistreham, a small port between Trouville and Cherbourg in Lower Normandy.

Julie bursts into tears! Julie cannot understand! Julie begs him to speak to her! And he looks at her calmly, pleasantly, the way he looks at everyone.

Captain Joris had disappeared from Ouistreham on 16 September. It is now the end of October.

What has happened to him while he was missing for six weeks?

'He went out to the lock to work the tide, as usual. An evening tide. I went off to bed. The next morning, he wasn't in his room . . .'

On account of the fog that night, everyone thinks Joris had slipped and fallen into the water. They hunted for him with grappling hooks. Then they assumed he had simply gone off for some peculiar reason of his own.

'Lisieux! . . . Departure in three minutes!'

Maigret goes to stretch his legs on the platform and refill his pipe. He has smoked so much since Paris that the air in the compartment has turned grey.

'All aboard!'

In the meantime Julie has powdered her nose; her eyes are still a bit red from weeping.

It's strange . . . There are moments when she is pretty, with a certain polish. At other times, though it would be hard to say why, she seems like a gauche little peasant.

She straightens the wig on the captain's head, for *her monsieur*, as she puts it, and looks at Maigret as if to say: 'Haven't I every right to take care of him?'

For Joris has no family. He has lived alone, for years, with Julie, whom he calls his housekeeper.

'He treated me like his daughter . . .'

As far as anyone knows, he has no enemies! Has had no adventures, no love affairs, no grand passions!

A man who, after sailing the seven seas for thirty years, could not resign himself to idleness and, despite his retirement, applied for the position of harbourmaster at Ouistreham. He had a small house built there . . .

And one fine evening, on 16 September, he vanished – then reappeared in Paris six weeks later in this sorry state.

Having never seen him in anything but a naval officer's uniform, Julie had been dismayed to find him wearing an off-the-peg grey suit.

She is anxious, uneasy. Whenever she looks at the captain, her face reflects both pity and a nameless fear, a haunting anguish. It really is him, obviously! It's *her monsieur*, all right. And yet, he is no longer completely himself.

'He'll get well again, won't he? I'll take good care of him . . .'

The mist is now turning into large, blurry drops on the windows. Maigret's big, stolid face rocks a little from side to side as the train rattles along. Placidly, he goes on watching his companions: Julie, who pointed out to him that they might just as well have travelled third class, as she normally does, and Joris, who is waking up only to look around him vacantly. One more stop, at Caen. Then on to Ouistreham.

'Around a thousand people live in the village,' a colleague originally from there had told Maigret. 'The harbour is small but important, because of the canal linking the roadstead to the city of Caen. The canal can handle ships of five thousand tons or more.'

Maigret doesn't bother trying to imagine what the place looks like; he knows that's a fool's game. He waits, and his eyes keep turning to the wig, which hides the raw pink scar.

When Captain Joris disappeared, he had thick, dark brown hair with only a touch of silver at the temples. Another torment for Julie, who can't bear the sight of his bare skull . . . Every time the wig slips, she quickly straightens it.

'In short, someone tried to kill him . . .'

He was shot, and that's a fact. But he was also given the very best of medical care. He had no money when he vanished – yet was found with five thousand francs in his pocket.

But there is more to come. Julie suddenly opens her handbag.

'I forgot! I brought along the captain's mail.'

Almost nothing. Brochures for marine supplies. A receipt for dues paid to the Association of Merchant Navy Captains. Postcards from friends still in the service, including one sent from Punta Arenas . . .

A letter from the Banque de Normandie, in Caen. A printed form, the blanks filled in on a typewriter.

> . . . beg to inform you that the sum of three hundred thousand francs has been transferred as per your instructions from the Dutch Bank in Hamburg and credited to your Account No. 14173 . . .

And Julie has already insisted over and over that the captain is not a wealthy man! Maigret looks from one to the other of the pair seated across from him.

Salted cod's roe . . . Hamburg . . . The made-in-Germany shoes . . . And only Joris could explain all this. Joris, who beams a nice broad smile his way because he sees that Maigret is looking at him . . .

'This station is Caen! Passengers for Cherbourg remain on board; change here for Ouistreham, Lion-sur-Mer, Luc . . .'

It is seven o'clock. The air is so humid that the lights on the platform can barely shine through the milky mist.

'How do we go on to our destination now?' Maigret asks Julie as the other passengers push past them.

'Well, the local train runs only twice a day in the winter . . .'

There are taxis outside the station. Maigret is hungry. Having no idea what awaits him in Ouistreham, he prefers to have dinner in the station buffet.

Captain Joris is still behaving well and eats what he is served, like a child who trusts those in charge of him. A passing railway employee pauses at their table to consider the captain.

'Isn't that the harbourmaster of Ouistreham?' he asks Maigret, and twirls a finger at his temple. At a nod from Maigret he goes on his way, visibly amazed.

As for Julie, she takes refuge in practical matters.

'Twelve francs for a dinner like this, and it wasn't even cooked with butter! As if we couldn't simply have eaten when we got home . . .'

As she speaks, Maigret is thinking, 'A bullet in the head . . . Three hundred thousand francs . . .'

He stares searchingly into the captain's innocent eyes, while his mouth sets in a hard line.

The next taxi in line, once a fine limousine, has lumpy seats and creaking joints. The three passengers must crowd together in the back because the jump seats are broken, and Julie is pinned between the two men, squashed by first one, then the other, as the car swerves.

'I'm trying to remember if I locked the garden gate!' she murmurs, increasingly concerned about her domestic duties as they get closer to the house.

Leaving the village, they literally drive into a wall of fog. A horse and cart appear abruptly, barely two metres away, like phantoms, and the trees and houses flitting by on both sides of the road seem like ghosts as well.

The driver slows down. They're going barely ten kilometres an hour, which doesn't prevent a man on a bicycle from bursting out of the fog and into the side of the taxi, which stops. The cyclist is unhurt.

As they go through Ouistreham, Julie rolls down the partition window to speak to the driver.

'Keep going to the harbour and across the swing bridge . . . Then stop at the cottage that's right by the lighthouse!'

Between the village and the harbour lies about a kilometre of road, now deserted, outlined by the feeble glow of streetlamps. At one corner of the bridge they see a lighted window and hear voices.

'That tavern is the Buvette de la Marine,' Julie points out. 'Everyone in the harbour spends most of their time in there.'

Beyond the bridge there's hardly any road at all, and what little there is goes wandering through the marshes along the banks of the Orne, leading at last only to the lighthouse and a cottage surrounded by a garden.

When they stop, Maigret watches the captain, who gets out of the taxi as calmly as you please and walks over to the gate.

'Did you see that, inspector!' cries Julie delightedly. 'He recognizes the house! I'm sure he'll eventually be completely himself again.'

She fits the key into the lock, pushes open the squeaky gate and heads up the gravel path. After paying the driver, Maigret quickly joins her, but now that the taxi is gone it is pitch dark.

'Would you mind striking a match? I can't find the keyhole . . .'

A tiny flame; the door is opened. A dark form brushes past Maigret's legs. Already inside, Julie switches on the light and, looking curiously along the floor, asks softly, 'That was the cat going outside just now, wasn't it?'

She takes off her hat and coat with practised ease, hangs them on a coat peg, pushes open the door to the kitchen and turns on the light, thus inadvertently revealing that this is the room where everyone usually gathers.

A well-lit kitchen with tiled walls, a big sand-scoured pine table, sparkling copper pots and pans. And the captain goes automatically to sit in his wicker armchair over by the stove.

'But I'm sure I put the cat out when I left, the way I always do . . .'

She's worried, talking to herself.

'Yes, I'm certain of it. I left all the doors locked. Oh, inspector, would you please go through the house with me? I'm frightened . . .'

So much so that she hardly dares to go first. She opens the door to the dining room, where all is in such perfect order, with the furniture and parquet polished to a fare-thee-well, that it's clear the room is never used.

'Look behind the curtains, would you?'

There are pieces of Chinese lacquerware and porcelain the captain must have brought back from the Far East, and an upright piano.

Then the living room, just as tidy, with the furniture as spotless as on the day it was bought. The captain is tagging along, pleased, almost blissful. They go upstairs, walking on a red carpet runner. There are three bedrooms, one of which is a spare.

And everywhere, that same cleanliness, that meticulous order, that faint smell of cooking and countryside.

No one is hiding there. The windows are shut and bolted. The garden gate is locked, although the key has been left outside.

'Perhaps the cat came in through a basement window,' Maigret tells her.

'There are none.'

They return to the kitchen; she opens a cupboard.

'May I offer you a drop of something?'

And it is now, amid these ritual movements, while pouring a liqueur into tiny glasses decorated with painted flowers, that she feels her anguish most deeply and begins to sob.

She looks furtively at the captain, who is back in his armchair. The sight of him is so painful that she looks away and, stammering with the effort to pull herself together, tells Maigret, 'I'll make the guest room ready for you.'

She can hardly get the words out. She takes an apron hanging on the wall to wipe her eyes.

'I would rather stay at the hotel. I suppose there is one . . .'

Julie looks up at a small china clock, the kind often won at a fairground, a clock that ticks along like the comforting soul of the household.

'Yes! You'll still find someone there at this hour. It's on the other side of the lock, just behind the Buvette de la Marine.'

She wishes he would stay, however, and seems afraid to be left alone with the captain, whom she no longer dares look at.

'You don't think there's anyone in the house?'

'As you saw for yourself.'

'You'll come back tomorrow morning?'

She goes with him to the front door, which she shuts firmly behind him.

And Maigret finds himself plunging into fog so dense that he cannot even see his feet. He does manage to find the gate. He can feel that he is walking on grass, then on the rough, stony road. He also becomes aware of a distant noise that he will need some time to identify.

It resembles the lowing of a cow, but sadder, more desolate.

'Idiot!' he finally growls between his teeth. 'It's only the foghorn . . .'

He's no longer sure where he is. And now, right in front of his feet, he looks down at water that appears to be steaming. He is on the wall of the lock! He hears the screech of cranks turning somewhere. He can't remember where the taxi crossed the water and, spotting a narrow footbridge, he is about to step on to it.

'Watch out!'

He is stunned: the voice is so close to him! Just when Maigret was feeling absolutely alone, a man has turned up within three metres of him – and the inspector must strain to make out even his silhouette.

Now he understands that warning: the footbridge he was about to cross is moving. It's the gate of the lock itself that is opening, and the sight becomes even more hallucinatory because quite close by, a few metres away, it's no longer a man that appears but an entire wall, as high as a house. On top of this wall are lights shining fitfully through the mist.

A ship is passing – and Maigret could reach out to touch it! When the end of a hawser thuds down near him, someone picks it up, lugs it to a bollard and makes it fast.

'Slow astern! . . . Stand by!' shouts someone up on the bridge of the steamer.

A few moments earlier, the place had seemed dead, deserted. And now Maigret, walking the length of the lock, sees that the mist is full of human figures. Someone is turning a winch. Another man runs up with a second mooring line. Customs officials are waiting for the gangway to be lowered to allow them aboard. And none of them can see a thing, in the thick mist that pearls in droplets on the men's moustaches.

'You want to cross over?'

The voice is quite close. Another lock-gate.

'Hurry up, or you'll have to wait a good fifteen minutes . . .'

He goes across holding on to the handrail, hears water boiling beneath his feet and, still in the distance, the moaning of the foghorn. The more Maigret advances, the more this world of mist fills with teeming, mysterious life. A light draws him on; approaching, he sees a fisherman, in a boat moored to the dock, lowering and raising a net attached to some poles.

The man glances at him without interest, then begins to sort through a basket of small fish.

The lights illuminating the mist around the ship make it easier to see what is going on. Up on deck, they're speaking English; a man in an officer's cap is initialling documents at the edge of the quay.

The harbourmaster! The replacement for Captain Joris . . .

Like Joris, the man is short, but he's thinner, more lively, and jokes around with the ship's officers.

The world has dwindled to a few square metres of patchy

illumination and a vast black hole where water and terra firma make their invisible presence felt. The sea is over there, to the left, barely murmuring at all.

Wasn't it on a night like this that Joris suddenly vanished from the scene? He was checking papers, like his colleague now, and probably cracking jokes, too. He was keeping track of the sluicing water and all the activity. He had no need to see everything; a few familiar sounds would have been enough. Look at the way no one here watches where he's going!

Maigret has just lit a pipe and begins to scowl; he does not like to feel clumsy. He's angry with himself for being a ponderous landlubber for whom the sea is a source of fear or wonder.

The lock-gates open. The ship enters a canal almost as wide as the Seine in Paris.

'Forgive the interruption: are you the harbourmaster? . . . Detective Chief Inspector Maigret, of the Police Judiciaire. I've just brought home your colleague.'

'Joris is here? So it really is he? . . . I heard about it this morning . . . But, is it true he's . . .'

And he gently taps his forehead.

'For the moment, yes. Will you spend all night here?'

'Never more than five hours at a stretch. As long as the tide lasts, basically! There are five hours during each tide when the ships have enough water to enter the canal or set out to sea, and this window shifts every day. Tonight, we've just begun and we'll be busy here until three in the morning . . .'

A straightforward man, who treats Maigret as a colleague, a public servant like himself.

'Would you excuse me?'

Then the harbourmaster looks out towards the open water, where there is nothing to see, and remarks, 'A sailing ship from Boulogne has tied up at the jetty to wait her turn at the canal.'

'Do you always know what ships to expect?'

'Most of the time. Especially the steamers. They're generally on a regular schedule, bringing coal from England, heading back from Caen loaded with ore.'

'Will you join me in a drink?'

'I can't, not until the tide has ebbed. I have to stay here.'

And the harbourmaster shouts orders to invisible men, knowing exactly where they are.

'You are conducting an inquiry?' he asks.

Just then they hear footsteps, coming from the village. A man goes across one of the lock-gates and as he passes a light, it gleams on the barrel of a rifle.

'Who is that?'

'The mayor, off to hunt ducks. He has a blind down by the Orne. His assistant must already be there getting things ready for tonight.'

'You think I'll find the hotel still open?'

'The Hôtel de l'Univers? Yes, but you'd best hurry . . . The owner will soon finish playing cards and head off to bed. And once there, he stays there!'

'Until tomorrow, then.'

'Fine. I'm due back here at ten, for the morning tide.'

They shake hands, like two phantoms in the mist. And life goes on in the fog, where one may suddenly bump into an invisible man.

The experience does not feel sinister, really; it's something else: a vague uneasiness, a faint oppressive anxiety, the impression of an unknown world with its own life going on all around you. A world in which you are a stranger.

That darkness peopled by invisible beings . . . That sailing ship, for example, waiting nearby for its turn, although you would never even guess it was there.

About to pass the fisherman again, sitting motionless under his lantern, Maigret tries to think of something to say.

'They biting tonight?'

And the other man merely spits into the water as Maigret walks on, kicking himself for having said something so stupid.

The last thing he hears before entering the hotel is the slamming of the upstairs shutters over at Captain Joris' cottage.

Julie, who is frightened! The cat escaping when they entered the house . . .

'That foghorn going to wail all night?' grumbles Maigret impatiently, as the landlord comes to greet him.

'As long as there's fog about . . . You get used to it . . .'

Maigret slept fitfully, the way one does with indigestion or as a child tosses and turns the night before some great event. Twice the inspector got up to lean his face against the cold windowpanes and saw nothing but the empty road and revolving lighthouse beam, which seemed to keep stabbing at a cloudbank. The eternal foghorn sounded harsher, more aggressive.

The second time, he checked his watch: four o'clock, and fishermen with baskets on their backs were clattering off to the harbour in their clogs.

Almost immediately there was a frantic pounding on his door, which opened without waiting for his response and revealed the anguished face of the landlord.

Some time had passed, however: although the foghorn was still going strong, sunshine now gleamed at the windows.

'Hurry! The captain is dying . . .'

'What captain?'

'Captain Joris . . . Julie's just rushed to the harbour to send for both you and a doctor.'

Maigret, his hair unbrushed, was already pulling on his trousers. He jammed his feet into his shoes without lacing them up and forgot to attach the stiff collar to his shirt before putting on his jacket.

'You'll have nothing before you go? A cup of coffee? A tot of rum?'

No – he hadn't time! It was sunny outdoors, but quite chilly. The road was still damp with dew.

Hurrying across the lock, Maigret caught a glimpse of the sea, but only a small strip of it, perfectly still and pale blue; the rest was hidden by a long fogbank hanging just offshore.

Someone called to him from the bridge.

'Are you the detective chief inspector from Paris? I'm with the local police. I'm glad you've come . . . Have you already heard?'

'Heard what?'

'They say it's awful! . . . Wait a minute . . . There's the doctor's car . . .'

Fishing boats in the outer harbour were rocking gently, casting red and green reflections across the water. Some sails were set, probably to dry, and showed their black identity numbers.

Two or three women waited out by the lighthouse, in front of the captain's cottage. The door was open.

The doctor's car passed Maigret and the policeman, who was sticking close to the inspector.

'They're talking about poison,' the officer continued. 'It seems he's turned a greenish colour . . .'

Maigret entered the cottage just when Julie was coming slowly downstairs in tears, her eyes swollen, her cheeks flushed. She had been shooed out of the bedroom so the doctor could examine the dying man.

Under a hastily donned coat, she still wore a long white night-gown and her feet were bare in their slippers.

'It's terrible, inspector! You can't imagine . . . Go up, quickly! Maybe . . .'

The doctor had been bending over his patient and was just straightening up when Maigret entered the bedroom. The inspector could see from his face that it was hopeless.

'Police . . .'

'Ah! Well, it's the end. Maybe two or three minutes more . . . Either I'm way off course, or it's strychnine.'

Joris seemed to be straining to breathe, so the doctor opened a window. And there again was that dreamlike tableau: the sun, the harbour, the boats and their unfurled sails, fishermen pouring brimming baskets of glittering fish into crates.

What a contrast: the dying man's face seemed yellower, or greener, an indescribable colour. A neutral tone incompatible with any ordinary conception of flesh. His limbs were writhing, jerking spasmodically, yet his face remained calm, in seeming repose, as he stared at the wall in front of him.

Holding one of his patient's wrists, the doctor was tracking the weakening pulse when Maigret saw a look come over his face that said, 'Watch closely! He's going now . . .'

Then something amazing and quite poignant happened. The captain's face had been so empty that no one could tell if the wretched man had recovered his reason, but now this face came back to life. As if he were a boy on the verge of tears, his features crumpled into a pitiful expression of misery so deep that it cannot go on.

And two great tears welled up, about to spill over . . .

Almost at the same instant, the doctor announced softly, 'It's over.'

Could that have happened? Could death have come at the very moment Joris was weeping?

And while those tears were still alive, trickling down to vanish within his ears, the captain himself was dead.

They heard footsteps in the stairwell. Surrounded by women, Julie was sobbing and gasping below. Maigret went out to the landing.

'No one,' he said slowly, 'is to enter this room!'

'Is he . . . ?'

'Yes!' he replied firmly.

And he went back to the sunny room, where the doctor, for his own peace of mind, was preparing to administer a heart injection.

Out on the garden wall, there was a pure white cat.

2. The Inheritance

Somewhere downstairs, probably in the kitchen, they could hear Julie's shrill cries as she struggled with her grief, restrained and surrounded by women from the neighbourhood.

The window was still wide open, and Maigret saw villagers arriving at a kind of half-run. Kids on bikes, women carrying babies, men in clogs – it was a disorganized and lively little procession that poured over the bridge and on towards the captain's house, just as if they had been drawn there by a travelling circus or a traffic accident.

Maigret soon had to close the window against the noise outside, and the muslin curtains softened the light. The atmosphere in the bedroom became milder, more subdued. The wallpaper was pink. The furniture of pale wood was well polished. A vase full of flowers held pride of place on the mantelpiece.

The inspector watched the doctor as he held up to the light a glass and a carafe of water he had taken from the bedside table. He even dipped a finger into the water and touched it to his tongue.

'That's what did it?'

'Yes. The captain must have liked to have a glass of water handy at night. As far as I can tell, he drank some at around three this morning, but I don't understand why he didn't call for help.'

'For the very good reason that he couldn't speak or even make the slightest sound,' muttered Maigret.

He summoned the policeman and told him to inform the mayor and the public prosecutor at Caen of what had happened. People were still coming and going downstairs, while outside, on that bit of road leading nowhere, the local folk were standing around in groups. A few, to be more comfortable, were sitting on the grass.

The tide was coming in, already invading the sandbanks by the entrance to the harbour. Smoke on the horizon betrayed a ship waiting for the right time to head in to the bay.

'Do you have any idea of . . .' the doctor began, but fell silent when he realized that the inspector was busy. Maigret had opened a mahogany writing desk that stood between the two bedroom windows and was making a list of what was in the drawers, with the obstinate frown he always wore on such occasions. Seen like that, the inspector looked somewhat brutish. He had lit his fat pipe, which he smoked in slow puffs, and his big fingers handled the things he was finding without any apparent care or respect.

Photographs, for example. There were dozens. Many were of friends, almost all of them in naval uniform and about the same age as Joris would have been at the time. Evidently he had kept in touch with his classmates at the marine academy in Brest, and they wrote to him from every corner of the world. Photos in postcard format, artless and banal, whether they arrived from Saigon or Santiago: 'Hello from Henry,' or 'At last! My third stripe! Hooray! Eugène.'

Most of these cards were addressed to 'Captain Joris, aboard the *Diana*, Compagnie Anglo-Normande, Caen'.

'Had you known the captain long?' Maigret asked the doctor.

'For a good while. Ever since he came here. Before that, he sailed on one of the mayor's ships. Captained her for twenty-eight years.'

'The mayor's ships?'

'Yes, Monsieur Ernest Grandmaison! The chairman of the Compagnie Anglo-Normande. In effect, the sole owner of the company's eleven steamships.'

Another photograph: Joris himself this time, at twenty-five, already stocky, with a broad, smiling face, but a hint of stubbornness, too. A real Breton!

Finally, in a canvas folder, certificates, from his school diploma all the way to a master's certificate in the Merchant Navy, as well as official documents, his birth certificate, service record, passports . . .

Maigret picked up an envelope that had fallen to the floor. The paper was already yellowing with age.

'A will?' asked the doctor, who was at a loose end until the examining magistrate arrived.

The household of Captain Joris must have been run on trust, because the envelope was not even sealed. Within was a sheet of paper; the writing was in a neat, elegant hand.

> I the undersigned Yves-Antoine Joris, born in Paimpol, a captain in the Merchant Navy, do hereby bequeath all my property, real and personal, to Julie Legrand, in my employ, in recompense for her years of devoted service.
>
> I direct her to make the following bequests:
>
> My canoe to Captain Delcourt; the Chinese porcelain dinner service to his wife; my carved ivory-headed cane to . . .

Almost everyone in that little harbour-town world, which Maigret had seen bustling in the fog the night before, had been remembered. Even the lock-keeper, who was to receive a fishing net, 'the trammel lying under the shed', as the captain had put it.

Just then there was a strange noise in the house. While the women in the kitchen were busy fixing Julie a hot toddy 'to buck her up', she had dashed upstairs and now entered the bedroom, looking wildly all around her. She then rushed towards the bed only to draw back, speechless before the spectacle of death.

'Is he . . . Can he be . . . ?'

She collapsed on to the carpet, wailing almost unintelligibly, but one could just make out: '. . . It can't be . . . My poor *monsieur* . . . my . . . my . . .'

Solemnly, Maigret stooped to help her to her feet and guide her, still shuddering in distress, into her bedroom next door. The place was in disorder, with clothes lying on the bed and soapy water in the wash basin.

'Who filled the water carafe sitting on the bedside table?'

'I did . . . Yesterday morning . . . When I put flowers in the captain's room . . .'

'Were you alone in the house?'

Julie was panting, slowly recovering her composure, yet beginning to wonder at the inspector's questions.

'What are you thinking?' she cried abruptly.

'I'm not thinking anything. Calm down. I've just read the captain's will.'

'And?'

'You inherit everything. You'll be rich . . .'

His words simply provoked fresh tears.

'The captain was poisoned by the water in the carafe.'

She glared at him with bristling contempt.

'What are you trying to say?' she shouted. 'What do you mean?'

She was so overwrought that she grabbed his forearm, shook it in fury and even seemed about to start hitting and clawing at him.

'Julie, compose yourself, listen to me! The inquiry has only just begun. I am not insinuating anything. I am gathering information.'

A loud knock at the door; the policeman had brought news.

'The magistrate cannot get here before early this afternoon. The mayor, who was out hunting last night, was in bed. He will come as soon as he's ready.'

Everyone was on edge. Throughout the house there was a

fever of anxiety. And that crowd outside, waiting without really knowing what it was waiting for, increased the feeling of tension and disturbance.

'Are you planning on staying here?' Maigret asked Julie.

'Why not? Wherever would I go?'

The inspector asked the doctor to leave the captain's bedroom, then locked the door behind him. He permitted only two women to remain with Julie, the wife of the lighthouse-keeper and a lock-worker's wife.

'Allow no one else in,' he told the policeman. 'If necessary, try to send these curiosity seekers away without making a fuss.'

The inspector himself left the cottage, made his way through the onlookers and walked to the bridge. The foghorn was still sounding in the distance, but only faintly now, with the wind blowing offshore. The air was mild. The sun shone more brightly with each passing hour. The tide was rising.

Two lock workers were already arriving from the village to begin their shifts. On the bridge, Maigret saw Captain Delcourt, with whom he had spoken the previous evening and who now came towards him.

'Tell me! Is it true?'

'Joris was poisoned, yes.'

'Who did it?'

The people over at the cottage were beginning to disperse. The policeman seemed to be the reason, going from group to group, telling them God knows what and gesturing emphatically. Now, however, the crowd had fixed on the inspector and observed him intently.

'Are you already on duty?'

'Not yet. Not until the tide rises a good metre more. Look! That steamship you see at anchor in the roadstead has been waiting since six this morning.'

Customs officials, the head lock-keeper, the water bailiff and the skipper of the coastguard cutter were among the onlookers hovering nearby, not daring to approach the two men, but the lock workers were getting ready to start their shifts.

So Maigret was now seeing in broad daylight the men he had sensed had been working all around him the previous night, hidden in the fog. The Buvette de la Marine was only a few steps away, its windows and glass door providing a fine view of the lock, the bridge, the jetties, the lighthouse and Joris' cottage.

'Will you come and have a drink?' the inspector asked Captain Delcourt.

He had the feeling that this was customary, that with each tide this little fraternity would repair to their local hangout. The captain checked the level of the water.

'I've got half an hour,' he announced.

They both entered the simple wooden tavern, gradually followed – after some hesitation – by the others. Maigret beckoned to them to join him and his companion at their table.

He had to break the ice, introducing himself to everyone to inspire their trust and even gain some sort of access to their circle.

'What'll you have?'

They all glanced at one another, still a bit ill at ease.

'This time of day, it's usually coffee laced with a warming drop . . .'

A woman served them all. The crowd returning from the cottage tried to see inside the bar and, reluctant to go on home, scattered through the harbour to await developments.

After filling his pipe, Maigret passed his tobacco pouch around. Captain Delcourt preferred a cigarette, but the head lock-keeper, reddening slightly, tucked a pinch of tobacco inside his lip and mumbled, 'If you don't mind . . .'

Maigret finally made his move.

'A strange business, this, don't you think?'

They had all been expecting this moment, but the sally still met with an uncomfortable silence.

'Captain Joris seems to have been quite a fine fellow . . .'

And the inspector waited, darting discreet glances at the men's faces.

'Indeed!' replied Delcourt, who was a bit older than his predecessor, less tidy in his appearance and apparently not averse to drink.

Nevertheless, while speaking he kept a careful eye, through the curtains, on both the progress of the tide and the ship now weighing anchor.

'He's starting a mite early! The current in the Orne will shortly drive him on to the sandbanks . . .'

'Your health!' said Maigret. 'I take it, then, that none of you knows what happened on the night of the 16th of September . . .'

'No one. It was a foggy evening, like last night. I myself was not on duty. I stayed on here, though, playing cards with Joris and these other men here with you now.'

'Did you get together here every evening?'

'Just about . . . Not much else to do in Ouistreham. Three or four times, that night, Joris left his hand to someone else when he had to go and attend to a boat in the lock. By nine thirty, the tide had gone out. He set out into the fog, as if he were heading home.'

'When did you realize he was missing?'

'The next day. Julie came to ask about him. She'd gone to sleep before he got home and the next morning was astonished not to find him in his bedroom.'

'Joris had had a few drinks?'

'Never more than one!' insisted the customs man, growing eager to have his say on this subject. 'And no tobacco!'

'And . . . How shall I put this . . . He and Julie? . . .'

An exchange of looks, some hesitation, several smiles.

'No way to know. Joris swore there was nothing. It's just that . . .'

The customs man picked up the thread.

'I'm not speaking ill of him when I say that he didn't entirely fit in with the rest of us. He wasn't a prideful man, no, that's not the right word! But he paid attention to appearances, you understand? He'd never have come on duty in clogs, like Delcourt sometimes does. He played cards here of an evening, but never came by during the day. He never spoke familiarly to the lock workers . . . I don't know if you see what I'm getting at . . .'

Maigret saw perfectly. He had spent several hours in Joris' modest, cosy, neat little house. And now he considered the regulars at the Buvette de la Marine, a rowdier, more unbuttoned crew. This was a place for hearty drinking, where voices surely grew boisterous, the atmosphere thick with smoke, and the talk a touch coarse.

Joris came here simply to play cards, never chatted about his personal life, had only the one drink before leaving.

'She's been at his house for about eight years now. She was sixteen when she arrived, a little country girl, bedraggled and badly dressed . . .'

'And now . . .'

The waitress arrived as if on cue with a bottle of home-made brandy and poured another shot into the glasses, where only a little coffee remained. This, too, appeared to be the custom of the place.

'Now? She is what she is . . . At our dances, for example, she won't step out on the floor with just anyone. And in the shops, when she's treated with easy familiarity, like a maid, she gets angry. It's hard to explain . . . Even though her brother . . .'

The head lock-keeper gave the customs man a sharp look – but Maigret caught him at it.

'Her brother?'

'The inspector will find out anyway!' continued the man, who was obviously not on his first spiked coffee of the day. 'Her brother did eight years in prison. He was drunk, one night, in

Honfleur. With a few others, loud and disorderly in the streets. When the police stepped in, the fellow hurt one officer so badly that he died the next month.'

'He's a sailor?'

'He served on ocean-going vessels in the foreign trade before coming back home. He's currently sailing on a schooner out of Paimpol, the *Saint-Michel*.'

Captain Delcourt had begun fidgeting nervously.

'Let's go!' he announced. 'It's time . . .'

'Before the steamer's even in the lock!' sighed the customs officer, clearly in less of a hurry.

Only three men were left. Maigret signalled to the waitress, who returned with her bottle.

'Does the *Saint-Michel* sometimes come through here?'

'Sometimes, yes.'

'Was she here on the 16th of September?'

'Well, it's going to be right there for him in the lock-keeper's log,' the customs man remarked to his neighbour and turned to Maigret: 'Yes, she was here. She even had to stay in the outer harbour on account of the fog and left only at daybreak.'

'Going where?'

'Southampton. I'm the one who looked over their papers. The cargo was grindstone grit, from Caen.'

'And Julie's brother hasn't been seen here since?'

This time the customs officer sniffed thoughtfully and paused before draining his glass.

'You'll have to ask those who claim to have spotted him yesterday . . . Me, I haven't seen a thing.'

'Yesterday?'

A shrug. An enormous steamer came gliding between the stone walls of the lock, a vast black mass towering over the countryside, its funnel taller than the trees lining the canal.

'I've got to get over there . . .'

'Me too . . .'

'How much does it come to, mademoiselle?' Maigret asked the waitress.

'The landlady isn't here just now, but I'm sure you'll be back.'

The people still waiting outside the captain's cottage for something to happen now gratefully turned their attention to the English steamer passing through the lock.

As Maigret left the bar, a man was arriving from the village; the inspector assumed he was the mayor, whom he had seen only briefly the night before.

A somewhat beefy fellow between forty-five and fifty, quite tall, with a rosy complexion. He was wearing a grey hunting coat and aviator gaiters. Maigret went over to him.

'Monsieur Grandmaison? I am Detective Chief Inspector Maigret of the Police Judiciaire.'

'Pleased to meet you,' came the casual reply.

The mayor looked at the Buvette de la Marine, then Maigret, then the tavern again as if to say, 'Strange company for an important official to keep!'

And he kept walking towards the lock on his way to the cottage.

'Joris is dead, I hear?'

'It's true,' replied Maigret, who did not much like the man's attitude.

An attitude that could hardly have been more traditional: that of the big fish in a small pond, someone who thinks himself the centre of the world, dresses like a country gentleman and pays a token tribute to democracy by shaking hands half-heartedly with his fellow citizens, saluting them with mumbled greetings and the occasional inquiry after their children's health.

'And you've caught the murderer? Since it was you who brought Joris here and who – excuse me . . .'

He went over to speak to the water bailiff, who apparently attended him when he went duck hunting.

'The left-hand reeds of the blind need straightening. And one of the decoys is useless, it looked half dead this morning.'

'I'll see to it, sir.'

The mayor rejoined Maigret, pausing en route to shake the harbourmaster's hand with a murmured greeting.

'How are you?'

'Fine, sir.'

'Where were we, inspector? Ah! What's all this I hear about a patched-up fractured skull, insanity and so on?'

'Were you a particular friend of Captain Joris?'

'He was in my employ for twenty-eight years, a fine man, assiduous in his duties.'

'Honest?'

'Almost all my employees are.'

'What was his salary?'

'That would depend, because of the war, which disrupted things everywhere. Enough for him to buy his little house, in any case. And I wager he had at least twenty thousand francs in the bank.'

'No more?'

'Oh, perhaps five thousand francs or so more, at most.'

The upstream lock-gate was opening to let the steamer into the canal; another ship, coming down from Caen, would take its place and head out to sea.

The day was beautifully calm. Everyone was watching Maigret and the mayor. Up on their ship, the English sailors glanced nonchalantly at the crowd while going about their duties.

'What is your opinion of Julie Legrand?'

The mayor hesitated for a moment before grumbling, 'A silly creature who had her head turned because Joris treated her far too nicely. She thinks she's . . . How shall I . . . Anyway, she fancies herself better than she is.'

'And her brother?'

'Never laid eyes on him. I'm told he's a scoundrel.'

They had left the lock behind and were approaching Joris' front gate, where a few kids were still playing and hoping to see some interesting developments.

'What did the captain die of?'

'Strychnine!'

Maigret was wearing his most pigheaded expression. He walked slowly, hands in his pockets, pipe clenched in his teeth. And this pipe seemed to match his big face, for it held a quarter-packet's worth of shag tobacco.

The white cat, stretched full-length in the sunshine atop the garden wall, leaped down in a flash as the two men arrived.

'You're not going in?' asked the mayor in surprise when Maigret stopped short at the cottage gate.

'Just a moment. In your opinion, was Julie the captain's mistress?'

'How would I know that!' exclaimed Monsieur Grandmaison impatiently.

'Did you often visit the captain here?'

'Never! Joris was one of my employees. So you see . . .' And he smiled in what he imagined to be a lordly manner. 'If it's all the same to you, inspector, we'll deal with this as swiftly as possible. I'm expecting guests for lunch.'

'Are you married?'

Frowning in concentration, Maigret kept pursuing his thought, his hand still on the front-gate latch.

Monsieur Grandmaison, who was just over six feet tall, looked down at the inspector, who noticed that although the mayor wasn't exactly cross-eyed, his irises were slightly asymmetrical.

'I should warn you, sir,' said the mayor, 'that if you continue to address me in that tone, you might well come to regret it. Now show me what it is you wish me to see.'

And after pushing open the gate himself, he walked up to and through the front door, where the policeman on guard stepped swiftly out of his way.

Through a glass panel in the kitchen door Maigret could see right away that something was amiss: the two women were there, but he did not see Julie.

'Where is she?'

'She went up to her room! Locked herself in and refused to come down.'

'Just like that, out of the blue?'

'She was doing better,' explained the lighthouse-keeper's wife. 'Still crying, but not as hard, and was talking with us a little. I told her she should eat something, so she opened the cupboard . . .'

'And?'

'I don't know . . . She seemed frightened! She dashed up the stairs, and next thing, we heard the key to her bedroom turning in the lock.'

There was nothing in the cupboard but crockery, a few apples in a basket, a dish of marinating herrings and two greasy plates that had probably held some cold meat.

'I am still waiting!' snapped the mayor, who had stayed out in the front hall. 'It is eleven thirty. What that young woman has been up to should hardly . . .'

Maigret locked the cupboard, pocketed the key and walked heavily to the stairs.

3. The Kitchen Cupboard

'Julie, open up!'

No reply, but the sound of someone collapsing on a bed.

'Open this door!'

Nothing. So Maigret slammed his shoulder into the door – and the screws popped out of the lock plate.

'Why didn't you open the door?'

She was not crying. She was not agitated. No, she was curled up on her bed staring fixedly straight in front of her. When the inspector came too close, she jumped down and attempted to reach the door.

'Leave me alone!' she said loudly.

'Well then, give me the note, Julie.'

'What note?'

She spoke aggressively, hoping to camouflage her lie.

'Did the captain allow your brother to come and visit you?'

No answer.

'Which means that he did not permit it! Your brother used to come and see you anyway. It seems he came here the night Joris disappeared . . .'

A hard, almost hateful look.

'The *Saint-Michel* was in that day. So it was only natural that he would come and see you. One question: when he comes, he usually has something to eat, doesn't he?'

'You're horrible!' she muttered between her teeth.

'And he came here while you were in Paris. Not finding you at home, he left you a note. To make sure that no one else but you would find it, he left it in the kitchen cupboard. Now give me the note . . .'

'I don't have it any more!'

Maigret looked at the empty fireplace, the closed window.

'Give it to me!'

She was rigid in protest, but not like an intelligent woman would be, and she so resembled an angry child that the inspector, catching one of her outraged looks, grumbled softly, 'Silly goose!'

The note was simply under her pillow, where Julie had been lying a minute before. Instead of giving up, however, she went back on the attack, trying to snatch the note from the inspector with a fury that amused him.

Pinioning her hands, he said sternly, 'Are you done now?'

And he read these lines of wretched handwriting, riddled with mistakes.

> If you comm back with yor boss be carefull with him for theres bad fellos that have got it in for him. I wil be back in 2 or 3 days with the ship. Dont look for the cuttletts I ate them. Yor brother for life.

Maigret bowed his head, thrown so off-balance that he paid no further attention to Julie.

Fifteen minutes later, Captain Delcourt was telling him that the *Saint-Michel* was probably in Fécamp and that if the north-westerly winds held steady, the ship would arrive the following night.

'Do you know the position of every single vessel?'

And Maigret, uneasy, looked out at the shimmering sea, with only a single plume of smoke visible in the distance.

'The ports are all in contact with one another,' replied the harbourmaster. 'Look! There is the list of all the ships due in today.'

He pointed to a blackboard hanging on the wall of the office, with the list written out in chalk.

'Have you discovered something? Well, don't rely too much

on what people say. Even important people! If you only knew how much petty jealousy can flourish around here . . .'

After waving to the captain of a freighter heading out to sea, the harbourmaster looked out of his office window at the Buvette de la Marine and sighed.

'You'll see . . .'

By three o'clock, the officials from the public prosecutor's office had finished their work. A dozen or so men filed out of Joris' cottage and walked through the little green gate towards the four cars that awaited them, surrounded by onlookers.

The deputy public prosecutor gazed around him appreciatively.

'The duck hunting here must be superb!' he remarked to Monsieur Grandmaison.

'We've had a disappointing season. But last year—'

The mayor suddenly dashed over to the first car as it was pulling away.

'You'll all stop in at my house for a moment, I hope? My wife will be expecting us . . .'

When Maigret was the only man left, the mayor turned to him with just enough bonhomie to appear polite.

'Ride back with us, inspector. You are invited as well, naturally.'

Only Julie and the two women remained in Captain Joris' cottage, along with the local policeman at the door, to await the hearse that would deliver the body to Caen.

The atmosphere in the cars had already taken on the festive air that often enlivens the trip when convivial companions return from a funeral. While Maigret perched uncomfortably on a jump seat, the mayor was chatting with the deputy public prosecutor.

'If it were up to me, I would stay here all year round, but my wife is not that fond of country living. So we spend most of our time at our house in Caen – although my wife has only just got back from Juan-les-Pins, where she spent a month with the children.'

'How old is your boy now?'

'Fifteen.'

The lock workers watched the cars drive by. And almost immediately, on the road to Lion-sur-Mer, they arrived at the mayor's residence, a large Norman villa on a property surrounded by white fencing and strewn with animal lawn ornaments.

Standing in the front hall in a dark silk dress, Madame Grandmaison welcomed her guests with the delicately aloof smile befitting her station in life. The drawing room was at their disposal; cigars and liqueurs were set out on a table in the smoking room.

All these people knew one another. The social elite of Caen were having a reunion. A maid in a white apron took everyone's hats and coats.

'Really, judge: you've never visited Ouistreham – and you've lived in Caen for *how* long?'

'Twelve years, dear madame . . . Ah! Here's Mademoiselle Gisèle!'

A girl of fourteen had come in to curtsey slightly to the guests, already holding herself like quite the lady – and, like her mother, acutely conscious of her social position. Meanwhile, however, no one had remembered to introduce Maigret to the mistress of the house.

Turning to the deputy public prosecutor, that lady inquired, 'I suppose that after what you've all just been through you would prefer something a little stronger than tea? A liqueur brandy, then? . . . And your wife, is she still in Fontainebleau?'

Everywhere, people were talking. Maigret heard snatches of conversations.

'No, ten ducks per night is the limit . . . But I assure you, it isn't cold at all! The blind is heated . . .'

On another side: '. . . hit hard by the drop in business?'

'That depends on the company. Here we've been relatively unaffected. Locally, none of our vessels is in trouble. The smaller concerns, on the other hand, especially those with only schooners for the coastal trade, are beginning to suffer. I might even say that those companies depending on schooners are in general looking to sell them, for they cannot cover their expenses . . .'

'No, madame,' insisted the deputy public prosecutor soothingly, 'there is no reason for alarm. The mystery – if there is one – of this man's death will soon be resolved. Isn't that so, inspector? . . . But . . . Haven't you been introduced? May I present Detective Chief Inspector Maigret, a man of stellar reputation from the Police Judiciaire.'

Maigret stood stiffly with a most unwelcoming expression on his face, and when young Gisèle smilingly held out to him a plate of petits fours, he gave her an odd look.

'No, thank you.'

'Really? You don't like cakes?'

'To your good health!'

'Here's to our charming hostess!'

The public prosecutor, a tall, thin man of about fifty who could barely see through the thick lenses of his glasses, now took Maigret aside.

'I'm giving you carte blanche, of course. But telephone me every evening to keep me up to date. What do you think of this case? A sordid affair, is it not?' Noticing Monsieur Grandmaison approaching, he added in a louder voice, 'And besides, you are lucky to be dealing with a mayor like Grandmaison here, who will be of great assistance in your inquiry. Is that not so, dear friend? I was just telling the inspector . . .'

'If he wants,' replied the mayor, 'we'd be delighted to have him stay in our house. I suppose you are at present at the hotel?'

'I am,' replied the inspector, 'and thank you for your invitation, but the hotel is so conveniently situated . . .'

'And you believe you will ferret something out at the tavern? A word of warning, inspector! You don't know Ouistreham! Consider what people who spend their lives in a tavern can conjure up through sheer imagination! They'd point the finger at their own parents simply to have a good tale to tell.'

'Why don't we talk about something else?' suggested Madame Grandmaison with a gracious smile. 'Inspector, a petit four? . . . Really? . . . You don't like sweets?'

For the second time! Unbelievable! And Maigret was almost moved to pull out his big fat pipe in protest.

'If you will excuse me. There are some matters I must attend to.'

No one tried to detain him. All things considered, they were no more enamoured of his presence than he was of theirs. Outside, he filled his pipe and walked slowly back to the harbour. The local people knew him now, knew that he had stood a round of drinks at the bar, so they greeted him with a hint of friendliness.

As he approached the quay, he noticed the hearse carrying the captain's body drive away towards Caen and saw Julie's face, framed in a downstairs window at the cottage. The other women were trying to cajole her back into the kitchen.

A fishing boat had just come in, and people gathered around it as the two fishermen sorted out their catch. The customs officials up on the bridge parapet whiled away the slow hours of their shift.

'I've just had a confirmation!' called out Captain Delcourt, hurrying over to Maigret. 'The *Saint-Michel* will arrive tomorrow! She was laid up for three days in Fécamp having her bowsprit repaired.'

'Say, tell me: does she ever carry salted cod's roe as cargo?'

'Cod's roe? No. The Norwegian roe comes in on Scandinavian schooners or small steamers. They don't unload at Caen, though, they make directly for the sardine ports, like Concarneau, Les Sables-d'Olonne, Saint-Jean-de-Luz . . .'

'What about seal oil?'

This time the captain stared at him in surprise.

'Why would they carry that?'

'I don't really know . . .'

'The answer's no, in any case. These coasters almost always carry the same cargo: vegetables, and onions in particular, for England, coal for the Breton ports, stone, cement, slates . . . By the way, I asked some lock workers about the *Saint-Michel*'s last call here. On the 16th of September, she came in from Caen at the tail end of the tide, when everyone was about to go off duty. Joris pointed out that the water in the channel was too low for safe access to the sea, especially when it was so foggy. The skipper insisted on going through the lock anyway, though, so that he could leave the next morning at first light. She spent the night here, in the outer harbour, moored to some pilings. At low tide, they were high and dry, couldn't leave until nine the next morning.'

'And Julie's brother was aboard?'

'He must have been! There were only three of them: the skipper, who also owns the boat, and two crew. Big Louis—'

'He's the ex-convict?'

'Yes. He's called Big Louis because he's big, bigger than you are and could strangle a man with one hand . . .'

'A bad sort?'

'If you ask the mayor or anyone well-to-do in these parts, they'll say yes. Me, I never knew him before he went off to prison. He doesn't turn up here very often. All I know is, he has never caused any trouble in Ouistreham. He does drink, of course. Although . . . It's difficult to tell, he always seems half-soused. He hangs around the harbour. He's gimpy in one leg and his head and shoulders are hunched to one side, which makes him look a bit shifty. Still, the skipper of the *Saint-Michel* is happy enough with him.'

'He was here yesterday, while his sister was in Paris.'

Not daring to deny it, Captain Delcourt looked away. And Maigret understood then and there that there was a fraternal bond among these men of the sea, that they would never tell him all they knew.

'He's not the only one . . .'

'What do you mean?'

'Nothing, really. I heard about a stranger seen prowling around . . . But nothing definite.'

'Who saw him?'

'I don't know. People talk, that's all . . . Could you manage a quick drink?'

For the second time, Maigret settled into the bar, where he was welcomed with handshakes.

'Well! Those gentlemen from the public prosecutor's office certainly got their job done in a hurry.'

'What's your pleasure?'

'I'll have a beer.'

The sun had been out all day long. But now streamers of mist were threading their way from tree to tree, and vapour began rising from the canal.

'Another pea-souper,' sighed the captain.

And at the same instant, they heard the fog horn.

'It's the light buoy, out at the entrance to the harbour channel.'

'Did Captain Joris go often to Norway?' asked Maigret abruptly.

'When he sailed for the Compagnie Anglo-Normande, yes! Especially right after the war, when there was a shortage of wood. It's a lousy cargo, wood is – gets in the way of handling the ship.'

'Did you work for the same company?'

'Not for long. I was mostly with Worms, in Bordeaux. I ran the "ferry", we called it, just the one run: Bordeaux to Nantes, Nantes to Bordeaux. For eighteen years!'

'What's Julie's background?'

'A fishing family, Port-en-Bessin. If you can call them fisherfolk . . . The father never did much of anything. Died during the war. The mother must still be peddling fish in the streets, when she isn't swilling red wine in bistros . . .'

For the second time, thinking of Julie, Maigret smiled to himself. He remembered her arriving in his office in Paris, neat as a pin in her blue suit, a determined little thing . . .

And that very morning, when she struggled so clumsily, like a child, to keep him from taking her brother's letter.

Joris' house was already fading into the mist. There was no light any more upstairs, where the body had lain, or in the dining room, only the light in the front hall and probably at the back of the house, in the kitchen, where the two women were keeping Julie company.

Some lock workers now came in from the harbour but, sizing up the situation, went off to a table in the back to play some dominoes. The lighthouse lit up.

'The same again!' called the captain, pointing to the glasses. 'This one's on me.'

When Maigret asked the next question, his voice sounded strangely soft, almost velvety.

'If Joris were alive right now, where would he be? Here?'

'No! At home. In his slippers.'

'In the dining room? In his bedroom?'

'In the kitchen. With the evening paper. And then he'd read one of those books on gardening. He'd fallen head over heels for flowers. Just look at his garden! Still full of them, although it's late in the season.'

The other men laughed, but were a trifle chagrined at not having a passion for flowers instead of haunting their beloved tavern.

'He never went hunting?'

'Not often . . . A few times, when he was invited.'

'With the mayor?'

'When the shooting was good, they'd go off to the duck blind together.'

The place was so poorly lit that it was difficult to see the domino players through the smoky haze. A big stove made the air even heavier. Outside, it was almost evening, but the fog turned this darkness more oppressive, almost sinister. The fog horn was still sounding. Maigret's pipe made faint sizzling noises.

Leaning back in his chair, he half closed his eyes, trying to piece together his scattered clues floating in a formless mass.

'Joris vanished for six weeks only to return with a cracked and patched-up skull,' he murmured, without realizing that he was speaking out loud.

Then poison is waiting for him on the day he comes home!

And Julie doesn't find her brother's note in the pantry cupboard until the next day . . .

Maigret heaved a great sigh and muttered, 'So: someone tried to kill him. Then someone got him back on his feet. Then someone finished him off. Unless . . .'

For these three statements did not fit together. Then he had an outlandish idea, so outlandish that it startled him.

'Unless this someone wasn't trying to kill him that first time? And was only trying to affect his reason?'

Hadn't the doctors in Paris affirmed that his operation could only have been performed by a highly skilled surgeon?

But does one fracture a man's skull to steal away his mind?

And besides! What proof was there that Joris had lost his mind for ever?

The others watched Maigret in respectful silence. The customs official simply signalled to the waitress for another round.

And they sat off in their corners in the fug of the tavern, each in a reverie slightly blurred by drink.

They heard three cars go by: the public prosecutor's party was returning to Caen after the Grandmaisons' reception. By now Captain Joris' body was already in a cold room at the Institut Médico-Légal.

No one spoke. Dominoes clicked on the unvarnished wooden table. The puzzling crime, it seemed, had gradually come to weigh heavily on everyone's mind. They felt it hanging, almost visibly, over their heads. Their faces creased into scowls.

The youngest of the customs officials grew so uneasy that he rose and blurted out, 'Time I was getting home to the little woman . . .'

Maigret handed his tobacco pouch to his neighbour, who filled his pipe and passed the tobacco along. Then Delcourt stood up as well to escape the now oppressive atmosphere.

'How much does it come to, Marthe?'

'These two rounds? Nine francs seventy-five. And the gentleman's from yesterday, that's three francs ten.'

Everyone was on his feet. Moist air swept in through the open door. There were handshakes all around.

Once outside, the men strode off into the mist in every direction, as the fog horn boomed over the sound of their footsteps.

Maigret stood listening to all the footsteps heading off in every direction. Heavy footsteps, sometimes pausing, or suddenly darting away . . .

And he realized that somehow there was now fear in the air. They were afraid, all those men going home, afraid of nothing, of everything, of some nebulous danger, some unforeseeable disaster, afraid of the dark and the lights in the mist.

'What if it isn't over?'

Maigret knocked the ashes from his pipe and buttoned his overcoat.

4. The Saint-Michel

'Do you like it?' inquired the hotel-owner anxiously about each dish.

'It's fine! Fine!' replied the inspector, who wasn't actually quite sure what he was eating.

He was alone in a hotel dining room spacious enough for forty or fifty guests. The hotel was for Ouistreham's summer visitors. The furniture was the kind found in any seaside hotel. On the tables, small vases of flowers.

No connection at all with the Ouistreham that the inspector found interesting and was beginning to understand.

That was what pleased him. What he hated the most, in an inquiry, were the first steps, with all the attendant false moves and misinterpretations.

The word Ouistreham, for example. In Paris, it had conjured up a complete fantasy, a port city like Saint-Malo. The evening he arrived, Maigret had decided that it was really a forbidding hole full of gruff, taciturn people.

Now he had got his bearings. Felt more at home. Ouistreham was an ordinary village at the end of a bit of road planted with small trees. What truly counted was the harbour: a lock, a lighthouse, Joris' cottage, the Buvette de la Marine.

And the workaday rhythm of this harbour as well: the twice-daily tides, the fishermen lugging their baskets, the handful of men exclusively devoted to the constant traffic through the lock.

Some words now meant more to Maigret: captain, freighter, coaster. He was watching all that in action and learning the rules of the game.

The mystery had not been resolved. He still could not explain the things that had stymied him from the first. But at least now the cast of characters was clear: all were accounted for, with their settings and little everyday routines.

'Will you be staying here long?' asked the hotel-owner as he served the coffee himself.

'That I don't know.'

'If this had happened during the season it would have hit us hard.'

Now Maigret could distinguish among precisely four Ouistrehams: the Harbour, the Village, the Villas, the Seaside Resort – this last temporarily on holiday itself.

'You're going out, inspector?'

'Just a stroll before bedtime.'

The tide was almost full in. The weather was much colder than it had been; the fog, while still opaque, was turning into droplets of icy water.

Everything was dark. Everything was closed. Only the misty eye of the lighthouse was visible. And up on the lock, voices called to one another.

A short blast from a ship's whistle. A green light and a red one drawing near; a mass gliding along, level with the wall . . .

Maigret had learned the drill. A steamer was coming in. The shadowy figure now approaching would pick up the hawser and secure it to the nearest bollard. Then, up on the bridge, the captain would give the order to reverse engines.

Delcourt passed close by the inspector, looking anxiously out towards the jetties.

'What's going on?'

'I can't tell . . .'

The harbourmaster squinted hard, as if it were possible to see into the pitch dark through sheer force of will. Two men were already moving to close the lock-gates.

'Wait a minute!' Delcourt yelled to them.

And exclaimed in astonishment:

'It's them!'

Just then a voice not fifty metres away called out, 'Hey there! Louis! Down jib and stand by to come alongside port side-to . . .'

The voice had come from the darkness below, over by the jetties. A firefly of light was coming closer. Someone seemed to be moving around; canvas fell as rings clattered along a stay.

Then a mainsail slipped past, close enough to touch.

'How in heaven did they pull that off!' grumbled Delcourt, who then turned towards the schooner and yelled, 'Get her nose in under the port quarter of the steamer, so's we can close the gates!'

A man had leaped ashore with a mooring line and now stood looking around him, hands on his hips.

'The *Saint-Michel*?' Maigret asked Delcourt.

'The same . . . They must have flown over the water.'

There was only a small lantern down on the schooner's deck, illuminating a confused scene: a cask, a pile of gear, the silhouette of a man leaving the tiller to dash forwards to the schooner's bows.

The lock workers seemed particularly interested in the boat, arriving one after the other to take a look at it.

'The lock-gate winches, men! Back to work! Let's go!'

With the gates closed, water roared in through the sluices, and both vessels began to rise. The lantern's pale light drew closer. As the schooner's deck drew level with the quay, the man there hailed the harbourmaster.

'All's well?'

'All's well,' replied Delcourt guardedly. 'Didn't expect you so soon!'

'Had the wind at our backs, and Louis put up all the canvas we had. We even left a freighter in our wake!'

'Heading for Caen?'

'We'll be unloading there, yes. Anything new around here?'

Maigret was a few paces away, Big Louis a bit further off, but they could barely see each other. Only Delcourt and the *Saint-Michel*'s captain were talking, and now the harbourmaster, at a loss, looked over at Maigret.

'I heard it's in the paper that Joris has come back. Is that true?'

'He came back and he left again,' replied Delcourt.

'What do you mean?'

Big Louis had taken a step closer. With his hands in his pockets and the one shoulder crooked, he looked rather flabby in the darkness, like a shapeless hulk.

'He's dead . . .'

Now Big Louis went right up to Delcourt.

'Is that true?' he grunted.

Hearing his voice for the first time, Maigret found that flabby, too, in a way: hoarse, and somewhat drawling. He still could not see his face.

'The first night he was home,' explained Delcourt, 'he was poisoned. And here,' he quickly pointed out, 'is the inspector from Paris who's in charge of the case.'

Having worried for some time how to prudently reveal this information, the harbourmaster now seemed relieved. Had he been afraid the men of the *Saint-Michel* might accidentally get themselves into trouble?

'Ah! So this gentleman is with the police . . .'

The schooner was still rising. Her skipper swung his legs over the rails and dropped down on to the quay, but then hesitated before shaking hands with Maigret.

'Hard to imagine . . .' he said slowly, still thinking about Joris.

He seemed worried as well, and even more obviously than Delcourt.

Louis, his tall form swaying, his head tilted to one side, barked out something the inspector could not understand.

'What did he say?'

'He was grumbling in dialect. He said: "a filthy business"!'

'What was a filthy business?' the inspector asked the ex-convict, but Big Louis simply looked him in the eye. They had moved closer and could now see each other's faces. Big Louis' features looked swollen; one cheek was bigger than the other, or simply seemed so because of the way he always tilted his head to one side. Puffy flesh, and big eyes that seemed to start from his head.

'You were here yesterday!' said the inspector sharply.

The water was at the proper level; the upper gates were opening. The steamer moved smoothly into the canal, and Delcourt hurried over to record her tonnage and provenance.

A voice shouted down from the bridge: 'Nine hundred tons! . . . Rouen!'

The *Saint-Michel* remained in the lock, however, and each of the men stationed there to deal with her, aware that something unusual was happening, waited, wrapped in shadows, listening carefully.

Delcourt returned, writing the necessary information in his notebook.

'Well?' asked Maigret impatiently.

'Well, what?' grumbled Louis. 'You says I was here yesterday! That's 'cause I was . . .'

It was hard to understand him, because he had a peculiar way of chewing on his words with his mouth almost closed, as if he were eating. Not to mention his thick local accent . . .

'Why did you come here?'

'See my sister.'

'And, not finding her at home, you left her a note.'

In the meantime, Maigret was stealthily observing the schooner's captain, who was dressed just like Louis. There was nothing special about him; indeed, he seemed more like a seasoned bosun's mate than the skipper of a coaster.

'We were three days at Fécamp for repairs,' the man now piped up, 'so Louis grabbed his chance to come here and see Julie!'

All around the lock, the men on duty must have been straining to listen in, keeping as quiet as possible. The fog horn still moaned in the distance, and the fog itself was growing wetter, leaving the cobblestones black and gleaming.

A hatchway opened in the schooner's deck, and a man's head emerged, with unkempt hair and a bushy beard.

'What's wrong? Why're we sitting here?'

'Shut it, Célestin!' said his skipper quickly.

Delcourt was stamping up and down the quay to warm himself up – and perhaps to save face as well, for he didn't know if he should stay there or not.

'Louis, what made you think that Joris was in danger?'

'Huh!' said Louis, and shrugged. 'He'd already had his skull stove in, hadn't he, so it wasn't hard to work out.'

It was so difficult to make out the syllables all mashed together in the man's grunting that Maigret could have done with an interpreter.

The atmosphere felt intensely uncomfortable and in a way, mysteriously threatening.

Louis looked towards the cottage but couldn't see a thing, not even a darker patch in the night.

'She's there, our Julie?'

'Yes. Are you going to go and see her?'

Louis shook his head with big sweeps, like a bear.

'Why not?'

'Sure she'll cry.'

It sounded like 'Shore shale crah' – and in the disgusted tone of a man who can't take the sight of tears.

They were still standing there; the fog was thickening, soaking their shoulders, and Delcourt decided to intervene.

'Anyone for a drink?'

A lock worker chimed in, off at his post in the darkness.

'They just closed the bar!'

'We could go below to the cabin, if you like,' offered the *Saint-Michel*'s captain.

★

There were four of them: Maigret, Delcourt, Big Louis and the skipper, whose name was Lannec. The cabin wasn't large, and the small stove gave off heat so intense that the air was hazy with humidity. The paraffin lamp, set in gimbals, looked almost red hot.

Cabin walls of varnished pitch pine. A scarred oak table, so worn that the entire surface was uneven. Dirty dishes still sat out, along with some sturdy but gummy-looking glasses and a half-bottle of red.

On either side of the cabin were wide, rectangular recesses, like cupboards without doors, for the beds of the captain and Louis, the first mate. Unmade beds, with dirty boots and clothing tossed on to them. Whiffs of tar, alcohol, cooking and stuffy bedrooms, but most of all, that indescribable smell of a boat.

Everyone looked less unsettling in the lamplight. Lannec had a brown moustache and sharp, bright eyes. He had taken a bottle from a locker and was rinsing glasses by filling them with water he then poured out on the floor.

'It seems that you were here on the night of the 16th of September, Captain Lannec.'

Big Louis was sitting hunched over with his elbows on the table.

'Right, we were here,' replied Lannec, pouring out the drinks.

'Wasn't that unusual? Because spending the night in the outer harbour would mean you'd have to keep an eye on your moorings, because of the tide.'

'It happens,' said Lannec casually.

'Like that you can often get underway a few hours earlier in the morning,' added Delcourt, who seemed determined to keep things cordial.

'Captain Joris didn't come and see you aboard?'

'While we were in the lock . . . Not later on.'

'And you neither saw nor heard anything out of the ordinary?'

'Cheers! . . . No, nothing.'

'You, Louis, you went to bed?'
'Must have.'
'What's that?'
'I said must have . . . Was some time ago.'
'You didn't visit your sister?'
'Mebbe so. Not for long . . .'
'Didn't Joris forbid you to set foot in his house?'
'Bunk!'
'What do you mean by that?'
'Nothing. It's all rubbish . . . You finished with me now?'

Maigret couldn't really charge him with anything. Besides, he had no desire at all to arrest him.

'Finished for today.'

Louis spoke with his skipper in Breton, rose, emptied his glass and touched his cap in farewell.

'What did he say to you?' asked the inspector.

'That I didn't need him on the Caen run, so he'll rejoin me back here after I've delivered our cargo.'

'Where is he going?'

'He didn't tell me.'

Delcourt hurried to look out of the hatchway, listened for a little while and returned.

'He's over on the dredger.'

'The what?'

'You didn't notice the two dredgers in the canal? They're simply moored there for the moment. They have sleeping quarters there. Sailors would rather kip on an old boat than in a hotel.'

'Another round?'

And after looking intently about the cabin, Maigret made himself more comfortable.

'What was your first port of call after leaving Ouistreham, on the 16th of last month?'

'Southampton. Delivering a cargo of stone.'

'Then?'

'Boulogne.'

'You haven't been up to Norway since then?'

'I've been there only once, six years ago.'

'Did you know Joris well?'

'Us, we know everyone, you see. From La Rochelle to Rotterdam. Cheers! . . . In fact, this here is good Dutch gin I got in Holland. Cigar?'

He took a box from a drawer.

'Cigars that cost ten cents over there. One franc!'

They were fat, smoothly rolled with gold bands.

'It's strange,' sighed Maigret. 'I was told that Joris definitely came aboard your boat when you were in the outer harbour, and that someone else was with him.'

Lannec was busy cutting the tip of his cigar, however, and when he looked up, his face wore no expression.

'I wouldn't have any reason to hide that.'

Outside, someone jumped on to the bridge with a loud thud. A head appeared at the top of the hatchway ladder.

'The steamer from Le Havre's coming in!'

Delcourt sprang up and turned to Maigret.

'I have to clear the lock for her, so the *Saint-Michel* will be moving out.'

'I assume I may continue my run?' added the captain.

'To Caen?'

'Yes. The canal doesn't go anywhere else! We'll probably be finished unloading by tomorrow evening.'

They all seemed like honest men, all had frank, open faces, and yet everything about them rang false! But so subtly that Maigret couldn't have said what or where the trouble was.

Lannec, Delcourt, Joris, everyone at the Buvette de la Marine, they appeared to be the salt of the earth. And even Big Louis, the ex-con, hadn't made such a bad impression!

'Don't get up, Lannec, I'll cast off for you,' said the harbour-master, and went topside to clear the hawser from its bollard.

Célestin, the old fellow who had stuck his head up out of the fo'c'sle, now hobbled across the deck muttering, 'That Big Louis, he's 'scaped off again!'

And after letting out both the jib and flying jib, he poled the schooner off with a boat hook. Maigret leaped ashore just in time. The mist had definitely turned to rain, making the men at work, the harbour lights and the steamer from Le Havre, now whistling with impatience in the lock, visible once again.

Winches clanked; water raced through the open sluices. The schooner's mainsail blocked the view up the canal. From the lock bridge, Maigret could make out the two dredgers, great ugly boats with complicated shapes and grim upper works encrusted with rust. He made his way over there with great care because the surrounding area was strewn with junk, old cables, anchors and scrap iron. He was walking along a plank used as a gangway when he saw a light glimmering through a split seam in the hulk.

'Big Louis!' he called.

The light vanished immediately. Louis' head and torso emerged from a hatchway missing its cover.

'What d'you want?'

But as he spoke something was moving below him, in the belly of the dredger. A vague shape was slipping away with the utmost caution. The sheet iron was echoing with knocks and bumps . . .

'Who's that with you?'

'With me? Here?'

When Maigret tried to look around, he almost plummeted into a metre or so of slimy mud, stagnating in the hold of the dredger.

Someone had definitely been there, but he was long gone: the banging noises were now coming from a different part of the vessel. And the inspector wasn't sure where he might safely walk. He was completely unfamiliar with the mess decks of this apocalyptic boat – and now banged his head smartly against one of the dredger's buckets.

'You've got nothing to say?'

An indistinct grunt. This seemed to mean, 'I don't know what you're talking about.'

To search the two dredgers at night, the inspector would have needed ten men – men who knew their way around them, too! Maigret beat a retreat. The rain made voices carry surprisingly far, and he could hear someone in the harbour saying, '. . . lying right across the channel.'

He followed the voice. It was the first mate of the steamer from Le Havre, who was pointing out something to Delcourt. And the harbourmaster seemed quite disconcerted when Maigret showed up.

'It's hard to believe they'd lose it and never notice,' the mate went on.

'Lose what?' asked the inspector.

'The dinghy.'

'What dinghy?'

'This one here, that we bumped into just inside the jetties. It belongs to the schooner that was ahead of us. Her name is on the stern: *Saint-Michel*.'

'It must have come loose,' observed Delcourt dismissively. 'That happens!'

'It did not come loose, for the very good reason that in this weather, the dinghy would not have been in tow, but on deck!'

And the lock workers, still at their posts, were trying to hear every word.

'We'll see about it in the morning. Leave the dinghy here.'

Turning to Maigret, Delcourt gave him a crooked smile.

'You can see what an odd sort of job I have,' he murmured. 'There's always something . . .'

Maigret did not smile back, however. In fact, he replied with the utmost gravity.

'Listen: if you don't see me anywhere tomorrow morning at seven, or perhaps eight, then telephone the public prosecutor at Caen.'

'But what . . .'

'Goodnight! And make sure that the dinghy does stay here.'

To lay a false trail, he walked off along the jetty, hands in his pockets, his overcoat collar turned up. The sea rumbled and sighed beneath his feet, ahead of him, on his right, on his left. The air he breathed into his lungs smelled strongly of iodine.

When almost at the end of the jetty, he bent down to pick something up.

5. Notre-Dame-des-Dunes

At dawn Maigret plodded back to the Hôtel de l'Univers in his sodden overcoat with a parched throat, having smoked pipe after pipe. The hotel seemed deserted but he found the hotel-owner in the kitchen, lighting the fire.

'You were out all night?'

'Yes. Would you bring some coffee up to my room as soon as possible? Oh, and is there any way I can have a bath?'

'I'll have to fire up the boiler.'

'Then don't bother.'

A grey morning with the inevitable fog, but it was a light, luminous one. Maigret's eyelids were stinging, and his head felt empty as he stood at the open window in his room, waiting for the coffee.

A strange night. He had done nothing sensational. Made no great discoveries. Yet he had made progress in his understanding of the crime. Many nuggets of information had been added to his growing store.

The arrival of the *Saint-Michel*. Lannec's behaviour. Was the skipper's attitude ambiguous? Dubious? Not even that! Yet he was a slippery fellow. But Delcourt as well was sometimes less than forthcoming. They all were, if they had anything to do with this harbour! Big Louis, for example, was definitely acting suspiciously. He hadn't gone on to Caen with the schooner. He was holed up on an empty dredger. And Maigret was sure that he wasn't there alone.

Then he had learned that the *Saint-Michel* had lost its dinghy shortly before entering the harbour. And at the end of a jetty, he had made a most unusual find: a gold fountain-pen.

It was a wooden jetty supported by pilings. At its far end, near the green light, an iron ladder went down to the water. The dinghy had been found in that area. In other words, the *Saint-Michel* had been carrying someone who did not want to be seen in Ouistreham. After landing in the dinghy, this passenger had let it drift away, and, as he had leaned over at the top of the ladder to hoist himself on to the jetty, the gold fountain-pen had slipped from his pocket.

The man had taken refuge in the dredger, where Louis was to join him.

This scenario was just about airtight. There could be no other interpretation of the facts.

Conclusion: an unknown man was hiding in Ouistreham. He had not come here without a reason: he had a job to do. And he belonged to a milieu in which men used gold fountain-pens!

So: not a sailor. Not a tramp . . . The expensive pen suggested clothing of equally good quality. The man must be a gentleman – a 'gent' as they say in the countryside . . . And off-season, in Ouistreham, a 'gent' would not pass unnoticed. He would have to lie low all day in the dredger. But wouldn't he come out at night to accomplish whatever he had come here for?

Maigret had therefore resigned himself, grumpily, to mounting guard. A job for a junior inspector! Spending hours in the drizzle peering at the inordinately complicated shadows of the dredger.

Nothing had happened. No one had come ashore. Day had dawned, and now the inspector was furious at not being able to enjoy a hot bath. Contemplating his bed, he considered snatching a few hours' rest.

The hotel-owner came in with his coffee.

'You're not going to sleep?'

'I haven't decided yet. Would you take a telegram to the post office for me?'

He was summoning Lucas, a trusted colleague, for Maigret had no desire to keep an eye on the dredger again that night.

The window looked out on the harbour, Joris' cottage and the sandbanks now emerging as the ebb tide left the bay.

While the inspector wrote his telegram, the hotel-owner looked outside, remarking off-handedly, 'Well! Captain Joris' maid is going for a walk . . .'

Looking up, Maigret saw Julie, who closed the front gate and set out briskly for the beach.

'What's over there?'

'What do you mean?'

'Where can one go? Are there any houses?'

'Nothing at all! Only the beach, but no one goes there because it's interrupted by breakwaters and mud sinkholes.'

'No path or road?'

'No. You reach the mouth of the Orne, and the banks are marshy all along the river. Wait, now . . . There are some duck blinds there for hunting.'

Maigret was already heading out of the door with a determined frown. He strode across the lock bridge, and by the time he reached the beach Julie was just a few hundred metres ahead of him.

The place was deserted. The only living creatures in the morning mist were the gulls, shrieking as they flew. To avoid being seen, the inspector went up into the dunes on his right.

The air was cool and the sea, calm. The white hem of the surf subsided with a rhythm like breathing and the crunching of broken shells.

Julie was not out for a walk. She advanced quickly, holding her little black coat tightly closed. She hadn't had time, since Joris' death, to order mourning clothes, so she was wearing all her black or dark things: an old-fashioned coat, woollen stockings, a hat with a downturned brim.

She staggered along, her feet sinking into the soft sand. Twice she turned around but did not see Maigret, hidden by the rolling dunes.

About a kilometre from Ouistreham, however, she almost spotted him when she went abruptly off to the right.

Maigret had thought she was making for a duck blind, but there was nothing like that out in the landscape of sand and coarse beach grass.

Nothing but a tumbledown structure missing one entire wall. Facing the ocean, five metres in from the high-tide line, there was a small chapel, probably constructed a few centuries earlier.

It had a semicircular vault, and the missing wall allowed Maigret to judge the thickness of the others: almost one metre of solid stone.

Julie went inside to the back of the chapel, and the inspector could now hear small objects being moved, almost certainly shells, from the sound of them.

He moved forwards cautiously and could see a small recess in the far wall, closed with a metal grille. Beneath was a kind of tiny altar, over which hovered Julie, looking for something.

She whipped around and recognized Maigret, who had had no time to hide.

'What are you doing here?' she exclaimed.

'And you?'

'I . . . I've come to pray to Notre-Dame-des-Dunes . . .'

She was nervous, and everything about her showed that she was hiding something. Her red eyes betrayed an almost sleepless night, and two locks of untidy hair stuck out from beneath her hat.

'Ah! This place is a Lady chapel?'

And indeed, in the niche behind the grille was a statue of the Virgin, so old and eaten away by time that it was almost unrecognizable.

The stone all around the niche was covered with a tangle of supplications written in pencil or incised with a sharp rock or pocket-knife.

★

Help Denise pass her exam . . . Notre-Dame-des-Dunes, make Jojo quickly learn to read . . . Grant good health to the whole family and especially Grandmother and Grandfather . . .

There were more earthly inscriptions, too, with hearts pierced by arrows.

Robert & Jeanne for ever . . .

Dried stalks that had once been flowers still hung from the grille, but what made this chapel different from so many others were the shells piled high on the ruins of the altar. Shells of every shape and kind, and there were words written on all of them, mostly in pencil, in the clumsy handwriting of children and simple souls, or sometimes the firmer script of more literate supplicants.

May the fishing be good in Newfoundland and Papa need never sign up again . . .

The floor was of beaten earth. Where the wall had fallen, the view was of sandy beach and silvery sea in the white haze. And in spite of herself, having no idea how to handle the situation, Julie kept glancing anxiously at the shells.

'Did you bring one here?' asked Maigret.

Julie shook her head.

'When I arrived, though, you were going through them. What were you looking for?'

'Nothing, I . . .'

'You . . . ?'

'Nothing!'

And she glared stubbornly, clutching her coat more tightly around her.

Now it was the inspector's turn to pick up the shells one by one to read what was written on them. Suddenly, he smiled. On an enormous clam shell he read, 'Notre-Dame-des-Dunes, help my brother Louis succeed so we will all be happy.'

The date on it was 13 September. So this primitive ex-voto had been brought here three days before Captain Joris vanished!

And hadn't Julie come here to remove it?

'Is this what you were hunting for?'

'What business is it of yours?'

Her eyes never left the shell. She seemed ready to jump at Maigret to tear it from his hands.

'Give it to me! Put it back where it belongs!'

'All right, I'll leave it here, but you must, too. Come on, we'll talk about it on the walk back.'

'I've nothing to say to you.'

They set out, leaning forwards because their feet sank into the soft sand. The wind was so sharp that their noses were red and their cheeks gleamed.

'Everything your brother has done has gone wrong, hasn't it?'

She stared straight ahead at the beach.

'Some things are impossible to hide,' he continued. 'I'm not talking only about . . . about what landed him in prison.'

'Of course! It's always that! After twenty years they'll still be saying—'

'No, no, Julie! Louis is a good sailor. Even an excellent one, I hear, able to serve as a first mate. Except that one fine day he gets drunk with some fellows he's just met and does some stupid things, doesn't return to his boat, drags around for weeks without a job. Am I right? At times like that, he asks you for help. You – and just a few weeks ago, Joris. Then he becomes responsible and hardworking again for a while.'

'So?'

'What was the plan that you wanted, on the 13th of September, to make turn out well?'

Julie stopped and looked into his face. She was much calmer now. She had had time to reflect. And there was an appealing gravity in her eyes.

'I knew it would bring us trouble. And yet, my brother did nothing! I swear to you that if he had killed the captain, I would have been the first to pay him back in kind.'

Her voice was low and heavy with emotion.

'It's just that, there *are* some coincidences, and then that time in prison always hanging around his neck. Whenever anyone does something wrong, Louis gets blamed for everything that happens afterwards.'

'What was the plan Louis had?'

'It wasn't a plan. It was quite simple. He'd met a really rich man, I don't remember any more if it was in England or at Le Havre. He didn't tell me his name. A gentleman who'd had enough of life ashore and wanted to buy a yacht and travel. He asked Louis to find him a boat.'

They were still standing on the beach, where all they could see of Ouistreham was the lighthouse, a raw white tower set off by the paler sky.

'Louis talked to his skipper about it. Because for some time, on account of the slump, Lannec had been wanting to sell the *Saint-Michel*. And that's the whole of it! The *Saint-Michel* is the best coaster anyone could find for turning into a yacht. In the beginning my brother was supposed to get ten thousand francs if the deal was made. Next the buyer talked about keeping him aboard as captain, someone he could trust.'

Immediately regretting those last words, she glanced at Maigret and seemed grateful to him for not smiling ironically at the idea of someone trusting an ex-con.

Instead, Maigret was thinking things over. Even he was startled by the frank simplicity of her story, which had the troubling ring of truth.

'But you haven't any idea who this buyer is?'

'No.'

'Or where your brother was going to meet him again?'

'No.'

'Or when?'

'Very soon. The refitting was supposed to be done in Norway, he said, and the yacht would leave within a month for the Mediterranean, bound for Egypt.'

'A Frenchman?'

'I don't know.'

'And you were at Notre-Dame-des-Dunes just now to retrieve your shell?'

'Because I thought that, if it were found, everyone would think something completely different from the truth. Admit it: you don't believe me . . .'

Instead of an answer, another question.

'Did you see your brother?'

She shuddered in surprise.

'When?'

'Last night . . . or this morning.'

'Louis is here?'

She seemed frightened, disoriented.

'The *Saint-Michel* has arrived.'

His words appeared to reassure her, as if she had been afraid that her brother had shown up without the schooner.

'So he's on his way to Caen?'

'No, he spent the night aboard one of the dredgers.'

'Let's go – I'm cold . . .'

The wind from the ocean was freshening as the overcast deepened.

'Does he often sleep on an empty old boat?'

When she didn't reply, the conversation died on its own. They walked on, hearing only the sand crunching softly underfoot and the snapping leaps of tiny crustaceans, disturbed at their feast of seaweed swept in by the tide.

Maigret was seeing two images come together in his mind's eye: a yacht . . . and a gold fountain-pen.

Then his thoughts came like clockwork. Earlier that morning, the pen had been difficult to explain because it didn't fit in with the *Saint-Michel* or its rough-and-ready crew.

A yacht . . . and a fountain-pen. That made more sense! A wealthy, middle-aged man is looking for a pleasure yacht and loses a gold pen.

But how to explain why this man, instead of going ashore at the quay, took the schooner's dinghy, hauled himself up the jetty ladder and hid in a waterlogged dredger?

'The night Joris vanished, when your brother came to see you, did he talk about this buyer? He didn't mention, for example, that the man was aboard the *Saint-Michel*?'

'No. He simply said that the deal was almost settled.'

They were approaching the foot of the lighthouse. Joris' cottage was just to the left, and flowers planted by the captain were still blooming in the garden.

Julie's face fell. She seemed sad and looked around vacantly like someone who no longer knew what to do with her life.

'You'll probably be going to see Joris' lawyer soon, for the reading of the will. You're a wealthy woman, now.'

'Fat chance!' she said curtly.

'What do you mean?'

'You know perfectly well. All this nonsense about a fortune, huh . . . The captain wasn't rich.'

'You don't know that.'

'He didn't keep secrets from me. If he'd had hundreds of thousands of francs, he would have told me. And he wouldn't have hesitated, last winter, to buy himself a two-thousand-franc shotgun! He really wanted that gun . . . He'd had a look at the mayor's and found out how much it cost.'

They had reached the front gate.

'Are you coming in?'

'No. Perhaps I'll see you later.'

She hesitated before going inside the cottage, where she would be all alone.

Nothing much happened over the next few hours. Maigret hung around the dredger like someone with time on his hands and a deep fondness for strange sights. There were chains, capstans, dredging buckets, huge pipes . . .

Towards eleven, he had an aperitif with the bar regulars.

'Has anyone seen Big Louis?'

They had seen him, rather early that morning. He had downed two glasses of rum there and taken off along the main road.

Maigret was drowsy. Perhaps he had caught a chill the night before. In any case, he felt as if he were coming down with the flu and looked it, too. He seemed lethargic.

But it didn't appear to bother him – and that bothered everyone else! His companions stole worried glances at him; the general mood was subdued.

'What should I do with the dinghy?' asked Delcourt.

'Tie it up somewhere.'

Maigret tossed out another disquieting question.

'Has a stranger been seen around here, this morning? Or anything unusual, over by the dredgers?'

No, nothing! But now that he had asked, they all felt something was in the offing.

It was funny: they all expected high drama! A presentiment? The feeling that this chain of events still had one more link to go?

A boat sounded its horn at the lock. The men stood up. Maigret trudged to the post office to see if there were any messages for him. A telegram from Lucas announced his arrival at 2.10.

And when that time came, so did the little train that runs along the canal from Caen to Ouistreham. With its 1850-model carriages, it looked like a child's toy when it appeared in the distance, but it pulled into the station with squealing brakes and a cloud of hissing steam.

Lucas came towards Maigret with his hand outstretched – and was surprised by the inspector's weary gloom.

'What's wrong?'

'I'm fine.'

Lucas couldn't help laughing at that, even though Maigret was his boss.

'You certainly don't look it! Well, since I haven't had any lunch . . .'

'Come to the hotel, they must still have something there to eat.'

They sat in the main dining room, where the hotel-owner served the sergeant himself. He hovered around Maigret and Lucas as they talked quietly and when he brought over the cheese he saw his chance to speak up.

'Did you hear what happened to the mayor?'

Maigret reacted with such alarm that the man was taken aback.

'Oh, nothing serious! It's just that a little while ago, at home, he fell while coming downstairs. No one knows how he managed to do that, but his face is so battered that he had to take to his bed.'

Then Maigret had a brainwave. That is the right word, for his intellect deciphered the incident in an instant.

'Is Madame Grandmaison still in Ouistreham?'

'No, she took the car and left early this morning with her daughter. I suppose they went to Caen.'

Maigret's flu vanished.

'Are you going to sit there all day?' he grumbled.

'Of course,' replied Lucas placidly, 'it's easy for someone with a full stomach to wax impatient watching a hungry man tuck into his food. Let's say, three minutes more . . . Oh! Don't take the camembert away yet please!'

6. The Fall Down the Stairs

The hotel-owner had not been lying, but the news he had passed on had been somewhat exaggerated, for Monsieur Grandmaison was not laid up in bed.

When Maigret arrived at the Norman villa, after sending Lucas to keep his eye on the dredger, he saw through the picture window a form sitting in the classic pose of the patient who must stay home to convalesce.

Although the inspector could not see his features, it was obviously the mayor.

Further from the window stood another man, but that was all Maigret could determine.

After ringing the bell, he heard more comings and goings inside than were necessary to open a front door. The maid arrived at last, a middle-aged, rather pinch-faced creature who must have felt infinite contempt for all visitors, for she never bothered to unclench her teeth.

Having opened the door, she went back up the few steps leading to the front hall and left Maigret to shut the door himself. Then she knocked on a double door and stood aside as the inspector entered the mayor's study.

There had been something peculiar about that whole performance. Nothing blatantly bizarre, but jarring little things and a slightly uneasy atmosphere.

The house was a large one, almost new, in the prevailing style of the French seaside, but given the wealth of the Grandmaison family, chief stockholders in the Compagnie Anglo-Normande, a touch more luxury might have been expected. Perhaps they had saved such embellishment for their residence in Caen?

Maigret had hardly entered the room when he heard: 'Here you are, inspector!'

The voice came from over by the window. Monsieur Grandmaison was ensconced in a massive club chair with his legs propped up on another chair. It was difficult to see him, because of the backlighting, but he was clearly wearing a scarf loosely knotted around his throat instead of a stiff collar, and covering the left half of his face with one hand.

'Do sit down.'

Maigret took a tour of the room, then finally went to sit facing the ship-owner. He struggled to repress a smile, for the mayor was quite a sight.

His left cheek, which his hand could not entirely conceal, was puffy, and his upper lip swollen, but what he was most intent on hiding was a stunning black eye.

The man's face wouldn't have seemed that funny if he hadn't been trying so hard to be as dignified as usual in spite of it! He was undaunted and stared at Maigret with frank suspicion.

'You've come to report the results of your inquiry?'

'No. You received me so graciously the other day, with the gentlemen from the public prosecutor's office, that I wished to thank you for your hospitality.'

There was never a hint of irony in Maigret's smiles. On the contrary! The more mocking he was, the more studiously solemn his face.

He looked around the study again. The walls were full of technical drawings of freighters and photographs of the ships of the Compagnie Anglo-Normande. The furniture was nondescript, good-quality mahogany, but nothing more. On the desk, a few files, some letters, telegrams.

And the inspector seemed to gaze with particular pleasure at the beautifully waxed floor.

'It seems you've had an accident?'

Sighing, the mayor shifted his legs and grumbled, 'A misstep, coming down the stairs.'

'This morning? Madame Grandmaison must have been terrified!'

'My wife had already left.'

'The weather is hardly suitable for a seaside vacation, true! Unless one is an avid duck hunter . . . I suppose that Madame Grandmaison is at Caen with your daughter?'

'Paris, actually.'

The ship-owner was carelessly dressed. Dark trousers, a dressing gown over a grey flannel shirt, felt slippers.

'What was there at the foot of the stairs?'

'What do you mean?'

'What did you land on?'

A venomous look. A strained reply.

'The floor, obviously.'

A lie, a whopper! Falling on the floor never gave anyone a black eye. Still less the marks of fingers tightly wrapped around one's throat!

As it happened, whenever the scarf moved the tiniest bit, Maigret could easily see the bruises it was intended to conceal from him.

'You were alone in the house, naturally.'

'Why "naturally"?'

'Because such accidents always happen when there's no one around to come and help!'

'The maid was doing her shopping.'

'She's the only servant here?'

'I also have a gardener, but he has gone to Caen. He had some errands there.'

'You must have been in real pain.'

What worried the mayor the most was precisely this solemnity on Maigret's part. He sounded sincerely sympathetic!

Although it was only 3.30, evening was already coming on, and the room was growing dark.

'May I?'

The inspector pulled his pipe from his pocket.

'If you'd like a cigar, there are some on the mantelpiece.'

There was a whole pile of packing-cases in a corner. A bottle of aged Armagnac, on a tray. The tall doors were of varnished pitch pine.

'And what about your investigation?'

Maigret gestured vaguely, making an effort not to look over at the door to the drawing room, a door that was vibrating for some mysterious reason . . .

'Nothing to report?'

'Nothing.'

'Would you like my opinion? It was a mistake to let people think that this was a complicated matter.'

'Evidently!' grunted Maigret. 'As if there were anything complicated about what happened! One evening, a man disappears and gives no sign of life for well over a month. He's found in Paris six weeks later, with a skilfully repaired bullet wound in his skull, having lost his memory. Brought home, he is poisoned that same night. Meanwhile, three hundred thousand francs have been deposited, from Hamburg, into his bank account. It's simple! Clear as day!'

This time, there was no mistaking the inspector's meaning, despite his genial tone.

'Well, perhaps the matter is less complicated than you think, in any case,' insisted the mayor. 'And supposing that this death truly is mysterious, it would be better, I believe, not to wantonly create an atmosphere of anxiety. By speaking of such things in certain cafés, one ends by unsettling minds that alcohol has already made only too unstable.'

Directing his stern, authoritative gaze at Maigret, he spoke slowly, carefully, as if delivering an indictment.

'And on the other hand, the police have made no effort to obtain information from the proper authorities! Even I, the local mayor, know nothing of what's happening down in the harbour.'

'Does your gardener wear espadrilles?'

The mayor looked immediately at the shining parquet, where footprints were clearly visible on the waxy surface. The pattern of rope-soled shoes was unmistakable.

'I have no idea!'

'Pardon me for interrupting you! A thought that occurred to me . . . You were saying?'

But Monsieur Grandmaison had lost the thread of his speech.

'Would you reach me down that box of cigars? . . . That's it, thank you.'

He lit one, moaning faintly because he was opening his jaws too wide.

'In short, how far have you got? Surely you've come up with *some* interesting leads by now.'

'Not really!'

'That's curious, because those people down in the harbour aren't lacking in imagination, in general, and certainly not after a few aperitifs.'

'I suppose you've sent Madame Grandmaison off to Paris to spare her the distress of all this drama? And any unpleasantness that might be still to come?'

They were not fighting out in the open. Yet they were sparring with a certain covert hostility fuelled simply, perhaps, by the social divide between them.

Maigret drank down at the Buvette de la Marine with fishermen and lock workers.

The mayor entertained guests from the public prosecutor's office with tea, liqueurs and petits fours.

Maigret was simply a man, impossible to categorize.

Monsieur Grandmaison belonged to a very definite social milieu. He was the most important man in a small town, the scion of an old bourgeois family, a prosperous and respectable ship-owner.

True, he put on democratic airs and cheerfully greeted the members of his constituency in the streets of Ouistreham. But this was a condescending, electoral democracy! He was patronizing them.

Maigret looked so rock-solid it was almost frighteningly impressive. Monsieur Grandmaison, with his pink face and rolls of fat, was fast losing a grip on his authority and sang-froid.

So he waxed indignant to regain the upper hand.

'Monsieur Maigret,' he began.

And it was a thing of beauty, the way he said those first two words!

'Monsieur Maigret . . . I take the liberty of reminding you that, as mayor of this town—'

So placidly that the mayor could only stare at him, the inspector rose and walked to a door that he opened as casually as you please.

'Do come in, Louis! It's irritating to watch a door that can't stop shaking and to hear you breathing behind it.'

Maigret must have been disappointed if he had hoped to create a dramatic scene: Big Louis did as he was told. He came into the study with his head and shoulders awry, as usual, and stood looking at the floor like both a simple sailor overawed by the villa of a local magnate and a man suddenly finding himself in a difficult stuation.

As for the mayor, he was puffing heavily on his cigar and staring straight ahead.

Daylight was almost gone from the study. A gas lamp outside was already lit.

'May I turn on the light?' asked Maigret.

'Just a minute . . . Close the curtains, first. There's no need for people going by to . . . That's it, the cord on the left, pull it slowly.'

Big Louis remained standing motionless in the middle of the study. Maigret switched the light on, walked over to the slow-combustion stove and automatically began to poke the fire.

It was a great habit of his. As was the way he would stand in front of a fire with his hands clasped behind him, toasting his back, when he was absorbed in reflection.

Had the situation changed? Be that as it may, there was a glint of mockery in the look Monsieur Grandmaison gave the inspector, who was thinking hard.

'Was Big Louis here when you . . . had your accident?'

'No!'

'Too bad! That's how you might have, for example, in tumbling down the stairs, landed on his bare fist . . .'

'And it would have allowed you to stir up anxiety in the little harbour cafés, by telling fanciful tales. Best wrap this business up, don't you think, inspector? There are two of us . . . We are both working on this case. You come here from Paris . . . You've brought with you Captain Joris, in a pitiful state, and all the evidence indicates that it was not in Ouistreham that he met with such injury . . . You were here when he was killed . . . You go about your inquiry in your own way.'

The man's voice was positively cutting.

'As for me, I have been the mayor here for ten years. I know my constituents. I consider myself responsible for their well-being. As mayor I am also the local chief of police. Well . . .'

When he paused to take a long puff on his cigar, the ash dropped off and crumbled over his dressing gown.

'While you've been patronizing the harbour bistros, I, too, have been busy with this case, if you please!'

'And you summoned Big Louis.'

'As I will summon others if I see fit. And now, I suppose that you have nothing more of importance to tell me?'

He rose, a trifle stiffly, to see his visitor to the door.

'I trust,' murmured Maigret, 'that you will have no objection if Louis comes with me? I already questioned him last night, but there are a few more things I'd like to ask him.'

Monsieur Grandmaison gestured dismissively by way of reply. It was Big Louis who stayed right where he was, staring at the floor as if nailed to it.

'Are you coming?'

'Nah! Not right now.'

It was more grunting than speaking, like everything Julie's brother said.

'Let me point out,' observed the mayor, 'that I have no objection at all to his going with you! I insist that you take note of this, so that you will not accuse me of trying to stymie your investigation. I sent for Big Louis to inquire about certain matters. If he prefers to stay, it's probably because he has something else to tell me.'

All the same, there was tension in the air, and even fear – and not just in the air, for there was almost panic in the mayor's eyes.

And the smile on Big Louis' face was one of brutish satisfaction.

'I'll wait for you outside,' the inspector told him.

But the reply he received was from the mayor.

'It was nice seeing you, Detective Chief Inspector Maigret.'

The inspector left the study. Hurrying from the kitchen, the maid sullenly showed him to the front door without a word and closed it behind him.

The road was deserted. In the window of a house a hundred metres away, Maigret saw a light; there were a few others, but at long intervals, for the villas on the Riva-Bella road are surrounded by extensive gardens.

Hands in his pockets, hunched over, Maigret walked to the front gate and looked out over empty ground, since all that part of Ouistreham runs alongside the dunes. Beyond the gardens lie only sand and beach grass.

A form in the darkness; a voice . . .

'That you, inspector?'

'Lucas?'

They quickly drew together.

'What are you doing here?'

Without taking his eyes from the villa's grounds, the sergeant whispered, 'The man from the dredger . . .'

'He came out?'

'He's here!'

'Has he been here long?'

'Barely fifteen minutes . . . Right behind the house.'

'Came in over the fence?'

'No. It looks as if he's waiting for someone. I heard your footsteps, so I came to check.'

'Show me where.'

They went around the garden to the back of the villa, where Lucas swore softly.

'What's the matter?'

'He's gone.'

'You're sure?'

'He was over by the clump of tamarisks.'

'You think he went inside?'

'No idea.'

'Stay here. No matter what happens.'

Maigret ran back to the road. No one . . . A ray of light showed at the study window, but the sill was out of reach.

He hurried back through the garden to ring at the door. The maid opened it almost immediately.

'I think I left my pipe in the study.'

'I will go and see.'

She left him on the threshold, but as soon as she had gone he went quietly to the study door and peeked in.

The mayor was still in his chair with his legs propped up. A small table had been set next to him. And on the other side of it sat Big Louis.

They were playing draughts.

The ex-con moved a piece and barked, 'Your turn!'

The mayor, looking up in exasperation at the maid still hunting for the pipe, exclaimed, 'You can see for yourself that it's not here! Tell the inspector he must have left it somewhere else. Your move, Louis.'

Perfectly at home, Louis called after her, 'And then bring us something to drink, Marguerite!'

7. Orchestrating Events

When Maigret left the villa, Lucas could tell there was trouble coming. The inspector was ready to explode, with staring eyes that seemed to see nothing.

'Didn't find him?'

'I don't think it's even worth looking for him. We'd need too many men to hunt down someone hiding in the dunes.'

His overcoat buttoned all the way up, Maigret thrust his hands into his pockets and chewed the stem of his pipe.

'See that gap between the curtains?' he said, pointing to the study window. 'And that low wall, right in front? Well, once you're standing on the wall, I think you could see into the room.'

Lucas was almost as big as his boss, but not as tall. He hoisted himself on to the wall with a sigh, checking both ways along the road to make sure no one was coming.

The wind had picked up at sundown, a sea wind that strengthened with each passing minute and shook the trees.

'Anything?'

'I'm not up high enough. Fifteen or twenty centimetres short.'

Maigret walked over to a heap of stones by the road and brought back a few.

'Try these.'

'I can see the edge of the table, but not the people.'

And the inspector went to fetch more stones.

'That does it! . . . They're playing draughts. The maid's bringing them some steaming glasses, must be hot grog.'

'Stay there.'

Maigret began pacing up and down the road. A hundred metres on: the Buvette de la Marine, then the harbour. A baker's van went by. The inspector almost stopped it to make sure no one was hiding inside, but instead he just shrugged.

There are some seemingly simple police operations that prove impracticable. Hunting for the man who had vanished into thin air behind the mayor's villa, for example! A search of the dunes, along the beach, in the harbour and village? Roadblocks everywhere? Twenty policemen would not be enough. And a smart fellow would slip through the net anyway.

Maigret didn't even know who he was or what he looked like.

The inspector returned to the wall, where Lucas was still standing in an awkward position.

'What are they doing?'

'Still playing draughts.'

'Talking?'

'Not a peep. The convict has both elbows on the table and is already on his third grog.'

Fifteen minutes later, something rang inside the house. Lucas called Maigret over.

'Phone call. The mayor's trying to get up . . . but Big Louis got there first.'

Although they couldn't hear the conversation, it seemed to have pleased Big Louis.

'They're done?'

'Back to the draughts.'

'Stay there!'

Maigret went off to the bar. A few of the evening regulars were playing cards and invited the inspector to join them for a drink.

'Thanks, not now. Is there a telephone here, mademoiselle?'

It was on the wall in the kitchen. An old woman was cleaning fish.

'Hello! Ouistreham switchboard? Police! Would you tell me who just called the mayor's villa?'

'Caen, sir.'

'What number?'

'It was 122. That's the train station café.'

'Thank you.'

He left the kitchen and for a good long moment stood lost in thought in the middle of the bar.

Suddenly he murmured, 'It's twelve kilometres from here to Caen . . .'

'Thirteen!' Delcourt informed him, having just walked in. 'And how's it going, inspector?'

Maigret hadn't heard him.

' . . . On a bike, that's barely half an hour . . .'

He remembered that the lock workers, most of whom lived in the village, came down to the harbour on bikes that sat all day right across from the bar.

'Would you mind seeing that none of the bicycles is missing?'

Then Maigret's brain went into gear and moved smoothly through the chain of events.

'Damn! It's my bike that's gone . . .'

Unsurprised, the inspector asked no further questions but returned to the phone in the kitchen.

'Give me the Caen police . . . Yes . . . Thank you . . . Hello! Police headquarters? Detective Chief Inspector Maigret here, Police Judiciaire. Is there still a train for Paris tonight? . . . What's that? . . . Not before eleven? . . . No, but listen, please write this down.

'First, make sure that Madame Grandmaison – the ship-owner's wife, yes! – did in fact leave for Paris in her car.

'Next, find out if any stranger showed up at Grandmaison's office or residence today . . . Yes, that's easy, but there's more. You are taking all this down, right?

'Finally, check all the garages in Caen. How many are there? Around twenty? . . . Then only those renting out cars will be of interest. Start with the ones close to the train station . . . Right! You're looking for someone who rented a car, with or without a driver, for Paris – or who might have bought a second-hand car . . . Hello? Don't hang up, damn it! . . . The man probably abandoned a bicycle in Caen.

'Yes, that's it. But do you have enough officers to take care of all that? . . . Good, that's it then . . . And as soon as you have any information whatsoever, call me at the Buvette de la Marine in Ouistreham.'

The harbour men at their aperitifs in the overheated main room had heard every word. When Maigret walked back in, their faces were grave, tense with anxiety.

'You think my bike . . . ?' began one lock worker, but in vain.

'A grog!' Maigret called out curtly.

Gone was the fellow who had smilingly raised a glass with them all over the past few days. He hardly saw or recognized them now.

'The *Saint-Michel*, she's not back from Caen?'

'Supposed to be here in time for the evening tide, but with this weather she may not be able to get out.'

'A storm?'

'We're in for some rough weather at least. And the wind's veering to the north, that's not good news. Can't you hear?'

And there was a kind of hammering, from the waves breaking on the jetty pilings. Wind gusts rattled the door.

'If there's a call for me, let me know. I'll be about a hundred metres up the road.'

'Right by the mayor's house?'

Maigret had a terrible time lighting his pipe outside. The massive clouds running low across the sky seemed to snag on the crowns of the poplars lining the road. From five metres away, he couldn't make out Lucas standing on his wall.

'Anything?'

'They've stopped playing draughts. All of a sudden Louis just swept the pieces off the board as if he were tired of the game.'

'What are they doing?'

'The mayor's slumped in his chair. The other one's smoking cigars and drinking grogs. He's already picked a dozen cigars to pieces, with a sarcastic look on his face, as if to provoke Grandmaison on purpose.'

'How many grogs?'

'Five or six.'

Maigret couldn't see anything but that thin strip of light down the façade. Some builders going home after work pedalled past towards the village. Next came a farmer's cart. Sensing a human presence in the darkness, the driver whipped up his horse and looked back nervously a few times.

'The maid?'

'Haven't seen her. She must be in her kitchen. Will I be up here much longer? Because in that case, you'd best get me more stones, so I don't have to stand on tiptoe.'

Maigret brought some. The din of the ocean was growing louder. All along the beach, the waves must have been almost two metres high, crashing into white foam on the sand.

Down by the harbour, a door opened and closed. It was the bar. A figure appeared, trying to see in the darkness, and Maigret ran over to him.

'Ah! It's you. You're wanted on the phone.'

Caen was calling back already.

'Hello? Detective Chief Inspector? How did you know! . . . Madame Grandmaison went through Caen this morning, heading for Paris. She left at noon, in a car. Her daughter stayed at home in the care of the governess. And regarding the stranger, you were right. At the very first garage we checked, the one across from the station, we learned that a man had arrived by bicycle and wanted to rent a car, no driver. They told him that the garage did not arrange that sort of thing.

'The man seemed impatient and asked if he could at least buy a car in a hurry, second-hand if possible, so they sold him one for twenty thousand francs, which he paid, cash on the barrel.

It's a yellow touring car, bearing the letter W because it was for sale.'

'Do they know which way he went?'

'The man asked for directions for the road to Paris through Lisieux and Évreux.'

'Telephone the national and local police in Lisieux, Évreux, Mantes and Saint-Germain. Warn Paris that all the entrances to the city must be watched, especially Porte Maillot.'

'We're to stop the car?'

'And arrest its occupant, yes! Do you have a description?'

'From the garage-owner . . . A rather tall man, middle-aged, in an elegant, light-coloured suit.'

'Same instructions as before: phone me at Ouistreham as soon as—'

'Excuse me, sir: it's almost seven o'clock, and the Ouistreham exchange shuts down at seven. Unless you go to the mayor's house . . .'

'Why is that?'

'Because the phone number there is 1 and is directly linked at night to Caen.'

'Send someone to the post office. If any call coming through their telephone exchange asks for the mayor, listen in on the conversation. Do you have a car?'

'Yes, a small one.'

'That will be enough to come and alert me. At the Buvette de la Marine, as before.'

Back in the main room, Captain Delcourt was bold enough to ask, 'Is it the murderer you're after?'

'I've no idea!'

The men there could not understand how Maigret, so cordial and friendly until then, could now be so distant and even cantankerous. He left without telling them anything. Outside, he plunged again into the roar of the wind and the sea and had to button his overcoat up tightly, especially to cross the bridge, which was shaking in the storm.

Standing in front of Joris' cottage, he hesitated for a moment, then looked through the keyhole. He saw the kitchen door, its glass panels lit up. Behind them a form went back and forth between the stove and the table.

He rang. Julie froze, holding a dish, then set it down, opened the door and came into the front hall.

'Who is it?' she asked anxiously.

'Inspector Maigret!'

She opened the door and stood aside. She was nervous. Her eyes were still red and she kept glancing fearfully around her.

'Come in, I'm glad you're here. If you knew how scared I am, by myself in this house! I don't think I'll be staying on.'

The inspector entered the kitchen, which was as clean and neat as always. On the white oilcloth covering the table sat only a small bowl and some bread and butter. A pot on the stove was giving off a sweet aroma.

'Hot chocolate?' exclaimed the inspector, surprised.

'I haven't any heart to cook just for myself . . . So I made some chocolate.'

'Pretend I'm not here. Go on, eat . . .'

She fussed a bit, then did fill her bowl and added big pieces of buttered bread to soak. Staring straight ahead, she ate this with a spoon.

'Your brother hasn't come to see you yet?'

'No! I don't understand . . . I went as far as the harbour, just now, hoping to see him. When they're at loose ends, sailors always hang around the harbour.'

'Did you know your brother was a friend of the mayor?'

She looked at him as if in shock.

'What do you mean?'

'They're busy playing draughts together.'

She thought he was joking and, when persuaded that he was not, she became frightened.

'I don't understand . . .'

'Why?'

'Because the mayor keeps his distance from people . . . And he certainly does not like Louis. He's tried to make trouble for him a few times. He didn't even want to let him live here.'

'And with Captain Joris?'

'What about him?'

'Was Monsieur Grandmaison friends with the captain?'

'The way he is with everyone! A handshake in passing. He makes a little joke. A remark about the weather. But that's all. Sometimes, I already told you this, he would take the captain along hunting . . . although that was simply so he wouldn't be alone.'

'Have you received a letter from the lawyer yet?'

'Yes! It says I'm the sole legatee. What exactly does that mean? Is it true that I'll inherit the house?'

'Along with three hundred thousand francs, yes!'

She calmly kept eating, then shook her head and murmured, 'That's impossible . . . It makes no sense. I've told you, I'm certain the captain never had three hundred thousand francs!'

'Where did he sit? Did he eat in the kitchen?'

'Where you are, in the wicker armchair.'

'Did you eat together?'

'Yes . . . Except that I would get up to do my cooking and handle the plates. He liked to read his paper while he ate . . . Once in a while he'd read an article out loud.'

Maigret was not in a mood for sentiment. And yet, something about the restful atmosphere was getting to him. The clock seemed to tick more slowly than clocks anywhere else. The long reflection from the brass pendulum swung back and forth on the wall in front of him. And the sweet smell of the chocolate . . . The wicker of the armchair creaked familiarly at his slightest movement, as it must have when Captain Joris was sitting in it.

Julie was afraid, off in the cottage on her own. And yet she was loath to leave it! Maigret realized that there was something keeping her in this snug and comfortable place.

Julie rose and went to the door. He watched her. She let in the white cat, which went over to a dish of milk at the foot of the stove.

'Poor Puss!' she said. 'Her master was fond of her . . . After dinner, Puss would sit on his lap until he went to bed.'

A calm so intense that it became in some way threatening! A warm, heavy calm . . .

'Do you really have nothing to tell me, Julie?'

She looked up at him questioningly.

'I believe I'm about to discover the truth. A word from you might help me . . . That's why I'm asking you if you have anything else to say.'

'I swear to you . . .'

'About Captain Joris?'

'Nothing!'

'About your brother?'

'Nothing, I swear.'

'About anyone who came here whom you didn't know!'

'I don't understand . . .'

She kept eating that sugary mush, the mere sight of which nauseated the inspector.

'Well, I'd best be going.'

She seemed disappointed; she would be alone again. She was anxious to ask him one last question.

'Tell me, about the funeral . . . I suppose they can't go on waiting much longer? A dead person . . . I mean . . .'

'He's on ice,' said Maigret reluctantly.

And a great shiver ran through her.

★

'Are you there, Lucas?'

It was pitch black, impossible to see anything now. And the roar of the storm drowned out everything else. In the harbour, each man at his post awaited the arrival of a boat from Glasgow that had missed the channel and could be heard whistling out between the jetties.

'I'm here.'

'What are they doing?'

'Eating. I wish I were. Some shrimp, clams, an omelette and what looks like cold veal.'

'At the same table?'

'Yes. Big Louis is still leaning on his elbows.'

'Talking?'

'Not much. Every now and then their lips move, but they must not be saying much.'

'Drinking?'

'Louis, yes! There are two bottles of wine on the table. Nice old bottles. The mayor keeps filling Louis' glass.'

'Trying to make him drunk?'

'Right. The maid's face is something to see. Whenever she has to go behind the sailor, she gives him a wide berth.'

'No more phone calls?'

'No. Now here's Louis blowing his nose in his napkin and standing up. Wait. He's fetching a cigar. The box is on the mantelpiece. He's holding it out to the mayor, who's shaking his head. The maid's bringing in the cheese.

'If I could just sit down!' added Sergeant Lucas plaintively. 'My feet are ice-cold. I'm afraid to move for fear I might tumble off . . .'

It wasn't enough to impress Maigret, who had been in similar situations at least a hundred times.

'I'll bring you something to eat and drink.'

The inspector's place was set at his table in the Hôtel de l'Univers. Without sitting down, he simply devoured a piece of pâté and some bread. He then made a sandwich for his colleague and carried off the rest of the bottle of Bordeaux.

'And here I've prepared a bouillabaisse for you the likes of which you'd not find even in Marseilles!' wailed the hotel-owner.

But nothing could touch the inspector, who returned to the wall to ask the same question for the tenth time.

'What are they doing?'

'The maid has cleared the table. The ship-owner, in his armchair, is chain-smoking. I do believe Louis is falling asleep. He still has his cigar between his teeth, but I don't see the slightest wisp of smoke.'

'Did he have any more to drink?'

'A full glass of the bottle that was on the mantelpiece.'

'Armagnac,' muttered Maigret.

'Hold on! There's a light upstairs . . . It must be the maid going to sleep. The mayor is standing up. He—'

The sound of voices over by the bar. A car engine. Some faint words . . .

'A hundred metres on? In the house?'

'No, outside.'

Maigret set out to intercept the car, which was heading his way. He saw the uniformed men inside and stopped it some distance from the villa so as not to alert the mayor.

'Any news?'

'Évreux has informed us that the man in the yellow car has been arrested.'

'Who is it?'

'Well, listen – he's protesting the arrest! He threatens to inform his ambassador.'

'He's a foreigner?'

'Norwegian! Évreux gave us the name over the phone, but it was impossible to understand. Martineau, or Motineau . . . His papers seem to be in order, and the police want to know what they should do.'

'Have them bring him here, with the yellow car. They must have an officer who can drive. Hurry, get back to Caen and try to find out where Madame Grandmaison stays when she goes to Paris.'

'They already told us that a little while ago, it's the Hôtel de Lutèce, Boulevard Raspail.'

'Telephone from Caen to find out if she arrived and what she's doing. Wait! If she is there, phone the Police Judiciaire for me and ask them to have her discreetly followed by an inspector.'

The car needed to back up at three different angles to turn around on the narrow road. Maigret went back once again to Lucas on his wall but found him clambering down.

'What are you doing?'

'There's nothing more to see.'

'They've left?'

'No, but the mayor came over to the curtains and drew them tightly closed.'

A hundred metres away, the boat from Glasgow moved gently into the lock as orders were given in English. A sudden gust carried the inspector's hat off in that direction.

The topmost light in the villa suddenly went out, leaving the façade in complete darkness.

8. The Mayor's Inquiry

Maigret was standing in the middle of the road, both hands in his pockets, frowning.

'Something worrying you?' asked Lucas, who knew his boss.

'Inside is where we should be,' grumbled the inspector, studying the villa's windows one after the other.

But they were all closed tight. There was no way to get into the house. Maigret went quietly up to the front door, leaned down and listened, gesturing to Lucas for silence. In the end they both had their ears glued to the oak panel.

They heard no voices, could identify no words. There were footsteps in the study, however, and some steady, dull thuds.

Were the two men fighting? Unlikely, for the pounding was too evenly spaced. Two struggling men would come and go, staggering and bumping into furniture, with pauses and flurries of punches. This was like a pile-driver. And they could even distinguish the rhythmic breathing of the man landing the blows: 'Huh! . . . Huh! . . . Huh! . . .'

In counterpoint, low moaning.

The two policemen looked at each other. The inspector turned towards the lock and pointed; the sergeant understood and pulled a set of skeleton keys from his pocket.

'Don't make any noise,' whispered Maigret.

The house seemed silent now. Ominously quiet. No more blows. No more footsteps. Maybe – but this was hard to tell – the hoarse gasping of an exhausted man.

Lucas signalled. The door opened. Dim light filtered into the hall from around the study door on the left. Maigret shrugged with irritation and anger. He was exceeding his authority – by a considerable extent, even, and in the home of a hostile official like the mayor of Ouistreham.

'Too bad!'

From the hall he could clearly hear breathing, but only one person's. No movement. Lucas had his hand on his revolver. Maigret opened the door with one shove.

He stopped short, as stunned and confused as he had ever been. Had he been expecting to catch someone red-handed?

This was something else! And completely baffling. Monsieur Grandmaison's lip was split, his chin and dressing gown all bloodied, his hair mussed up, and he looked as punch-drunk as a boxer who had stumbled to his feet after a knock-out.

And he seemed barely able to stand, propped up against a corner of the mantelpiece but leaning so far back that it seemed impossible for him to stay upright.

A few steps away, a rough-looking Big Louis with blood on his still-clenched fists. The mayor's blood!

It was Big Louis' panting they had heard out in the corridor. He was the one out of breath, doubtless from beating the other man. He smelled of alcohol. The glasses on the small table had been tipped over.

The policemen were so astounded and the others so exhausted that it was a good minute at least before anyone said a word.

Then Monsieur Grandmaison wiped his lip and chin with a corner of his dressing gown and stammered, while trying to stand up straight, 'What the . . . What . . . ?'

'Do excuse me,' said Maigret courteously, 'for having entered your home unannounced. I heard a noise, and the front door was not locked.'

'That's not true!'

The mayor had evidently recovered his spirits.

'In any case, I'm glad we arrived in time to protect you and . . .'

He glanced over at Big Louis, who did not seem the least bit upset and was now even smiling strangely while studying the mayor's reaction.

'I do not need to be protected.'

'But this man has attacked you . . .'

Standing at a mirror, Monsieur Grandmaison was trying to make himself more presentable and seemed frustrated at failing to stop his lip from bleeding.

It was an extraordinary and unsettling display of strength and weakness, self-assurance and cowardice.

With his impressive shiner, wounds and bruises, his face had lost its slightly childish, rosy-cheeked glow, and there was a dull look in his eyes.

He was recovering his aplomb surprisingly quickly, though, and, leaning against the mantelpiece, he soon challenged the policemen.

'I take it that you broke into my house.'

'Pardon me: we wished to come to your rescue.'

'Not true, because you did not know that I was in any danger at all! And . . . I . . . was . . . not!'

Maigret studied the impressive figure of Big Louis from head to toe.

'Nonetheless, I trust that you will allow me to take this gentleman away.'

'Absolutely not!'

'He beat you. And rather brutally at that.'

'We've sorted it all out! And it's nobody's business but my own!'

'I have every reason to believe that it was on him that you fell this morning, while going a bit quickly downstairs.'

Big Louis' grin was as pretty as a picture. He was in heaven. While he was getting his breath back, he missed nothing of what was happening and found these developments delightful. He, at least, must have understood all the hidden facets of the situation and could savour the jest to the full!

'I did tell you earlier today, Monsieur Maigret, that I'd undertaken my own investigation. I am not meddling with yours. Do me the favour of not interfering with mine. And don't be surprised if I file a complaint against you for illegal entry.'

It was hard to tell whether he cut a tragic or comic figure. He was standing on his dignity and drawing himself up imposingly – with a bleeding lip! And a face that was one big bruise! And a dressing gown in tatters!

Big Louis even seemed to be egging him on.

The main thing was what had just happened, and it wasn't hard to picture: the ex-convict, punching so hard and so much and so well that he wore himself out.

'Please forgive me if I don't leave right away, Monsieur Grandmaison. Given that you are the only person in Ouistreham with a telephone connection at night, I've taken the liberty of having a few calls directed here.'

The mayor's only response was, 'Shut the door!' – for it had been left wide open.

Then he picked up one of the cigars lying scattered on the mantelpiece and tried to light it, but its contact with his lip must have been painful, for he threw it violently away.

'Lucas, would you get Caen on the line for me?'

Maigret kept studying the mayor, then Big Louis, then the mayor again. And he was having difficulty marshalling his thoughts.

For example, a first impression might suggest that, of the two opponents, it was Monsieur Grandmaison who was the underdog, the weakest not only physically but morally.

He had been beaten, discovered in the most humiliating circumstances.

Well, not at all! Within a few minutes he had recouped his sang-froid and some of his bourgeois respectability.

He was almost calm. His look, haughty.

Big Louis had the easy part. He had been the winner. He was

neither wounded nor even bruised. Moments before, his blissful smile had evoked an almost childlike joy. And now he was the one beginning to look uneasy, unsure of what to do, where to go, even where to look.

So Maigret wondered . . . Assuming that one of these two was the boss, which was it? He just didn't know. Grandmaison, at times; Louis, at others.

'Hello? Caen, Police Headquarters? . . . Detective Chief Inspector Maigret asked me to tell you that he will be at the mayor's house all night . . . Yes . . . That's telephone number 1 . . . Hello! Do you have any news? Lisieux already? . . . Thanks . . . Yes.'

Turning to Maigret, Lucas announced, 'The car just went through Lisieux. It'll be here very soon.'

'I believe I heard you say—'

'That I would spend the entire night here, yes. With your permission, of course. Twice, now, you have mentioned the inquiry you have personally undertaken, and I believe the best thing would be for you to authorize me to pool the information we have both gathered on our own.'

Maigret was not being sarcastic. He was furious. Furious at the unbelievable situation in which he had landed himself. Furious at being flummoxed by the case.

'Would you explain to me, Big Louis, why, when we arrived, you were busily . . . um . . . punching the daylights out of the town mayor?'

But Big Louis said nothing, looking at the mayor himself as if to say, 'You, speak up!'

'That is my affair,' remarked Monsieur Grandmaison crisply.

'Of course! Everyone has the right to have himself beaten up if he likes that!' grumbled Maigret. 'Lucas, get me the Hôtel de Lutèce.'

The shot hit home. Monsieur Grandmaison's hand tightened its grip on the marble mantelpiece. He opened his mouth to speak.

Lucas was talking on the phone.

'A three-minute wait? . . . Thank you . . . Yes.'

'Don't you find that this inquiry is taking an odd turn?' asked Maigret. 'By the way, Monsieur Grandmaison, perhaps you can be of help here. As a ship-owner, you must know people from many countries. Have you heard of a certain . . . just a moment . . . a certain Martineau . . . or Motineau . . . from Bergen or Trondheim . . . A Norwegian, in any case?'

Silence! Big Louis' eyes had gone hard. He reached automatically for one of the glasses lying on the table and poured himself a drink.

'Well, it's too bad you don't know him. He's on his way here.'

That was it. Not worth adding a single word. They wouldn't answer. They wouldn't even flinch. It was obvious from the poses they had taken.

In a change of tactics, Monsieur Grandmaison, still leaning against the mantelpiece, was contemplating the floor with studied indifference while he toasted his calves before the fire of coal briquettes.

But what a face! Slack features, splotched with blue and red, bruises and a bloody chin! A mixture of focused energy and panic, or distress.

Big Louis? He had parked himself astride a chair. After yawning three or four times, he seemed to be dozing.

The phone rang. Maigret grabbed the receiver.

'Hello? The Hôtel de Lutèce? . . . Don't cut me off: I'd like to speak to Madame Grandmaison . . . Yes! She should have arrived this afternoon or this evening . . . Yes, I'll wait.'

'I assume,' said the mayor in a flat voice, 'that you have no intention of involving my wife in your . . . rather bizarre actions at this moment?'

No reply. Maigret waited, the receiver at his ear, staring at the tablecloth.

'Hello, yes! . . . Repeat that? . . . She has already left? . . . One moment . . . From the beginning. When did the lady arrive? . . . Seven o'clock, fine . . . With her car and driver . . . You say she dined at the hotel, then was summoned to the telephone . . . She left directly afterwards? . . . Thank you . . . No! . . . That's enough.'

No one faltered. Monsieur Grandmaison seemed calmer. Maigret hung up, then picked up the receiver again.

'Hello! Caen central? Police here. Would you tell me if anyone at this number put through a call to Paris today at any time before this present call? . . . Yes? . . . About fifteen minutes ago? . . . The Hôtel de Lutèce, wasn't it? . . . Thank you.'

Beads of perspiration stood out on Maigret's forehead. He slowly filled a pipe with little taps of his index finger. Then he poured himself a drink, using a glass from the table.

'I suppose you realize, inspector, that everything you're doing now is illegal. You broke into my house. You're staying here without my permission. You might very well cause great upset to my family and, finally, you are treating me like a criminal in the presence of a third person. You will pay for all this.'

'Understood!'

'Since I am no longer master in my own house, either, I would like permission to go to bed.'

'No!'

Maigret caught the sound of a car in the distance.

'Go and wait for them at the door, Lucas.'

He tossed a shovelful of coal into the fireplace out of habit and turned around at the very moment when the new arrivals entered: two policemen from Évreux flanking a man in handcuffs.

'Leave us,' he told the escorts. 'Wait for me outside, even if it takes all night.'

The mayor had not budged. Neither had the sailor. You would have thought that they hadn't seen a thing, or didn't want to. As for the newcomer, he was relaxed, and a smile hovered about his lips when he noticed Monsieur Grandmaison's swollen face.

'Who is in charge here?' he asked, glancing around.

Maigret, raising his shoulders as if in surprise at the policemen's effrontery, pulled a small key from his pocket and removed the handcuffs.

'Thank you. I was rather astonished at—'

'At what?' thundered Maigret angrily. 'At being arrested? Are you sure you were really all that astonished?'

'That's to say, I'm still waiting to learn what I'm supposed to have done.'

'Let's start with stealing a bicycle!'

'Correction! Borrowed! The garage-owner from whom I bought the car will tell you that! I left him with the bicycle and instructions to send it back to Ouistreham with some monetary compensation for its owner.'

'Really! . . . But, you don't actually seem to be Norwegian . . .'

The man neither looked nor sounded Norwegian. He was tall, well built, still young. His nicely tailored clothes were a bit the worse for wear.

'Excuse me! I am Norwegian, perhaps not by birth, but I've been naturalized.'

'And you live in Bergen?'

'Tromsø, near the Lofoten islands.'

'Are you a businessman?'

'I own a factory for processing waste products from cod-fishing.'

'Including, for example, salted cod's roe.'

'The roe and other things. With the heads and livers we make oil. With the bones, fertilizer.'

'Perfect! That's just perfect! Now all I need to know is what you were doing in Ouistreham on the night of the 16th of September.'

Without turning a hair, the man looked slowly around and said, 'I was not in Ouistreham.'

'Where were you?'

'And where were you? What I mean is,' he said with a smile, 'would you be able, out of the blue, to say what you were doing at a given hour on a given day after more than a month had gone by?'

'Were you in Norway?'

'Probably.'

'Look.'

And Maigret held out to him the gold fountain-pen, which the Norwegian put in his pocket as calmly as you please.

'Thank you.'

He was a really good-looking man, the mayor's age and height, but slimmer, yet muscular. His dark eyes were intensely alive. And the smile on his thin lips betrayed his immense self-confidence.

Politely, pleasantly, he answered the inspector's questions.

'I rather feel there must be some mistake, and I'd very much like to continue on my way to Paris.'

'That's a different matter. Where did you first meet Big Louis?'

Maigret was disappointed: the man's eyes did not flick over to the sailor.

'Big Louis?' he repeated.

'You met Joris during his voyages as a merchant ship captain?'

'Sorry, I don't understand.'

'Evidently! And if I ask you why you preferred to sleep aboard a laid-up dredger instead of in a hotel you'll look at me with big round eyes . . .'

'Certainly. Well, put yourself in my place.'

'Yet you arrived yesterday in Ouistreham on the *Saint-Michel*. You came ashore in the dinghy before she entered the harbour. You holed up in the dredger and spent the night there. This afternoon, you walked around this very villa, then . . . borrowed a bicycle and sped off to Caen. Purchased a car. Left for Paris. Is it Madame Grandmaison you were going to join at the Hôtel de Lutèce? If so, don't bother to continue your journey. Unless I'm much mistaken, she'll arrive here later tonight.'

Silence. The mayor had become a statue, and his stare was so vacant that it seemed devoid of life. Big Louis was scratching his head and yawning, still astride his chair, with everyone else standing around him.

'So your name is Martineau?'

'Jean Martineau, yes.'

'Well, Monsieur Jean Martineau, why don't you think things over? Consider whether you might not have something to tell me after all. The chances are good that someone here in this room will one day be committed for trial.'

'Not only have I nothing to say to you, but I would like permission to contact my consul so that he may take the usual steps . . .'

That made two of them! Grandmaison had threatened to file a complaint; Martineau was going to follow suit. Only Big Louis wasn't trying to warn him off, instead reacting philosophically to whatever happened, as long as there was something to drink.

Outside the tempest was raging and, at high tide, it had reached its full strength.

What Lucas thought showed in his face: 'Now we're in hot water! Either we come up with something, or we're cooked.'

Maigret was tramping up and down the room, puffing ferociously at his pipe.

'So neither of you knows anything about Captain Joris' disappearance or his death?'

Grandmaison and Martineau shook their heads. Silence. Maigret kept looking over at Martineau.

Then, hurried footsteps outside; a nervous rapping at the front door. After a moment's hesitation, Lucas went to open it. Someone ran in: Julie, all out of breath, who gasped, 'Inspector . . . My . . . My brother . . .'

And she was struck dumb at the sight of Big Louis, who stood up, dwarfing her with his great size.

'Your brother?' Maigret prompted her.

'Nothing . . . I . . .'

She tried to smile as she caught her breath but, retreating backwards, she bumped into Martineau.

'Sorry, monsieur,' she stammered, without seeming to recognize him.

The wind roared in through the forgotten front door, left wide open.

9. The Conspiracy of Silence

Julie was explaining why she had come, in short, hesitant sentences.

'I was alone in the house . . . I was frightened. . . . I'd gone to bed with all my clothes on . . . Someone started pounding on the door . . . It was Lannec, my brother's skipper.'

'The *Saint-Michel* is in?'

'She was in the lock when I passed by. Lannec wanted to see my brother right away . . . Seems they're in a hurry to set out. I told him Louis hadn't even come to visit! And the skipper's the one who got me worried, muttering things I didn't understand . . .'

'Why did you come here?' asked Maigret.

'I asked Lannec, was Louis in any danger – and he told me yes, that maybe it was already too late . . . So I asked around in the harbour, and they told me you were here.'

Big Louis was staring at the floor, looking irritated. He shrugged, as if to indicate that women get all worked up about nothing.

'You're in danger?' asked Maigret, trying to meet his eyes.

Big Louis laughed. A great booming noise, much more simple-minded than his usual laughter.

'Why was Lannec worried?'

'Now how would I know?'

'In short,' said Maigret pensively, looking around at everyone, 'you don't know anything. None of you do!' he added, with an edge of bitterness. 'You, Monsieur Grandmaison, you've never met Monsieur Martineau and don't know why Big Louis – who makes himself at home in your house, playing draughts with you and eating at your table – would suddenly begin punching your face into pudding.'

Not a word.

'What am I saying? You seem to find this perfectly natural! You don't defend yourself! You won't file a complaint! You won't even throw Big Louis out of your house.'

He turned to Big Louis.

'You, you haven't a clue either! You sleep aboard the dredger but have no idea who else is with you there. You repay the hospitality of this house by using the master of it as a punchbag. You have never seen Monsieur Martineau in your life . . .'

Not a flicker of response. Everyone was stubbornly studying the carpet.

'And you, Monsieur Martineau, you're just the same. Do you even know how you got from Norway to France? No! You'd rather sleep in a bunk in the abandoned dredger than in a hotel bed. You take off on a bike, buy a car to drive to Paris. But you know nothing. You've never met Monsieur Grandmaison, Big Louis, or Captain Joris. And of course you, Julie, know even less than the others.'

Discouraged, he looked over at Lucas. His sergeant understood. They couldn't arrest them *all* . . . Every single one of them was guilty of inexplicable behaviour, lying or conflicting statements.

But not one thing that would stand up in court!

It was eleven o'clock. Maigret knocked out his pipe in the fireplace.

'I must ask you all,' he intoned grumpily, 'to remain at the disposal of the judicial authorities . . . I will certainly have occasion to question you further, in spite of your ignorance. I take it, Mayor Grandmaison, that you have no intention of leaving Ouistreham?'

'No.'

'Thank you. Monsieur Martineau, you could take a room at the Hôtel de l'Univers, where I am staying.'

The Norwegian bowed slightly.

'Accompany Monsieur Martineau to the hotel, Lucas.'

He turned to Julie and Big Louis.

'You two, come with me.'

Once outside, Maigret dismissed the two policemen waiting for him there, then watched Lucas and Martineau set off immediately for the hotel, where the proprietor was waiting up for his guests.

Julie had rushed from the cottage without her coat, and her brother, seeing her shivering, made her put on his jacket.

The storm made talking too difficult. They had to walk bent over with the wind constantly whistling in their ears and chilling their faces so badly that their eyelids hurt.

The bar in the harbour was lit up, full of lock workers who were dashing in, between vessels, to get warm and down hot grogs. Their faces turned towards the trio, who plodded on through the gale, over the bridge.

'Is that the *Saint-Michel*?' asked Maigret.

A schooner was leaving the lock, making for the outer harbour, but he thought it seemed much taller than the one he remembered.

'She's in ballast,' grunted Louis.

Meaning that the *Saint-Michel* had unloaded in Caen and was travelling empty to pick up a fresh cargo.

Just as they were coming to Joris' cottage, a shadowy figure approached them. They had to peer into his face to recognize him. The man spoke shakily to Big Louis.

'There y'are at last. Hurry, let's get under way!'

Maigret looked hard at the little Breton skipper, then at the waves attacking the jetties in an endless roar. The sky was a startling panorama of furious, roiling clouds.

The *Saint-Michel*, moored to a piling in the darkness, showed only one tiny light from a lamp on the deckhouse.

'You mean to go out in this?'

'Of course!'

'Where to?'

'La Rochelle, for a cargo of wine.'

'You absolutely must have Big Louis?'

'You really think just two could manage her in this blow?'

Standing there listening, stamping her feet, Julie was cold. Her brother kept looking back and forth between Maigret and the *Saint-Michel*, her rigging creaking in the storm.

'Go and wait for me aboard!' Maigret told the skipper.

'But we . . .'

'But what?'

'Tide's on the ebb, we've got only two hours left.'

There was something in his eyes . . . He was clearly uneasy, apprehensive, kept shifting from one foot to the other and couldn't look at anything for more than a second or two.

'Me, I've got my living to earn!'

Maigret caught an exchange of glances between the skipper and his mate. There are moments when intuition goes into high gear, and Maigret was sure he had read the little captain right: 'Boat's not far, only one line to cast off; a single swing at this police fellow and we're away . . .'

'Go and wait for me aboard!' repeated Maigret.

'But . . .'

The inspector signalled to the two others to follow him inside.

Maigret was seeing the brother and sister alone together for the first time. They were all three in Captain Joris' kitchen, where a good fire was drawing so well in the iron stove that the purring flames would sometimes snap and crackle.

'How about something to drink?' said the inspector to Julie, who fetched a carafe of spirits and some matching glasses with painted flowers on them.

He was in the way, he could tell. Julie would dearly have liked to be alone with Big Louis, who watched her attentively with what was clearly great affection and a kind of brutish tenderness.

Like the consummate housekeeper she was, Julie did not sit down after serving the two men but restoked her fire.

'To the memory of Captain Joris,' said Maigret, raising his glass.

There was a long silence. This suited the inspector. He wanted everyone to have time to absorb the warm, quiet atmosphere of the kitchen.

The steady humming of the fire gradually joined with the tick-tock of the pendulum clock into a kind of music. Safe from the chilly winds outside, their cheeks grew pink, and their eyes shone brightly. And the pungent aroma of calvados perfumed the air.

'Captain Joris,' said Maigret softly. 'Here I am, sitting at his place, in his armchair . . . A wicker chair that creaks with every move I make. If he were alive, he'd be coming in from the harbour and probably asking for another glass, to warm himself up. Right, Julie?'

She looked at him, wide-eyed, then turned away.

'He wouldn't go right up to bed. I bet he'd take off his shoes . . . You'd fetch him his slippers . . . He'd say, "Dirty weather – but the *Saint-Michel* still insisted on heading out to sea, may God keep her!"'

'How did you know?'

'What?'

'That he used to say, "May God keep her"? That's it, exactly . . .'

She was deeply moved, and there was a touch of gratitude in the look she gave Maigret.

Big Louis hunched over a little more.

'Well, he won't ever say it again. Too bad! He was a happy man. He had a pretty little house, a garden full of flowers he loved, his savings . . . Everyone really liked him, it seems. And yet there was someone who put an end to all that, suddenly, with a sprinkling of white powder in a glass of water.'

Julie's face seemed to collapse. She fought hard to hold back her tears.

'A pinch of white powder and it's all over! And whoever did it will probably be happy, he will, because no one knows who he is! He was doubtless just with us a little while ago . . .'

'Be quiet!' begged Julie with clasped hands, and the tears finally streamed down her face.

But the inspector knew where he was going. He kept speaking in a low voice, slowly, giving each word its due. And there wasn't much play-acting in it, for he was caught up in the mood himself. He too felt the nostalgia of that atmosphere in which he conjured up the sturdy form of the late harbourmaster.

'Dead, he has only one friend left . . . Me! A lone man who is fighting to find out the truth, to prevent Joris' murderer from living happily ever after . . .'

Overwhelmed by her sorrow, Julie was sobbing as Maigret went on.

'The thing is, everyone around the dead man keeps silent, everyone lies, as if everyone had some reason to feel guilty, as if they were all accomplices in what happened!'

'That's not true!' wailed Julie.

Big Louis, growing more and more uncomfortable, poured himself more calvados and refilled the inspector's glass.

'Big Louis, first of all, remains silent.'

Julie looked at her brother through her tears, as if struck by the true meaning of those words.

'He knows something,' continued Maigret. 'He knows many things. Is he afraid of the murderer? . . . Is he in danger in some way?'

'Louis!' cried his sister.

And Louis looked away, with a face made of stone.

'Say it isn't true, Louis! . . . Won't you listen to me?'

'Don't know what the inspector . . .'

He just couldn't remain still any longer. He got to his feet.

'Louis is the biggest liar of the bunch! He claims not to know the Norwegian but he does! He claims not to have any dealing with the mayor, and I find him in the man's house, beating him to a pulp . . .'

That vague smile appeared on the ex-convict's lips. But Julie wasn't mollified.

'Oh, Louis! Is that true?'

When he didn't answer, she clutched at his arm.

'Then why don't you tell the truth? You haven't done anything, I know you haven't!'

He pulled away, but looked torn . . . Perhaps he was weakening. Maigret didn't give him time to pull himself together.

'Just one tiny truth, a single scrap of information in this whole mess of lies would probably be enough to untangle everything!'

But, no. In spite of his sister's pleading looks, Louis shook himself like a giant harassed by furious little enemies.

'I don't know anything.'

'Why won't you talk?' said Julie sternly, already growing suspicious.

'I don't know anything!'

'The inspector says—'

'I don't know anything!'

'Listen, Louis . . . I've always believed in you, you know that. And I defended you, even to Captain Joris . . .'

Flushed with regret over that last remark, she quickly went on.

'You must tell the truth. I can't take this any more. And I won't stay any longer in this house, by myself.'

'Stop talking, Julie,' sighed her brother.

'What do you want him to tell you, inspector?'

'Two things. First, who Martineau is. Then, why the mayor let himself be beaten up.'

'You hear that, Louis? . . . It's not so bad!'

'I don't know anything.'

Now she was getting angry.

'Louis, listen to me! I'm going to end up thinking that . . .'

And the fire kept on purring. And the ticking of the clock was slow, stretching the reflected lamplight along on its copper pendulum.

Louis was too tall, too strong, too rough, with his lopsided head and shoulder, for that tidy little cottage kitchen. He didn't know what to do with his big callused hands. His shifty eyes could find no place to rest.

'You must speak!'

'I got nothing to say.'

He tried to pour himself another drink, but she pounced on the carafe.

'That's enough! There's no point in you getting any drunker.'

She was painfully anxious. She had the confused feeling that real tragedy was at stake, at that very moment. She clung to her hope that one word might make everything clear.

'Louis, that man, that Norwegian . . . He's the one who was supposed to buy the *Saint-Michel* and become your boss, isn't he?'

'No!' barked Louis.

'Then who is he? We've never seen him around here. And foreigners don't come here off-season . . .'

'I don't know.'

Julie kept at him, with a subtle feminine instinct.

'The mayor always hated you. Did you really eat supper at his house tonight?'

'That's true.'

She was almost dancing with impatience.

'But then, tell me something! You must! Or I swear I'll start believing that . . .'

She couldn't go on. She was wretched. She looked around at the wicker armchair, the familiar stove, the clock, the carafe with its painted flowers.

'You were fond of the captain, I know it! You said so a hundred times, and if you two fell out it's because . . .'

But now she had to explain all that.

'Don't go thinking the wrong thing here, inspector! My brother was fond of Captain Joris, and the captain liked him as well, it's just that there was . . . But nothing serious! Louis goes a little wild when he's got money in his pocket and then he spends it all, any old which way . . . The captain knew that he used to come here to wheedle my savings out of me. So he lectured him . . . That's all! If he ended by forbidding him to come here, it was for that, so that he wouldn't go off with any more of my money! But he'd tell me that Louis was really a good fellow at heart, whose only fault was that he was weak.'

'And Louis,' said Maigret slowly, 'might have known that, with Joris dead, you would inherit three hundred thousand francs!'

It happened so quickly that the inspector almost got the worst of it. As Julie uttered a piercing scream, Big Louis leaped with all his strength at Maigret, trying to get his hands around his throat.

The inspector managed to grab one of his wrists on the fly, and with slow but steady pressure, he twisted the sailor's arm behind his back, growling, 'Hands off!'

Julie wept even more piteously, her elbows up against the wall, her head buried in her crossed arms.

'My God,' she moaned faintly, 'my God . . .'

'Don't you want to talk, Louis?' said Maigret sternly, releasing his grip on him.

'I have nothing to say.'

'And if I arrest you?'

'So what!'

'Follow me.'

Julie cried out:

'Inspector! I'm begging you! For the love of God, Louis, talk to him!'

They were already at the kitchen door. Big Louis turned around, his face red, his eyes glittering. His expression was beyond words. He reached with one hand for his sister's shoulder.

'My Lilie, I swear to you . . .'

'Don't touch me!'

He hesitated, took a step towards the front hall, then turned again.

'Listen . . .'

'No! No, get out!'

So he followed Maigret, dragging his feet. Stopping at the threshold, he was tempted to look back . . . but did not. The front door closed behind them. They had not taken five steps into the storm when the door flew open on the young woman's pale form.

'Louis!'

Too late. The two men walked straight ahead, into the night.

A gust of rain soaked them in a matter of seconds. They couldn't see a thing, not even the edges of the lock. A voice hailed them, though, rising up through the darkness.

'That you, Louis?'

It was Lannec, aboard the *Saint-Michel*. He had heard their footsteps and stuck his head up through the hatchway. He must have known that his first mate was not alone, for he then spoke rapidly in Low Breton, saying, 'Jump on to the fo'c'sle and we'll head out.'

Maigret, who had understood, now waited, unable to find the true outline of the *Saint-Michel* in the pitch dark. All he could see of his companion was a wavering mass of a man, his shoulders gleaming in the rain.

10. The Three Men of the Saint-Michel

A glance at the black hole of the ocean; a more furtive one at Maigret. With a shrug, Big Louis grunted to the inspector, 'You coming aboard?'

Maigret now saw that Lannec held something in his hand: the end of a mooring line. Tracing it with his eyes, he saw that it passed once around a bollard and went back aboard. In other words, the *Saint-Michel* had been made fast in a way that allowed the skipper to cast off without putting a man ashore.

The inspector said nothing. He knew the harbour was deserted. Julie was doubtless sobbing in her kitchen 300 metres away, and there was no one else nearby but the people sheltering in the warmth of the Buvette de la Marine.

He stepped on to the bulwarks handrail and jumped down to the deck, followed by Louis. Even protected by the jetties, there was rough water in the outer harbour, and the *Saint-Michel* rose on each wave as if on a man's heaving chest.

Nothing in the darkness but yellow glints on wet things. On the fo'c'sle, a vague form: the captain, looking at Louis in astonishment. He wore tall rubber boots, an oilskin slicker, a sou'wester, and he was still clutching the mooring line.

No one did anything. They all waited . . . The three men of the *Saint-Michel* must have been studying Maigret, who cut such a strange figure with his velvet-collared overcoat and bowler hat, held clamped to his head to preserve it from the gale.

'You will not leave tonight!' he announced.

No protest. But a look passed between Lannec and Louis that meant, 'We sail anyway?' . . . 'Better not.'

The wind was now so violent that they could barely stand

upright, and again it was Maigret who took the lead by going to the hatchway, which he remembered from his first visit.

'We'll talk – and bring that other sailor down too!'

He did not want anyone left up on deck, out of his sight. The four men went down the hatch.

Off came boots and oilskins. The gimballed lamp was lit, and there were glasses on the table next to a greasy sea-chart heavily marked with pencil lines.

Lannec put two coal briquettes into the small stove but looked askance at Maigret and seemed hesitant to offer him a drink. As for old Célestin, he went to huddle in a corner, peevish and uneasy, wondering why he had been brought down to the cabin.

Everyone's attitude clearly meant the same thing: no one wanted to speak up, because no one knew how matters stood. The puzzled skipper stared at Louis, who looked back at him helplessly.

What he had to say would require such long, complicated explanations!

'You've thought it over?' muttered Lannec hoarsely, after coughing to clear his throat a little.

Maigret was sitting on a bench, elbows on the table, playing absently with an empty glass so smudged that it was now opaque.

Standing there, Big Louis had to bow his head to avoid touching the roof.

Lannec fiddled around in the cupboard to give himself something to do.

'Thought what over?'

'I don't know which legal powers you have. What I do know is, I answer only to the maritime authorities. They alone can stop a vessel from entering or leaving a port.'

'Meaning?'

'You're keeping me from leaving Ouistreham. I've got cargo to take on in La Rochelle, plus there's penalties to pay for every day I'm late.'

They were getting off on the wrong foot, with this serious, semi-official approach. Maigret knew that game by heart! Hadn't the mayor threatened him almost in the same way? And hadn't Martineau then talked of appealing, not to the maritime authorities, but to his consul?

He paused a moment to take a deep breath and give them all a rapid – and now strangely cheerful – glance.

'Why don't you give all that a rest!' he said in Breton. 'And pour us a drink instead.'

It was a long shot. The old sailor was the first one to turn towards Maigret in amazement. Big Louis' face relaxed.

'You're a Breton?' asked Lannec, still wary.

'Not quite. I'm from the Loire, but I studied for some time in Nantes.'

What a look! The face coastal Bretons make at the mention of inland Bretons, and especially the halfway Bretons around Nantes.

'Any of that Dutch gin left from the other day?'

Lannec brought the bottle and slowly filled the glasses, happy to have something to do. Because he still didn't know what to do about Maigret. There he was: big, affable, pipe between his teeth, his bowler pushed back on his head, settling in nicely.

'You can sit down, Big Louis.'

The first mate obeyed. The uneasy atmosphere still lingered some, but in another way. The sailors felt awkward, not being able to return the inspector's cordiality, but they had to remain on their guard.

'Your health, boys! And admit it: by keeping you here tonight I'm saving you from a nasty run.'

'It's the harbour channel, mostly,' murmured Lannec. A swallow of gin, and then, 'Once we're out of the gat, we're clear . . . But with that current from the Orne, and all those sandbanks, the channel's tough. Every year she grounds some ships.'

'The *Saint-Michel*'s never had real trouble?'

The captain quickly touched wood. Célestin growled angrily at the mere mention of bad luck.

'The *Saint-Michel*?' exclaimed Lannec. 'She's maybe the best schooner on the coast. Listen! Two years ago, in dense fog, she fetched up on the rocky English coast in a hell of a surf. Any ship but her would have left her bones there. Well! She floats away on the next tide, didn't even need to lie up in dry dock.'

Maigret felt they could get along fine in this vein, but he wasn't in the mood to talk ships all night. Their wet clothes were beginning to steam. Water was snaking down the ladder. And the ever-increasing heaving of the ship, which slammed now and then into the pilings, was beginning to tell on the inspector.

'She'll make a fine yacht!' he exclaimed, looking off into the distance.

So that was it! Lannec flinched.

'Yes, she'd make a fine one,' he countered. 'With only the deck to change. And a little less canvas, especially aloft.'

'Has the Norwegian signed the contract?'

Lannec looked sharply at Louis, who sighed. They would have given a great deal, those two, to talk privately for even a few seconds. What had Louis already revealed? What could the captain safely say?

Big Louis was wearing his stubborn look. He knew the fix they were in but had no way of explaining what was going on to the skipper. It was too complicated!

And would all end badly, of course. He had best have a drink. He poured himself one, drank it straight off and faced the inspector. He wasn't even really feeling up for a fight, but simply resigned.

'What Norwegian?'

'Well, the Norwegian who isn't exactly a Norwegian. Martineau. Anyway, it certainly wasn't in Tromsø that he saw the *Saint-Michel*, since she never went that far north.'

'Mind you, she could! Could handle all the way to Archangel, right enough.'

'When's he taking delivery?'

The old sailor snorted derisively, off in his corner. His contempt was not directed at Maigret, but at the three men of the *Saint-Michel*, himself included.

'I don't know what you mean,' replied Lannec lamely.

Maigret elbowed him gaily in the ribs.

'Come off it! Really, boys. Stop looking as if you were all at a funeral! And wipe those grumpy looks off your pig-headed Breton faces . . . Martineau promised to buy the schooner, but has he actually purchased it?'

Inspiration struck.

'Show me the muster roll.'

He felt that shot strike home.

'I've no idea where it . . .'

'I told you to give that stuff a rest, Lannec! Show me the crew list, damn it all!'

He was playing the pretend bully, the good-hearted brute. The skipper went to the cupboard for a well-worn briefcase, grey with age. It was full of official documents and business letters from ship-brokers' firms. One thing was new, a big yellow folder containing some impressively large pages: it was the muster roll. It had been drawn up and dated only a month and a half before, on 11 September. Five days before Captain Joris disappeared.

> Schooner Saint-Michel, 270 gross tons, licensed for the coastal trade. Owner of record: Louis Legrand, Port-en-Bessin. Captain: Yves Lannec. Seaman: Célestin Grolet.

Big Louis poured himself another. Lannec hung his head in embarrassment.

'Look at this! You're the present owner of this boat, Big Louis?'

No reply. Off in his corner, old Célestin bit off a great chunk of his chewing tobacco.

'Listen, boys. There's no point in wasting time over this. I'm not a complete fool, eh? Granted, I'm no expert on life at sea, but Big Louis is flat broke. A boat like this one is worth at least a hundred and fifty thousand francs.'

'I'd never have sold her for that!' Lannec shot back.

'Let's say two hundred thousand. So Big Louis bought the *Saint-Michel* on someone else's behalf! And let's say . . . on behalf of Jean Martineau. For some reason or other, the Norwegian doesn't want anyone to know he owns the schooner . . . cheers!'

Célestin shrugged, as if deeply disgusted by the entire business.

'Was Martineau in Fécamp on the 11th of September, when the sale took place?'

The others just frowned. Louis picked Célestin's quid up from the table and bit off his own chunk of tobacco while the deck-hand spattered the cabin floor with great spurts of brown spittle.

There was a lull in the conversation because the wick of the lamp was charring for lack of fuel. Lannec had to fetch more from the can on deck and returned soaked through. The others sat for a minute in darkness, and when the lamp was relit none of them had moved.

'Martineau was there, I'm sure of it! The boat was purchased in Big Louis' name, and Lannec was to stay aboard, perhaps permanently, perhaps only for a while.'

'For a while . . .'

'Right! I thought so. Long enough to captain the *Saint-Michel* on a most unusual voyage.'

Lannec got to his feet in such agitation that he chewed through his cigarette.

'You came to Ouistreham. On the night of the 16th, the schooner was moored in the outer harbour, ready to head out to sea. Where was Martineau?'

The captain sat down again, still distressed but determined to keep silent.

'On the morning of the 17th, the *Saint-Michel* sails. Who is aboard? Is Martineau still there? Is Joris there too?'

Maigret did not seem like a judge or even a police officer. His voice was still pleasant; there was a glint of mischief in his eyes. It was as if he were playing a game of riddles with his companions.

'You sail to England. Then you set a course for Holland. Is that where Joris and Martineau leave you? Because they have further to go. I have good reasons to believe they go all the way up to Norway.'

Big Louis grunted at that.

'What did you say?'

'That you'll never get anywhere.'

'Was Joris already wounded when he came aboard? Was he injured during your voyage, or only up in Scandinavia?'

He no longer waited for replies.

'All three of you continue your business as usual. You stick close to the northern coast. You're waiting for a letter or telegram informing you of a rendezvous. Last week, you were in Fécamp, the port where Martineau met you the first time. Big Louis learns that Captain Joris has been found in Paris, in a bad way, and will be brought home to Ouistreham. He travels here by train. There is no one in the captain's cottage. He leaves a note for his sister. He returns to Fécamp.'

Maigret sighed, took his time lighting his pipe.

'And here we are! Getting close to the end. You return with Martineau and set him ashore at the entrance to the harbour, which proves he did not want to be seen. Big Louis joins him on the dredger . . . cheers!'

He poured his own drink and drained his glass under the mournful gaze of the three men.

'In a nutshell, the only thing left in order to make sense of everything is to discover why Big Louis went to the mayor's house while Martineau was speeding off to Paris. A bizarre mission: thumping silly a man with the reputation of not suffering common folk lightly.'

Big Louis couldn't help grinning angelically at the memory of his punching sessions.

'There you have it, my friends! Now, try to get it through your skulls that the whole truth will come out in the end. The sooner the better, don't you think?'

And Maigret knocked out his pipe against his shoe, refilled it and started all over.

Célestin had fallen deeply asleep. He was snoring, open-mouthed. Big Louis, his head tipped to one side, was looking at the dirty floor, while Lannec tried in vain to catch his eye and solicit some advice.

At last the captain muttered, 'We have nothing to say.'

There was a noise up on deck. As if a rather heavy object had fallen. Maigret started; Big Louis stuck his head out of the hatchway, leaving nothing to see except his legs on the ladder.

If he had disappeared up on to the deck, the inspector would no doubt have followed him. There was nothing to hear besides the hammering of the rain and some creaking blocks.

This pause lasted for half a minute, no more. Big Louis came back down, his hair plastered to his forehead by the rain streaming down his cheeks, but at first offered no explanation.

'What was it?'

'A pulley block.'

'How . . . ?'

'Banged into the bulwarks.'

The captain replenished the stove. Did he believe what Louis had just said? In any case, instead of responding to his pleading looks, Louis was shaking Célestin.

'Go and rig the mizzen sheet . . .'

The old man rubbed his eyes, still drowsy. The order was

repeated twice more. Then he donned his oilskins and sou'wester and climbed the ladder, stiff with the comfort of recent sleep and angry at being sent out into the cold and rain. He wore clogs that clattered up and down the deck, over their heads.

Big Louis poured himself what was at least his sixth glass, yet he showed no signs of intoxication.

His face was always the same: uneven, a trifle bloated, with big eyes that almost bulged from his head. He seemed to be a man plodding glumly through life.

'What do you think, Louis?'

'About what?'

'Idiot! Have you thought about the fix you're in? Don't you understand that you're the one who'll get it in the neck? Your record, first of all. An ex-convict! Then this schooner you now own even though you haven't a sou to your name. Joris barred you from his house because you'd sponged off him too often! The *Saint-Michel*, here in Ouistreham the evening he vanished. You were here the day he was poisoned . . . And your sister then inherits three hundred thousand francs!'

Did Big Louis have a single thought in his head? His eyes were as vacant as could be. China-doll eyes, staring absently at the wall.

'What's he doing up there?' asked Lannec anxiously, looking over at the half-open hatch. Rainwater was pooling on the floor.

Maigret had not had a lot to drink, albeit enough to bring the blood to his head, especially in that stuffy cabin. And enough to inspire a moment of reverie.

Now that he knew the three men, he could imagine their lives in the world of the *Saint-Michel*.

The one man in his bunk, fully dressed most of the time. Always a bottle and some dirty glasses on the table. At least one man on deck; the comings and goings of his clogs or boots . . . Then that dull, steady sound of the sea . . . The compass in the binnacle with its tiny light . . . The other lamp, swaying up on the mizzen-mast . . .

Eyes peering into the darkness, hunting for the firefly gleam of the lighthouse . . . And the loading docks . . . Two or three days with nothing to do, spending hours in bistros that are everywhere the same . . .

Strange noises were heard overhead. Was Big Louis also sinking into a deep slumber? A small alarm-clock showed it was already three o'clock. The bottle was almost gone . . .

Lannec yawned, felt around in his pockets for some cigarettes.

Hadn't the ship's company spent the night this way, in this same hothouse atmosphere smelling of close quarters and coal tar, on the day Captain Joris had disappeared? And had the captain been among them then, drinking, struggling against drowsiness?

This time, voices were heard on deck, although the tempest reduced them to a whisper down in the cabin.

Maigret stood up with a frown, saw Lannec pouring himself another drink, saw Big Louis' chin touching his chest and his eyes half closed.

He felt for the revolver in his pocket and climbed the almost vertical ladder.

The hatchway was exactly big enough for a man, and the inspector was much taller and bulkier than the average sailor.

So he couldn't even fight back! Hardly had his head emerged from the hatchway when a gag was placed over his mouth and tied behind his neck.

That was the work of the men on deck, Célestin and someone else.

Meanwhile, down below, the revolver was torn from his right hand and his wrists were bound behind him.

He kicked violently back with his foot and hit something that felt to him like a face, but an instant later a rope coiled around his legs.

'Heave ho!' said the flat, indifferent voice of Big Louis.

That was the hard part. He was heavy. He was pushed from below; pulled from above.

The rain was coming down like a waterfall. The wind was blasting up the channel with unbelievable force.

He thought he saw four silhouettes, but the ship's lantern had been put out, and the passage from warmth and light to freezing night had bewildered his senses.

'One . . . Two . . . And away!'

They swung him over like a sack. He sailed fairly high and landed on the wet stones of the quay.

Louis went over after him and bent down to make sure all his bonds were tight. For a moment the inspector had the ex-convict's face quite close to his and had the impression the man was reluctantly carrying out a sad duty.

'You got to tell my sister . . .' he began.

Tell her what? Louis himself didn't know. Aboard the *Saint-Michel* there were hasty footsteps, creaking, grinding sounds, muttered orders. The jibs were unfurled. The mainsail rose slowly up the mast.

'Remember, you must tell her, I'll see her again one day . . . And maybe you, too.'

He jumped heavily back on deck. Maigret was lying facing out to sea. A lantern on a halyard ran up to the masthead. There was a black figure by the tiller.

'Cast off!'

The mooring rope snaked off the bollards, hauled in from the boat. The jibs snapped in the wind for an instant or two . . . The bow paid off, and the schooner almost swung completely around, so ferociously was she attacked by the storm.

But no – a heave on the tiller brought her into the wind's eye. She hesitated, seeking her way and, heeling over, shot suddenly between the jetties.

A black mass in the blackness. A tiny dot of light on the deck. Another, on high, at the masthead, already seemed like a star wandering lost in a whirlwind sky.

Maigret could not move. He lay inert, in a puddle, at the edge of infinite space.

Out there, wouldn't they buck themselves up by polishing off that bottle? A few more briquettes would go into the fire.

One man at the tiller; the others in the damp bunks.

Perhaps there was one salty drop among the pearly ones streaming down the inspector's face.

A big, powerful man, in the prime of life, perhaps the most dignified and manly officer of the Police Judiciare, abandoned there until dawn, at the end of a harbour quay, next to a bollard.

Had he been able to turn around, he would have seen the small wooden awning of the Buvette de la Marine, now closed for the night.

11. The Black Cow Shoal

The sea was draining away fast. Maigret heard the surf at the end of the breakwaters at first, then further out as the sand of the beach was laid bare.

With the ebb tide, the wind eased, as almost always happens. The piercing rain lost some of its sting. By the time the lowest-lying clouds were paling at the approach of day, the deluges of the night had become a light but even more chilling rain.

Objects were gradually emerging from their inky shrouds. The slanting masts of fishing boats now stranded at low tide stuck up above the mudflats of the outer harbour.

Off inland, the distant lowing of a cow. The church bell ringing gently, discreetly, to announce the low mass at seven o'clock.

But he would have to wait a while longer. Any churchgoers would not be passing through the harbour. The lock workers would have no business there before high tide. Only a fisherman, perhaps, might show up . . . But did fishermen bother getting out of bed in such weather?

Maigret, now a sodden heap, thought about all the beds in Ouistreham, the sturdy wooden beds with their enormous down quilts, beds where everyone was snuggling lazily in the warmth of their covers, peeking out resentfully at the blanching window panes and granting themselves a tiny respite before sticking their bare feet down on the floor.

Was Sergeant Lucas in bed, too? No! Because in that case, what had just happened was inexplicable.

The inspector had reconstructed those events this way: Jean Martineau had somehow managed to get rid of Lucas. Why not by tying him up, as he had with Maigret himself? The Norwegian then went straight to the *Saint-Michel*, where, hearing Maigret's voice, he waited patiently for someone to appear. Then Big Louis stuck his head out the hatch. Martineau whispered instructions to him or showed him a note he had written.

The rest was simple. There had been that noise up on deck. Louis sent Célestin up from the cabin. Martineau and the old sailor talked, luring Maigret up to investigate.

And when he was halfway there, the team on deck silenced him while those below immobilized his arms and legs.

By now the schooner must have been well outside the three-mile limit for territorial waters. Unless she were to put in at a French port, which wasn't likely, Maigret had no way to intercept her.

Maigret kept still. He had noticed that every time he moved, a little water crept in under his overcoat.

He had one ear on the ground and began identifying the successive sounds he heard. He recognized the noise of the pump in Joris' garden: Julie was up! She must have been out in her clogs, pumping water for her morning ablutions. But she would not come into town. Day hadn't properly dawned yet, so her kitchen light would be on.

Footsteps . . . A man was crossing the bridge . . . Stepping on to the stone wall . . . Walking slowly . . . He threw something that sounded like a bundle of ropes from the top of the quay into a dinghy.

A fisherman? Maigret struggled to change his position and saw the man, twenty metres away, about to go down the iron jetty ladder to the water. In spite of his gag, he managed to make muffled cries.

Looking around, the fisherman spied the black heap and stared at it suspiciously for a long time. At last he made up his mind to draw closer.

'What're you doing there?'

And having vaguely remembered what precautions to take at

a crime scene, he added cautiously, 'Mebbe I'd best go fetch the police first.'

He did remove the gag, however. The inspector negotiated with him, and the man, still somewhat dubious, began to untie the bonds, muttering curses at whoever had tied such knots.

The waitress over at the bar was just opening the shutters. Even though the wind had fallen, the sea was still running high, but the waves were no longer thundering in as they had during the night. There were massive swells that rose up over the sandbanks to crest at least three metres and more in waves that crashed in a dull boom, as if the whole continent were being shaken.

The fisherman was a little old man with a bushy beard who remained leery of the situation but unsure of what to do.

'The local police still need to know . . .'

'But I keep telling you: I am a kind of plain-clothes police officer!'

'A plain-clothes police officer,' repeated the old fellow hesitantly.

The old salt's eyes turned naturally to the sea, swept along the horizon, stopped at a point to the right of the jetties, off towards Le Havre, then fixed their appalled gaze on Maigret.

'What's the matter with you?'

The man was too upset to reply, and Maigret only understood why after looking out to sea himself.

The bay at Ouistreham was almost completely high and dry. The sand, the colour of ripe wheat, stretched out for more than a mile, to the purling, pure white surf.

And to the right of the jetty, not more than a kilometre away, was a vessel stranded half on the sand, half in the water, which was attacking the hull like a battering ram.

Two masts, one of them bearing a square lantern. A Paimpol schooner. It was the *Saint-Michel*.

In that direction, sky and sea were indistinguishable, an expanse of greyish-white.

Nothing else there but the black hulk of the beached ship.

'Must've tried leaving too late after the tide turned,' murmured the stunned fisherman.

'Does that happen often?'

'At times . . . Not water enough in the gat! And that Orne current drove her on to Black Cow shoal.'

There was a silent sense of desolation, made even more forlorn by the drizzle in the air. Seeing the schooner almost completely beached, however, it was hard to imagine that her company had been in any real danger.

When she had set out, though, the sea had still been breaking at the foot of the dunes, adding at least ten battle lines of massive swells.

'Got to tell the harbourmaster . . .'

A small detail. The old man turned automatically towards Joris' cottage, then mumbled, 'Except that . . .'

And he walked off in the opposite direction. The wreck had been spotted by others, now, perhaps from the church porch, for Captain Delcourt arrived looking as if he had dressed in a hurry, followed by three other men.

Delcourt shook hands distractedly with Maigret without noticing that the inspector was rather wet.

'I told them!'

'They'd let you know they were leaving?'

'Well, it's just that when I saw them tie up down here, I had the feeling they wouldn't wait for the next tide. I warned the skipper to watch out for that current.'

Everyone was walking out on to the beach. The wet sand made it heavy going, and there were pools of water thirty centimetres deep. It was a long slog.

'Are the crew in danger?' asked Maigret.

'I doubt they're still aboard. Otherwise, they'd have hoisted the distress flag, tried to signal for help . . . But, wait a minute,' he exclaimed, suddenly uneasy. 'They didn't have their dinghy along! You remember? When the steamer brought it in, we kept it in the dock.'

'So?'

'So they must have had to swim to shore . . . Or . . .'

Delcourt was worried. Certain things bothered him.

'I'm surprised they didn't prop her up, keep her from heeling over . . . Unless she went right over when she grounded on the shoal. But still . . .'

They approached the *Saint-Michel*, and she was a sorry sight. They could see her keel, thick with green under-water paint, and the barnacles encrusting her hull. Sailors were already examining the schooner for any damage, but finding none.

'An ordinary grounding.'

'Nothing serious?'

'It means that at the next tide a tug will probably get her out of there. But what I don't understand is . . .'

'What don't you understand?'

'Why they abandoned her! It's not like them to cut and run. They know the schooner's rock-solid. Look how stoutly she's made! . . . Hey! Jean-Baptiste! Fetch me a ladder!'

The tilting hull still put the bulwark rail more than six metres above the sand.

'No need!'

A snapped shroud was hanging down. Jean-Baptiste used it to clamber up the ship's side like a monkey, then swing over the deck and drop down to it. A few minutes later, he lowered a ladder.

'No one aboard?'

'Not a soul.'

Several kilometres further along the coast they could see the houses of Dives, factory chimneys, then Cabourg and Houlgate, not quite as clearly, and the rocky point concealing Deauville and Trouville.

Maigret climbed up the ladder out of a sense of duty, but he felt unpleasantly dizzy on the sloping deck. An anxious vertigo worse than if the ship had been tossing on a furious sea!

In the cabin, broken glass on the floor, the cupboard doors hanging open . . .

And the harbourmaster didn't know what he should do about all this. He was not the captain of the ship! Should he take responsibility for refloating her and send to Trouville for a tug to heave her off?

'If she goes through another tide she'll be kindling!' he muttered.

'Well, then, do everything possible to save her. You can say that I'm the one who decided . . .'

There was a mournful sense of foreboding in the quiet scene. All eyes kept turning towards the deserted dunes as if expecting to see the *Saint-Michel*'s crew.

Men and children were coming out from the village now. When Maigret returned to the harbour, Julie ran up to him.

'Is it true? Have they been wrecked?'

'No. They ran aground. A strong young man like your brother will surely have pulled through.'

'Where is he?'

The whole affair was ominous, disturbing. The owner of the Hôtel de l'Univers came out to hail Maigret.

'Your two friends haven't come down yet. Should I wake them?'

'Don't bother.'

The inspector went upstairs himself to Lucas' room and found his sergeant almost as tightly bound as Maigret had been.

'There's an explanation . . .'

'Don't need one! Come on.'

'Something's happened? You're all wet . . . And you look exhausted.'

Maigret took him along to the post office, at the highest spot in the village, opposite the church. People were standing out on their doorsteps. Those who could go were dashing down to the beach.

'No chance to defend yourself?' asked Maigret.

'We were going upstairs, and that's where he jumped me. He was behind me, then suddenly pulled my legs out from under me, and the rest was so fast I couldn't fight back. Have you seen him?'

Maigret was causing quite a stir for he appeared to have spent the night up to his neck in water. He couldn't even write his messages in the post office. He was soaking the paper.

'Take the pen, Lucas. Telegrams to all the police stations and town halls in the district: Dives, Cabourg, Houlgate. Those on this side as well: Luc-sur-Mer, Lion . . . Check the map: include even the smallest villages up to ten kilometres inland.

'Four descriptions: Big Louis; Martineau; Captain Lannec; the old sailor answering to the name of Célestin.

'After you've sent the telegrams, call the closest local places, that'll save us some time.'

He left Lucas dealing with his phone and wire assignments.

In a bistro across from the post office, he gulped down a steaming grog while some kids outside pressed their noses to the windows, trying to get a look at him.

Ouistreham was awake now, a nervous, worried village that gazed or hurried towards the sea. And news was travelling . . . Distorted, exaggerated news.

Out on the road, Maigret ran into the old fisherman who had freed him at daybreak.

'You didn't say anything about . . .'

'I said that I found you,' replied the man with indifference.

The inspector gave him twenty francs and returned to the hotel to change. He was shivering all over, felt both hot and cold. He had a bristly growth of beard and great circles under his eyes.

In spite of his fatigue, though, his brain was at work. Even more than usual. He managed to notice everything around him, to question and answer people without losing his train of thought.

When he returned to the post office, it was almost nine o'clock. Lucas was just completing his list of phone calls. The telegrams had already been sent. In reply to his questions, every police station was reporting no sign yet of the four wanted men.

'Monsieur Grandmaison hasn't made any calls, mademoiselle?'

'One hour ago. To Paris.'

She gave him the number. He looked in the phone book: a boys' school, the Collège Stanislas.

'Does the mayor often call that number?'

'Rather often. I think it's his son's boarding school.'

'It's true, he does have a son . . . Of about fifteen, yes?'

'I believe, but I've never seen him.'

'Has Monsieur Grandmaison called Caen?'

'It was Caen that called him. Someone in his family or one of his employees, because the call came from his house there.'

The telegraph was clicking. A message for the harbourmaster: 'Tug Athos arriving noon. Signed: Trouville Harbourmaster's Office.'

And the Caen police phoned in at last.

'Madame Grandmaison arrived in Caen at four in the morning. She slept at her home in the Rue du Four. She has just left by car for Ouistreham.'

When Maigret looked out at the beach from the harbour, the sea had retreated so far that the stranded boat was about halfway between the water and the dunes. Captain Delcourt was morose. Everyone was watching the horizon with dread.

Because there could be no mistake. The wind had fallen with the tide, but the storm would return with a vengeance around noon, when the tide turned. That much was clear from the unhealthy grey colour of the sky and the treacherous green of the waves.

'Has anyone seen the mayor?'

'He had his maid inform me that he is ill,' replied Delcourt, 'and that he's leaving me in charge of the rescue operation.'

Maigret headed wearily towards the villa with his hands in his pockets. He rang. It was almost ten minutes before the door opened.

The maid tried to speak but he did not listen, walking into the front hall with such a determined expression that she decided simply to hurry ahead to the study door.

'It's the inspector!' she cried.

Maigret entered the room he was beginning to know so well, tossed his hat on to a chair, nodded to the man stretched out in his armchair.

The bruises of the previous day were much more visible, having turned from red to blue. An enormous coal fire was burning in the fireplace.

One look told Maigret that the mayor intended to say nothing and even to ignore his visitor.

Maigret did the same. He removed his overcoat and went to stand with his back to the fire, like a man intent only on warming himself. The flames felt good on his calves. He smoked his pipe in short, hurried puffs.

'Before the day is over, this whole affair will be resolved!' he finally said, as if musing to himself.

The other man made an effort not to react. He even picked up a newspaper lying within reach and pretended to read it.

'We might, for example, be obliged to go to Caen together.'

'To Caen?'

Monsieur Grandmaison had looked up with a frown.

'To Caen, yes! I should have told you earlier, which would have spared Madame Grandmaison the trouble of coming here for nothing.'

'I don't see what my wife—'

'Has to do with all this!' broke in Maigret. 'Neither do I!'

And he went over to the desk for some matches to relight his pipe.

'It isn't important anyway,' he continued in a lighter tone, 'since it'll all be cleared up soon. By the way, do you know who the current owner of the *Saint-Michel* is, which Delcourt will be attempting to refloat? . . . Big Louis! Except that he's obviously a straw man, acting on behalf of a certain Martineau.'

The mayor was trying to see where Maigret was going with this, but had no intention of talking or – above all – asking him any questions.

'You'll see the chain of events here. Big Louis buys the *Saint-Michel* as a cat's paw for this Martineau five days before Captain Joris disappeared. The schooner is the only boat that left Ouistreham soon after that disappeance, and she went on to England and Holland before returning to France. From Holland, there must be coasters of the same type making regular runs to Norway . . . Martineau happens to be Norwegian. And before turning up in Paris, with a cracked and repaired skull, Captain Joris went to Norway.'

The mayor was listening closely.

'That isn't all. Martineau returns to Fécamp to rejoin the *Saint-Michel*. Big Louis, who is his factotum, is here a few hours before Joris' death. The *Saint-Michel* arrives a little later, with Martineau. And last night, he tries to make a run for it, taking with him most of the men I asked to remain at the disposal of the judicial authorities . . . Except you!'

Maigret paused, and sighed.

'What's still unclear is why Martineau returned and tried to reach Paris, and why you telephoned your wife to have her rush back here.'

'I hope you're not insinuating . . .'

'Me? Not a bit. Listen! There's a car coming. I bet it's Madame

Grandmaison arriving from Caen. Would you do me the favour of not telling her anything?'

The doorbell. The maid's footsteps in the hall. The sounds of low voices in conversation, then the maid's face looking in through the half-open door. But why wasn't she saying anything? Why such anxious looks at the master of the house?

'Well?' said he, impatiently.

'It's just that . . .'

Maigret pushed her aside and saw no one in the hall but the uniformed chauffeur.

'You've lost Madame Grandmaison en route?' he demanded bluntly.

'Well . . . Well, she . . .'

'Where did she get out of the car?'

'At the crossroads linking Caen and Deauville. She did not feel well.'

In his study, the mayor was on his feet, breathing heavily. The look on his face was grim.

'Wait for me!' he shouted to the chauffeur.

And finding his way blocked by Maigret's massive form, he hesitated.

'I suppose you're ready to confess . . .'

'Everything. You're right. *We* must go there together.'

12. The Unfinished Letter

The car stopped at a bare crossroads. The chauffeur looked back over his shoulder for instructions. Ever since leaving Ouistreham, Monsieur Grandmaison had not been the same man.

On his home ground he had always managed to control himself, trying to maintain his dignity even under the most distressing circumstances.

Not any more! He was now in a state close to panic, which his battered face made even more obvious. His restless gaze roamed constantly around the passing countryside.

When the car stopped, he looked at Maigret expectantly, but the inspector simply asked, with quiet mischief, 'What shall we do now?'

Not a soul on the road or in the orchards nearby. Madame Grandmaison had clearly not left her car intending to sit down by the roadside. If she had sent her chauffeur on, after alighting there, it was because she was meeting someone or had suddenly seen a person with whom she wished to speak in private.

The trees were dripping with rain. The air smelled strongly of damp earth. Cows stared at the car, chewing their cud . . .

The mayor peered all around, perhaps expecting to spot his wife behind a hedge or tree trunk.

'Look closely!' said Maigret, as if training a rookie.

There were some recognizable tracks on the road to Dives. A vehicle had stopped there, had some trouble turning around on the narrow road and driven off again.

'An old van. Let's go, driver!'

They did not drive far. Well before Dives, the tracks vanished near a stony side road. Monsieur Grandmaison was still tense, his eyes glittering with both anxiety and hatred.

'What do you think?'

'There's a small village that way, about five hundred metres on.'

'In which case, we'd best leave the car here.'

Exhaustion gave Maigret a look of inhuman indifference. He was literally asleep on his feet. He seemed to advance thanks only to his own momentum. Anyone watching them walk along that road would have thought the mayor was in charge, and the inspector, some underling following placidly in his wake.

They passed a little house surrounded by chickens, where a woman stared at the two men in amazement. Then they arrived at the back of a church not much bigger than a thatched cottage and, to the left, a tobacconist's shop.

'You don't mind?' asked Maigret, bringing out his empty pouch.

He stepped inside the little shop, which sold groceries and all sorts of household items. An elderly man emerged from a room with a vaulted ceiling and summoned his daughter to bring Maigret his tobacco. While the door was open, the inspector glimpsed a wall telephone.

'At what time did my friend come here to place a call this morning?'

'A good hour ago,' replied the girl promptly.

'So the lady has arrived?'

'Oh, yes. She even came in here for directions. They're not complicated, it's the last house, the lane on the right.'

Maigret left, still moving like a sleepwalker. He found Monsieur Grandmaison standing in front of the church, looking all around in a manner certain to arouse the suspicions of the entire village.

'It occurs to me,' murmured Maigret, 'that we should split up. You search off to the left, by the fields, while I look on the right.'

He caught a gleam of delight in the man's eye. The mayor could not hide his hope of finding his wife on his own and talking privately with her.

'Good idea,' he replied, feigning indifference.

The hamlet consisted of no more than twenty poky little houses that clumped together enough in one area to give the illusion of a street, which did not prevent real manure from piling up there. It was still raining, a rain so fine it was almost a mist, and no one was outdoors. Curtains were twitching, however. One could just imagine, behind them, the usual wrinkled old women peering out from their dimly lit homes.

At the very end of the hamlet, in front of the fenced-in meadow where two horses were galloping around, there was a single-storey building with a crooked roof and two front steps. Maigret looked back, heard the mayor's footsteps at the other end of the village, then walked into the house without knocking.

Something moved in the shadows that pressed in on the glowing hearth. A black shape; the white patch of an old woman's house cap.

She hobbled over, bent almost in two.

'What d'you want?'

The stuffy room smelled of straw, cabbage and chicken coops. There were even chicks pecking around by the fireplace.

Maigret's head almost touched the ceiling. Noticing a door at the far end of the room, he realized that speed was in order. Without a word, he marched over and opened the door: Madame Grandmaison was busy writing, with Jean Martineau standing next to her.

There was a moment of surprise and dismay. The woman rose from her straw-bottomed chair. Martineau's first impulse was to grab and crumple up her piece of paper. Both of them instinctively drew close together.

The cottage had only these two rooms, and this was the old woman's bedroom. On the whitewashed walls, two portraits and some cheap chromos in black-and-gold frames. A very high bed. The table where Madame Grandmaison had been writing was the wash stand, from which the basin had been set aside.

'Your husband will be here in a few minutes!' announced Maigret, by way of an introduction.

'Is that your doing?' demanded Martineau angrily.

'Hush, Raymond.'

She had used his first name – and called him not Jean, but Raymond. Reflecting on these details, Maigret went to listen briefly at the front door.

'Will you give me the letter you were writing?'

The couple looked at each other. Madame Grandmaison was pale and wan. Maigret had seen her once before, but only in the performance of her most sacred duties as a woman of her social standing: receiving guests at home.

At that time he had been impressed by her perfect performance and the conventional graciousness with which she could offer a cup of tea or respond to a compliment.

He had imagined her life: the cares of a household in Caen, the social occasions, the children's upbringing. Two or three months spent at health spas or luxury resorts. A certain level of vanity, but more concern about her dignity than her beauty.

Something of all that doubtless remained in the woman now before him, but there was a new element. She was in fact showing more sang-froid, even more raw nerve than her companion, who seemed on the verge of real collapse.

'Give him the paper,' she said, as Martineau was about to tear it up.

There was almost nothing on it.

Dear Headmaster,
Would you be kind enough to . . .

The large, backwards-sloping hand of every girl educated at boarding school at the turn of the century.

'You received two telephone calls this morning, didn't you? One from your husband . . . Or rather, you were the one who called, to tell him you would be arriving in Ouistreham. Then a call from Monsieur Martineau, asking you to come here. He had you picked up at the crossroads by a small van.'

Just then Maigret saw something he hadn't noticed before, on the table, behind the ink pot: a neat pile of thousand-franc bills.

Martineau followed his eyes . . . Too late to do anything! And too much for him: he collapsed in sudden lethargy on the edge of the old woman's bed and stared despondently at the floor.

'Are you the one who brought him that money?'

And once again, there was the same feeling that had marked this entire case. The same atmosphere as when Maigret had caught Big Louis beating the mayor in his villa in Ouistreham – and both men had refused to talk! The same atmosphere as when the crew of the *Saint-Michel* had refused to answer him the night before!

A fierce refusal, an absolute determination not to explain anything at all.

'I suppose this letter is addressed to the headmaster of a boarding school. Your son is at Stanislas, so the letter probably concerns him. As for the money . . . Of course! Martineau must have abandoned the grounded schooner to swim to shore, and in his hurry he probably left his wallet behind. You brought him some money so that—'

Maigret abruptly changed the subject, and his tone:

'And the others, Martineau? All safe and sound?'

The man hesitated, but could not keep himself, in the end, from blinking in affirmation.

'I won't ask you where they're hiding. I know you won't tell.'

'True!'

'*What's true?*'

Someone had just pushed the front door wide open. The outraged voice was the mayor's – and he was unrecognizable. Panting with anger, fists clenched, tensed to spring at the enemy, he glared at his wife, at Martineau, at the money still lying on the table.

But the menace in his eyes betrayed fear, too, and the dread of disaster.

'What's true? What did he say? What new lies is he telling? . . . And her? She's the one . . .'

Choking, he couldn't get the words out. Maigret watched, prepared to intervene.

'What's true? What's going on! . . . Are they plotting something? . . . And whose money is that?'

The old woman was bustling about in the front room, calling her chickens to the door.

'Here, chick-chick! Chick-chick!'

The scattered corn clattered softly down on the bluestone steps. A neighbour's hen was fended off with a foot.

'G'won home with you, Blackie . . .'

In the bedroom, nothing. Heavy silence. As pallid and depressing as the sky that rainy morning.

People possessed by fear. Because they were afraid! All of them! Martineau, the woman, the mayor . . . It was as if each one of them were alone with that fear . . . Each one afraid in a different way!

Then Maigret spoke slowly and solemnly, like a judge.

'I have been instructed by the public prosecutor to find and arrest the murderer of Captain Joris, wounded by a bullet to the head and, six weeks later, poisoned in his bed with strychnine. Does anyone here wish to make a statement regarding this crime?'

Until that moment, no one had noticed that the room was unheated. Yet suddenly, they felt cold . . . Each syllable had rung out as if in a church. The words still seemed to linger in the air.

Poisoned . . . Strychnine . . .

Especially Maigret's last question.

Does anyone here wish to make a statement? . . .

Martineau was the first to hang his head. Madame Grandmaison, her eyes gleaming, kept looking back and forth between him and her husband.

But no one said a thing. No one dared face the look in Maigret's eyes, which seemed to grow darker.

Two minutes . . . Three minutes . . . The old woman put a few logs on the fire in the next room.

Then Maigret's voice, again, deliberately curt and stripped of all emotion.

'In the name of the law, Jean Martineau, I arrest you.'

A woman's scream. Madame Grandmaison flung herself desperately at Martineau but fell in a faint almost at the same instant.

With a savage look, the mayor turned towards the wall.

And Martineau heaved a sigh of weary resignation, not daring even to go to help the unconscious woman.

It was Maigret who bent down to her, then looked around for the water jug from the wash stand.

He went to ask the old woman for some vinegar, the smell of which now mingled with the already complex odour of the cottage.

A few moments later Madame Grandmaison came to, and, after a few uncontrollable sobs, sank into an almost complete state of prostration.

'Do you think you can walk?'

She nodded. She could walk, but in a jolting, uneven way.

'You will follow me, gentlemen, will you not? I trust that I may count, *this time*, on your compliance?'

The old woman watched them cross her kitchen in some consternation. Only after they were outside did she rush to the door.

'You're coming back for lunch, then, Monsieur Raymond?'

Raymond! It was the second time he had been called that. The man shook his head.

The four of them walked on through the village. Martineau stopped in front of the little shop, hesitated, and turned to Maigret.

'Please forgive me, but as I'm not sure I'll ever return here, I don't wish to leave any unpaid debts behind. I owe these people for a phone call, a grog and a pack of cigarettes.'

It was Maigret who paid. They walked around the church and at the end of the stony road found the car waiting for them. After telling them all to get in, the inspector paused to think before speaking to the driver.

'To Ouistreham. There you will stop first at the police station.'

The journey took place in complete silence. Rain still fell from a sky of solid grey as a freshening wind shook the dripping trees.

Outside the police station, Maigret had Martineau get out and gave instructions to Lucas.

'Keep him in the lock-up. You're responsible for him! Anything new here?'

'The tug's arrived. They're waiting for the tide to come in.'

The car drove away. When they swung by the harbour, Maigret made another short stop.

It was noon. The lock workers were at their posts, because a steamer was due in from Caen. The strip of sand along the beach had narrowed and the foaming waves were almost licking at the dunes.

On the right, a crowd watched a fascinating spectacle: the tug from Trouville was anchored not 500 metres off the coast. A dinghy was fighting its way over to the *Saint-Michel*, now half righted with the incoming tide.

Maigret noticed that the mayor was also watching the drama, from inside the car. Then Captain Delcourt came out of the bar.

'Will it work?' asked Maigret.

'I think we'll save her. For the last two hours we've been lightening her, removing ballast. If we can keep her from breaking adrift . . .'

And he looked up at the sky as if reading the vagaries of the wind on a map.

'It's just that we have to finish before the tide turns again.'

Glimpsing the mayor and his wife inside their car, he nodded to them deferentially, then gave Maigret a questioning look.

'Anything new?'

'Don't know.'

Lucas was approaching, and he did have news, but he drew his chief aside before delivering it.

'We've got Big Louis.'

'What?'

'He slipped up! This morning the police in Dives found tracks through some fields. The footsteps of a man walking straight ahead and clambering over the hedgerows. The trail led to the Orne, to the place where a fisherman kept his rowing boat hauled up on the bank. Except that the boat was on the other side of the river.'

'The officers followed him?'

'Yes, and came to the beach, more or less opposite the *Saint-Michel*. At the edge of the dunes over there is a—'

'Ruined chapel!'

'You already know?'

'Notre-Dame-des-Dunes.'

'Right. They nabbed Big Louis there. He was holed up, watching the salvage operation. When I arrived he was begging the officers not to take him away yet, so that he could watch from the beach until the job was done. I gave permission. He's still there, in handcuffs. And shouting instructions! He's afraid they'll lose his boat . . . Don't you want to see him?'

'I don't know . . . maybe, in a little while.'

For the Grandmaisons were still waiting in the car.

'You think we'll ever get to the bottom of this?'

No reply.

'Personally,' continued Lucas, 'I'm beginning to think we won't. They're all liars! And the ones who aren't lying won't talk, even though they know something! It's as if everyone around here were responsible for Joris' death . . .'

But the inspector simply shrugged and walked away muttering, 'See you later . . .'

Back in the car, he surprised the chauffeur by telling him, 'Back to the house, now,' as if he were speaking of his own home.

'The house in Caen?'

To tell the truth, the inspector hadn't meant that, but the chauffeur had given him an idea.

'Yes, in Caen!'

Monsieur Grandmaison scowled. His wife, though, could not react at all. She seemed to be allowing events to carry her along and offered not the slightest resistance.

Between the city gates and Rue du Four, a good fifty hats were doffed. Everyone appeared to recognize Monsieur Grandmaison's car. And the greetings were respectful. The ship-owner was like a nobleman travelling through his domain.

'A simple formality,' said Maigret casually when they arrived at the house. 'Please excuse me for having brought you here, but as I mentioned this morning, this affair must be resolved by tonight.'

A calm street, lined with imposing mansions of a kind found only in the provinces these days. The house, its stones dark with age, was fronted by a courtyard. And on the gate was a brass plaque with the name of the family's shipping company.

Inside the courtyard, a sign with an arrow: 'Office'.

Another sign, another arrow: 'Cashier's Office'.

And one last notice. 'Office Hours: 9 a.m. to 4 p.m.'

It was shortly past noon. The drive from Ouistreham had taken only ten minutes. Most of the firm's employees had already left for lunch by then, but a few were still at their desks, in dark, solemn offices with thick carpets and heavy Louis-Philippe furniture.

'I will probably ask you later on to spare me a few moments of your time, madame, but for the moment, would you like to retire to your rooms?'

The entire ground floor was given over to offices. The vestibule was spacious, flanked with large cast-iron candelabra. A marble staircase led up to the first floor, where the family lived.

The mayor of Ouistreham was waiting gloomily for Maigret to deal with him.

'What is it you want from me?' he asked quietly.

He turned up his collar and jammed his hat down to keep his staff from seeing what Big Louis' fists had done to him.

'Nothing in particular. Simply permission to come and go, to get the feel of the house.'

'Do you need me for anything?'

'Not at all.'

'In that case, if I may, I will go and join Madame Grandmaison.'

His respectful reference to his wife was in sharp contrast with that morning's events in the old woman's cottage. After watching him vanish upstairs, Maigret went to the far end of the vestibule to make sure the building had only one exit.

Leaving the mansion, he found a local policeman and stationed him near the front gate.

'Got it? Let everyone leave, except Monsieur Grandmaison. Will you recognize him?'

'Well, of course! But, what's he done? A fine man like him . . . He's president of the chamber of commerce, you know!'

'So much the better!'

In the vestibule, an office on the right: 'Secretary'. Maigret knocked, pushed open the door, smelled a whiff of cigar, but saw no one.

The office on the left: 'Director'.

Again, the same resolutely solemn atmosphere, the same dark-red carpets, the gilt wallpaper, the elaborate ceiling mouldings.

The impression that within these walls, no one would dare to raise his voice. Dignified gentlemen in morning coats and striped trousers would smoke fat cigars and pontificate.

A solid business indeed! A well-established provincial firm, handed down from father to son for generations.

'Monsieur Grandmaison? His signature is as good as gold.'

And here was Maigret in his office, which was furnished in the opulent Empire style, more suitable for an important businessman. On the walls, statistical tables, graphs, colour-coded schedules, photographs of ships.

As he was walking around, his hands in his pockets, a door opened, and a rather anxious, white-haired old man popped his head in.

'What's the . . .'

'Police!' replied Maigret sharply, as if savouring the explosive effect of his words in that place.

And the old fellow went into a terrified dither.

'Don't worry, monsieur. Your employer has asked me to look into a few things. And you are . . .'

'The head cashier,' replied the man hastily.

'Then you would be the man who's been with the firm for . . . for . . .'

'Forty-two years. I began here in Monsieur Charles' time.'

'Right. And that's your office, next door? In short, you're now the one who runs everything, aren't you? At least that's what I hear . . .'

Maigret was sitting pretty. He had seen the house, and one look at this old man was all he needed.

'It's only natural, isn't it! When Monsieur Ernest is not here . . .'

'Monsieur Ernest?'

'Yes, well, Monsieur Grandmaison! I've known him since he was a boy, so I still call him Monsieur Ernest.'

Maigret had eased himself into the old man's office, a place devoid of luxury and apparently not open to outsiders. And here files and documents were piled up in profusion.

On a cluttered table, some sandwiches sitting on their butcher's paper. On the stove, a small steaming coffee pot.

'You even eat here, monsieur . . . Forgive me, I've gone and forgotten your name.'

'Bernardin. But everyone here calls me Old Bernard. As I live alone, there's no point in me going home for lunch like the others. In fact, is it about that small theft last week that Monsieur Ernest has called you in? . . . He should have spoken to me, because it's all sorted out now. A young man who'd taken two thousand francs, and his uncle has paid us back. The young man swore . . . Well, you know, at that age! . . . He'd fallen into some bad company.'

'We'll see about that presently. But do go on with your lunch . . . So, you were already Monsieur Charles' trusted lieutenant before being his son's.'

'I was the cashier. Back then there was no chief cashier – and I might even say that the position was created just for me!'

'Monsieur Ernest was an only son?'

'Yes. There was a daughter, married off to a businessman in Lille, but she died in childbirth along with her infant.'

'But what of Monsieur Raymond?'

The old man's head jerked up in surprise.

'Ah! Monsieur Ernest has told you?'

Old Bernard now seemed more on his guard.

'Wasn't he part of the family?'

'A cousin. A Grandmaison, but a poor relation. His father died out in the colonies. It happens in every family, doesn't it . . .'

'Indeed it does!' Maigret agreed readily.

'Monsieur Ernest's father more or less adopted him . . . That is, he found a place for him here . . .'

Maigret needed more information and dropped all pretence.

'One moment, Monsieur Bernard! I'd like to make sure I've got everything straight. The founder of the Anglo-Normande was Monsieur Charles Grandmaison, correct? Monsieur Charles Grandmaison had an only son, Monsieur Ernest, currently in charge.'

'Yes.'

The inspector's inquisitorial tone puzzled the old man, who was beginning to get worried.

'Good! Monsieur Charles had a brother who died in the colonies and who also had a son, Monsieur Raymond Grandmaison.'

'Yes, but I—'

'Just a moment! And go on with your lunch, please. This Monsieur Raymond, a penniless orphan, was taken in here by his uncle. A position was found for him in the firm. Which one, exactly?'

'Well,' replied the old man hesitantly, 'he was assigned to the freight department. As a kind of office manager.'

'Fine. Monsieur Charles Grandmaison died. Monsieur Ernest took over. Monsieur Raymond was still here.'

'Yes.'

'They quarrelled. One moment! Was Monsieur Ernest already married at the time?'

'I'm not sure that I should say anything.'

'I advise you strongly to cooperate if you don't want to have problems with the law, elderly though you may be.'

'The law! Has Monsieur Raymond returned?'

'Never mind that. Was Monsieur Ernest married?'

'No. Not yet.'

'Right. Monsieur Ernest was the boss. His cousin, Raymond, still an office manager. What happened?'

'I'm not sure I have the right . . .'

'I give you the right.'

'It's like this in every family. Monsieur Ernest was a responsible, reliable man, like his father. Even at the age when boys naturally rebel against authority, he was already as serious as he is now.'

'And Monsieur Raymond?'

'Quite the opposite!'

'And?'

'I'm the only one here who knows, aside from Monsieur Ernest. Some irregularities were discovered in the accounts . . . Involving large sums . . .'

'So?'

'Monsieur Raymond disappeared. That's to say, instead of having him arrested, Monsieur Ernest strongly advised him to go and live abroad.'

'In Norway?'

'I don't know. I never heard his name mentioned again.'

'Monsieur Ernest was married soon after that?'

'That's right. A few months later.'

The walls were lined with filing cabinets of a doleful green. The faithful old man was eating without any appetite, still worried, feeling guilty for letting the inspector worm information out of him.

'And how long ago was that?'

'Let me see . . . It was the year they widened the canal. Fifteen years ago, or just about.'

Footsteps had been going back and forth in the room above their heads for a few minutes now.

'The dining room?' asked Maigret.

'Yes.'

And then the footsteps overhead went faster . . . A dull thud – as a body fell to the floor.

Old Bernard was whiter than the butcher's paper on his desk.

13. The House Across the Street

Monsieur Grandmaison was dead. Lying across the carpet, his head near a table leg, his feet over by the window, he seemed enormous. Very little blood. The bullet had entered between two ribs and lodged in his heart.

As for the revolver, it lay next to his lifeless hand.

Madame Grandmaison was not weeping. She stood leaning against the monumental mantelpiece, staring at her husband as if she had not yet grasped what had happened.

'It's over,' said Maigret simply, and got to his feet.

A large room, sad and severe. Dark curtains at windows that let in a bleak light.

'Did he say anything to you?'

She shook her head, then made an effort to speak.

'Ever since we got home,' she stammered, 'he'd been pacing up and down. Several times he turned to me, and I thought he was going to tell me something . . . Then suddenly, the shot came – and I hadn't even seen the gun!'

She spoke as women do when they are profoundly shaken and struggling to make sense of their own thoughts, but her eyes were dry.

It was clear that she had never loved Grandmaison, at least not passionately. He was her husband. She was a dutiful wife. A kind of affection had sprung up as they'd grown used to living together.

But before his dead body, she displayed none of those wrenching emotions that betoken real love.

Instead, dazed and exhausted, she asked, 'Was it him?'

'It was.'

Then there was silence around the immense body bathed in harsh daylight. The inspector watched Madame Grandmaison. He saw her look out at the street, searching for something across the way, and a feeling of nostalgia seemed to soften her features.

'Would you allow me to ask you two or three questions before the others arrive?'

She nodded.

'Did you know Raymond before you met your husband?'

'I lived across the street.'

A grey house much like the one they were in. Above the front door, the brass plate of a notary.

'I loved Raymond. He loved me. His cousin was courting me as well, but in his own way.'

'Two quite different men, weren't they?'

'Ernest was already as you knew him. A cold man, who seemed never to have been young. Raymond, well, he had a bad reputation because his life was too big and wild to fit into the small-town mould. That and his lack of fortune were why my father did not want me to marry him.'

It was eerie, listening to these personal confessions murmured next to a corpse. They were like the dismal summing-up of a whole life.

'Were you Raymond's mistress?'

She blinked in affirmation.

'And he left?'

'Without telling a soul. One night. I learned about it from his cousin. Left with some of the company money.'

'And Ernest married you. Your son is not his, I take it?'

'He is Raymond's son. You see, when he left and I was on my own, I knew I was going to have a child. And Ernest was asking me to marry him. Look at these two houses, this street, this city where everyone knows everyone else.'

'You told Ernest the truth?'

'Yes. He married me anyway. The child was born in Italy; I stayed there for more than a year to avoid nasty gossip. I thought my husband had been a kind of hero . . .'

'And?'

She turned away: she had just caught sight of the body again.

'I don't know,' she sighed. 'I believe that he did love me,' she continued reluctantly, 'but after his own fashion. He wanted me. He got me. Can you understand? A man incapable of impulse, of spirit. Once married, he lived as before: for himself. I was part of his household. Somewhat like a trusted employee. I don't know if he received any news of Raymond later on, but when the boy came across a picture of him one day and asked Ernest about him, he simply said, "A cousin who turned out badly."'

Maigret seemed gripped by some profound concern, for it was a whole way of life he was attempting to piece together. More than that, it was the life of a family business, of the very family itself!

That life had lasted fifteen years! New steamships had been bought. There had been receptions in this very room, bridge parties and afternoon teas. There had been baptisms.

Summers at Ouistreham and in the mountains.

And now, Madame Grandmaison was so weary that she collapsed into an armchair, passing a limp hand over her face.

'I don't understand,' she stammered. 'This captain whom I never saw . . . You really think . . . ?'

Maigret turned away to listen, then went to open the door. The old man was on the landing, fearful but too deferential to enter the room. He looked searchingly at the inspector.

'Monsieur Grandmaison is dead. Call the family doctor. Do not announce the news to the employees and servants until later.'

He closed the door, almost took his pipe from his pocket and shrugged.

To his surprise, he felt growing respect and sympathy for this woman, who had struck him, the first time he had seen her, as an ordinary 'lady of the house'.

'Was it your husband, yesterday, who sent you to Paris?'

'Yes. I hadn't known that Raymond was in France. My husband simply asked me to get my son at Stanislas and spend a few days with him in the South of France. Although I thought this somewhat peculiar, I did as he asked, but when I arrived at the Hôtel de Lutèce, Ernest telephoned to ask me to return home without going on to the boarding school.'

'And this morning, Raymond called you here?'

'Yes, with an urgent request. He begged me to bring him a little money. He swore that our lives – all our lives – would otherwise be torn apart.'

'He did not accuse your husband of anything?'

'No. Back there, in the cottage, he never even mentioned him, but spoke of friends, a few seamen to whom he had to give some money so that they could leave the country. He spoke of some kind of shipwreck.'

The doctor arrived, a friend of the family who stared at the corpse in consternation.

'Monsieur Grandmaison has killed himself!' announced Maigret firmly. 'It is for you to discover what illness has carried him off. You understand me? And I will deal with the police . . .'

He went to take leave of Madame Grandmaison, who finally summoned the courage to say, 'You have not told me why . . .'

'Raymond will tell you one day. Ah, one last question. On the 16th of September, your son was in Ouistreham with your husband, was he not?'

'Yes. He stayed there until the 20th . . .'

Maigret bowed himself out, tramped downstairs and walked through the offices with drooping shoulders and a heavy heart.

Outdoors, he breathed more deeply and stood bareheaded in the rain, as if to refresh himself, to dispel the oppressive atmosphere of that house.

Turning, he took one last look up at the windows. Another at those across the street, where Madame Grandmaison had spent her youth.

A sigh.

'Come on!'

Maigret stood in the open door to the empty room where Raymond had been kept. He beckoned to him to follow, then led him out to the street and the road to the harbour.

Raymond was surprised and somewhat worried by this unexpected release.

'Haven't you anything to tell me?' grumbled Maigret with a show of irritation.

'No!'

'You won't defend yourself against the charges?'

'I'll keep telling the court that I haven't killed anyone!'

'But you won't tell the truth?'

Raymond hung his head.

They were beginning to catch glimpses of the sea and could hear the tug whistling as it moved towards the jetties, towing the *Saint-Michel* at the end of a steel cable.

It was then that Maigret announced impassively, as if it were the most natural thing in the world: 'Grandmaison is dead.'

'What? . . . What did you say?'

Raymond caught Maigret's arm in a fierce grip.

'He's . . . ?'

'He killed himself an hour ago, in his house.'

'Did he say anything?'

'No. He paced up and down his dining room for a quarter of an hour and then shot himself. That's it!'

They kept walking. In the distance they could see the excited crowd on the jetties, watching the salvage operation.

'So now you can tell me the truth, Raymond Grandmaison.

Besides, I already know the gist of it. You were trying to get your son back, weren't you!'

No reply.

'You had help from Captain Joris, among others. And unfortunately for him, as it turned out.'

'Don't say it! If you only knew . . .'

'Come this way, there will be fewer people.'

The narrow path led down to a deserted beach pounded by waves.

'Did you really take off with some of the company funds?'

'Is that what Hélène told you?' Now his voice was bitter. 'Yes . . . Ernest must have told her his own version of what happened . . . I'm not claiming to have been a saint, far from it! I was looking for a good time, as they say. And above all, at least for a while, I was enthralled by gambling. I won, I lost. Then came the day when, yes, I helped myself to some company money. My cousin found out.

'I promised to pay it back over time and pleaded with him to keep the whole thing quiet. He really did want to call in the police but agreed not to, on one condition: that I leave the country and never set foot in France again! You understand? He wanted Hélène . . . and he got her.'

Smiling sadly, Raymond was quiet for a few moments.

'Others head down south or out east, but I went north and set myself up in Norway. I never heard any news from home . . . The letters I wrote to Hélène went unanswered, and yesterday I learned that she'd never received them.

'I wrote to my cousin, too, with no more success.

'I won't pretend to be better than I am or try to make you feel sorry for me with a tale of unhappy love. No . . . In the beginning I didn't think much about it. There, you can see I'm being sincere! I was working, having all sorts of problems . . . But at night, I felt a kind of dull, aching nostalgia.

'There were disappointments . . . I started a business; it ended badly. For years I went through ups and downs in a country where I was an outsider.

'I'd changed my name there. To try tipping the scales in my favour as a businessman, I became a naturalized citizen as well.

'Now and then I'd entertain officers from some French ship, and that's how I discovered one day that I had a son.

'I wasn't sure! But when I thought about the dates . . . I couldn't stop thinking about it and wrote to Ernest. I begged him to tell me the truth, to let me come home to France, if only for a few days.

'He sent me a telegram: "Arrest at French border".

'Years went by; I was bent on making money. There's not much to say about that, except that there was a hollow place in my heart.

'In Tromsø there are three months of endless night every year. Regrets and longings grow sharper . . . Sometimes I would have attacks of hysterical rage.

'I set myself a goal: to become as rich as my cousin. And I did! Thanks to the cod roe business. But it was when I achieved this success that I felt the most miserable.

'Then suddenly, I came back here. I was determined to act. Yes! After fifteen years! I was looking around Ouistreham and . . . I saw my boy, on the beach. I saw Hélène, at a distance . . .

'And I wondered how I had ever managed to live without my son. Do you understand me?

'I bought a boat. If I had acted openly, my cousin would not have hesitated for a moment to have me arrested. Because he had kept all the evidence he needed!

'You saw the men helping me: good men, no matter what they look like. Everything was arranged.

'Ernest Grandmaison and the boy were alone in the house that night. To be even more certain of success, to increase the odds in my favour, I'd asked Captain Joris to help. I'd met him in Norway, when he was still going to sea. He knew the mayor and was to visit him under some pretext and distract him while Big Louis and I were spiriting my son away.

'And that – *that* was what caused the tragedy. While Joris was with my cousin in the study, Big Louis and I had come in through the back door, but unfortunately, we knocked over a broom in the corridor.

'Grandmaison heard the noise, thought someone was after him and got his revolver from the desk drawer.

'What happened next . . . I truly don't know, there was such confusion! Joris followed Grandmaison out to the corridor, which was completely dark. A shot – and of all the bad luck, Joris was hit!

'I was beside myself with anguish. I didn't want any scandal, especially for Hélène's sake. How could I have told that whole story to the police!

'Big Louis and I carried Joris aboard the *Saint-Michel*. He needed medical attention, so we headed for England and arrived there a few hours later. But we couldn't go ashore without passports! There were police officers and watchmen on the quay.

'I'd studied a little medicine once upon a time and did my best for Joris on the ship, but it was nowhere near enough. We set out for Holland. That's where the surgeons cleaned up the wound. The clinic could not keep him there, however, without informing the authorities.

'We sailed on, a ghastly voyage! Can you imagine us all on the ship, and Joris at death's door? He needed weeks of rest and care. I almost took him to Norway on the *Saint-Michel*, but then we encountered a schooner bound for the Lofoten islands. I moved Joris with me to that schooner; we were safer at sea than on land.

'He stayed a week at home with me in Tromsø. Again, though, people began to wonder who my mysterious guest was, and we had to set out again. Copenhagen, Hamburg . . . Joris was getting better; the wound had scarred over, but he'd lost his reason and was unable to speak.

'What could I do with him, I ask you? And wouldn't he stand a better chance of recovering his reason in his own home, in familiar surroundings, instead of while running from pillar to post?

'I wanted at least to secure his material comfort. I sent three hundred thousand francs to his bank, signing his name for deposit to his account.

'I still had to get him home! It was too risky for me to bring him here to Ouistreham myself. Releasing him in Paris . . . Would that not bring him inevitably to the attention of the police, who would identify him and send him home?

'And that's what happened. There was only one thing I couldn't have anticipated: that my cousin, terrified that Joris might one day reveal who'd shot him, would do away with the captain in that cowardly way.

'Because he is the one who put the strychnine in the water carafe. He simply went in the cottage through the back door when he was going off duck hunting.'

'And you got back to work,' said Maigret slowly.

'What else could I do! I wanted my son! But now my cousin was on his guard. The boy was back at Stanislas, beyond my reach.'

Maigret knew about that part. And now, looking around at the setting he had come to know so well, he understood more clearly what was at stake in the secret battle between the two men.

And not just between the two of them! A struggle against *him*, Maigret!

The police had to be kept in the dark, for neither one of the cousins could afford to tell the truth.

'I came here on the *Saint-Michel* . . .'

'I know! And you sent Big Louis to the mayor's house.'

Raymond couldn't help smiling as the inspector went on.

'A Big Louis primed for battle, who took revenge on Grandmaison for all the powerful men who'd persecuted him! He could pound him to his heart's content, knowing that his victim would never let out a peep to the police. He must have forced him to write a letter authorizing you to take the boy out of school.'

'Yes. I was behind the villa with your colleague on my heels. Big Louis left the letter in a pre-arranged spot, and I shook off your man. I took a bicycle; I bought a car in Caen. I had to move fast. While I was getting my son, Big Louis stayed with the mayor to keep him from alerting the school. A waste of time, as it turned out, since he'd already sent Hélène to pick up the boy ahead of me.

'Then you had me arrested.

'It was all over . . . I couldn't go after her while you were stubbornly digging up the truth.

'Our only recourse was to escape. If we stayed, you would inevitably work everything out.

'And that explains last night. Bad luck just wouldn't let us go . . . The schooner grounded on the shoal, and we had a hard time of it, swimming ashore. To cap it all, I lost my wallet.

'No money! The police on our track . . . All I could do was call Hélène to ask her for a few thousand francs, enough to get the four of us to the border . . . In Norway, I could pay my companions what I owed them. And Hélène came at once.

'But so did you! You, whom we constantly found blocking our way. You, relentless, to whom we could say nothing, whom I could hardly warn that you might provoke more harm through your inquiry!'

His eyes now betrayed a sudden misgiving, and in a faltering voice he asked:

'Did my cousin *really* kill himself?'

Had Maigret lied to him, perhaps, to induce him to speak?

'Yes, he did kill himself, when he realized that the truth would come out in the end. And he understood *that* when I arrested you. He guessed that I'd done that simply to give him time to think things over.'

The two men had been walking as they talked; now they stopped abruptly together on the jetty. The *Saint-Michel* was going slowly past, with an old fisherman proudly at the wheel.

Someone ran up, pushing his way roughly through the gawking crowd, the first man to leap on to the schooner's deck.

Big Louis!

He had given his captors the slip, snapped the chain between his handcuffs! Hustling the fisherman aside, he grabbed the wheel.

'Slow down, for God's sake!' he yelled to the men aboard the tug. 'You'll bash her up!'

'And the other two?' Maigret asked Raymond.

'This morning you passed within a metre of them. They're hiding out in the village, in the old woman's woodshed.'

Lucas was making his way through the crowd towards Maigret, looking surprised.

'Listen, we've got them!'

'Who?'

'Lannec and Célestin . . .'

'They're here?'

'The Dives police have just brought them in.'

'Well, tell them to let those two go. And have them both come to the harbour.'

They stood facing Captain Joris' cottage and his garden, its last roses stripped of their petals by the storm. Behind a curtain, someone looking out: it was Julie, wondering if the man at the wheel on the schooner was really her brother. Near Captain Delcourt, the lock workers and harbour men stood together, watching.

'Those fellows . . . The trouble they caused me, with their half-truths and evasions!' sighed Maigret.

Raymond smiled.

'They're sailors!'

'I know! And sailors don't like a landlubber like me sticking my nose into their business.'

He filled his pipe with little taps of his index finger. Puffing gently on the fresh pipe, he frowned.

'What will we tell them?'

Ernest Grandmaison was dead. Must they reveal that he was a murderer?

'Perhaps we could . . .' Raymond began.

'I don't know . . . Claim that it was some old feud? A vengeful sailor, a foreigner, who's gone back to his country . . .'

The crew of the tug was tramping off to the Buvette de la Marine, beckoning the lock workers to join them.

And Big Louis was bustling about his boat, patting and touching it as if he were checking a lost dog come home, making sure she wasn't hurt.

'Hey there!' Maigret called to him.

Big Louis gave a start but hesitated to step forwards – or more likely, to leave his schooner again. When he noticed Raymond standing there too, he seemed as surprised as Lucas had been.

'What the . . . ?'

'When can the *Saint-Michel* go back to sea?' asked Maigret.

'Right away if need be! No damage anywhere! She's a trim little ship, I promise you.'

Big Louis was looking questioningly at Raymond, who announced, 'In that case, take off on a sail-about with Lannec and Célestin . . .'

'They're here too?'

'They're coming . . . Go on a sailing spree for a few weeks. And far enough away that they forget about the *Saint-Michel* around here.'

'Well, I might take my sister along as ship's cook . . . She's fearless, you know, our Julie.'

Still, he was a bit hangdog around Maigret. He hadn't forgotten the ship's run for it the night before and had no idea if he could treat it lightly.

'You weren't too cold, at least, were you?' he asked the inspector.

Big Louis was now standing at the edge of the dock, off which Maigret sent him splashing with one push.

'I believe I've got a train at six o'clock,' he observed pleasantly.

Still, he made no move to leave. He looked around him with a pang of nostalgia, as if he had already grown fond of the little harbour town.

Didn't he know it in all its nooks and crannies, in all its moods, in shivery morning sunshine and blustery tempest, fogbound or streaming with rain?

'Will you be going to Caen?' he asked Raymond, who was sticking close to his side.

'Not right away. I think it would be better . . . to let . . .'

'Some time pass . . . Yes.'

When Lucas returned fifteen minutes later and asked after Maigret, he was waved over to the Buvette de la Marine, which had just lit its lamps.

He could see the inspector through the misted-over windows. An inspector solidly straddling a cane-seated chair, pipe clenched in his teeth, a glass of beer within reach, listening to the stories being told around him by men in rubber boots and sailor caps.

And on the ten o'clock train that evening, that same inspector sighed, 'They must be snug and warm in the cabin, all three of them . . .'

'What cabin?'

'Aboard the *Saint-Michel*! With the gimballed lamp, the nicked-up table, those thick glasses and that bottle of Dutch gin . . . And the purring stove . . . Say, have you got a match?'

Maigret

Translated by ROS SCHWARTZ

MAIGRET

GEORGES SIMENON

ROMAN

6 Fr.

A. FAYARD & Cie
PARIS

1.

Maigret struggled to open his eyes, frowning, as if distrustful of the voice that had just shouted at him, dragging him out of a deep sleep:

'Uncle!'

His eyes still closed, he sighed, groped at the sheet and realized that this was no dream, that something was the matter, because his hand had not encountered Madame Maigret's warm body where it should have been.

Finally he opened his eyes. It was a clear night. Madame Maigret, standing by the leaded window, was pulling back the curtain while downstairs someone was banging on the door and the noise reverberated throughout the house.

'Uncle! It's me!'

Madame Maigret was still looking out. Her hair wound in curling pins gave her a strange halo.

'It's Philippe,' she said, knowing full well that Maigret was awake and that he was turned towards her, waiting. 'Are you going to get up?'

Maigret went downstairs first, barefoot in his felt slippers. He had hastily pulled on a pair of trousers and shrugged on his jacket as he descended the staircase. At the eighth stair, he had to duck to avoid hitting his head on the beam. He usually did so automatically, but this time he forgot and banged his forehead. He groaned and swore as he reached the freezing hall. He went into the kitchen, which was a little warmer.

There were iron bars across the door. On the other side, Philippe was saying to someone:

'I won't be long. We'll be in Paris before daylight.'

Madame Maigret could be heard padding around upstairs. Maigret pulled open the door, surly from the knock he had just given himself.

'It's you!' he muttered, seeing his nephew standing in the road.

A huge moon floated above the leafless poplars, making the sky so light that the tiniest branches were silhouetted against it while, beyond the bend, the Loire was a glittering swarm of silvery spangles.

'East wind!' thought Maigret mechanically, as would any local on seeing the surface of the river whipped up.

It is one of those country habits, as is standing in the doorway without saying anything, looking at the intruder and waiting for him to speak.

'I hope I haven't woken Aunt up, at least?'

Philippe's face was frozen stiff. Behind him the shape of a G7 taxi stood out incongruously against the white-frosted landscape.

'Are you leaving the driver outside?'

'I need to talk to you right away.'

'Come inside quickly, both of you,' called Madame Maigret from the kitchen where she was lighting an oil lamp.

She added to her nephew:

'We haven't got electricity yet. The house has been wired, but we're waiting to be connected to the power supply.'

A lightbulb was dangling from a flex. People notice little details like that for no reason. And when they are already on edge, it is the sort of thing that can irritate them. During the minutes that followed, Philippe's eyes kept returning to that bulb, which served no purpose other than to emphasize everything that was antiquated about this rustic house, or rather everything that is precarious about modern comforts.

'Have you come from Paris?'

Maigret was leaning against the chimney breast, not properly awake yet. The presence of the taxi on the road made the question as redundant as the lightbulb, but sometimes people speak for the sake of saying something.

'I'm going to tell you everything, Uncle. I'm in big trouble. If you don't help me, if you don't come to Paris with me, I don't know what will become of me. I'm going out of my mind. I'm in such a state I even forgot to give my aunt a kiss.'

Madame Maigret stood there, having slipped a dressing gown over her nightdress. Philippe's lips brushed her cheek three times, performing the ritual like a child. Then he sat down at the table, clutching his head in his hands.

Maigret filled his pipe as he watched him, while his wife stacked twigs in the fireplace. There was something strange in the air, something threatening. Since Maigret had retired, he had lost the habit of getting up in the middle of the night and he couldn't help being reminded of nights spent beside a sick person or a dead body.

'I don't know how I could have been so stupid!' Philippe suddenly sobbed.

He poured out his tale of woe in a sudden rush, punctuated by hiccups. He looked about him like a person seeking to pin his agitation on something, while, in contrast to this outburst of emotion, Maigret turned up the wick of the oil lamp and the first flames leapt up from the fireplace.

'First of all, you're going to drink something.'

The uncle took a bottle of brandy and two glasses from a cupboard that contained some leftover food and smelled of cold meat. Madame Maigret put on her clogs to go and fetch some logs from the woodshed.

'To your good health! Now try to calm down.'

The smell of burning twigs mingled with that of the brandy. Philippe, dazed, watched his aunt loom silently out of the darkness, her arms filled with logs.

He was short-sighted and, seen from a certain angle, his eyes looked enormous behind his spectacle lenses, giving him the appearance of a frightened child.

'It happened last night. I was supposed to be on a stakeout in Rue Fontaine—'

'Just a moment,' interrupted Maigret, sitting astride a straw-bottomed chair and lighting his pipe. 'Who are you working with?'

'With Chief Inspector Amadieu.'

'Go on.'

Drawing gently on his pipe, Maigret narrowed his eyes and stared at the lime-plastered wall and the shelf with copper saucepans, caressing the images that were so familiar to him. At Quai des Orfèvres, Amadieu's office was the last one on the left at the end of the corridor. Amadieu himself was a skinny, sad man who had been promoted to divisional chief when Maigret had retired.

'Does he still have a drooping moustache?'

'Yes. Yesterday we had a summons for Pepito Palestrino, the owner of the Floria, in Rue Fontaine.'

'What number?'

'Fifty-three, next to the optician.'

'In my day, that was the Toréador. Cocaine dealing?'

'Cocaine initially. Then something else too. The chief had heard rumours that Pepito was mixed up in the Barnabé job, the guy who was shot in Place Blanche a fortnight ago. You must have read about it in the papers.'

'Make us some coffee!' said Maigret to his wife.

And, with the relieved sigh of a dog who finally settles down after chasing its tail, he leaned his elbows on the back of his chair and rested his chin on his folded hands. From time to time, Philippe removed his glasses to wipe the lenses and, for a few moments, he appeared to be blind. He was a tall, plump, auburn-haired boy with baby-pink skin.

'You know that we can no longer do as we please. In your day, no one would have batted an eyelid at arresting Pepito in the middle of the night. But now, we have to keep to the letter of the law. That's why the chief decided to carry out the arrest at eight o'clock in the morning. In the meantime, it was my job to keep an eye on the fellow . . .'

He was getting bogged down in the dense quiet of the room, then, with a start, he remembered his predicament and cast around helplessly.

For Maigret, the few words spoken by his nephew exuded the whiff of Paris. He could picture the Floria's neon sign, the doorman on the alert for cars arriving, and his nephew turning up in the neighbourhood that night.

'Take off your overcoat, Philippe,' interrupted Madame Maigret. 'You'll catch cold when you go outside.'

He was wearing a dinner-jacket. It looked quite incongruous in the low-ceilinged kitchen with its heavy beams and red-tiled floor.

'Have another drink—'

But in a fresh outburst of anger Philippe jumped up, wringing his hands violently enough to crush his bones.

'If only you knew, Uncle—'

He was on the verge of tears, his eyes stayed dry. His gaze fell on the electric lightbulb again. He stamped his foot.

'I bet I'll be arrested later!'

Madame Maigret, who was pouring boiling water over the coffee, turned around, saucepan in hand.

'What on earth are you talking about?'

And Maigret, still puffing on his pipe, opened his nightshirt collar with its delicate red embroidery.

'So you were on a stakeout opposite the Floria—'

'Not opposite. I went inside,' said Philippe, still on his feet. 'At the back of the club there's a little office where Pepito has set up a camp bed. That's where he usually sleeps after closing up the joint.'

A cart rumbled past on the road. The clock had stopped. Maigret glanced at his watch hanging from a nail above the fireplace. The hands showed half past four. In the cowsheds, milking had begun and carts were trundling to Orléans market. The taxi was still waiting outside the house.

'I wanted to be clever,' confessed Philippe. 'Last week the chief yelled at me and told me—'

He turned red and trailed off, trying to fix his gaze on something.

'He told you—?'

'I can't remember—'

'Well I can! If it's Amadieu, he probably came out with something along the lines of: "You're a maverick, young man, a maverick like your uncle!"'

Philippe said neither yes nor no.

'Anyway, I wanted to be clever,' he hastily went on. 'When the customers left, at around 1.30, I hid in the toilet. I thought that if Pepito had got wind of anything, he might try and get rid of the stuff. And do you know what happened?'

Maigret, more solemn now, slowly shook his head.

'Pepito was alone. Of that I'm certain! Suddenly, there was a gunshot. It took a few moments for it to dawn on me, then it took me a few more moments to run into the bar. It looked bigger, at night. It was lit by a single lightbulb. Pepito was lying between two rows of tables and as he fell he'd knocked over some chairs. He was dead.'

Maigret rose and poured himself another glassful of brandy, while his wife signalled to him not to drink too much.

'Is that all?'

Philippe was pacing up and down. And this young man, who generally had difficulty expressing himself, began to wax eloquent in a dry, bitter tone.

'No, that's not all! That's when I did something really stupid! I was scared. I couldn't think straight. The empty bar was sinister, it felt as if it was shrouded in greyness. There were streamers strewn on the floor and over the tables. Pepito was lying in a strange position, on his side, his hand close to his wound, and he seemed to be looking at me. What can I say? I took out my revolver and I started talking. I yelled out some nonsense and my voice scared me even more. There were shadowy corners everywhere, drapes, and I had the impression they were moving. I pulled myself together and went over to have a look. I flung open a door and yanked down a velvet curtain. I found the switchbox and I wanted to turn on the lights. I pushed the switches at random. And that was even more frightening. A red projector lit the place up. Fans started humming in every corner. "Who's there?" I shouted again.'

He bit his lip. His aunt looked at him, as distressed as he was. He was her sister's son and had been born in Alsace. Maigret had wangled him a job at police headquarters.

'I'd feel happier knowing he was in the civil service,' his mother had said.

And now, he panted:

'Please don't be angry with me, Uncle. I don't know myself how it happened. I can barely remember. In any case, I fired a shot, because I thought I saw something move. I rushed forwards and then stopped. I thought I heard footsteps, whisperings. But there was nothing but emptiness. I would never have believed the place was so big and full of obstacles. In the end, I found myself in the office. There was a gun on the table. I grabbed it without thinking. The barrel was still warm. I took out the chamber and saw that there was one bullet missing.'

'Idiot!' groaned Maigret between clenched teeth.

The coffee was steaming and Madame Maigret, sugar bowl in hand, stood there not knowing what she was doing.

'I had completely lost my mind. I still thought I could hear a noise over by the door. I ran. It was only later that I realized I had a gun in each hand.'

'Where did you put the gun?'

Maigret's tone was harsh. Philippe stared at the floor.

'All sorts of things were going through my mind. If it was a murder, people would think that since I'd been alone with Pepito—'

'Dear God!' groaned Madame Maigret.

'It only lasted for a few seconds. I put the gun near Pepito's hand, to make it look like a suicide, then—'

Maigret rose to his feet and took up his favourite position in front of the fireplace, his hands clasped behind his back. He was unshaven. He had put on a little weight since the days when he used to stand like that in front of his stove at Quai des Orfèvres.

'When you left, you ran into someone, am I right?'

He knew it.

'Just as I was closing the door behind me, I bumped into a man who was walking past. I apologized. Our faces were almost touching. I don't even know whether after that I closed the door properly. I walked to Place Clichy. I took a taxi and gave the driver your address.'

Madame Maigret put the sugar bowl down on the beech table and slowly asked her husband:

'Which suit are you wearing?'

For half an hour, it was a mad rush.

Maigret could be heard shaving and getting dressed in the bedroom. Madame Maigret cooked some eggs and questioned Philippe.

'Have you heard from your mother?'

'She's well. She was planning to come to Paris for Easter.'

The driver was invited in, but he refused to remove his heavy brown overcoat. Droplets of water trembled in his moustache. He sat down in a corner and stayed put.

'My braces?' shouted Maigret from upstairs.

'In the top drawer.'

Maigret came down wearing his coat with a velvet collar and his bowler hat. He pushed away the eggs waiting for him on the table and, defying his wife, drank a fourth glass of brandy.

It was 5.30 when the door opened and the three men stepped outside and got into the taxi. It took a while for the engine to start. Madame Maigret stood shivering in the doorway while the oil lamp made the reddish reflections dance on the little window panes.

The sky was so light, it felt like daybreak. But this was February and it was the night itself that was silver-coloured. Each blade of grass was rimed with frost. The apple trees in the neighbouring orchard were iced so white that they looked as fragile as spun glass.

'See you in two or three days!' yelled Maigret.

Philippe, embarrassed, shouted:

'Goodbye, Aunt!'

The driver slammed the car door again and crunched the gears for a moment.

'Please forgive me, Uncle—'

'What for?'

What for? Philippe didn't dare say. He was asking forgiveness because there was something dramatic about this departure. He recalled his uncle's silhouette earlier, by the fireplace, with his nightshirt, his old clothes, his slippers.

And now, he barely dared look at him. It was indeed Maigret who was beside him, smoking his pipe, his velvet collar upturned, his hat perched on his head. But it wasn't an enthusiastic Maigret. It wasn't even a Maigret who was sure of himself. Twice he turned round and watched his little house receding.

'Did you say that Amadieu will arrive at Rue Fontaine at eight?' he asked.

'Yes, at eight o'clock.'

They had time. The taxi was going quite fast. They drove through Orléans, where the first trams were setting out. Less than an hour later, they reached the market in Arpajon.

'What do you think, Uncle?'

It was draughty in the back of the car. The sky was clear. There was a golden glow in the east.

'How could Pepito have been killed?' sighed Philippe, who received no reply.

They stopped after Arpajon to warm up in a café and almost at once it was daylight, with a pale sun slowly rising where the fields met the horizon.

'There was no one but him and me in—'

'Be quiet!' said Maigret wearily.

His nephew huddled in his corner with the look of a child caught misbehaving, not daring to take his eyes off the door.

They entered Paris as the early-morning bustle was beginning. Past the Lion de Belfort, Boulevard Raspail, the Pont-Neuf . . .

The city looked as if it had been washed in clean water, so bright were the colours. A train of barges was gliding slowly up the Seine and the tugboat whistled, puffing out clouds of immaculate steam to announce its flotilla.

'How many passers-by were there in Rue Fontaine when you came out?'

'I only saw the man I ran into.'

Maigret sighed and emptied his pipe, tapping it against his heel.

The driver pulled down the glass partition and inquired: 'Where to?'

They stopped for a moment at a hotel on the embankment to drop off Maigret's suitcase, then they got back into the taxi and made their way to Rue Fontaine.

'It's not so much what happened at the Floria that worries me. It's the man who bumped into you.'

'What are you thinking?'

'I'm not thinking anything!'

He came out with this favourite expression from the past as he turned round to glimpse the outline, once so familiar, of the Palais de Justice.

'At one point I thought of going to the big chief and telling him the whole story,' muttered Philippe.

Maigret did not answer and, until they reached Rue Fontaine, he kept his gaze fixed on the view of the Seine as it flowed through a fine blue and gold mist.

They pulled up a hundred metres from number 53. Philippe turned up the collar of his overcoat to conceal his dinner-jacket, but at the sight of his patent-leather shoes, people turned round to stare all the same.

It was only 6.50. A window-cleaner was washing the windows of the corner café, the Tabac Fontaine, which stayed open all night. People on their way to work stopped off for a quick *café crème* with a croissant. There was only a waiter serving since the owner did not get to bed before five or six in the morning and rose at midday. He was a swarthy young southern-looking fellow with black hair. There were cigar ends and cigarette butts lying on a table next to a slate used for keeping score for card games.

Maigret bought a packet of shag and ordered a sandwich, while Philippe grew impatient.

'What happened last night?' asked Maigret, his mouth full of bread and ham.

And, gathering up the change, the waiter answered bluntly:

'People are saying the owner of the Floria was killed.'

'Palestrino?'

'I don't know. I'm on the day shift. And during the day, we don't have anything to do with the nightclubs.'

They left. Philippe did not dare say anything.

'You see?' grumbled Maigret.

Standing on the kerb, he added:

'That's the work of the man you bumped into, you realize. Theoretically, no one should know anything before eight o'clock.'

They walked towards the Floria, but they stopped fifty metres short. They spotted the peaked cap of a Paris police sergeant standing in front of the door. On the opposite pavement, a knot of people had gathered.

'What shall I do?'

'Your chief is bound to be at the scene. Go up to him and tell him—'

'What about you, Uncle?'

Maigret shrugged and went on:

'—Tell him the truth.'

'Supposing he asks where I went next?'

'Tell him you came to fetch me.'

There was resignation in his voice. They had got off on the wrong foot, and that was all! It was a stupid business and Maigret felt like gnashing his teeth.

'I'm sorry, Uncle!'

'No emotional scenes in the street! If they let you go free, meet me in the Chope du Pont-Neuf. If I'm not there, I'll leave you a note.'

They did not even shake hands. Philippe headed straight for the Floria. The sergeant did not know him and tried to bar him from entering. Philippe had to show his badge, then he vanished inside.

Maigret remained at a distance, his hands in his pockets, like the other onlookers. He waited. He waited for almost half an hour, without the least idea of what was going on inside the club.

Detective Chief Inspector Amadieu came out first, followed by a short, nondescript man who looked like a waiter.

And Maigret needed no explanations. He knew that this was the man who had bumped into Philippe. He could guess Amadieu's question.

'Was it right here that you bumped into him?'

The man nodded. Inspector Amadieu beckoned Philippe, who was still inside. He came out, looking as nervous as a young musician, as if the entire street were aware of the suspicions that were about to engulf him.

'And was this the gentleman who was coming out at that

moment?' Amadieu must have been saying, tugging his brown moustache.

The man nodded again.

There were two other police officers. The divisional chief glanced at his watch and, after a brief discussion, the man sauntered off and went into the Tabac Fontaine while the policemen went back inside the Floria.

Fifteen minutes later, two cars arrived. It was the public prosecutor.

'I've got to go back to repeat my statement,' the man from the Floria told the waiter at the Tabac Fontaine. 'Another white wine and Vichy, quick!'

And, discomfited by Maigret's insistent stare as he stood nearby drinking a beer, he lowered his voice and asked:

'Who's that?'

2.

Maigret sat with his head bent over his work with the application of a schoolboy. He drew a rectangle and placed a little cross somewhere in the centre. Then he stared at his effort and frowned. The rectangle represented the Floria, and the cross, Pepito. At the far end of the rectangle, Maigret drew another, smaller one: the office. And in this office he placed a dot indicating the gun.

This was pointless. It meant nothing. The case wasn't a geometry problem. Maigret doggedly continued all the same, scrunched the page into a ball and started all over again on a fresh sheet.

Only now he was no longer concerned with placing crosses in rectangles. Poring over the page, deeply engrossed, he tried to pin down a snatch of conversation, a look, an unwitting attitude.

He sat alone at his former table at the back of the Chope du Pont-Neuf. And it was too late to wonder whether he had been right or wrong to come. Everyone had seen him. The owner had shaken his hand.

'How's it going with the chickens and rabbits?'

Maigret was sitting by the window and he could see the Pont-Neuf bathed in a rosy glow, the steps of the Palais de Justice, the gates of the police headquarters. A white napkin under his arm, the beaming owner was in a chatty mood:

'So life's good! Dropping in to see your old pals?'

The beat officers were still in the habit of playing a hand of *belote* in the Chope before setting off on their rounds. There were some new faces who didn't know Maigret, but the others, after greeting Maigret, spoke to their colleagues in hushed tones.

That was when he had drawn his first rectangle, his first cross. The hours dragged by. At aperitif time, there were a dozen 'boys' in the place.

Trusty Lucas, who had worked with Maigret on a hundred cases, came over looking slightly sheepish.

'How are you, chief? Come for a breath of Paris air?' Lucas still called him chief, in memory of the old days.

And Maigret, between two puffs of smoke, merely muttered:

'What did Amadieu have to say?'

There was no point lying to him. He could see their faces and he knew the Police Judiciaire well enough to know what was going on. It was midday, and Philippe had not yet put in an appearance at the Chope.

'You know what Inspector Amadieu is like. We've had a few problems at HQ recently. Things are a bit tricky with the public prosecutor. So—'

'What did he say?'

'That you were here, of course. That you were going to try to—'

'Let me guess. His words were "act the wise guy".'

'I have to go,' stammered Lucas, embarrassed.

Maigret ordered another beer and became absorbed in drawing his rectangles while most of the tables were talking about him.

He ate lunch at the same table, now in the sunlight. The photographer from the criminal records office was eating nearby. As he drank his coffee, Maigret repeated to himself, pencil in hand:

'Pepito was here, between two rows of tables. The murderer was concealed somewhere. There's no shortage of hiding places. He fired, unaware of the presence of that idiot Philippe, then went into the office to get something. He had just put his gun down on the desk when he heard a noise and so he hid again. And from then on, the two of them played cat and mouse.'

It was simple. Pointless looking for any other explanation.

The murderer had eventually reached the door without being seen and made it out into the street while Philippe was still inside.

So far, nothing extraordinary. Any fool would have done the same thing. The clever part was what happened next: the idea of ensuring that someone would recognize Philippe and testify against him.

And, a few moments later, it was done. The murderer had found his man, in an empty street in the dead of night. This person bumped into Philippe as he emerged and rushed off to fetch the policeman on duty in Place Blanche.

'I say, officer, I've just seen a suspicious-looking character coming out of the Floria. He was in such a rush that he didn't bother to close the door.'

Maigret, without looking at his former colleagues, who were drinking beers, could guess what the old-timers were whispering to the new boys:

'Have you heard of Detective Chief Inspector Maigret? That's him!'

Amadieu, who didn't like him, must have announced in the corridors of the Police Judiciaire:

'He's going to try and act the wise guy. But we'll show him!'

It was four in the afternoon and Philippe had not appeared yet. The newspapers came off the presses with details of the murder, including his alleged confession. Another dirty trick of Amadieu's.

Quai des Orfèvres was in turmoil, phones ringing, files dredged up, witnesses and informers brought in for questioning.

Maigret's nostrils were quivering as he sat hunched on the banquette patiently doing little drawings with the tip of his pencil.

He had to find Pepito's killer at all costs. But he was not on good form, he felt afraid, anxious as to whether he would succeed. He watched the young police officers and tried to fathom what they thought of him.

Philippe did not arrive until 5.45. He stood there for a moment, as if dazzled by the light. As he sat down beside Maigret, he attempted a smile and stammered:

'It went on for ages!'

He was so exhausted that he wiped his hand across his brow as if to collect his thoughts.

'I've been at the prosecutor's office. The examining magistrate questioned me for an hour and a half. But before that, he made me wait in the corridor for two hours.'

Everyone was watching them. And while Philippe talked, Maigret looked at the men facing them.

'You know, Uncle, it's much more serious than we thought.'

For Maigret, each word was loaded with significance. He knew the examining magistrate, Gastambide, a stocky Basque who was meticulous and contemptuous, who weighed up his words, spent several minutes formulating his sentences then letting them drop as if to declare:

'What can you say to that?'

And Maigret was familiar with that corridor, filled with defendants under police guard, the benches crammed with restless witnesses, women in tears. If Philippe had been made to wait, it was deliberate.

'The magistrate told me not to deal with any cases, to take no action before the end of the investigation. I am to consider myself suspended from duty and I must remain at his disposal.'

It was aperitif hour, the noisiest time at the Chope du Pont-Neuf. All the tables were full. The air was thick with pipe and cigarette smoke. From time to time, a newcomer greeted Maigret from across the room.

Philippe did not dare look at anyone, not even his companion.

'I'm very sorry, Uncle.'

'What else has happened?'

'Everyone thought, naturally, that the Floria would be closed, at least for a few days. But it isn't going to be. Today, there was a series of phone calls, some baffling developments. Apparently, the Floria was sold two days ago and Pepito was no longer the owner. The buyer has friends in high places and tonight the joint will be open for business as usual.'

Maigret frowned. Was it because of what he had just heard, or because Detective Chief Inspector Amadieu had just walked in with a colleague and sat down at the other end of the room?

'Godet!' Maigret shouted.

Godet was an inspector from the vice squad who was playing cards three tables away. He turned round, cards in hand, unsure whether to get up.

'When you've finished your game!'

And Maigret screwed up all his scraps of paper and threw them on to the floor. He downed his beer in one gulp and wiped his mouth, looking over in Amadieu's direction.

Amadieu had heard him. He watched the scene from a distance as he poured water into his Pernod. Intrigued, Godet finally went over to Maigret's table.

'Did you want to speak to me, sir?'

'Hello, old friend!' said Maigret, shaking his hand. 'A simple piece of information. Are you still with the Vice? Good. Can you tell me whether Cageot showed his face at HQ this morning?'

'Hold on. I think he came into the office at around eleven.'

'Thank you, my friend.'

That was all! Maigret looked at Amadieu. Amadieu looked at Maigret. And now it was Amadieu who was uncomfortable and Maigret was the one suppressing a smile.

Philippe did not dare speak. The case had just moved up a rung. The game was being played over his head and he didn't even know the rules.

'Godet!' bawled a voice.

This time, all the police officers in the room shuddered as they watched the inspector get up again, still holding his cards, and walk over to Chief Inspector Amadieu.

There was no need to hear what was said. It was clear that Amadieu wanted to know:

'What did he ask you?'

'Whether I'd seen Cageot this morning.'

Maigret lit his pipe, let the match burn down to the very end and finally rose, calling:

'Waiter!'

Drawn up to his full height, he waited for his change, glancing casually around the room.

'Where are we going?' asked Philippe once they were outside.

Maigret turned to him, as if surprised to see him there.

'You're going to bed,' he said.

'What about you, Uncle?'

Maigret shrugged, thrust his hands in his pockets and walked off without answering. He had just spent one of the most unpleasant days of his life. Hours on end stuck in his corner. He had felt old and feeble, with no energy, no inspiration.

Then the shift happened. A little flame shot up. But he had to take advantage of it right away.

'We'll see, damn it!' he grunted to boost his spirits.

Normally, at this hour, he would be reading his newspaper under the lamp, his legs outstretched in front of the log fire.

'Do you come to Paris often?'

Maigret, propping up the bar of the Floria, shook his head and merely replied:

'Uh-huh, from time to time . . .'

He was feeling buoyant again. He did not express his good humour in smiles, but he had an inner feeling of well-being. One of his gifts was the ability to laugh inwardly without betraying his outer gravitas. A woman was sitting next to him. She asked him to buy her a drink and he nodded in acquiescence.

Two years ago, a prostitute would never have made that mistake.

But his overcoat with its velvet collar and his standard black, hard-wearing serge suit and tie told her nothing. If she mistook him for a provincial out on the town, it meant he had changed.

'Something happened here, didn't it?' he muttered.

'The boss got bumped off last night.'

She also misread the look in his eye, which she thought was one of interest. But things were not so straightforward! Maigret was back in a world he had long since left behind. This nondescript little woman, he knew her without knowing her. He was certain that she did not have a record and that, on her passport, her occupation was given as *artiste* or *dancer*. As for the Chinese barman who served them, Maigret could have recited his criminal history. The cloakroom attendant, on the other hand, had clocked him and had greeted him anxiously, trying to place him.

Among the waiters, there were at least two whom Maigret had brought into his office in the past for questioning in cases similar to Pepito's killing.

He ordered a brandy with water. He vaguely watched the room and instinctively positioned crosses, as he had done on paper. Customers who had read the papers were asking questions and the waiters were explaining, pointing out the spot near the fifth table where the body had been found.

'Would you like to share a bottle of champagne?'

'No, dear.'

The woman almost guessed, and was at least intrigued as Maigret's gaze followed the new owner, a young man with fair hair whom he had known as the manager of a Montparnasse dance hall.

'Will you see me home?'

'Of course! In a while.'

In the meantime, he went into the toilets and guessed where Philippe had hidden. At the back of the main room, he could glimpse the office with its door ajar. But that was of no interest. He knew the scenario before setting foot in Rue Fontaine. The actors too. Going round the room, he could point to each person, saying:

'At this table, we have a newlywed couple from the South out for a night on the town. This young man who is already drunk is a young German who will end the night minus his wallet. Over there, the gigolo with a criminal record and packets of cocaine in his pockets. He is in cahoots with the head waiter, who has done three years inside. The plump brunette spent ten years at Maxim's and is winding up her career in Montmartre—'

He returned to the bar.

'Can I have another cocktail?' asked the woman, for whom he had already bought a drink.

'What's your name?'

'Fernande.'

'What were you doing last night?'

'I was with three young men, boys from good families, who wanted to take ether. I went with them to a hotel in Rue Notre-Dame-de-Lorette.'

Maigret did not smile, but he could have continued the story for her.

'First, we went into the pharmacy in Rue Montmartre separately and bought a little bottle of ether each. I wasn't entirely sure what was going to happen. We got undressed. But they didn't even look at me. All four of us lay down on the bed. When they inhaled the ether, one got up and said in this strange voice: "Oh! There are angels on top of the wardrobe . . . Aren't they lovely . . . I'm going to catch them . . ." He tried to get up and fell on to the rug. Me, the smell made me feel sick. I asked them if that was all they wanted from me and I got dressed again. But I did laugh. There was a bug on the pillow between two of their heads, and I can still hear the voice of one of the boys saying, as if in a dream: "There's a bug in front of my face!" "And mine!" sighed the other one. And they didn't budge. They were both squinting.'

She downed her drink in one go, and decreed:

'Barmy!'

All the same, she was starting to grow anxious.

'You're keeping me for the night, aren't you?'

'Of course! Of course!' replied Maigret.

There was a curtain dividing the bar from the lobby where the cloakroom was. From his seat, Maigret could see through the slit in the curtain. Suddenly he jumped down from his stool and took a few steps. A man had just walked in, and said to the cloakroom attendant:

'Nothing new?'

'Good evening, Monsieur Cageot!'

It was Maigret speaking, his hands in his jacket pockets, his pipe in his mouth. The man he was addressing, who had his back to him, slowly turned around, looked him up and down, and grunted:

'So you're here!'

The red curtain and the music were behind them, and in front of them the door opened on to the cold street where the doorman was pacing up and down. Cageot was reluctant to take off his overcoat.

Fernande, feeling uneasy, poked her nose out, but withdrew immediately.

'Will you have a drink?'

Cageot had finally made up his mind and handed his overcoat to the cloakroom attendant, watching Maigret all the while.

'If you like,' he agreed.

The head waiter hurried over to show them to a free table. Without looking at the wine list, the newcomer muttered:

'Mumm 26!'

He was not in evening dress, but was wearing a dark-grey suit as ill-fitting as Maigret's. He was not even freshly shaven and a greyish stubble ate into his cheeks.

'I thought you'd retired?'

'So did I!'

This seemed pretty innocuous, yet Cageot frowned, and signalled to the girl selling cigars and cigarettes. Fernande sat at the bar, wide-eyed. And young Albert, who was playing the part of the owner, wondered whether or not he should go over to them.

'Cigar?'

'No thank you,' said Maigret, emptying his pipe.

'Are you in Paris for long?'

'Until Pepito's killer is behind bars.'

They did not raise their voices. Next to them, high-spirited men in dinner-jackets were pelting each other with cotton-wool balls and throwing paper streamers. The saxophonist wandered solemnly from table to table playing his instrument.

'Have they called you back to investigate this case?'

Germain Cageot had a long, lifeless face and bushy eyebrows the colour of grey mould. He was the last man one would expect to meet in a place where people go to have fun. He spoke slowly, frostily, gauging the effect of each word.

'I came of my own accord,' Maigret replied.

'Are you working for yourself?'

'One could say that.'

It seemed unimportant. Fernande herself must have been thinking that it was pure chance that her companion knew Cageot.

'How long ago did you buy the place?'

'The Floria? You're mistaken. It belongs to Albert.'

'As it did Pepito.'

Cageot did not deny it, but merely smiled mirthlessly and stopped the waiter who was about to pour him some champagne.

'What else?' he asked in the tone of someone casting around for a topic of conversation.

'What's your alibi?'

Cageot gave another smile, even more neutral, and reeled off without batting an eyelid:

'I went to bed at nine as I had a touch of flu. The concierge brought me up a hot toddy and gave it to me in bed.'

Neither of them paid any attention to the hubbub that surrounded them like a wall. They were used to it. Maigret smoked his pipe, and Cageot a cigar.

'Still drinking Pougues mineral water?' asked the former chief inspector as Cageot poured him a glass of champagne.

'Still.'

They sat facing each other, grave and slightly sullen like two soothsayers. At a neighbouring table, some woman who didn't know better was aiming cotton-wool balls at their noses.

'You were quick to get the place re-opened!' commented Maigret between two puffs of smoke.

'I'm still pretty well connected with the "boys".'

'Are you aware that there's a kid who's stupidly compromised in this business?'

'I read something along those lines in the papers. A young cop who was hiding in the toilet and who panicked and killed Pepito.'

The jazz band struck up again. An Englishman, all the more priggish for being drunk, brushed past Maigret murmuring:

'Excuse me.'

'Go ahead.'

And Fernande, at the bar, was watching him with a worried look. Maigret smiled at her.

'Young police officers are hot-headed,' sighed Cageot.

'That's what I said to my nephew.'

'Is your nephew interested in these matters?'

'He was the kid hiding in the toilet.'

Cageot could not turn pale, because his face was always ashen. But he took a hasty sip of mineral water, then wiped his mouth.

'That's too bad, isn't it?'

'That's exactly what I said to him.'

Fernande jerked her chin at the clock, which showed 1.30. Maigret signalled that he was coming.

'To your health,' said Cageot.

'To yours.'

'Is it pleasant, where you're living? I've heard you've moved out to the country.'

'It is pleasant, yes.'

'Winter in Paris is unhealthy.'

'I thought the same thing when I heard about Pepito's death.'

'Be my guest, please,' protested Cageot as Maigret opened his wallet.

Maigret still put fifty francs down on the table and stood up, saying:

'So long!'

He just walked past the bar and whispered to Fernande:

'Come on.'

'Have you paid?'

In the street, she wasn't sure whether to take his arm. He still had his hands in his pockets and walked with big, slow strides.

'D'you know Cageot?' she asked shyly at length, slipping into informality

'He's from my part of the world.'

'You know, you should be careful. He's a bit of a dodgy character. I'm telling you this because you seem like a good man.'

'Have you slept with him?'

Then Fernande, who had to take two steps to Maigret's every stride, replied simply:

'He doesn't sleep with anyone!'

In Meung, Madame Maigret was fast asleep in the house that smelled of wood smoke and goat's milk. In his hotel room in Rue des Dames, Philippe had finally fallen asleep too, his glasses on the bedside table.

3.

Maigret perched on the edge of the bed while Fernande, her legs crossed, gave a contented sigh as she slipped off her shoes. With the same lack of inhibition she hitched up her green silk dress to undo her garters.

'Aren't you getting undressed?'

Maigret shook his head, but she didn't notice as she was pulling her dress over her head.

Fernande had a small apartment in Rue Blanche. The red-carpeted staircase smelled of wax floor polish. There were empty milk bottles standing outside every door on the way up. Once inside the apartment, they had crossed a living room cluttered with knick-knacks and Maigret had a glimpse of a spotless kitchen where all the items were arranged with meticulous care.

'What are you thinking about?' asked Fernande as she peeled off her stockings to reveal her long, white legs and then examined her toes with interest.

'Nothing. May I smoke?'

'There are cigarettes on the table.'

Maigret paced up and down, his pipe between his teeth, and stopped in front of an enlarged portrait of a woman in her fifties, then in front of a copper pot in which a plant stood. The floor was waxed and near the door were two pieces of felt shaped like shoe soles, which Fernande must have used to walk around so as not to mark the floor.

'Are you from the North?' he asked, without looking at her.

'How can you tell?'

Finally he went over and stood in front of her. Her hair was vaguely blonde, with an auburn tinge, her features irregular – an elongated mouth, a pointed nose covered in freckles.

'I'm from Roubaix.'

You could tell from the way the apartment was arranged and polished and from the spick-and-span kitchen in particular. Maigret was sure that in the morning, Fernande sat there by the stove and drank a big bowl of coffee while she read the paper.

Now she gazed at her companion with a hint of anxiety.

'Aren't you getting undressed?' she repeated, rising and going over to the mirror.

Then, immediately suspicious:

'Why did you come?'

She sensed something was not quite right. Her mind was busy working it out.

'You're right, I didn't come for *that*,' admitted Maigret with a smile.

His grin broadened as she grabbed a bathrobe, suddenly overcome with modesty.

'So what *do* you want?'

She could not guess. Even though she was adept at categorizing men. She took in her visitor's shoes, tie and eyes.

'But you're not from the police, are you?'

'Sit down. We're going to have a nice friendly chat. You're not entirely mistaken, because I was a detective chief inspector with the Police Judiciaire for many years.'

She frowned.

'Don't be afraid. I'm not there any more! I've retired to the countryside and the reason I'm in Paris now is because Cageot's up to his old tricks.'

'So that's why!' she said under her breath as she recalled the two men sitting at the table and behaving oddly.

'I need proof, and there are people whom I can't question.'

She no longer treated him like a punter – now she addressed him formally.

'You require my help? Is that it?'

'You've guessed it. You know as well as I do, don't you, that the Floria is full of crooks and scum?'

She sighed to signal her assent.

'The real boss is Cageot, who also owns the Pélican and the Boule Verte.'

'People say he's opened a place in Nice too.'

Now they were sitting at the table facing each other, and Fernande asked:

'Would you like a hot drink?'

'Not now. You've heard about the business in Place Blanche, a couple of weeks ago. A car drove past, with three or four men inside, at around three in the morning. Between Place Blanche and Place Clichy, the door opened and one of the men was thrown out on to the road. Dead. He'd just been stabbed.'

'Barnabé!' said Fernande.

'Did you know him?'

'He used to come to the Floria.'

'Well, that was Cageot's doing. I don't know if he was in the car himself, but Pepito was with them. And last night, he copped it.'

She said nothing. She was thinking and her brow was furrowed, making her resemble an ordinary housewife.

'What's it to you?' she protested at length.

'If I don't catch Cageot, my nephew will be convicted in his place.'

'The tall redhead who looks like a tax clerk?'

Now it was Maigret's turn to be surprised.

'How do you know him?'

'He's been hanging around the bar at the Floria for the last couple of days or so. I clocked him because he didn't dance and he spoke to no one. Last night, he bought me a drink. I tried to worm some information out of him and he more or less admitted it, stammering that he couldn't tell me anything, but that he was on an important mission.'

'The fool!'

Maigret rose and got straight to the point.

'So, are we agreed? There'll be two thousand francs for you if you help me nail Cageot.'

She couldn't help smiling. She found this entertaining.

'What do I have to do?'

'First of all, I need to know whether or not Cageot showed his face in the Tabac Fontaine last night.'

'Shall I go there tonight?'

'Right away if you like.'

She shrugged off her bathrobe and, dress in hand, looked at Maigret for a moment.

'Do you really want me to put my clothes back on?'

'Yes,' he sighed, putting a hundred francs on the mantelpiece.

They walked up Rue Blanche together. On the corner of Rue de Douai, they shook hands and parted company, and Maigret headed down Rue Notre-Dame-de-Lorette. When he arrived at his hotel, he was surprised to catch himself whistling.

By ten in the morning, he was ensconced at the Chope du Pont-Neuf, where he had chosen a table that was intermittently in the sun, as the passers-by kept casting shadows. Spring was already in the air. Street life was more cheerful, the sounds sharper.

At Quai des Orfèvres, it was time for the morning briefing. At the end of the long corridor of offices, the head of the Police Judiciaire was meeting his colleagues, who had all brought their case files. Detective Chief Inspector Amadieu was in his element. Maigret could imagine the scenario.

'Well, Amadieu, what's new in the Palestrino case?'

Amadieu leaning forwards, twiddling his moustache, saying with an amiable smile:

'Here are the reports, chief.'

'Is it true that Maigret is in Paris?'

'So rumour has it.'

'So why the hell hasn't he come to see me?'

Maigret smiled. He was certain that this was how the conversation would go. He could picture Amadieu's long face growing even longer. He could hear him insinuating:

'Perhaps he has his reasons.'

'Do you really think young Philippe fired that shot?'

'I'm not making any accusations, chief. All I know is that his fingerprints are on the gun. We found a second bullet in the wall.'

'Why would he have done that?'

'Panic . . . We're given young inspectors who haven't been trained to—'

Just then, Philippe walked into the Chope du Pont-Neuf and made a beeline for his uncle, who asked:

'What are you drinking?'

'A *café crème*. I've managed to get everything you asked for, but it wasn't easy. Amadieu has got his eye on me! The others are wary of me.'

He wiped the lenses of his glasses and fished some papers out of his pocket.

'First of all, Cageot. I looked him up in the files and copied his details. He was born in Pontoise and he's fifty-nine years old. He started out as a solicitor's clerk in Lyon and he was sentenced to a year for forgery and falsification of records. Three years later, he was given six months for attempted insurance fraud. That was in Marseille.

'There's no trace of him for several years, but then he turned up again in Monte-Carlo, where he worked as a croupier. From that point he was a police informant, which didn't prevent him from being mixed up in a gambling case that was never solved.

'Finally, five years ago, in Paris, he was manager of a low-down dive called the Cercle de l'Est. The place was soon closed down, but Cageot wasn't bothered. That's the lot! Since then, he's lived in an apartment in Rue des Batignolles where there's just a cleaning woman. He's still a regular visitor to the Ministry of the Interior in Rue des Saussaies and at Quai des Orfèvres. He owns at least three nightclubs which are managed by front men.'

'Pepito?' asked Maigret, who had taken notes.

'Age twenty-nine. Born in Naples. Deported from France twice for drug trafficking. No other offences.'

'Barnabé?'

'Born in Marseille. Age thirty-two. Three convictions, including one for armed robbery.'

'Has the stuff been found at the Floria?'

'Nothing. No drugs, no documents. Pepito's killer took the lot.'

'What's the name of the fellow who bumped into you and then called the police?'

'Joseph Audiat. A former waiter who's mixed up in horse-racing. I think his job is to collect the bets. He is of no fixed address and has his post delivered to the Tabac Fontaine.'

'By the way,' said Maigret, 'I met your lady friend.'

'My lady friend?' echoed Philippe, turning beetroot.

'A tall girl in a green silk dress. You bought her a drink at the Floria. We almost slept together.'

'Well I didn't!' said Philippe. 'If she told you otherwise—'

Lucas had just come in and stood dithering in the doorway. Maigret beckoned him over.

'Are you handling the case?'

'Not exactly, chief. I just wanted to let you know that Cageot is at headquarters again. He arrived a quarter of an hour ago and shut himself up with Detective Chief Inspector Amadieu.'

'Do you want a beer?'

Lucas filled his pipe from Maigret's tobacco pouch. It was the hour when the waiters were setting up, polishing the mirrors with whiting and scattering sawdust between the tables. The owner, already in a black jacket, was inspecting the hors-d'œuvres lined up on a serving table.

'Do you think it's Cageot?' asked Lucas, dropping his voice and reaching for his beer.

'I'm convinced of it.'

'That's no joke!'

Philippe kept quiet, awed by his companions, who had worked together for nearly twenty years. From time to time, between puffs on their pipes, the two veterans would utter a few syllables.

'Did he see you, chief?'

'I went there and told him I'd get him. Waiter! Two more beers!'

'He'll never confess.'

La Samaritaine delivery lorries rumbled past the windows, bright yellow in the sunshine. Long trams followed them, clanging their bells.

'What do you plan to do?'

Maigret shrugged. He had no idea. His beady eyes were staring beyond the bustle of the street at the Palais de Justice on the other side of the Seine. Philippe toyed with his pencil.

'I have to run!' sighed Sergeant Lucas. 'I've got to investigate a kid from Rue Saint-Antoine, some Pole who's been up to some funny business. Will you be here this afternoon?'

'Most likely.'

Maigret rose too. Philippe grew anxious:

'Shall I come with you?'

'I'd rather you didn't. Go back to Quai des Orfèvres. We'll meet back here for lunch.'

Maigret boarded the omnibus and half an hour later he was climbing the stairs to Fernande's apartment. It took her a few minutes to open the door, because she was still in bed. Sunlight was streaming into the room. The sheets on the unmade bed were bright white.

'Already!' exclaimed Fernande, clutching her pyjama top over her chest. 'I was asleep! Wait a moment.'

She went into the kitchen, lit the gas ring and filled a saucepan with water, talking all the while.

'I went to the Tabac Fontaine, like you asked me to. Naturally they aren't wary of me. Did you know that the owner also has a hotel in Avignon?'

'Go on.'

'There was a table where some men were playing cards. Me, I acted like I'd been out all night and was tired.'

'Did you happen to notice a small, dark man called Joseph Audiat?'

'Wait! There was a Joseph, at any rate. He was telling the others how he'd spent the afternoon being questioned by an examining magistrate. But you know how it goes. They play. *Belote! Rebelote!* Your turn, Pierre . . . Then one of them says something . . . Someone answers from the bar . . . Pass! . . . Pass again! . . . Your go, Marcel! . . . The owner was playing too . . . There was an African . . . "Do you want a drink?" a tall, dark-haired man asked me, pointing to a chair near him. "I don't mind if I do." He showed me his hand. "In any case," said the man they called Joseph, "I think it's risky to involve a cop. Tomorrow, they're going to bring me face to face with him. He looks like a right idiot, of course . . ." "Hearts trumps." "*Quatrième haute!*"' Fernande interrupted herself:

'Will you have a cup of coffee too?'

And soon the smell of coffee filled the three-room apartment.

'So anyway, I couldn't suddenly start asking them about Cageot, could I? I said to them, "So do you fellows come here every night?" "Looks like it," said the one sitting next to me. "And you didn't hear anything, last night?"'

Maigret, having removed his coat and hat, had half opened the window, allowing the street noises to enter the room. Fernande went on:

'He gave me a funny look and he said: "Are you a bad girl?" I could see he was getting aroused. Still playing cards, he stroked my knee. And he went on: "Us lot, we don't hear anything, you understand? Apart from Joseph, who saw what he had to see . . ." That made them all roar with laughter. What could I do? I didn't dare move my leg away. "Spades again! *Tierce haute* and *belote!*" "He's one hell of a guy!" said Joseph, who was drinking a hot toddy. But the fellow who was stroking my leg coughed then grumbled: "I'd rather he didn't spend so much time with the cops, if you know what I mean."'

Maigret felt as if he were in the room. He could have put a name to almost each face. He already knew that the owner ran a brothel in Avignon. And the tall, dark-haired man must be the owner of the Cupidon, in Béziers, and of a brothel in Nîmes. As for the African, he belonged to a local jazz outfit.

'They didn't mention any names?' Maigret asked Fernande, who was stirring her coffee.

'No names. Two or three times they said *the Lawyer*. I thought they meant Cageot. He looks like a degenerate lawyer. But wait, I haven't finished! Aren't you hungry? It must have been three in the morning. You could hear them pulling down the shutters at the Floria. My neighbour, who was still rubbing my knee, was beginning to annoy me. That's when the door opened and Cageot came in. He touched the brim of his hat, but he didn't say a general hello.

'Nobody looked up. You could feel they were all giving him shifty glances. The owner scooted over to the bar.

'"Give me six *Voltigeur* cigars and a box of matches," said Cageot.

'Little Joseph didn't bat an eyelid. He stared at the bottom of his toddy glass. Cageot lit a cigar, put the others in his jacket pocket, and looked for a note in his wallet. You could have heard a pin drop.

'The silence didn't bother him. He turned round, looked

at everyone, calmly, coolly, then touched his hat again and left.'

As Fernande dunked her buttered bread in her coffee, her pyjama top had fallen open, revealing a pert breast.

She must have been in her late twenties, but she had the body of a girl and her barely formed nipples were pale pink.

'They didn't say anything after he left?' questioned Maigret who couldn't help turning down the gas ring on which the kettle was beginning to sing.

'They looked at each other and exchanged winks. The owner sat down again, sighing: "Is that all?" Joseph, who looked awkward, explained: "It's not that he's proud, you know!"'

At this time of day, Rue Blanche was almost provincial. You could hear the clatter of the hooves of the horses harnessed to a heavy brewer's dray.

'The others sniggered,' added Fernande. 'The one who was groping my leg groaned: "It's not that he's proud, no! But he's shrewd enough to land us all in it. I tell you, I'd like it better if he didn't go to Quai des Orfèvres every day!"'

Fernande had told her story taking care not to forget anything.

'Did you go straight home?'

'That wasn't possible.'

Maigret looked none too pleased.

'Oh!' she hastily added, 'I didn't bring him back here. It's best not to show those people that you've got a few bits and pieces. He didn't let me go until five o'clock.'

She rose and went to get a breath of fresh air by the window.

'What should I do now?'

Maigret paced up and down, preoccupied.

'What's his name, your lover-boy?'

'Eugène. There are two gold initials on his cigarette case: E.B.'

'Do you want to go back to the Tabac Fontaine tonight?'

'If I have to.'

'Pay attention to the one called Joseph in particular, the little guy who fetched the police.'

'He took no notice of me.'

'I'm not asking you to do *that*. Just listen carefully to what he says.'

'Now, if you don't mind, I have to clean my place up,' said Fernande tying a kerchief over her hair.

They shook hands. And as he descended the stairs, Maigret had no idea that there would be a raid in Montmartre, and that the police would swoop on the Tabac Fontaine and take Fernande to the station.

Cageot knew.

'I should inform you of half a dozen women who are in an irregular situation,' he was saying at that very moment to the chief of the vice squad.

Fernande above all, who was going to be carted off in a meat wagon!

4.

Maigret had just finished shaving and was cleaning his razor when there was a knock on his door. It was nine in the morning. He had been awake since eight, but, for once, he had lain in bed for ages watching the sun's slanting rays and listening to the sounds of the city.

'Come in!' he shouted.

And he took a sip of the cold coffee stagnating at the bottom of his cup. Philippe's hesitant footsteps echoed in the room and finally reached the bathroom.

'Good morning, son.'

'Good morning, Uncle.'

Maigret knew from his voice that something was wrong. He buttoned up his shirt and looked at his nephew, who had red eyelids and puffy nostrils like a child who had been crying.

'What's happened?'

'I've been arrested!'

Philippe said this as gloomily as if he were announcing that he would be going in front of a firing squad in five minutes.

He held out a newspaper. Maigret glanced at it while continuing to get dressed.

Despite Inspector Philippe Lauer's denials, examining magistrate Gastambide reportedly decided to have him arrested this morning.

'My photo's splashed all over the front page of the *Excelsior*,' Philippe added melodramatically.

His uncle said nothing. There was nothing to be said. His braces dangling, slippers on his bare feet, he padded to and fro in the sunshine, hunting for his pipe, then his tobacco and finally a box of matches.

'You didn't drop by there this morning?' asked Maigret.

'I've come from Rue des Dames. I saw the paper when I was having my coffee and croissant in Boulevard des Batignolles.'

It was an exceptional morning. The air was fresh, the sun joyful, and the intense, animated bustle of Paris a frenzied dance. Maigret opened the window and the room reverberated with the throbbing life of the riverbanks, while the slow-moving Seine shimmered in the sunlight.

'Well, you have to go, my boy! What can I say?'

He didn't want to get all sentimental over this kid who had forsaken his green valley in the Vosges for the corridors of the Police Judiciaire!

'Naturally, it won't be as cushy as home!'

His mother was Madame Maigret's sister, and that said it all. She mollycoddled the boy: *Philippe will be home soon . . . Philippe will be hungry . . . Have Philippe's shirts been ironed? . . .*

And tasty little dishes, home-made desserts and liqueurs! And sprigs of lavender in the linen cupboard!

'There's something else,' said Philippe while his uncle adjusted his detachable collar. 'Last night I went to the Floria.'

'Of course!'

'Why of course?'

'Because I advised you not to go there. Now what have you done?'

'Nothing. I chatted with that girl, Fernande, you know. She hinted that she was working with you and that she had some mission to carry out at the café on the corner of Rue de Douai. Since I was leaving anyway, I followed her, instinctively. It was on my way home. But on her way out of the café, she was yelled at by inspectors from the vice squad and bundled into a meat wagon.'

'You tried to step in, I'll bet!'

Philippe looked shamefaced.

'What did they say?'

'That they knew what they were doing.'

'Off you go now,' sighed Maigret, hunting for his tie. 'Don't worry.'

He put his hands on Philippe's shoulders, kissed him on both cheeks and, to cut the scene short, suddenly pretended to be very busy. Only when the door had opened and closed behind Philippe again did he look up, hunch his shoulders and mutter a few garbled syllables.

The first thing he did once on the riverbank was to buy the *Excelsior* from a news kiosk and look at the photo which was indeed on the front page with the caption:

Inspector Philippe Lauer, accused of killing Pepito Palestrino, who was under surveillance.

Maigret walked slowly over the Pont-Neuf. The previous evening, he had not gone inside the Floria but had paid a visit to Rue des Batignolles to sniff around Cageot's place. He lived in a residential building dating from the 1880s, like most of the apartment blocks in the neighbourhood. The corridor and the staircase were poorly lit. It was easy to imagine the dark, dismal apartments, grubby curtains at the windows and furniture with faded velvet upholstery.

Cageot's apartment was on the mezzanine. There was no one around at this time of day and Maigret had entered the building as if he were a regular visitor. He wandered up to the fourth floor and then came back down again.

There was a safety lock on Cageot's door, otherwise Maigret might have given in to temptation. He walked past the lodge and the concierge, face pressed up against the window, stared after him for a while.

What could that matter? Maigret crossed almost the entire

city on foot, his hands in his pockets, the same thoughts going round and round in his head.

Somewhere – at the Tabac Fontaine or elsewhere – there was a small group of crooks who were happily going about their illicit business. Pepito had been one of them. Barnabé too.

And one by one, Cageot, the big boss, was eliminating them, or having them eliminated.

Gangland killings! The police would hardly have bothered about them if that idiot Philippe—

Maigret had arrived at Quai des Orfèvres. Two inspectors on their way out greeted him with unconcealed surprise, and he went through the entrance, crossed the courtyard and walked past the vice squad.

Upstairs it was time for the morning briefing. In the vast corridor, fifty police officers stood in huddles, speaking in loud voices and passing on intelligence and records. Sometimes an office door opened and a name was yelled and summoned inside.

Maigret's arrival caused a few moments' silence and unease. But he sauntered past the groups looking perfectly at home, and the officers resumed their confabs to keep up appearances.

To the right was the chief's waiting room furnished with red velvet armchairs. Sitting in a corner, a lone visitor was waiting. Chin cupped in his hands, Philippe stared fixedly ahead of him.

Maigret walked off in the opposite direction, reached the end of the corridor and knocked at the last door.

'Come in!' answered a voice from inside.

And everyone saw him enter Detective Chief Inspector Amadieu's office, hat in hand.

'Hello, Maigret.'
'Hello, Amadieu.'

They touched fingertips as they used to do when they saw each other every morning. Amadieu signalled to an inspector to leave, then murmured:

'Did you want to talk to me?'

Maigret perched on the edge of the desk in a familiar pose and picked up a box of matches from the table to light his pipe.

His colleague had pushed back his chair and tilted it backwards.

'How's country life?'

'Fine, thanks. How are things here?'

'Still the same. I have to see the chief in five minutes.'

Maigret pretended not to know what that meant and began unbuttoning his overcoat, slowly and deliberately. He was very much at home in this office, which had been his for ten years.

'Are you worried about your nephew?' blurted out Amadieu, who was unable to keep quiet any longer. 'I want you to know that I'm even more concerned than you are. I'm the one who's carrying the can. It's gone all the way to the top, you know. The minister himself sent a note to the chief. I'm not even involved any more. It's the examining magistrate who's in charge. Gastambide was there in your day, wasn't he?'

The telephone rang. Amadieu held the receiver to his ear and muttered:

'. . . Yes, chief . . . Very good, chief . . . In a few minutes . . . I'm not alone . . . Yes . . . That's correct . . .'

Maigret knew what this conversation was about. At the other end of the corridor, Philippe had just been called into the chief's office.

'Did you want to ask me something?' said Amadieu, getting to his feet. 'You heard. The chief wants me.'

'Just a couple of questions. First of all, was Cageot aware that Pepito was about to be arrested?'

'I don't know. Besides, I don't see how that's relevant.'

'I'm sorry. I know Cageot. I know he's an informer. I also know that sometimes there's careless talk in front of informers. Did he come here two or three days before the murder?'

'I think so. Yes, I recall—'

'Another question: Do you know the address of Joseph Audiat, that waiter who was walking down Rue Fontaine and just happened to bump into Philippe?'

'He sleeps at a hotel in Rue Lepic, if I'm not mistaken.'

'Have you checked out Cageot's alibi?'

Amadieu feigned a smile.

'Now look, Maigret, I know how to do my job!'

But there was more to come. On the desk, Maigret had spotted a yellow cardboard folder with the vice squad's letterhead.

'Is that the report on Fernande Bosquet's arrest already?'

Amadieu looked away. He had seemed about to give Maigret a clear explanation, but now his hand was on the door knob and he merely mumbled:

'What do you mean?'

'I mean that Cageot had a girl arrested by the Vice. Where is she now?'

'I don't know.'

'May I have a quick look at the file?'

It was hard to say no. Maigret leaned over, read a few lines and concluded:

'She's probably having her fingerprints done as we speak.'

The telephone rang again. Amadieu raised his hand.

'I'm sorry, but—'

'I know. Mustn't keep the chief waiting.'

Maigret buttoned up his overcoat and left the office at the same time as Amadieu. Instead of heading back down the stairs, he walked with him to the waiting room with red velvet armchairs.

'Would you ask the chief if he can see me?'

Amadieu pushed open a padded door. The office boy also vanished inside the head of the Police Judiciaire's office where Philippe was being grilled. Maigret stood waiting, hat in hand.

'The chief is very busy and requests that you come back this afternoon.'

Maigret turned and walked back through the knots of

inspectors. His expression was a little grim, but he wanted to keep up appearances. He gave a joyless smile.

He did not go back out into the street, but sneaked off down the narrow corridors and up the winding staircases that led to the top floor of the Palais de Justice. He found his way to the criminal records department and pushed open the door. The women's session was over. In the grey room around fifty men who had been arrested the previous night were getting undressed, leaving their clothes in little piles on the benches lining the walls.

Once naked, one by one they went into the next room where staff in black overalls took their fingerprints, sat them down on the anthropometric chair and shouted out their measurements like sales assistants in a department store announcing a sale at the till.

There was a smell of sweat and filth. Most of the men were bewildered, awkward in their nakedness, allowing themselves to be shoved around from pillar to post and trying to obey instructions, many of them confused because they did not speak French.

Maigret cordially shook hands with the staff and heard the inevitable platitudes:

'Popping in to say hello?' 'How's life in the country?' 'It must be gorgeous in this weather!'

The neon lamp shed a crude light in the little room where the photographer worked.

'Were there a lot of women, this morning?'

'Seven.'

'Have you got their records?'

They were lying on a table since they had not yet been filed. The third one was Fernande's, with the prints of her five fingers, a clumsy signature and a horribly realistic mug shot.

'Did she say anything? Did she cry?'

'No. She was very docile.'

'Do you know where she's been taken?'

'I don't know whether they let her go or whether they'll make her do a few days in Saint-Lazare.'

Maigret's gaze roved over the naked men who stood in rows like soldiers. He raised his hand to his hat and said:

'Goodbye!'

'Are you leaving so soon?'

He was already on the stairs, where there was not a single step that he hadn't trodden a thousand times. Another staircase, to the left, narrower than the first, led to the laboratory whose every nook and cranny, every vial, he knew.

He was back on the second floor just after the troop of inspectors had left. Visitors began to take their places outside various doors – people who had been summoned, or who had come to lodge a complaint, or who had something they wanted to report.

Maigret had spent most of his life in this atmosphere but now he looked around him with a sort of disgust.

Was Philippe still in the chief's office? Probably not! By now he would have been arrested and two of his colleagues would be escorting him to the examining magistrate's chambers!

What had been said to him, behind the padded door? Had they spoken to him honestly and plainly?

'You have committed a blunder. The evidence against you is such that the public would not understand if you remained at liberty. But we will endeavour to uncover the truth. You will remain one of us.'

That was probably not what had been said. Maigret thought he could hear the chief, uncomfortable while waiting for Amadieu, mutter between coughs:

'Inspector, I am extremely displeased with you. It was easier for you to get into the police than for anyone else thanks to your uncle. Have you shown yourself worthy of that favour?'

And Amadieu would go further:

'As of now, you are in the hands of the examining magistrate.

With the best will in the world, there is nothing we can do for you.'

And yet this Amadieu, with his long pale face and his brown moustache, which he was always tapering, was not a bad man. He had a wife and three children, including a daughter he wanted to provide with a dowry. He had always believed that everyone around him was scheming, that they all wanted his job and were constantly seeking to compromise him.

As for the chief, in two years' time he would reach retirement age and until then it was best to avoid trouble.

This was a standard gangland killing, in other words, a run-of-the-mill case. Were they going to risk complications by protecting a rookie inspector who had gone astray and was Maigret's nephew to boot?

Cageot was a crook and everyone knew it. He himself didn't even hide it. He cashed in on all sides. And when he sold someone to the police, it was because that person was no longer useful to him.

Nevertheless, Cageot was a dangerous criminal. He had friends, connections. And above all, he was good at protecting himself. They would get him one day, for sure. They had him in their sights. They had checked his alibi and the investigation would follow the proper course.

But there was no need for overzealousness! And there was certainly no need for Maigret, with his habit of putting his foot in it.

Maigret had reached the little paved courtyard where a morose crowd waited outside the juvenile court. Despite the sunshine, there was a chill in the air and in the shade there was still a dusting of frost between the flagstones.

'That idiot Philippe!' grumbled Maigret almost sick with revulsion.

For he was well aware that he was going round and round like a circus horse. There was no point waiting for a brainwave;

in police matters, brainwaves were of no use. Nor was it a matter of discovering a phenomenal lead, or a clue that had eluded everyone else.

It was simpler and more brutal. Cageot had killed Pepito, or had him killed. The challenge was to get Cageot finally to admit that this was the truth.

Now Maigret was strolling along the riverbank, close to the laundry boat. He did not have the power to summon Cageot to an office and lock him in for a few hours, or to repeat the same question a hundred times, roughing him up if necessary to make him crack.

Nor could he summon the café owner, the waiter or the men who played *belote* every night a hundred metres from the Floria.

He had barely started using Fernande when she had literally been snatched away from him.

He reached the Chope du Pont-Neuf, pushed open the glazed door and went over to shake hands with Lucas, who was sitting at the bar.

'How are things, chief?'

'Not good!' replied Maigret.

'It's tough, isn't it?'

It wasn't tough. It was a hopelessly tragic situation.

'I'm getting old! Maybe it's the effect of rural life.'

'What are you drinking?'

'I'll have a Pernod!'

He said that almost defiantly. He remembered that he had promised to write to his wife, but he hadn't felt up to it.

'Is there some way I can help?'

Lucas was a curious character, always badly dressed, puny into the bargain, who had neither wife nor family. Maigret let his gaze rove around the place, which was beginning to fill up, and he had to crease his eyes when he turned to the window where the sun was streaming in.

'Have you worked with Philippe?'

'A couple of times.'

'Was he very disagreeable?'

'There are people who resent him because he doesn't say much. He's shy, you know. Have they banged him up?'

'Cheers.'

Lucas was concerned to see Maigret so tight-lipped.

'What are you going to do, chief?'

'I know I can trust you, so I'll tell you. I'm going to do *everything* that's necessary. Do you understand? It's best that someone knows, so if anything were to happen—'

He wiped his mouth on the back of his hand, and tapped a coin on the bar to attract the waiter's attention.

'Leave it! It's my round,' said Lucas.

'If you insist. I'll buy a round when this is over. Goodbye, Lucas.'

'Goodbye, chief.'

Lucas' hand lingered for a moment in Maigret's rough paw.

'All the same, you will take care, won't you?'

And Maigret, on his feet, boomed:

'I cannot stand cretins!'

He walked off alone. He had plenty of time, since he had no idea where he was going.

5.

As Maigret pushed open the door of the Tabac Fontaine, at around 1.30, the owner, who had just risen, was slowly making his way down a spiral staircase into the back of the café. Although not as tall as Maigret, he was just as broad and burly. As he crossed the room, he exuded a whiff of the bathroom – his hair reeked of cologne and there were traces of talcum powder behind his ears. He wore neither a jacket nor a collar. His lightly starched shirt was snowy white, fastened by a swivel stud.

He went behind the bar, shoving the waiter roughly aside, grabbed a bottle of white wine and a glass, diluted the wine with mineral water, threw back his head and gargled.

At that hour, there were just a few passing customers snatching a hurried coffee. Maigret went and sat by the window, but the owner, oblivious of him, tied on a blue apron and turned to a blonde girl seated at the till of the cigarette counter.

He said no more to her than to the waiter, opened the cash register, looked at a notebook and stretched, now fully awake. His day was beginning, and the first thing he noticed on inspecting his realm was Maigret staring placidly at him.

They had never met, but the owner still knitted his thick, black eyebrows. He appeared to be racking his brains. Unable to place Maigret, he scowled. And yet he could never have foreseen that this placid customer was going to sit there for twelve full hours!

Maigret's first task was to go over to the till and say to the girl:

'Have you got a telephone token?'

The booth was in a corner of the café. It only had a frosted glass door, and Maigret, sensing the owner had his eye on him, jiggled the handset making a series of loud clicks. Meanwhile, using the pen-knife he was holding in his other hand, he cut the cable at the point where it went under the floor, so that no one would notice that it had been severed.

'Hello! . . . Hello! . . .' he yelled.

He emerged fuming.

'Is your telephone out of order?'

The owner glanced over at the cashier, who looked surprised.

'It was working a few minutes ago. Lucien telephoned for some croissants. Didn't you, Lucien?'

'Barely a quarter of an hour ago,' confirmed the waiter.

The owner wasn't suspicious yet, but he was still watching Maigret covertly. He went into the booth and tried to make a call, persisting for a good ten minutes without noticing the severed cable.

Impassive, Maigret had returned to his table and ordered a beer. He was stocking up on patience. He knew that he was going to have to sit on that same chair for hours, in front of that fake mahogany pedestal table, confronted with the sight of the pewter bar and the glazed booth where the girl sold tobacco and cigarettes.

As he came out of the telephone booth, the owner kicked the door shut, walked over to the doorway and sniffed the air of the street for a moment. He stood very close to Maigret, who was staring fixedly at him. Finally becoming aware of that penetrating gaze, he spun round.

Maigret didn't move a muscle. He was still wearing his overcoat and hat, as if about to leave.

'Lucien! Run next door and telephone for someone to come and repair the phone.'

The waiter hurried out, a dirty napkin over his arm, and the owner himself served two builders who came in, their faces clown-like under an almost even layer of plaster dust.

An atmosphere of doubt hung in the air for perhaps another ten minutes. When Lucien announced that the engineer would not be coming until the next day, the owner turned to Maigret again and muttered under his breath:

'Bastard!'

He could have meant the tardy engineer, but the insult was chiefly addressed to the customer in whom he finally recognized a policeman.

It was 2.30 and this was the prologue to a long, drawn-out performance, which eluded everybody present. The owner's name was Louis. Customers who knew him came and shook his hand, exchanged a few words with him. Louis himself rarely served. Most of the time, he stayed in the background, behind the bar, between the waiter and the girl on the cigarette counter.

And he watched Maigret over their heads. He made no bones about it, and Maigret watched him with equal brazenness. The situation could have been comical, for they were both big, broad and heavy, and they were trying to outstare each other.

Neither was a fool, either. Louis knew exactly what he was doing when, from time to time, he glanced at the glass door, afraid of seeing a certain person walk in.

At that hour, Rue Fontaine was bustling with everyday activities like any other Paris street. Opposite the bar there was an Italian grocery where the local housewives came to do their shopping.

'Waiter! A calvados.'

The lethargic blonde cashier stared at Maigret with mounting curiosity. Meanwhile, the waiter had intuited that something was amiss, although he didn't know what exactly, and he gave the owner an occasional wink.

It was just after three when a big, light-coloured limousine pulled up outside. A tall, youngish, dark-haired man with a scar on his left cheek alighted and entered the café, extending his hand over the bar.

'Hello, Louis.'

'Hello, Eugène.'

Maigret had a direct view of Louis, and he could see the newcomer's reflection in the mirror.

'A mint-soda, Lucien. And make it quick.'

He was one of the *belote* players, probably the owner of a brothel in Béziers that Fernande had mentioned. He wore a silk shirt and his clothes were well tailored. He too smelled fragrant.

'Have you seen the—'

He broke off mid-sentence. Louis had signalled to him that someone was eavesdropping and Eugène looked up at Maigret's reflection.

'Hmm! Where's that iced soda, Lucien?'

He took a cigarette from a monogrammed case, and lit it from his lighter.

'Nice weather, isn't it!' said the owner, with irony, still eyeing Maigret.

'Nice weather indeed. But there's a funny smell in here.'

'What smell?'

'Something fishy.'

They both roared with laughter, while Maigret puffed gently on his pipe.

'See you later?' queried Eugène, extending his hand once again.

He wanted to know if they'd be meeting up as usual.

'See you later.'

This conversation galvanized Louis, who grabbed a dirty cloth and, with a grin, came over to Maigret.

'May I?'

He wiped the table so clumsily that he knocked over the glass, spilling the contents on to Maigret's trousers.

'Lucien! Bring the gentleman another glass.'

And, by way of apology:

'No extra charge!'

Maigret gave a vague smile in return.

★

By five o'clock the street lamps were lit, but it was still light enough outside to identify the customers as they crossed the road and reached for the door handle.

When Joseph Audiat walked in, Louis and Maigret looked at each other, as of one accord, and from that moment it was almost as if they had been exchanging protracted secrets. There was no need to mention the Floria, or Pepito, or Cageot.

Maigret knew, and Louis knew that he knew.

'Evening, Louis!'

Audiat was a short man, dressed in black from head to foot, with a slightly crooked nose and eyes that darted everywhere. He walked up to the bar and held his hand out to the blonde cashier, saying:

'Hello, sweetheart.'

Then to Lucien:

'A Pernod, young man.'

He talked a lot. He gave the impression of an actor on stage. But Maigret soon discerned a certain anxiety beneath his façade. Audiat also had a nervous twitch. As soon as his smile left his lips, he automatically struggled to recompose it.

'No one here yet?'

The café was empty. There were only two customers standing at the bar.

'Eugène's been in.'

The owner re-enacted the scene he had played earlier, pointing out Maigret to Audiat who, less diplomatic than Eugène, swung round, looked Maigret in the eye and spat on the floor.

'Anything else?' he said.

'Nothing. Did you win?'

'No. Zilch! I was given a tip that backfired. I was in with a chance for the third race, but the horse missed the start. Give me a packet of Gauloises, sweetheart.'

He could not keep still; he kept shifting from one foot to the other, gesticulating and waggling his head.

'Can I make a phone call?'

Louis looked daggers at Maigret.

'No you can't. The gentleman over there wrecked the phone.'

It was open war. Audiat was ill at ease. He was afraid of making a blunder, for he had no idea what had happened before his arrival.

'Are we seeing each other this evening?'

'As usual!'

Audiat downed his Pernod and left. Meanwhile, Louis came and sat down at the table next to Maigret, where the waiter brought him a hot meal which he had cooked on the gas ring in the back.

'Waiter!' Maigret called out.

'Here! Nine francs seventy-five—'

'Bring me two ham sandwiches and a beer.'

Louis was eating some reheated sauerkraut with two appetizing-looking sausages.

'Is there any ham left, Monsieur Louis?'

'There must be an old piece in the icebox.'

He chewed noisily, crudely exaggerating his movements. The waiter brought Maigret two dry, shrivelled sandwiches, but he pretended not to notice.

'Waiter! Some mustard—'

'There isn't any.'

The two hours that followed went faster, for the bar was invaded by passers-by dropping in for an aperitif. The owner condescended to serve them himself. The door kept opening and closing, sending a blast of cold air in Maigret's direction each time.

Now the temperature had dropped to freezing. For a while, the passing omnibuses were crammed full, and there were passengers standing on the platform at the rear. Then, gradually, the street grew empty. The seven o'clock flurry gave way to an unexpected quiet, a prelude to the very different bustle of the evening.

The toughest hour was between eight and nine. The place was deserted. The blonde girl behind the till had been replaced by a woman in her forties, who began sorting all the coins from the cash register into piles. Louis had gone up to his room, and when he came back down, he was wearing a jacket and tie.

Joseph Audiat was the first to put in an appearance, a few minutes after nine. He looked around for Maigret and strolled over to Louis.

'Everything OK?'

'Everything OK. There's no reason why it wouldn't be, is there?'

But Louis did not have the same energy as earlier. He was tired, and did not look at Maigret with the same cockiness. And Maigret himself seemed to exhibit a certain weariness. He must have drunk a little of everything – beer, coffee, calvados, mineral water. Seven or eight saucers were piled up on the table in front of him, and he had to order another drink.

'Look! Here come Eugène and his friend.'

The pale-blue limousine had drawn up alongside the kerb again, and two men came into the bar, Eugène first of all, dressed as he had been that afternoon, then a younger, timid-looking man who smiled at everyone.

'What about Oscar?'

'He's bound to come.'

Eugène winked, jerking his head in Maigret's direction, moved two tables together and went over to fetch the red mat and the chips from a drawer.

'Shall we begin?'

They were all putting on an act. But it was Eugène and the owner who were calling the tune. Especially Eugène, who was freshly arrived on the scene. He had brilliant white teeth and a genuine cheerfulness, and women must have gone crazy over him.

'At least we'll be able to see clearly tonight!' he said.

'Why?' asked Audiat, who was always a bit slow on the uptake.

'Because we have a luminary among us!'

That luminary was Maigret, who was smoking his pipe less than a metre away from the players.

Louis picked up the slate and the chalk with a ritual gesture. He was the one who usually kept score. He drew the columns headed with the players' initials.

'What are you drinking?' asked the waiter.

Eugène narrowed his eyes, glanced over at Maigret's calvados and replied:

'The same as the gentleman over there!'

'A strawberry cordial,' said Audiat, on edge.

The fourth man had a strong Marseille accent and could not have been in Paris long. He took his cue from Eugène, for whom he appeared to have a profound admiration.

'The hunting season's not over yet, is it, Louis?'

This time it was Louis who was bemused.

'How do I know? Why are you asking?'

'Because I was thinking about going after rabbits.'

Again, it was Maigret who was the butt of his comment. The explanation followed, as the cards were dealt and each player arranged them in a fan in his left hand.

'I went to see the man, earlier.'

Which translated as: 'I went to warn Cageot'.

Audiat abruptly looked up.

'What did he say?'

Louis frowned, probably thinking that they were going too far.

'He's laughing! Apparently he's on home ground and he's planning a little party.'

'Diamonds trumps . . . *Tierce haute* . . . OK?'

'Four of a kind.'

Eugène was all keyed up and it was clear he was not concentrating on the game but on coming up with fresh witticisms.

'The Parisians,' he stated, 'go and spend their holidays in the country – in the Loire, for example. The funny thing is, that the people from the Loire come and spend their holidays in Paris.'

At last! He hadn't been able to resist the urge to let Maigret know that he knew all about him. And Maigret sat there, puffing away on his pipe and warming his calvados in the hollow of his hand before taking a sip.

'Keep your eyes on the game,' retorted Louis, who kept darting anxious glances in the direction of the door.

'Trumps . . . and double trumps. A twenty-point bonus, plus ten for the last trick . . .'

An individual who looked like a modest Montmartre shopkeeper walked in and went over to wedge himself between Eugène and his friend from Marseille, without saying a word. He shook both their hands and sat slightly back, still without opening his mouth.

'All right?' asked Louis.

The newcomer's lips parted, and a thin, reedy sound came out. He had lost his voice.

'All right!'

'You got it?' Eugène bawled in his ear, revealing that the man was deaf as well.

'Twigged what?' replied the reedy voice.

They must have kicked him under the table. Finally the deaf man's gaze lighted on Maigret and rested on him for a long moment. He gave a faint smile.

'I get it.'

'Clubs trumps . . . Pass . . .'

'Pass . . .'

Rue Fontaine was coming back to life. The neon signs were lit and the doormen were at their posts on the pavement. The Floria's doorman came in to buy cigarettes, but no one took any notice of him.

'Hearts trumps . . .'

Maigret was hot. He felt stiff all over but he gave no sign of it and his expression remained the same as when he had begun his long vigil.

'I say!' said Eugène suddenly to his hard-of-hearing neighbour, whom Maigret had recognized as the owner of a brothel in Rue de Provence. 'What do you call a locksmith who doesn't make locks any more?'

The comical aspect of this conversation came from the fact that Eugène had to shout, while the other man answered in an angelic voice:

'A locksmith who—? I don't know.'

'Well, I'd call him a nobody.'

He played a card, picked up and played again.

'And a cop who's no longer a cop?'

The penny had dropped. His neighbour's face lit up and his voice was reedier than ever as he said:

'A nobody!'

Then they all burst out laughing, even Audiat, who gave a snigger. Something was stopping him from joining wholeheartedly in the general mirth. He was visibly anxious, despite the presence of his friends. And it was not solely on account of Maigret.

'Léon!' he shouted to the night waiter. 'Bring me a brandy and water.'

'You're drinking brandy now?'

Eugène had noticed that Audiat was losing his nerve and he was keeping a close eye on him.

'You'd better go easy.'

'Go easy on what?'

'How many Pernods did you have before dinner?'

'Damn you!' replied Audiat stubbornly.

'Calm down, boys,' broke in Louis. 'Spades trumps!'

By midnight, their cheerfulness was more forced. Maigret was still sitting immobile in his overcoat, his pipe in his mouth. He looked like part of the furniture. Or even better, he blended in with the walls. Only his eyes were alive, roving slowly from one player to the other.

Audiat had been the first to display signs of unease, and then the deaf man soon began to show some impatience. At length, he stood up:

'I have to go to a funeral tomorrow. I should go to bed.'

'Oh, drop dead!' said Eugène under his breath, certain he wouldn't be heard.

He said that the way he would have said anything else, to keep his spirits up.

'*Rebelote* . . . and trumps . . . and trumps again . . . Give me your cards . . .'

Despite the disapproving looks he was getting, Audiat had drunk three brandies and his face was furrowed. He had turned pale and his forehead was clammy.

'Where are you going?'

'I'm off too,' he said, rising.

He clearly felt sick. He had drunk his third brandy to perk himself up, but it had finished him off. Louis and Eugène exchanged glances.

'You look like a wet rag,' Eugène said after a moment.

It was just after one o'clock in the morning. Maigret took out his money and put it on the table. Eugène drew Audiat into a corner and spoke to him in hushed but urgent tones. Audiat was reluctant, but eventually allowed himself to be persuaded.

'See you tomorrow!' he said, his hand on the door handle.

'Waiter! How much?'

The saucers rattled. Maigret buttoned up his overcoat, filled a fresh pipe and lit it with the gas lighter by the bar.

'Good night, gentlemen.'

He left the café and identified the sound of Audiat's retreating footsteps. Meanwhile, Eugène slipped behind the bar, as if to have a word with the owner. Louis immediately understood and discreetly opened a drawer. Eugène plunged his hand inside then put it in his pocket and headed for the door with the man from Marseille in tow.

'See you later,' he said, stepping out into the night.

6.

In the glow from the nightclubs' neon signs, Rue Fontaine was busy with doormen on the pavement and drivers manoeuvring to park their cars. It was only after Place Blanche, when Maigret and his quarry turned right on to Boulevard Rochechouart, that the situation became clearer.

Joseph Audiat walked ahead with a feverish, irregular step, never once turning round.

Twenty metres behind him came Maigret's burly form taking great, calm strides, his hands thrust in his pockets.

Audiat and Maigret's footsteps echoed each other in the silence of the night, Audiat's more rapid, Maigret's tread heavier and more solemn.

Behind them, the purring of Eugène's engine could be heard – for Eugène and the man from Marseille had jumped into the car. They drove at a crawl, hugging the kerb and trying to keep a distance from the two men. Sometimes they had to change gear to maintain their speed. Sometimes too they would put on a sudden spurt and then slow down to allow Audiat and Maigret to get ahead.

Maigret had no need to look over his shoulder. He knew what was going on. He was aware that the big blue limousine was behind him. He could picture the faces behind the windscreen.

It was classic. He was following Audiat because he had the feeling that Audiat would allow himself to be intimidated more easily than the others. Meanwhile, the others, who knew this, were following him in turn.

At first, this made Maigret smile inwardly.

Then, he was no longer smiling, but frowning. Audiat was

not heading towards Rue Lepic, where he had a room, nor towards the centre of Paris. He continued along the boulevard beneath the overground section of the métro in the direction of La Chapelle, without stopping at the Barbès intersection.

It was highly unlikely that he had any business in this neighbourhood at such an hour. There could only be one explanation. Audiat had been instructed by the two men in the car to lure Maigret into the deserted back streets.

Already, the only signs of life were the occasional girl hidden in the shadows, or the hesitant form of a North African going from one to the other before making up his mind.

Maigret did not feel frightened straight away. He remained calm, puffing away on his pipe and listening to his footsteps, as regular as a pendulum.

The boulevard passed over the railway lines coming out of the Gare du Nord, which loomed in the distance with its illuminated clock and empty platforms. The time was 2.30. The car was still purring behind them, when, for no reason, it gave a little hoot of its horn. Then Audiat began walking faster, so fast that he seemed to be trying not to run.

For no apparent reason either, he crossed the road. Maigret crossed too. For a second, he was sideways on. He saw the car out of the corner of his eye, and that was when it dawned on him what they were up to.

The overground métro made the boulevard darker than any other part of Paris. A police cycle patrol rode past and one of the officers turned round to look at the car, saw nothing untoward and vanished with his colleagues.

The pace was hotting up. After a hundred metres, Audiat crossed the road again, but this time he lost his cool and ran the last few steps. Maigret stopped and he could hear the car revving up. The situation was perfectly clear. There were beads of perspiration on his forehead, for it was pure chance that he had avoided being run over.

So that was it! Audiat's job was to entice him through the empty streets. And then, when Maigret was halfway across the road, the car would mow him down.

As if in a nightmare, Maigret was conscious of the sleek limousine gliding through the streets and its two occupants, especially Eugène, with his brilliant white teeth and angelic smile, sitting with his hands on the wheel waiting for the right moment.

Could this be called a crime? Maigret was in danger of dying a stupid and horrible death any moment now: lying in the dirt, severely wounded, and howling with pain for hours before anyone would come to his aid.

It was too late to turn back. In any case, he didn't want to. He was no longer counting on Audiat, he had abandoned his plan of catching up with him and getting him to talk, but he was determined to continue following him. It was a question of self-respect.

His only precaution was to take his gun out of his trouser pocket and to cock it.

Then he walked a little faster. Instead of staying twenty metres behind Audiat, he was so close on his heels that Audiat thought Maigret was going to arrest him, and he too hastened his step. For a few seconds, it was comical, and the two men in the car must have realized what was going on because they came much closer.

The trees on the boulevard and the pillars supporting the overhead métro filed past. Audiat was afraid, afraid of Maigret and perhaps too of his accomplices. When the car hooted once more to prompt him to cross the road, he stopped, breathless, on the kerb.

Close on his heels, Maigret saw the car's headlamps, Audiat's soft hat and anxious eyes.

He was about to step off the pavement close behind his companion when a sixth sense held him back. Perhaps Audiat had the same intuition, but for him it was too late. He was already in the road, advancing one metre, two metres . . .

Maigret opened his mouth to shout a warning. He could see that the two men in the car, tired of this fruitless chase, had suddenly decided to put their foot down, even if it meant hitting their comrade at the same time as Maigret.

There was no scream. A rush of air, the sound of an engine going at full throttle. A dull thud too, and perhaps a vague shout.

The car's red rear lights were already receding, and then it vanished down a side street. On the ground, the little man in black was struggling to raise himself up on his hands, gazing wild-eyed at Maigret.

He looked like a madman or a child. His face was covered in dust and blood. His nose had changed shape, which distorted his entire face.

He managed to sit up and raise a hand to his forehead, limply, as in a dream, grimacing.

Maigret gathered him up and sat him down on the kerb, and, without thinking, went to pick up the hat that was sitting in the middle of the road. Then it took him a few moments to recover his own equilibrium, even though he had not been hit.

There were no passers-by. A taxi could be heard, but it was a long way off, probably near Barbès.

'You had a narrow escape!' grunted Maigret, leaning over the injured man.

He probed Audiat's head with his thumbs, slowly, to check whether his skull was fractured. He flexed his legs one after the other, for his trousers were torn, or rather ripped off below the right knee, and Maigret glimpsed an ugly wound.

Audiat seemed to have lost not only the power of speech, but also his mind. His jaw worked up and down, as if to get rid of a nasty taste in his mouth.

Maigret looked up. He had heard the sound of an engine. He was convinced it was Eugène's car driving down a back street.

Then the noise drew closer and the blue limousine shot across the boulevard barely a hundred metres from the two men.

They could not stay there. Eugène and his sidekick would not go away. They wanted to know what was going to happen. They drove around the neighbourhood in another big circle, the purring of the engine barely audible in the still night. This time, they drove along the boulevard within a few metres of Audiat. Maigret held his breath, expecting gunfire.

'They'll be back,' he thought. 'And next time . . .'

He lifted Audiat, carried him across the road and sat him down on the ground behind a tree.

And the car did drive past again. Eugène failed to spot the two men and pulled up a hundred metres further on. There must have been a brief discussion between him and the other man, and the outcome was that they gave up the chase.

Audiat groaned and writhed as the light from a gas lamp revealed a huge pool of blood on the ground in the spot where he had been knocked over.

There was nothing they could do but wait. Maigret did not dare leave the injured man to go off in search of a taxi, and he was loath to ring a doorbell and have a crowd gather. They only had to wait for ten minutes before a half-drunk Algerian came past, and Maigret got him to understand that he must fetch a taxi.

The night was cold. The sky had the same icy tinge as the night Maigret had left Meung. From time to time the whistle of a freight train reached them from the Gare du Nord.

'It hurts!' said Audiat at last in a mournful tone.

And he looked up at Maigret as if expecting him to alleviate his suffering.

Fortunately, the Algerian had done as he had been asked and a taxi pulled up. The driver was wary:

'Are you sure it was an accident?'

He couldn't make up his mind whether to turn off the engine and help Maigret or not.

'If you don't believe me, take us to the police station,' Maigret replied.

The driver was won over and a quarter of an hour later they pulled up opposite the Hôtel des Quais, where Maigret was staying.

Audiat, who had not closed his eyes, was watching people and things with such an ineffable gentleness that the sight made people smile. The hotel doorman misinterpreted it.

'Your friend looks as though he's had one too many.'

'Perhaps he was a bit drunk. A car knocked him over.'

They carried Audiat up to the room. Maigret ordered a rum and had towels brought. He did not need any help for the rest. While people slept in the neighbouring room, he silently removed his shoes, his jacket and his detachable collar and rolled up his shirt sleeves.

Half an hour later, he was still working on Audiat, who was stretched out on the bed, scrawny and naked, with the mark of his garters on his calves. The ugliest wound was the one on his knee. Maigret disinfected and dressed it. He had put sticking plasters on the few minor scratches and finally got the injured man to drink a large glass of rum.

The radiator was scalding hot. The curtains weren't drawn, and the moon was visible against a patch of sky.

'Well, your friends are utter bastards, aren't they?' sighed Maigret suddenly.

Audiat pointed to his jacket and asked for a cigarette.

'What alerted me was that you were so twitchy. You'd guessed that they'd go after you too!'

His gaze steadier, Audiat eyed Maigret with suspicion. When he did open his mouth, it was to ask a question.

'What does it matter to you?'

'Keep still, you're still very shaken. Let me tell you why it matters to me. A thug – someone you know – killed Pepito, probably because he was afraid he'd say too much about the

Barnabé business. At around two in the morning, the thug in question came looking for you at the Tabac Fontaine.'

Audiat knitted his brow and stared at the wall.

'You remember! Cageot called you outside. He asked you to bump into the fellow who'd be coming out of the Floria at any moment. And thanks to your testimony, that's the fellow who's been locked up. Now supposing that were a member of my family—'

His cheek on the pillow, Audiat murmured:

'Don't count on me!'

It was around four. Maigret sat down beside the bed, poured himself a glassful of rum and filled a pipe.

'We have plenty of time to chat,' he said. 'I've just looked at your papers. So far you only have four convictions and they're not serious: pickpocketing, fraud, accessory to the burglary of a villa—'

Audiat was pretending to be asleep.

'Only, if I've done my sums correctly, one more conviction and it's exile to the colonies for you. What do you think?'

'Let me sleep.'

'I'm not stopping you from going to sleep. But you won't stop me from speaking. I know that your friends aren't home yet. Right now, they're arranging things so that tomorrow, if I report their registration number, a garage owner will swear that their car didn't leave his garage this evening.'

Audiat's swollen lips stretched in a blissful smile.

'Except that I'll tell you one thing: I'll get Cageot! Whenever I've made up my mind to get someone, I've nabbed them in the end. Now the day when Cageot is hauled in, you will be too, and no matter how much you protest—'

By five in the morning Maigret had drunk two glasses of rum and the air was blue with pipe smoke. Audiat had tossed and turned so many times that he had ended up sitting up in bed, his cheeks red and his eyes shining.

'Was it Cageot who planned last night's little surprise? Most likely, eh? Eugène couldn't have thought of that all by himself. And if that is the case, you must be aware that your boss has no qualms about getting rid of you.'

A resident kept awake by Maigret's monologue stamped on the floor. The room was so hot that Maigret had removed his waistcoat.

'Give me some rum.'

There was only one glass, the water beaker, and the two men took it in turns to drink from it, without realizing how much alcohol they were downing. Maigret kept harking back to the same subject.

'I'm not asking much from you. Simply admit that, immediately after Pepito's death, Cageot came to fetch you from the café.'

'I didn't know that Pepito was dead.'

'You see! So you were at the Tabac Fontaine, as you were last night, with Eugène and probably the little hotel owner too. Did Cageot come in?'

'No!'

'Well, he knocked on the window. You must have had a pre-arranged signal.'

'I'm not talking.'

At six, the sky grew light. Trams rumbled past on the riverbank and a tugboat siren let out a heartrending wail as if, during the night, it had lost its barges.

Maigret's face was nearly as red as Audiat's, his eyes nearly as bright. The rum bottle was empty.

'I'm going to tell you, as a friend, what's going to happen now that they know that you came here and we talked. They'll repeat the operation as soon as they can, and this time they won't miss you. If you talk, what do you risk? We'll keep you in prison for a few days, for your own safety. When we've got the whole bunch of them banged up, we'll let you go and that will be it.'

Audiat listened attentively. He was clearly not entirely opposed to the idea, for he murmured, as if to himself:

'In the state I'm in, I'm entitled to go to the infirmary.'

'Of course. And you know the infirmary at Fresnes. It's even better than a hospital.'

'Can you check whether my knee is swollen?'

Maigret obeyed, removing the dressing. The knee had swollen, and Audiat, who was terrified of disease, prodded it anxiously.

'Do you think they'll have to amputate my leg?'

'I promise you that it will heal within a fortnight. You just have a little water on the knee.'

'Oh!'

He gazed at the ceiling and lay still for a few minutes. An alarm clock rang in another room. From the corridors came the muffled tread of the valet arriving on duty, then, from the landing, the relentless swish of a brush polishing shoes.

'Have you decided?'

'I don't know.'

'Would you rather end up in court with Cageot?'

'I'd like a drink of water.'

He was doing it deliberately. He was not smiling, but Maigret could sense his delight at being waited on.

'This water's warm!'

Maigret did not protest. His braces dangling, he ambled over and did everything the injured man asked of him. The horizon turned pink. A ray of sunshine licked the window.

'Who's in charge of the investigation?'

'Inspector Amadieu and the examining magistrate Gastambide.'

'Are they decent men?'

'There's no one better.'

'Admit that I was nearly a goner! How did I get run over?'

'By the car's left wing.'

'Was Eugène at the wheel?'

'It was him. The fellow from Marseille was with him. Who is he?'

'A young guy who arrived three months ago. He was in Barcelona, but apparently there's nothing going on there.'

'Now look here, Audiat. There's no point playing cat and mouse any longer. I'm going to call a taxi. The two of us are going to go to Quai des Orfèvres. Amadieu will arrive at eight o'clock, and you're going to tell him your story.'

Maigret yawned, so exhausted that he could barely speak.

'You're not saying anything?'

'All right, let's go and see what happens.'

Maigret gave his face a quick wash, adjusted his clothes and had two breakfasts brought up.

'You see, in a situation like yours, there is only one place where you are safe. And that's in prison.'

'Amadieu, isn't he the tall one, always pale-faced, with a droopy moustache?'

'Yes.'

'I don't like the look of him!'

The rising sun made Maigret think of his little house in the Loire and the fishing rods waiting for him in the bottom of the boat. Perhaps it was because he was so tired, but, for a split second, he was tempted to drop the whole thing. He looked at Audiat with round eyes, as if he had forgotten what he was doing there, and ran his hand through his hair.

'How can I get dressed, my trousers are all torn?'

They called the valet, who found Audiat an old pair of trousers. Audiat limped, groaned and leaned on Maigret with all his weight. The taxi drove over the Pont-Neuf and it was a relief to breathe in the sharp morning air. An empty van pulled out of police HQ, where it had just deposited its cargo of prisoners.

'Will you be able to walk up the stairs?'

'Maybe. In any case, I don't want a stretcher!'

Their destination was in sight. Maigret's chest felt tight with impatience. The taxi pulled up outside number 36. Maigret paid the fare and called over the uniformed orderly to help him get Audiat out of the car.

The orderly was talking to a man with his back to the street who wheeled round on hearing Maigret's voice. It was Cageot, wearing a dark overcoat, his cheeks grey with a two-day stubble. Audiat didn't spot him until he was out of the taxi, as Cageot, without even looking at him, resumed his conversation with the officer.

No words were exchanged. Maigret supported Audiat, who pretended to be much more seriously injured than he was.

Once they had crossed the courtyard, he sank down on to the first stair, like a man whose strength has failed him. Then, looking up, he sniggered:

'Ha, ha! I had you, didn't I! I've got nothing to say. I don't know anything. But I didn't want to stay in your room. Do I know you? How can I be sure it wasn't you who pushed me in front of the car?'

Maigret clenched his fist but kept it thrust in his overcoat pocket, hard as a rock.

7.

Eugène arrived first, just before eleven o'clock. Although it was not yet spring, his clothes reflected the sunny weather. He wore a light-grey linen suit, so soft that with every movement his muscles rippled beneath the fabric. His hat was the same shade of grey, and his shoes of fine buckskin. And when he pushed open the glass door of the Police Judiciaire, a gentle fragrance wafted into the corridor.

This was not the first time he had set foot inside Quai des Orfèvres. He glanced to the right and to the left, like a regular visitor, still smoking his gold-tipped cigarette. The morning briefing was over. People were waiting gloomily outside the inspectors' offices.

Eugène went up to the clerk, greeting him by raising a finger to his hat.

'Say, my good man, I believe Inspector Amadieu is expecting me.'

'Take a seat.'

He sat down casually, crossed his legs, lit another cigarette and opened a newspaper at the racing section. His blue limousine seemed to be stretching in front of the gate. Maigret spotted it from a window and went down into the street to inspect the left wing, but there were no scratches on it.

A few hours earlier, he had entered Amadieu's office without removing his hat, his expression wary.

'I've brought in a man who knows the truth.'

'That's a matter for the examining magistrate!' Amadieu had replied, continuing to leaf through a pile of reports.

Then Maigret had knocked on the chief's door and had gathered at once that his visit was not welcome.

'Good morning, sir.'

'Good morning, Maigret.'

They were both equally ill at ease and needed few words to communicate.

'Chief, I've worked all night and I've come to ask you to arrange for three or four individuals to be brought in for questioning.'

'That's up to the examining magistrate,' objected the head of the Police Judiciaire.

'The examining magistrate won't get anything out of them. You know what I mean.'

Maigret knew he was a thorn in everyone's side and that they would have liked to tell him to go to hell, but still he persisted. He stood there for ages, his massive bulk hovering over the chief, blocking his line of vision. Eventually the chief gave in and phone calls were made from one office to another.

'Come in here for a moment, Amadieu!'

'Coming, chief.'

Words were exchanged.

'Our friend Maigret tells me that . . .'

At nine, Amadieu steeled himself to go over to Gastambide's office via the back corridors of the Palais de Justice. When he returned twenty minutes later, he had in his pocket the necessary warrants to question Cageot, Audiat, the owner of the Tabac Fontaine, Eugène, the fellow from Marseille and the short deaf man.

Eugène was already in the building waiting to see Amadieu, and so was Audiat. Maigret had made him come upstairs, where, since early morning, he had been sitting scowling at the end of the corridor watching the police officers' comings and goings.

At 9.30, inspectors set off to round up the others, while Maigret, heavy with sleep, roamed the establishment to which he no longer belonged, sometimes pushing open a door, shaking the hand of a former colleague or emptying his pipe into the sawdust of one of the spittoons.

'How are you doing?'

'Fine!' he replied.

'They're furious, you know!' Lucas whispered.

'Who?'

'Amadieu . . . The chief . . .'

And Maigret waited, soaking up the atmosphere of the place that had been his home. Ensconced in a red velvet armchair, Eugène showed no sign of impatience. On catching sight of Maigret, he even gave a cheery half-smile. He was a good-looking fellow, high-spirited and brimming with confidence. He exuded health and a happy-go-lucky attitude through every pore, and his tiniest movements displayed an almost animal grace.

An inspector came in from outside and Maigret hurried over to him.

'Did you go to the garage?'

'Yes. The garage owner says that the car was in the garage all night and the night watchman confirms his statement.'

The answer was so predictable that Eugène, who must have overheard, did not even bother to smirk.

It was not long before Louis appeared, bleary-eyed, annoyance written all over his face.

'Detective Chief Inspector Amadieu!' he grunted at the office boy.

'Have a seat.'

Acting as if he didn't recognize Eugène, Louis sat down three metres from him, his hat on his knees.

Inspector Amadieu called Maigret in and once again they found themselves facing each other in the small office overlooking the Seine.

'Are your rogues here?'

'Not all of them.'

'Do you want to tell me exactly what questions you want me to ask them?'

The seemingly friendly and deferential little phrase sounded so innocent. But it was an affirmation of passive resistance. Amadieu knew as well as Maigret that it is impossible to determine in advance the questions that will be asked during an interrogation.

Nevertheless, Maigret dictated a number of questions for each witness. Amadieu took notes with the obedience of a secretary and with blatant satisfaction.

'Is that all?'

'That's all.'

'Shall we begin right away with the one called Audiat?'

Maigret shrugged to indicate that he was not bothered, and then Amadieu pressed a bell, issuing orders to the inspector who appeared. His secretary sat at the end of the desk, with his back to the light, while Maigret sat in the darkest corner.

'Have a seat, Audiat, and tell us what you were doing last night.'

'I wasn't doing anything.'

Even though he had the sun in his eyes, Audiat had spotted Maigret and managed to glower at him.

'Where were you at midnight?'

'I can't remember. I went to the cinema, then I had a drink in a bar in Rue Fontaine.'

Amadieu glanced at Maigret to signal:

'Don't worry. I'll take your notes into account.'

And, his pince-nez on his nose, he slowly read out:

'What are the names of the friends you met in this bar?'

The battle was lost before it had begun. The questioning had got off to a bad start. The inspector sounded as if he was trotting out a lesson. Audiat, sensing this, grew increasingly bold.

'I didn't meet up with any friends.'

'And you didn't even notice someone who is here in this room?'

Audiat turned to Maigret and jerked his head in his direction.

'That gentleman maybe. But I'm not sure. I didn't take any notice of him.'

'And then?'

'And then I left. The cinema gave me a headache, so I went for a stroll along the boulevards. As I was crossing the road, I was hit by a vehicle and I ended up sitting at the base of a tree, injured. That gentleman was there. He told me I'd been knocked down by a car. I asked him to take me home, but he refused and took me to a hotel room.'

A door had opened to admit the chief of the Police Judiciaire, who stood silently, leaning against the wall.

'What did you tell him?'

'Nothing at all. He's the one who did all the talking. He spoke of people I don't know and he wanted me to come here and state that they were friends of mine.'

A chubby blue pencil in his hand, Amadieu scribbled the occasional note on his blotting pad, while the secretary recorded the full statement.

'Excuse me!' broke in the chief. 'This is all very well. But tell us what you were doing at three in the morning on Boulevard de La Chapelle.'

'I had a headache.'

'I wouldn't try and be clever, if I were you. When you've got four convictions already—'

'Excuse me! For the first two, I was granted an amnesty. You're not allowed to mention them.'

Maigret merely watched and listened. He smoked his pipe, the smell filling the office while the smoke curled upwards in the sunshine.

'We'll see about that in a few minutes.'

Audiat was taken into a neighbouring room. Amadieu telephoned:

'Bring in Eugène Berniard.'

The latter entered, smiling and relaxed. He glanced quickly around the room to identify who was sitting where, and stubbed out his cigarette in the ashtray.

'What were you doing last night?' repeated Amadieu listlessly.

'Well, inspector, I had a toothache, so I had an early night. Why don't you ask the night watchman from the Hôtel Alsina?'

'What time did you go to bed?'

'Midnight.'

'And you didn't drop in to the Tabac Fontaine?'

'Where's that?'

'Just a moment! Do you know a certain Audiat?'

'What does he look like? One meets so many people in Montmartre!'

Maigret was finding it increasingly difficult to sit still.

'Bring in Audiat!' said Amadieu into the telephone.

Audiat and Eugène stared at each other with curiosity.

'Do you know each other?'

'Never seen him before!' grunted Eugène.

'Pleased to meet you!' joked Audiat.

They barely bothered to put on an act. Their eyes were laughing, belying their words.

'So you weren't playing *belote* together last night at the Tabac Fontaine?'

One stared wide-eyed, the other burst out laughing.

'I'm afraid you're mistaken, *monsieur l'inspecteur.*'

The fellow from Marseille had just arrived, and was brought in to face the other two. He held out his hand to Eugène.

'Do you know each other?'

'Of course! We were together.'

'Where?'

'At the Hôtel Alsina. Our rooms are next to each other.'

The chief of the Police Judiciaire signalled to Maigret to follow him.

They paced up and down one end of the corridor where Louis was still waiting, not far from Germain Cageot.

'What do you intend to do?' The chief shot his companion an anxious look.

'Is it true they tried to kill you?' he asked.

Maigret did not answer. Unfazed, Cageot watched him with the same irony as Audiat and Eugène.

'If only I could have questioned them myself,' Maigret sighed at length.

'You know that isn't possible. But we'll carry on with the face-to-face confrontations for as long as you wish.'

'Thank you, chief.'

Maigret knew that it would be pointless. The five men were in cahoots. They had taken precautions. And it wasn't the questions that Amadieu was asking in his lugubrious tone that would force them to confess.

'I don't know whether you are right or wrong,' the chief added.

They walked past Cageot, who got to his feet and greeted the head of the Police Judiciaire.

'Was it you who summoned me, sir?'

It was midday. Most of the inspectors had gone to lunch or were on an assignment. The long corridor was almost empty. Pausing outside his door, the chief shook Maigret's hand.

'What more can I say? All I can do is wish you the best of luck.'

He went to collect his coat and hat and headed for the stairs, shooting a parting glance at the office where the interrogation was still ongoing and giving Cageot a dirty look.

Maigret's nerves were on edge. Never had he felt so suffocated by a sense of helplessness. Sitting side by side, Cageot and Louis were patient and relaxed, both amused at his comings and goings.

From Amadieu's office came a calm murmur of voices. Questions and answers succeeded each other with no urgency. The inspector followed the plan outlined by Maigret as promised, but without adding anything, without taking any interest.

Philippe was in prison! Madame Maigret was waiting impatiently for the postman.

'Nice day, isn't it?' said Cageot suddenly to his neighbour Louis.

'Very nice day. There's an easterly wind, though,' replied the latter.

'Have you been summoned too?'

This was for Maigret's benefit, with the barefaced intention of making fun of him.

'Yes. I think they need some information from me.'

'Same here. Who called you?'

'A certain Amadieu.'

As Maigret brushed past him, Cageot half-opened his mouth in a snigger and suddenly there was a violent reflex, impossible to control. Maigret's hand had smashed into Cageot's cheek.

That was a blunder! But it was the result of a sleepless night, and a whole string of humiliations.

While Cageot was left stunned by the brutality of the attack, Louis jumped up and grabbed Maigret's arm.

'Are you mad?'

Were they about to fight in the corridors of the Police Judiciaire?

'What's going on here?'

It was Amadieu, who had just opened his door. On seeing the three breathless men, no one could fail to grasp the situation, but the detective chief inspector said calmly, as if he had no idea:

'Would you step this way, Cageot?'

Once again, the other witnesses had been taken into the neighbouring office.

'Have a seat.'

Maigret followed them in and stood against the door.

'I asked you to come in because I need you to identify certain individuals.'

Amadieu pressed a bell and Audiat was shown in.

'Do you know this man?'

Then Maigret stomped out, slamming the door and swearing

loudly. He could have cried. This charade appalled him.

Audiat did not know Cageot. Cageot did not know Audiat! Neither of them knew Eugène! And so it would go on ad nauseam! As for Louis, he knew no one!

Amadieu, who was questioning them, scored a point with each new denial. Huh! So Maigret dared to disrupt his little habits! Huh! He was trying to teach him his job! He would remain polite to the end, because he was well brought-up, unlike some! But time would tell!

Maigret descended the drab stairs, crossed the courtyard and walked past Eugène's powerful car.

The sun was shining on Paris, on the Seine, on the sparkling Pont-Neuf. The warm air abruptly turned chilly as soon as you stepped into a patch of shade.

In a quarter of an hour, or in an hour, the interrogations would be over. Eugène would slide behind the wheel, next to his friend from Marseille. Cageot would flag down a taxi. They would go their separate ways after exchanging winks.

'That damned fool Philippe.'

Maigret was talking to himself. His feet pounded the cobblestones. He didn't know where he was going. At one point, he had the impression that a woman he passed quickly looked away to avoid being recognized. He stopped and glimpsed Fernande, who hastened her step. A few metres further on, he caught up with her and grabbed her arm with unintended violence.

'Where are you off to?'

She looked alarmed, and did not answer.

'When did they release you?'

'Last night.'

He realized that the trust that had existed between them was ruined. Fernande was afraid of him. All she wanted was to be on her way again as soon as possible.

'Were you summoned?' he asked, glancing towards the buildings of the Police Judiciaire.

'No.'

This morning she was wearing a blue suit that made her look like a respectable woman. Maigret was all the more impatient since he had no further reason to detain her.

'Why are you going there?'

He followed Fernande's gaze, lighting on Eugène's blue car.

He understood. He felt offended, a pang of jealousy.

'Do you know he tried to kill me last night?'

'Who?'

'Eugène.'

She almost said something, but bit her lip.

'What were you about to say?'

'Nothing.'

The sentry was watching them. Upstairs, behind the eighth window, Amadieu was still taking the witness statements cooked up by the five men. The car was parked outside, lithe and light as its owner, and Fernande, her face set, was waiting for the chance to make her escape.

'Do you think it was me who had you locked up?' Maigret pressed her.

She said nothing and looked away.

'Who told you that Eugène was here?' he persisted in vain.

She was in love! In love with Eugène, with whom she had slept to please Maigret!

'Too bad,' he grunted finally. 'Off you go, dear!'

He hoped that she would retrace her steps, but she hurried towards the car and stood by the door.

The only person left on the pavement was Maigret. He filled his pipe, but was unable to light it, having tamped down the tobacco too hard.

8.

As he crossed the lobby of his hotel, Maigret tensed when a woman rose from a wicker armchair and started walking towards him. She kissed him on both cheeks with a sad smile and clasped his hand, keeping it in hers.

'This is terrible,' she moaned. 'I got here this morning and I've been running around so much that I don't know whether I'm coming or going.'

Maigret looked at his sister-in-law, who had turned up from Alsace. He needed to adjust to the sight of her, such a contrast was she from the images of the last few days and the morning, from the unsavoury world in which he was immersed.

Philippe's mother looked like Madame Maigret, but there was something more provincial about her. She wasn't plump but cuddly; she had a rosy complexion and carefully smoothed hair, and everything about her exuded cleanliness – her black and white outfit, her eyes, her smile.

It was the atmosphere of the countryside that she brought with her and Maigret thought he caught a whiff of her house, with its cupboards filled with home-made jam, the aroma of the little delicacies and desserts which she loved cooking.

'Do you think he'll be able to find a job after all this?'

Maigret picked up his sister-in-law's luggage, which was even more provincial than she was.

'Are you staying here?' he asked.

'If it's not too expensive . . .'

He showed her into the dining room, where he never set foot when he was alone, for it had an austere atmosphere and people only spoke in whispers.

'How did you get hold of my address?'

'I went to the Palais de Justice and I saw the examining magistrate. He wasn't aware that you were handling the case.'

Maigret said nothing but pulled a face. He could hear his sister-in-law's voice imploring: *You understand, sir. My son's uncle, Divisional Chief Inspector Maigret—*

'Then what?' he asked irritably.

'He gave me the address of the lawyer in Rue de Grenelle. I went there too.'

'You did all that carrying your suitcases?'

'I put them in left-luggage.'

It was astounding. She must have told the whole world her story.

'I tell you, when the photograph appeared in the newspaper, Émile didn't dare go to his office!'

Émile was her husband. Philippe had inherited his myopic squint.

'In our part of the world, it's not like Paris. Prison is prison. People say that there's no smoke without fire. Does he at least have a proper bed with blankets?'

They ate sardines and rounds of beetroot, and drank a carafe of table wine. From time to time Maigret made an effort to steer the conversation away from the obsessive topic of Philippe.

'You know Émile. He's very angry with you. He blames you. He says it's your fault that Philippe joined the police instead of looking for a good job in a bank. I told him that whatever will be, will be. By the way, how's my sister? Not finding the animals too much work?'

Luncheon lasted a good hour, for afterwards they had to have a coffee and Philippe's mother wanted to know exactly how a prison is built and how the prisoners are treated. They were in the lounge when the doorman came to inform them that a gentleman wished to speak to Maigret.

'Show him in!'

He wondered who it could be and was more than astonished

to see Inspector Amadieu, who greeted Madame Lauer awkwardly.

'Philippe's mother,' said Maigret.

And, to the detective chief inspector:

'Shall we go up to my room?'

They went upstairs in silence. Once inside the room, the inspector cleared his throat and put down his hat and the umbrella which never left his side.

'I thought I'd see you after the interrogation this morning,' he began. 'But you left without saying a word.'

Maigret watched him without speaking. He knew that Amadieu had come to make peace, but was not gallant enough to make things easier for him.

'Those boys are very good, you know! I realized it when they were brought face to face with each other.'

He sat down to give an impression of composure, and crossed his legs.

'Look, Maigret, I've come to tell you that I'm beginning to share your opinion. You see that I'm being honest with you and that I bear no ill will.'

But his voice did not sound entirely natural and Maigret sensed that this was a lesson learned and that Amadieu had not taken this step of his own accord. After that morning's interrogations, there had been a meeting between the chief of the Police Judiciaire and Amadieu, and it was the chief who had been in favour of Maigret's theory.

'Now, I'm asking you: what should we do?' said Amadieu solemnly.

'I have no idea!'

'Don't you need my men?'

Then, suddenly garrulous:

'I'll tell you what I believe. Because I thought long and hard while I was questioning those rogues. You know that when Pepito was killed, he'd been issued with a summons. We knew that there was a rather large drugs cache at the Floria. And it was to stop them from moving the drugs that I had posted an inspector there until the arrest, which was planned for dawn. Well, the stuff has vanished.'

Maigret appeared not to be listening.

'From that, I deduce that when we lay our hands on it we'll have the murderer too. I've a good mind to ask the magistrate for a search warrant and to pay a visit to our friend Cageot.'

'There's no point,' sighed Maigret. 'The man who masterminded this morning's face-to-face confrontation wouldn't have kept such a compromising package in his home. The stuff isn't at Cageot's, or Eugène's, nor at the homes of any of the others. By the way, what did Louis have to say about his customers?'

'He swears he's never seen Eugène, even less played cards with him. He thinks Audiat might have come in a few times to buy cigarettes, but he has never spoken to him. As for Cageot, while the name rings a bell, like everyone in Montmartre, he didn't know him personally.'

'And they didn't slip up, naturally?'

'Not once. They even exchanged amused looks as if the interrogation was a farce. The chief was furious.'

Maigret found it hard to repress a little smile, for Amadieu had admitted that his hunch was correct and that his own change of heart was thanks to the head of the Police Judiciaire.

'We could always have an inspector tail Cageot,' continued Amadieu, who found silences awkward. 'But he'll have no trouble shaking him off. Not to mention that he has protection and that he's capable of filing a complaint against us.'

Maigret pulled out his watch, which he gazed at insistently.

'Do you have an appointment?'

'Shortly, yes. If you don't mind, we'll go downstairs together.'

As they passed the doorman, Maigret inquired after his sister-in-law.

'The lady left a few minutes ago. She asked me which bus she should take to get to Rue Fontaine.'

That was typical! She wanted to see for herself the place where her son was accused of having killed Pepito. And she would go inside! She'd tell her story to the waiters!

'Shall we have a drink at the Chope on the way?' suggested Maigret.

They sat down in a corner and ordered a vintage Armagnac.

'You have to admit,' ventured Amadieu, tugging at his moustache, 'that your method is impossible to apply in a case like this one. The chief and I were arguing about it earlier.'

Well, well, the chief really was taking a close interest in the case!

'What do you mean by my method?'

'You know better than I do. Usually, you get involved in people's lives; you try to understand their thinking and you take as much interest in things that happened to them twenty years earlier as you do in concrete clues. Here, we're faced with a bunch about whom we know pretty much everything. They don't even try to put us off the scent. And I'm not even sure that, in private, Cageot would even bother to deny having killed.'

'He hasn't denied it.'

'So what do you plan to do?'

'What about you?'

'I'll start by spreading a net around them, that's the best thing. From this evening, I'll have each one of them followed. They'll have to go somewhere, talk to people. We'll question those people and—'

'And in six months' time Philippe will still be in prison.'

'His lawyer intends to request his interim release. As he is only accused of manslaughter, he's bound to obtain it.'

Maigret could no longer feel his tiredness.

'Another?' suggested Amadieu, pointing to the glasses.

'With pleasure.'

Poor Amadieu! How uncomfortable he must have felt when he walked into the hotel lounge! By now, he'd had the time to regain his composure and adopt a deceptive air of confidence, and even to speak of the case with a certain casualness.

'As a matter of fact,' he added, taking a sip of Armagnac, 'I wonder whether Cageot is actually the killer. I've been mulling over your hypothesis. Why wouldn't he have given Audiat the job of shooting? He himself could have been hiding in the street—'

'Audiat would never have retraced his steps to bump into my nephew and raise the alarm. He'd be likely to lose his bottle. He's a nasty little thug but small fry.'

'What about Eugène?'

Maigret shrugged, not because he believed Eugène to be innocent, but because he would have found it awkward to implicate him. It was very vague. Fernande had something to do with it.

Besides, Maigret was barely in the conversation. His pencil in his hand, he was doodling aimlessly on the marble table top. The room was hot. The Armagnac produced a mellow feeling of well-being, as if all his accumulated fatigue were gradually dissipating.

Lucas came in with a young inspector and gave a start on seeing Maigret and Amadieu sitting side by side. Maigret winked at him across the room.

'Why don't you come over to HQ?' suggested Amadieu. 'I'll show you the transcript of the interrogations.'

'What's the use?'

'What do you intend to do?'

He was on edge. What could be brewing behind Maigret's stubborn brow? Already he was being slightly less cordial.

'We mustn't let our efforts undermine each other. The chief is of the same opinion as me and it's he who advised me to reach an agreement with you.'

'Well, aren't we agreed?'

'About what?'

'About the fact that Cageot killed Pepito and that it was probably he who killed Barnabé a fortnight earlier.'

'Being agreed about it isn't sufficient grounds to arrest him.'

'Of course not.'

'So?'

'So nothing. Or rather, I will only ask one thing of you. I imagine it will be easy for you to get a summons against Cageot from Gastambide?'

'And then what?'

'Then I'd like there to be an inspector on duty at Quai des Orfèvres with that summons in his pocket. As soon as I telephone him, he should come and meet me.'

'Meet you where?'

'Wherever I am! It would be better if instead of one summons, he has several. You never know.'

Amadieu's glum face had grown longer.

'Fine,' he snapped. 'I'll talk to the chief.'

He called the waiter and paid for one round. Then he spent ages buttoning and unbuttoning his overcoat in the hope that Maigret would finally say something.

'Well! I wish you every success.'

'That's very kind. Thank you.'

'When do you think it will be?'

'Perhaps later today. Perhaps not until tomorrow morning. Actually, I think it would be better if it were to happen tomorrow morning.'

Just as his companion was heading off, Maigret had an afterthought.

'And thank you for coming!'

'You're welcome.'

Left on his own, Maigret paid for the second round, then paused at the table where Lucas and his colleague were sitting.

'Any news, chief?' asked Lucas.

'Soon. Where will I be able to get hold of you at around eight tomorrow morning?'

'I'll be at Quai des Orfèvres. Unless you'd rather I came here.'

'See you tomorrow here!'

Outside, Maigret stopped a taxi and asked to be dropped off in Rue Fontaine. Night was falling. Lights went on in the windows. As they drove past the Tabac Fontaine, he asked the driver to slow down.

In the little bar, the dozy girl was at the till, the owner behind the bar, while the waiter was wiping the tables. But there was no sign of Audiat, or Eugène or his friend from Marseille.

'I bet they're furious at being deprived of their game of *belote* this evening!'

A few moments later, the taxi drew up opposite the Floria. Maigret asked the driver to wait, and pushed the half-open door.

It was cleaning time. A single lamp was on, casting a wan light over the wall hangings and the red and green paintwork. The tablecloths had not yet been put on the unvarnished tables, and the musicians' instruments lay scattered around the stage still in their cases.

The overall effect was shabby and dismal. The office door, at the back, was open and Maigret had a fleeting glimpse of a woman's shape. He walked past a waiter sweeping the floor and suddenly emerged into the bright light.

'It's you!' exclaimed his sister-in-law.

Her face was flushed and she became flummoxed.

'I wanted to see the—'

A young man was leaning against the wall, smoking a cigarette. It was Monsieur Henry, the Floria's new owner, or rather Cageot's new front man.

'This gentleman has been very kind—' stammered Madame Lauer.

'I wish I could have done more,' apologized the young man. 'Madame has told me that she's the mother of the police officer who killed . . . I mean who's accused of shooting Pepito. I know nothing about it. I took over the place the following day.'

'Thank you again, monsieur. I can see that you understand what it's like to be a mother.'

She was expecting Maigret to read her the riot act. Once they were in the waiting taxi, she talked for the sake of talking.

'You came by car? There's a very good bus . . . I don't mind if you smoke your pipe . . . I'm used to it . . .'

Maigret gave the address of the hotel, then, on the way, he murmured in a strange voice:

'This is what we're going to do. We've got a long night ahead of us. Tomorrow morning, we must be fresh, our nerves steady and our minds alert. We can go to the theatre, how about that?'

'To the theatre, while poor Philippe's in prison?'

'Bah! This will be his last night.'

'Have you found out something?'

'Not yet. Let me do as I see fit. The hotel is depressing. There's nothing for us to do there.'

'And I was wanting to take this opportunity to go and tidy Philippe's room!'

'He would be furious. A young man doesn't want his mother going through his things.'

'Do you think that Philippe has a young lady?'

All her provincialism was distilled in these words. Maigret kissed her on the cheek.

'Of course not, silly goose! Sadly he hasn't. Philippe is a real chip off the old block.'

'I'm not certain that before Émile married me he—'

It was like bathing in clear water. When they arrived at the hotel, Maigret booked seats at the Palais-Royal theatre, then, before dinner, he wrote a letter to his wife. He appeared to have forgotten all about Pepito's murder and his nephew's arrest.

'You and I are going to paint the town red!' he told his sister-in-law. 'If you're a good girl, I'll even show you the Floria in full swing.'

'I'm not dressed for that!'

He kept his word. After an elegant dinner in a restaurant on one of the Grands Boulevards – because he didn't want to eat at the hotel – he took his sister-in-law to the theatre and enjoyed watching her laugh at the bedroom farce despite herself.

'I feel bad at what you're making me do,' she sighed during the interval. 'If Philippe were to know where his mother was right now!'

'And what about Émile! I hope he's not whispering sweet nothings to the maid.'

'She's fifty, poor thing.'

It was harder to get her to agree to set foot in the Floria. She was already overwhelmed by the neon lights in the entrance to the nightclub. Maigret steered her towards a table by the bar, brushing against Fernande, who was there with Eugène and his sidekick from Marseille.

As one might expect, there were smiles at the sight of the good woman being piloted by the former detective inspector.

And Maigret was thrilled! It was as if that was what he had been hoping for! Like a decent provincial fellow out for a good time, he ordered champagne.

'I'll be tipsy!' simpered Madame Lauer.

'Good!'

'Do you realize this is the first time I've set foot in a place like this?'

She really was a babe in the woods! She was a paragon of moral and physical virtue!

'Who's that woman who keeps staring at you?'

'That's Fernande, a friend of mine.'

'If I were in my sister's shoes, I'd be worried. She looks lovesick.'

It was true and yet it wasn't. Fernande had been making eyes at Maigret, as if she rued losing the intimacy that had been disrupted. But she immediately clutched Eugène's arm and made an exaggerated show of flirting with him.

'She's with a very handsome young man!'

'The sad thing is that tomorrow the handsome young man will be in prison.'

'What did he do?'

'He's one of the gangsters who got Philippe arrested.'

'Him?'

She couldn't believe it. And it was worse when Cageot poked his head through the curtain to see how things were going, as he did every night.

'You see that gentleman who looks like a lawyer?'

'With the grey hair?'

'Yes! Well, be careful. Try not to scream. He's the murderer.'

Maigret's eyes were laughing as if he already had Cageot and the others at his mercy. Then he was laughing out loud so hard that Fernande turned round in surprise and frowned, anxious and wistful all of a sudden.

A little later, she made her way to the toilets, glancing at Maigret as she walked past. He stood up to go and talk to her.

'Have you got any news?' she asked, almost spitefully.

'What about you?'

'Nothing. As you can see, we're having a night out.'

She watched Maigret closely and said after a silence:

'Is he going to be arrested?'

'Not straight away.'

She stamped her high-heeled foot on the floor.

'The love of your life?'

But she was already marching off.

'Don't know yet,' she retorted.

Madame Lauer was ashamed to be going to bed at two in the morning, while Maigret fell into a deep sleep as soon as his head touched his pillow, snoring as he had not done for a few days.

9.

At 7.50, Maigret dropped in to the hotel office just as the owner, who had just arrived, was reviewing the guest list with the night watchman. A bucket of dirty water stood in the middle of the corridor; there was a broom leaning up against the wall and Maigret, with the utmost seriousness, grabbed the broom and examined the handle.

'May I use this?' he asked the owner, who stammered:

'Feel free . . .'

Then he had second thoughts and asked anxiously:

'Is your room not clean enough?'

Maigret was smoking his first pipe of the day with unmitigated pleasure.

'My room is fine!' he replied, unperturbed. 'It's not the broom I'm interested in. I'd just like a little piece of the handle.'

The cleaning woman, who had appeared and was wiping her hands on her blue apron, must have thought he had gone mad.

'You wouldn't have a little saw, would you?' Maigret asked the night watchman.

'Go on, Joseph,' the owner said, 'go and fetch a saw for Monsieur Maigret.'

Thus the fateful day began on a comic note. It was another sunny morning. A chambermaid entered with a breakfast tray. The floor of the corridor had just been washed down. The postman came in and rummaged in his leather satchel.

Maigret, broom in hand, was waiting for a saw.

'There is a telephone in the lounge, I believe?' he asked the owner.

'Yes, there is, Monsieur Maigret. On the table to your left. I'll connect you right away.'

'There's no need.'

'Don't you want to make a call?'

'No thank you. It's not necessary.'

He entered the lounge with his broom, while the cleaning woman declared:

'I'd just like to say that it's not my fault I'm standing here twiddling my thumbs. You'd better not yell at me for not finishing the lobby!'

The night watchman returned with a rusty saw, which he had found in the basement. Meanwhile, Maigret reappeared with the broom, took the saw from him and began sawing off the end of the handle. He rested the broom on the desk. Sawdust fell on to the newly washed floor. The other end of the handle rubbed against the register while the owner looked on in dismay.

'There! Thank you very much,' said Maigret at length picking up the small round of wood which he had just sawn off and handing back the broom minus a few centimetres to the cleaning woman.

'Is that what you needed?' asked the hotel owner, keeping a straight face.

'Exactly.'

At the Chope du Pont-Neuf, where he met up with Lucas in the back room, cleaners and their buckets were everywhere, as at the hotel.

'You know that the squad worked all night, chief. When Amadieu left you, he got it into his head to beat you to it, and put everyone on the case. I even know that you went to the Palais-Royal theatre with a lady.'

'And then that I went to the Floria? Poor Amadieu! What about the others?'

'Eugène was at the Floria too. I expect you saw him. At 2.45 he left with a tart.'

'Fernande, I know. I bet he slept at her place in Rue Blanche.'

'You're right. He even left his car parked outside all night. It's still there.'

Maigret had raised an eyebrow, even though he wasn't in love. The other morning, it was he who had been in her sun-drenched apartment. Fernande had sat there half naked drinking her *café au lait* and there had been an intimate sense of trust between them.

It wasn't jealousy, but he was not very fond of men like Eugène, whom he could picture now, still in bed, while Fernande fussed around making coffee and bringing it to him. What a condescending smile he must have on his lips!

'He'll get her to do anything he wants,' he sighed. 'Go on, Lucas.'

'The Marseille sidekick hung around a couple of clubs and then went back to the Hôtel Alsina. He'll be asleep at this hour because he never rises before eleven or midday.'

'What about the little deaf man?'

'His name is Colin. He lives with his wife – turns out he is lawfully married – in an apartment in Rue Caulaincourt. She makes a scene when he comes home late. She used to be the madam in his brothel.'

'What's he doing right now?'

'He's at the market. He's the one who always does the shopping, wearing a long scarf around his neck and carpet slippers on his feet.'

'Audiat?'

'He went on a bar crawl and got drunk as a lord. He returned to his hotel in Rue Lepic at around one in the morning and the night watchman had to help him up the stairs.'

'And Cageot's at home, I imagine?'

On coming out of the Chope du Pont-Neuf, Maigret had the impression he could see his characters dotted around the Sacré-Cœur, whose white dome emerged from the Paris mist.

For ten minutes he issued instructions to Lucas in an undertone, murmuring as he shook his hand:

'Is everything clear? Are you sure you don't need more than half an hour?'

'Are you armed, chief?'

Maigret patted his trouser pocket and hailed a passing taxi.

'Rue des Batignolles!'

The door of the concierge's lodge was open and the gasman was standing in the doorway.

'Can I help you?' asked a voice with a northern accent as Maigret walked past.

'Monsieur Cageot, please.'

'On the mezzanine, to the left.'

Maigret paused on the threadbare doormat to get his breath back. He yanked the heavy silk cord, which set off a soft tinkling inside the apartment, sounding like a child's toy.

Here too a broom was sweeping the floor, occasionally hitting a piece of furniture. A woman's voice said:

'Are you going to open the door?'

Then there was the sound of muffled footsteps. A chain was taken off. A key turned in the lock and the door opened, but barely ten centimetres.

It was Cageot who had opened the door. He was in his dressing gown, his hair tousled, his eyebrows bushier than ever. He was not surprised. He looked Maigret in the eye and snarled:

'What do you want?'

'First of all, to come in.'

'Are you here officially, with a proper warrant?'

'No.'

Cageot wanted to shut the door again, but Maigret had wedged his foot in the gap so it wouldn't close.

'Do you not think it would be better if we talked?' he said.

Cageot realized that he wouldn't be able to close his door and his expression darkened.

'I could call the police—'

'Of course! Except that I think that it wouldn't do you any good and that a conversation between just the two of us would be preferable.'

Behind Cageot, a cleaning woman dressed in black had stopped work to listen. All the doors were open for her to clean the whole apartment. Leading off the corridor to the left Maigret had the impression there was a light-filled room overlooking the street.

'Come in.'

Cageot locked the door again, put the chain on and said to his visitor:

'To the right . . . in my office . . .'

It was a typical lower-middle-class Montmartre apartment, with a kitchen barely one metre wide looking on to the courtyard, a bamboo coat-stand in the hall, a gloomy dining room with gloomy curtains and wallpaper with a faded leaf pattern.

Cageot's 'office' had been designed to be the sitting room and was the only room in the apartment to have two windows letting in the light.

A polished wooden floor. In the centre were a worn rug and three upholstered armchairs that had taken on the same indefinable hue as the rug.

The walls were dark red, cluttered with a large number of paintings and photographs in gilt frames. And in the corners pedestal tables and shelves were laden with worthless knick-knacks.

A mahogany desk with an old morocco top stood near one of the windows. Cageot chose to seat himself behind it, tidying away some papers that had been lying carelessly on the right-hand side.

'Marthe! Bring me my hot chocolate in here.'

He did not look at Maigret. He waited, preferring to let his visitor launch the offensive.

Meanwhile, Maigret, sitting on a chair that was too spindly for his burly frame, had unbuttoned his overcoat and filled a pipe, tamping the tobacco down with his thumb, staring about him as he did so. A window was open, probably to air the place, and when the cleaning woman arrived with the hot chocolate Maigret asked Cageot:

'Do you mind if we shut the window? I caught a chill yesterday and I don't want to make my cold worse.'

'Close the window, Marthe.'

Marthe had taken a dislike to the visitor. It was clear from the way she busied herself around him, banging into his leg in passing and making no apology.

The room was filled with the smell of chocolate. Cageot cupped the bowl in his hands as if to warm them. Outside in the street, delivery lorries drove past, their roofs reaching almost to the windows, as did the omnibuses' metallic tops.

Marthe went out, leaving the door ajar, and continued cleaning the hall.

'I won't offer you a hot chocolate,' said Cageot, 'as I imagine that you have had your breakfast.'

'I have, yes. But if you had a glass of white wine—'

Everything mattered, every single word, and Cageot frowned, wondering why his visitor was asking for a drink.

Maigret understood, and smiled.

'I'm used to working outdoors. In winter, it's cold. In summer, it's hot. In both cases, a man needs a drink—'

'Marthe, bring some white wine and a glass.'

'Everyday wine?'

'That's right. I prefer everyday wine,' replied Maigret.

His bowler hat sat on the desk, next to the telephone. Cageot sipped his chocolate without taking his eyes off Maigret.

He was paler in the morning than in the evening, or rather his skin was drained of colour, his eyes the same dull grey as his hair and eyebrows. He had an elongated, bony face. Cageot was one of those men who it is impossible to imagine anything other than middle-aged. It was hard to believe that he had ever been a baby, or a schoolboy, or even a young man in love. He could never have held a woman in his arms and whispered loving words to her.

On the other hand, his hairy hands, which were nicely manicured, had always wielded a pen. The desk drawers must have been full of papers of all kinds – accounts, calculations, bills and memoranda.

'You're up relatively early,' commented Maigret after glancing at his watch.

'I don't sleep more than three hours a night.'

He was speaking the truth. It was hard to say how you could tell, but you could.

'So, do you read?'

'I read, or I work.'

They granted each other a moment's respite. There seemed to be a tacit understanding that the real conversation would begin once Marthe had brought in the white wine.

Maigret couldn't see a book case, but on a small table by the desk were some bound books: the penal code, Dalloz law manuals, legal tomes.

'Leave us, Marthe,' said Cageot as soon as the wine was on the table.

As she reached the kitchen, he nearly called her back to tell her to close the door, but changed his mind.

'I'll leave you to pour it yourself.'

Meanwhile, as if it were the most natural thing in the world, he opened a desk drawer and took out an automatic revolver, which he placed within reach. It did not even feel like a provocation. He was acting as though this were completely normal behaviour. Then he pushed away the empty bowl and rested his elbows on the arms of his chair.

'I'm ready to hear your proposal,' he said, with the air of a businessman meeting a client.

'What makes you think that I have a proposal to put to you?'

'Why else would you be here? You are no longer a member of the police, so you haven't come to arrest me. You can't be here to question me since you are no longer a sworn officer, and anything you say afterwards will be of no consequence.'

Maigret assented with a smile as he relit his pipe, which he had allowed to go out.

'On the other hand, your nephew is up to his neck in trouble and you can't see any way of getting him off.'

Maigret had put his box of matches on the brim of his hat and had to reach for it three times in quick succession, because the tobacco, which was probably packed too tightly, kept going out.

'So,' concluded Cageot, 'you need me but I don't need you. Well, I'm all ears.'

His voice was quite neutral, as colourless as his persona. With his face and a voice like that, he would have made a tremendous criminal judge.

'Fair enough!' decided Maigret, rising and taking a few steps. 'What would you want in exchange for getting my nephew off the hook?'

'Me? What can I do?'

Maigret smiled pleasantly.

'Come, don't be modest. It's always possible to undo what one has done. How much?'

Cageot remained silent for a moment, digesting this offer.

'I'm not interested,' he said at length.

'Why not?'

'Because I have no reason to help this young man. He deserves to go to prison for what he did. I don't know him.'

Maigret paused from time to time in front of a portrait, or in front of the windows, looking down into the street, where housewives jostled each other around little market barrows.

'For example,' he muttered softly, lighting his pipe yet again, 'if my nephew were exonerated, I would no longer have the slightest reason to involve myself in this case. You said so yourself, I am no longer a member of the police force. To be honest with you, I confess I'd jump on to the first train to Orléans and two hours later I'd be in my little boat, fishing.'

'You're not drinking!'

Maigret poured himself a full glass of white wine, which he drained in one gulp.

'As for what you can do,' he went on, sitting down and putting the matchbox back on the brim of his hat, 'there are a number of options. When the witnesses are brought face to face for the second time, Audiat could be less certain of his recollection and not formally identify Philippe. That happens all the time.'

Cageot grew pensive and, seeing his absent look, Maigret guessed that he was not listening, or barely paying attention. But no! He must have been asking himself:

'Why the devil has he come to see me?'

And from then on, Maigret's chief concern was to avoid looking in the direction of the hat and the telephone at all costs. It was also vital that he appear to mean what he said. Whereas in fact, he was wasting his breath. To loosen his tongue he filled another glass and drank it.

'Is it good?'

'The wine? Not bad. I know what you're going to say. If Philippe is exonerated, the investigation will be re-opened all the more energetically, since there will no longer be a culprit.'

Cageot looked up imperceptibly, curious as to what was to come. Maigret suddenly turned red as a thought struck him.

What would happen if, at the same moment, Eugène, or his friend from Marseille, or the owner of the Tabac Fontaine or anyone were to try to reach Cageot on the telephone? It was possible, probable even. The previous day, the entire gang had been hauled in to Quai des Orfèvres and they must all be feeling somewhat anxious. Wasn't Cageot in the habit of giving orders and receiving reports over the telephone?

But, for the time being, the telephone was out of action, and it would remain so for a few long minutes more, perhaps for an hour.

Maigret had put his hat down on the desk in such a way as to conceal the base of the telephone from Cageot's view. And each time he picked up the box of matches, he slid the little round of wood he had sawn off that morning under the receiver.

In other words, the call had begun. Lucas was stationed at the telephone exchange with two shorthand typists who would take everything down.

'I understand that you're lacking a culprit,' muttered Maigret staring at the rug.

What would happen if Eugène were to try to telephone Cageot and fail to get through was that he would come running. Maigret would be back to square one! Or rather it would be impossible to start again since Cageot would be on his guard.

'It's not difficult,' he went on, trying to keep a steady voice. 'You just need to find some boy who is of roughly the same build as my nephew. There's no shortage in Montmartre. And there must be one whom you wouldn't mind seeing locked up. Two or three testimonies into the bargain and it's in the bag.'

Maigret was so warm that he removed his overcoat and hung it over the back of a chair.

'May I?'

'We could open one of the windows,' suggested Cageot.

Oh no! With the noise from the street, the shorthand typists on the other end of the line wouldn't be able to hear half of the things that were said.

'Thank you, but it's my influenza that's making me sweat. The cold air would do me more harm. I was saying—'

He drained his glass and filled a fresh pipe.

'I hope the smoke doesn't bother you?'

They could still hear Marthe bustling around, but sometimes the noise stopped and she must have been eavesdropping.

'Just give me a figure. What's the price for an operation like that?'

'Jail!' retorted Cageot, bluntly.

Maigret smiled, but he was beginning to doubt his strategy.

'In that case, if you're afraid, suggest another scheme.'

'I don't need a scheme! The police have arrested a man they allege killed Pepito. That's their business. True, from time to time, I do a small favour for the Ministry of the Interior or for the police. As it happens, I know nothing. I wish for your sake that I did—'

He made as if to get up to put an end to the conversation. Maigret needed to think fast.

'Shall I tell you what's going to happen?' he enunciated slowly.

He took his time, speaking syllable by syllable:

'In the next two days, you will have to kill your little friend Audiat.'

The message struck home, that was certain. Cageot avoided looking at Maigret, who continued, for fear of losing his advantage:

'You know it as well as I do! Audiat is a kid. Furthermore, I suspect him of taking drugs, which makes him impressionable. Since he's been aware that I'm on to him, he has made one blunder after another, panicked and, the other night, in my room, he actually came clean. It was very clever of you to be waiting for us outside the Police Judiciaire to stop him from repeating what he'd told me. But you might not be so lucky another time. Last night, Audiat went on a bar crawl and got drunk. He'll do the same tonight. There'll be someone tailing him all the time.'

Cageot sat absolutely still, his eyes fixed on the dark-red wall.

'Go on,' he said in a perfectly normal voice.

'Do I have to? How will you go about eliminating a man under police surveillance day and night? If you don't kill him, Audiat will squeal, that's for certain! And if you kill him, then you'll be caught, because it's difficult to commit a murder under those conditions.'

The ray of sunshine filtering through the grimy window slid over the desk and, in a few minutes, would reach the telephone. Maigret smoked his pipe, taking rapid little puffs.

'What do you have to say to that?'

Without raising his voice, Cageot said:

'Marthe! Shut the door.'

She did so, grumbling. Then he lowered his voice, speaking so softly that Maigret wondered whether his words would carry down the telephone.

'And supposing Audiat were already dead?'

He didn't bat an eyelid as he said this. Maigret remembered his conversation with Lucas, in the Chope du Pont-Neuf. Hadn't the sergeant stated that Audiat, followed by an inspector, had gone back to his hotel in Rue Lepic, at around one o'clock in the morning? And the inspector must have kept a watch on the hotel for the rest of the night.

His hand resting on the worn leather desk top, a few centimetres from the revolver, Cageot went on:

'You see that your offer doesn't stand up. I thought you were better than that.'

And, as Maigret froze with dread, he added:

'If you want to know more, you can telephone the police station of the 18th *arrondissement*.'

As he spoke these words, he could have reached for the receiver and handed it to Maigret. But he didn't, and Maigret breathed again, saying hastily:

'I believe you. But I haven't quite finished yet.'

He didn't know what he was going to say. But he had to play for time. At all costs, he had to get Cageot to say certain words which he seemed to be avoiding like the plague.

So far, he had not once denied the murder. But nor had he said a single word that could be considered as a formal confession.

Maigret imagined Lucas growing impatient, the earpiece pressed to his ear, poor Lucas veering from hope to despair and saying to the typists:

'There's no need to type that.'

What if Eugène or someone else called?

'Are you sure that what you have to tell me is worth it?' persisted Cageot. 'It's time for me to get dressed.'

'Please give me another six minutes.'

Maigret poured himself a drink and rose like a very nervous man about to launch into a speech.

10.

Cageot did not smoke, did not move, had no nervous twitches that could provide an outlet for his jumpiness.

Maigret had not yet realized that it was precisely this stillness that bothered him, but it dawned on him when he saw Cageot reach out towards a comfit box that was on the desk, and help himself to a sugared almond.

It was a small detail, and yet Maigret's eyes lit up as if he had discovered the chink in Cageot's armour. The man was neither a smoker nor a drinker nor a womanizer, but he liked sweets, sucking a sugared almond and passing it slowly from one side of his mouth to the other!

'I could say that we are among professionals here,' said Maigret at length. 'And it's as a fellow professional that I'm going to tell you why, inevitably, you'll be caught.'

The sugared almond in his mouth moved faster.

'Let's take the first murder. I'm talking about the first murder in this series, because it is possible that you have others to your name. Wasn't the solicitor to whom you were chief clerk poisoned?'

'It was never proved,' said Cageot simply.

He was trying to work out what Maigret was leading up to. At the same time, Maigret's mind was working overtime.

'It doesn't matter! It's now three weeks since you decided to eliminate Barnabé. As far as I can tell, Barnabé was the link between Paris and Marseille, in other words, between you and the Turks who bring the drugs in by boat. I'm guessing that Barnabé wanted to take too big a cut. He was invited to get into a car at night. Suddenly, Barnabé feels a knife stabbing him in the back and a few moments later his body is thrown out on to the pavement. You see the error?'

Maigret picked up his matches to ensure that the round of wood was still in place. At the same time, he wanted to conceal a faint smile that he was finding hard to suppress, for Cageot was thinking, earnestly trying to spot the mistake like a diligent schoolboy.

'I'll tell you later,' promised Maigret, interrupting his train of thought. 'For the time being, I'll go on. The police, through some coincidence, are on to Pepito. Since the stuff is at the Floria and the Floria is being watched, the situation is dangerous. Pepito knows he's going to get caught. He threatens to squeal if you don't save him. You shoot him with a revolver at a time when he thinks he's alone in the empty club. Here, no mistakes.'

Cageot looked up and the sugared almond remained poised on his tongue.

'No mistakes so far. Are you beginning to follow me? But you realize there is a police officer inside the club. You exit. You can't resist the urge to get the police officer arrested. At first, it seems like a stroke of genius. And yet, that was the mistake, your second.'

Maigret was on the right track. All he needed to do was go on, without rushing things. Cageot listened and mulled things over while anxiety was beginning to gnaw away at his composure.

'Third murder, that of Audiat. Audiat too was about to talk. The police are watching him. The knife and the gun are out. I bet Audiat was in the habit of having a drink of water during the night. This time, he'll drink even more because he is drunk, and he won't wake up because the water in the jug has been poisoned. Third mistake.'

Maigret staked his all, but he was sure of himself! Things couldn't have happened any other way.

'I'm waiting to hear what the three mistakes were!' said Cageot after a moment, reaching for the box of sugared almonds.

And Maigret imagined the hotel in Rue Lepic, whose residents were mainly musicians, gigolos and prostitutes.

'In the Audiat case, the mistake is that someone put the poison in the jug!'

Cageot was baffled, sucked another sugared almond, and there was a faintly sweet smell in the air, a hint of vanilla.

'With Barnabé,' continued Maigret pouring himself a drink, 'you took at least two people with you: Pepito and the driver, probably Eugène. And it was Pepito who subsequently threatened to squeal.

'Are you with me? Result: the need to eliminate Pepito. You were only dealing with the shooting. But you added the extra touch of going to fetch Audiat, whose job was to bump into the inspector. What automatically happens? Eugène, Louis, the owner of the Tabac Fontaine, a *belote* player called Colin and Audiat are now in the know. It is Audiat who loses his nerve. And so you have to get rid of him!

'But, yesterday afternoon, you didn't go to Rue Lepic yourself. You must have used a resident at the hotel whom you contacted by telephone. Another accomplice! A man who might talk! Are you with me now?'

Cageot was still ruminating. The sun reached the nickel-plated telephone receiver. It was late. A crowd was swelling around the little barrows and the clamour from the street could be heard in the apartment despite the closed windows.

'You're good, that's clear. But then, why do you keep lumbering yourself with useless accomplices who are likely to give you away? You could have easily bumped off Barnabé at any time, he wasn't suspicious of you. You didn't need Audiat in the Pepito business. And yesterday, when you weren't under surveillance, you could have gone to Rue Lepic yourself. In these hotels, where there's no doorman, anyone can just walk straight in.'

Occasionally footsteps could be heard on the stairs, and Maigret had to force himself to appear calm and carry on talking as if nothing were amiss.

'Right now, there are five people at least who can have you put away. Now, five people have never managed to keep a secret like that for long.'

'I didn't stab Barnabé,' said Cageot slowly. He was gloomier than ever.

Maigret jumped at the opportunity and stated confidently:

'I know!'

Cageot looked at him in surprise and narrowed his eyes.

'A stabbing is more up the street of an Italian, like Pepito.'

He needed to make one more tiny effort, but just then the cleaning woman opened the door and Maigret thought his edifice was going to collapse.

'I'm off to the market,' she announced. 'What vegetables shall I get?'

'Whatever you like.'

'Can you give me some money?'

Cageot took two ten-franc coins from a sturdy, well-worn purse with a metal clasp, a real miser's purse. The wine bottle on the table was empty and he held it out to Marthe.

'Here! You can get the deposit back on this. You have the receipt.'

His mind was elsewhere, however. Marthe left without shutting the door, but she did close the kitchen door behind her and water could be heard boiling on the stove.

Maigret had been watching Cageot's every move, and forgotten about the telephone and the typists lying in wait on the other end of the line. He had a sudden intuition, he couldn't have said exactly when. He had talked a lot, without thinking too hard about what he was saying, and now he was within a hair's breadth of the truth.

Added to which were the sugared almonds in the comfit box, the purse and even the word 'vegetable'.

'I bet you're on a diet.'

'It's been twenty years.'

Cageot was no longer talking about throwing his visitor out. It even seemed as if he needed him. Seeing Maigret's empty glass, he said:

'Marthe will bring some more wine. There's never more than one bottle in the house.'

'I know.'

'How do you know?'

Because it fitted in with all the rest, of course! Because now, for Maigret, Cageot had stopped being an adversary and had become a man. And he knew this man better with each second. He felt him live, breathe, think, fear and hope. He could hear the irritating rattle of the sugared almond against his teeth.

The decor came to life too – the desk, the furniture, the paintings, as cloying as jam.

'Do you know what I think, Cageot?'

These were not just hollow words, but the culmination of a long chain of thought.

'I'm asking myself if you really did kill Pepito. Right now, I'm almost certain you didn't.'

His tone had changed. Maigret was fired up, leaning forwards to get a closer look at Cageot.

'I'm going to tell you straight away why I think that. If you had been capable of shooting Pepito yourself, you wouldn't have needed anyone to kill Barnabé and Audiat. The truth is that you're afraid.'

Cageot's lips were dry. Even so he attempted an ironic smile.

'Just you dare to tell me that you have slaughtered a chicken or a rabbit! Dare to tell me that you are capable of seeing blood flow from a wound!'

Maigret no longer had any doubts. He had understood. He charged ahead.

'Let's get this straight. You are afraid to kill with your own hands, but you have no compunction about doing away with a person! On the contrary! You are afraid of killing, afraid of dying. But that makes you all the more determined to order murders. Isn't that true, Cageot?'

Maigret's voice was devoid of hatred, devoid of pity. He studied Cageot with the fascination with which he studied human beings in general. And this man was terribly human in his eyes. Nothing had been left to chance, not even his first job as a solicitor's clerk.

Cageot was and always had been completely withdrawn. All alone, his eyes closed, he must dream up brilliant schemes, schemes of all kinds, financial, criminal and erotic.

Had he ever been seen with women? Of course not! Women were not capable of enacting his wild fantasies!

Cageot retreated into himself, into a lair filled with his thoughts, his dreams, his smell.

And when he looked out of his windows at the street below bathed in sunlight, where people teemed around the market stalls and packed buses rumbled past, what he was inclined to do was not to mingle with the living mass of humanity outside, but to use it as inspiration for his cunning schemes.

'You are a coward, Cageot!' thundered Maigret. 'A coward like all those who live only by their brains. You sell women, cocaine, and God only knows what else – for I believe you are capable of anything. But at the same time you are a police informer!'

Cageot did not take his grey eyes off Maigret, who was unstoppable.

'You had Barnabé killed by Pepito. And I'm going to tell you who you had kill Pepito. In your gang, there is a good-looking young man, who has everything going for him – women, money and success. He's happy-go-lucky and completely devoid of a conscience.

'Just you dare to tell me that the night of Pepito's murder you weren't at the Tabac Fontaine! There was the owner, then that brothel-owner Colin, who is even more of a coward than you, then Audiat, the fellow from Marseille and lastly Eugène.

'It was Eugène whom you sent to the Floria. Then, when he came back, having done the job, and told you there had been someone inside the club, you brought Audiat in.'

'And then what?' said Cageot. 'What use is all this to you?'

He gripped the arms of his chair with both hands as if he wanted to get up. He thrust his head slightly forwards, in a movement of defiance.

'What use is it to me? To prove to you that I'll get you, precisely because you are a coward and you have surrounded yourself with too many people.'

'I swear you won't ever get me.'

He had a mirthless smile. His pupils had contracted. He added slowly:

'The police have never been very clever! Earlier you mentioned poisoning. Seeing as you were once in the police, you can probably tell me how many poisonings they expose every year in Paris?'

Maigret did not have time to reply.

'Every year! You hear me? You can't be naive enough to believe that out of a population of four million, there aren't a few who succumb to an overdose of arsenic or strychnine?'

He got to his feet at last. Maigret had been expecting him to do this for some time. It was the release after too long an effort, and the release inevitably expressed itself in words.

'I could have killed you today. I thought about it. All I needed to do was poison your wine. You'll note that the bottle is already gone from the house. All I'd need to do is rinse your glass. You'd leave here and you'd go and die somewhere—'

Maigret had a doubt, but it lasted only a fraction of a second.

'You are right. I didn't kill Barnabé. I didn't kill Pepito. I didn't even kill that idiot Audiat!'

Cageot, comfit box in hand, spoke softly and continuously.

He was a ridiculous sight with his dressing gown that was too short and his unkempt hair giving him a strange halo. Had it not been for the telephone, Maigret would have opened a window to escape this oppressive atmosphere of a reclusive existence.

'What I say to you is of no consequence, since you are not a sworn police officer and there are no witnesses.'

As if overcome by doubt, he glanced at the corridor and even opened the door to his bedroom for a moment.

'The thing you have not understood, you see, is that they won't betray me, even if they want to, because legally they are guiltier than I am! Eugène has killed. It's Louis who supplied the gun and the key to the Floria. And do you know what might happen if Eugène tried to be clever? Little Monsieur Colin, as you call him, that half-deaf little runt with a stutter, has instructions to slip something in his glass one night while they're playing *belote*. I promise you, in this game, it's not as necessary as you might think to be capable of slitting a chicken's throat.'

Maigret had gone over to the desk to pick up his hat and his matches. His knees were trembling slightly. It was over. He had achieved his goal. All he had to do was to get out. The inspector waiting outside in the street had a summons in his pocket. At Quai des Orfèvres they were waiting for news and were probably laying bets on the outcome.

Maigret had been there for two hours. Eugène, in silk pyjamas, was perhaps having a late breakfast with Fernande. And where on earth might Philippe's dear mother be?

There were footsteps on the stairs, followed by a violent knocking on the apartment door. Cageot looked Maigret in the eyes, then gazed at his revolver, which was still lying on the desk.

While he went to open the door, Maigret put his hand on his gun pocket and stood stock-still in the middle of the room.

'What's going on?' came Eugène's voice from the hall.

The two men were instantly at the door to the office. There were more footsteps behind them, those of Fernande, who stared at Maigret in surprise.

'What the—?' repeated Eugène.

But already a car was pulling up outside with a squeal of brakes.

Eugène ran to a window.

'I knew it!' he groaned.

The police, who had been watching Fernande's place and had followed the couple, jumped out on to the pavement.

Cageot didn't budge. His revolver in his hand, he was thinking.

'Why have you come here?'

He was addressing Eugène, who was talking at the same time.

'I telephoned four times and—'

Maigret had inched backwards so as to have his back to the wall.

At that, Cageot glanced at the telephone. Just then a shot rang out, the room was filled with the smell of burnt gunpowder and a bluish cloud hung in the sunlight.

Maigret had fired. The bullet had hit Cageot's hand, causing him to drop the revolver.

'Don't move!' said Maigret, who was still pointing his gun.

Cageot stood rooted to the spot. In his mouth he still had a sugared almond, which made his left cheek bulge. He did not dare move a muscle.

There were footsteps on the stairs.

'Go and open the door, Fernande,' commanded Maigret.

She sought Eugène with her eyes to know whether she should obey, but her lover was staring stubbornly at the floor. So she walked resignedly across the hall, undid the chain and unlocked the door.

Blood was dripping from Cageot's hand, plopping on to the rug, where a brownish stain was spreading.

Suddenly, before Maigret could do anything, Eugène made a

dash for one of the windows, flung it open, breaking a pane, and jumped out.

Screams rose up from the street. Eugène had landed on the roof of a stationary car, leaped to the ground and started running in the direction of Rue des Dames.

At that moment, two inspectors appeared in the doorway.

'What's going on?' they asked Maigret.

'Nothing. You are going to arrest Cageot, against whom there is a summons. Have you got back-up downstairs?'

'No.'

Fernande had no idea what was happening. She stood gazing at the open window in a stupor.

'Then he'll run for a long time!'

As he spoke, Maigret picked up the round of wood and slipped it into his pocket. He had the feeling that something was afoot with Cageot, but it wasn't serious. Cageot had crumpled to the floor and rolled on the rug, where he lay inert.

He had fainted, probably at the sight of his blood splashing on to the rug, drop by drop.

'Wait till he comes round. Call a doctor if you must. The telephone is working now.'

Maigret shoved Fernande on to the landing and made her go down the stairs ahead of him. A crowd had gathered in front of the building. A beat sergeant was trying to fight his way through it.

Maigret elbowed his way out of the crush and he and Fernande found themselves outside the charcuterie on the corner of the street.

'The love of your life?' he asked.

Then he noticed that she was wearing a new fur coat. He felt it.

'Did he give it to you?'

'Yes, this morning.'

'By the way, do you know that he's the one who killed Pepito?'

'Oh!'

She hadn't batted an eyelid. He smiled.

'Did he tell you?'

She merely fluttered her eyelashes.

'When?'

'This morning.'

And she added, suddenly solemn, like a woman in love who believes it's the real thing:

'You won't get him!'

And she was right. A month later, she went to join Eugène in Istanbul, where he had opened a nightclub on the famous Grand Rue de Pera.

As for Cageot, he was a book-keeper in prison.

Madame Lauer wrote to her sister:

> I'm sending you by express delivery six plum tree saplings like the ones we have in the garden at La Tourelle, as you requested. I think they'll take very well in the Loire. But you should tell your husband that in my view he doesn't prune his fruit trees properly, he should take off more branches.
>
> Philippe is much better since he's been back home. He's a good boy who barely ever goes out and loves doing crosswords in the evening. But in the last few days, I've seen him hanging around the Scheffers' house (the owners of the gasworks) and I think there are wedding bells in the air.
>
> Tell your husband too that last night they put on the play that we saw together at the Palais-Royal. But it didn't go down as well as it did in Paris . . .

Maigret came in wearing his waders and holding three pike at arm's length.

'But we're not going to eat those, are we?' said his wife.

'Of course not!'

He said that in such an odd tone of voice that she raised her head to look at him. But no! He was already going into the shed to put away his fishing rods and take off his boots.

'If we had to eat everything we killed!'

The words formed in his mind of their own accord at the same time as a ridiculous image, that of an ashen, perplexed Cageot confronted with the bodies of Pepito and Audiat. It did not even bring a smile to his face.

'What soup have you made?' he shouted, sitting down on a crate.

'Tomato.'

'Good!'

And the rubber boots fell to the beaten earth floor one after the other as he heaved a contented sigh.

The Judge's House

Translated by HOWARD CURTIS

SIMENON

MAIGRET REVIENT...

CÉCILE EST MORTE
LES CAVES DU MAJESTIC
LA MAISON DU JUGE

LIBRAIRIE *nrf* GALLIMARD

1. The Customs Officer's Wife

'Fifty-six, fifty-seven, fifty-eight . . .' Maigret counted.

He didn't want to count. It was mechanical. His head was empty, his eyelids heavy.

'Sixty-one, sixty-two . . .'

He glanced outside. The bottom halves of the windows in the Café Français were frosted. Above the frosted section, all you could see were the bare trees on the square and the rain, the never-ending rain.

'Eighty-three, eighty-four . . .'

He was standing there, his billiard cue in his hand, and he could see himself in the mirrors that covered the walls of the café.

And Monsieur Le Flem, the owner, carried on playing, never saying a word, quite relaxed, as if this was all perfectly natural. He would go from one side of the green baize to the other, bend down then straighten up again, watching the movement of the balls with a distant look in his eyes.

'A hundred and twenty-two . . . A hundred and twenty-three . . .'

The room was vast. Near the window, the maid, a middle-aged woman, was sewing. That was all. Nothing but the three of them! With a cat sitting by the stove.

And it was only three o'clock! And it was only 13 January. Maigret could see the figure on a big calendar hanging behind the cash register. And it had been like this for three months! And . . .

He hadn't complained to anybody. Even Madame Maigret didn't know why he had fallen into disgrace and been transferred to Luçon. This was the hidden face of the profession, of no concern to those outside.

Madame Maigret was here, too, in an apartment they had rented above a piano shop, and they had already had some brushes with the landlord because . . . Well, never mind!

'How many points is that?' Monsieur Le Flem asked, not sure when to stop.

'A hundred and fifty . . .'

Maigret puffed gently at his pipe. Come on! A hundred and forty-seven, a hundred and forty-eight, a hundred and forty-nine, a hundred and fifty! The balls froze on the billiard table, the whites a nasty yellow, the red an unhealthy pink. The cues were placed back in their rack. Monsieur Le Flem went to the beer pump and poured two glasses, taking the heads off them with the help of a wooden knife.

'Cheers.'

What else could they have said to each other?

'It's still raining . . .'

Maigret put on his overcoat, placed his bowler hat well forward on his head and, a few moments later, his hands in his pockets, was walking along the streets of the town in the falling rain.

He opened the door to his office, its walls covered with administrative posters. His nose puckered at the smell of Inspector Méjat's brilliantine, a sickly odour that even ten pipes could not have overcome.

An old lady in a bonnet, with a shrivelled face, was sitting there on a chair, holding a huge dripping umbrella, of the kind common in the Vendée, in front of her. There was already a long trail of water on the floor, as if a dog had been caught short.

'What is it?' Maigret asked, walking through the barrier and leaning down towards his one inspector.

'It's for you. She only wants to talk to you.'

'What do you mean, to me? Did she say my name?'

'She asked for Detective Chief Inspector Maigret.'

The old woman realized they were talking about her and pursed her lips in a dignified manner. Before taking his coat off, Maigret, out of habit, fiddled with some of the papers awaiting him on his desk: the usual routine, a few Poles to keep an eye on, missing identity cards, rescindments of residence permits . . .

'I'm listening, madame. Please stay where you are. But before we start, I have a question for you: who told you my name?'

'My husband, inspector . . . Justin Hulot . . . When you see him, you're bound to remember him, he has the kind of face you can't forget. He was a customs officer in Concarneau when you were there on a case. He read in the paper that you'd been appointed to Luçon . . . Yesterday, when he realized the body was still in the room, he told me . . .'

'Excuse me! What body is this we're talking about?'

'The one in the judge's house.'

Clearly a woman who wouldn't be easily intimidated! For the moment, Maigret was looking at her without a great deal of interest, not suspecting that this sixty-four-year-old woman he had before him, Adine Hulot, would soon become much more familiar to him and that, like everyone else, he would end up calling her Didine.

'First of all, I should tell you that my husband has retired and that we've moved to the village I come from, L'Aiguillon . . . I have a little house there, near the harbour, which I inherited from my late uncle . . . I don't suppose you know L'Aiguillon?'

'That's what I thought. In that case, it won't be easy for you to understand . . . But who else could I turn to? Not the local policeman, who's drunk all day long and can't be bothered . . . The mayor's only interested in his mussels . . .'

'His mussels?' Maigret echoed.

'He's a mussel farmer, like my late uncle, like almost everybody in L'Aiguillon. He breeds mussels . . .'

That idiot Inspector Méjat saw fit to laugh sarcastically at this, and Maigret threw him an icy glance.

'You were saying, madame . . .'

She didn't need any encouragement. She was taking her time. She, too, had underlined with a glance the inappropriateness of Méjat's laughter.

'There are no stupid professions.'

'Of course not! Please go on.'

'The village of L'Aiguillon is quite far from the harbour. Not many people live there, only about twenty. The largest house is the judge's . . .'

'One moment. Who is this judge?'

'Forlacroix, his name is. He used to be a justice of the peace in Versailles. I think he got into trouble, and it wouldn't surprise me to hear that the government forced him to resign . . .'

She clearly didn't like the judge! And, small and wrinkled as she was, it was obvious this little old woman wasn't afraid to express her opinions about people!

'Tell me about the body. Is it the judge?'

'Unfortunately not! That kind of person never gets murdered!'

Excellent! Maigret had his answer, and Méjat laughed into his handkerchief.

'If you don't let me tell the story in my own way, you'll get me all mixed up . . . What day is it today? The 13th . . . My God, I hadn't even thought of that . . .'

She hastened to touch wood, then to make the sign of the cross.

'It was the day before yesterday, in other words, the 11th. The previous evening, they'd had people over . . .'

'Who's "they"?'

'The Forlacroixs . . . Dr Brénéol, with his wife and daughter, I mean his wife's daughter, because . . . It's a long story . . . Anyway, they'd had their little party, as they do every two weeks. They play cards until midnight, then they make a great racket starting their cars . . .'

'You seem to know a lot about what goes on in your neighbours' house.'

'I told you, our house – or rather, my late uncle's house – is more or less behind theirs. So even without meaning to . . .'

A gleam had come into the inspector's eyes that would have pleased Madame Maigret. He was smoking in a particular way, with short puffs, and he went and stoked the stove and then stood there with his back to the fire.

'About the body . . .'

'The next morning . . . I did say it was the 11th, didn't I? . . . The next morning, my husband took advantage of the fact that it was dry to prune the apple trees. I held the ladder. From up there, he could see over the wall. He was level with the first floor of the judge's house . . . One of the windows was open . . . Suddenly he comes back down and tells me, just like that:

'"Didine . . ." My name's Adine, but everybody calls me Didine . . . "Didine," he says, "there's someone lying on the floor in the bedroom . . ."

'"Lying on the floor?" I said. I didn't believe it. "Why would they be lying on the floor when there are plenty of beds in the house?"

'"That's the way it is . . . I'm going back up to have another look . . ."

'He goes back up. He comes down again . . . He's a man who never drinks and who, when he says something . . . And he's a man who thinks. After all, he was a public employee for thirty-five years . . .

'All day, I can see him thinking, thinking. After lunch he goes for his walk. He stops off at the Hôtel du Port . . .

'"It's odd!" he says when he comes back. "Nobody came in on the bus yesterday and nobody saw any cars."

'It was bothering him, you see? He asks me to hold the ladder for him again. He tells me the man is still lying on the floor . . .

'That evening, he watched the lights until they went off . . .'

'What lights?'

'The lights in the judge's house. The thing is, they never close the shutters at the back. They think nobody can see them. Well, the judge came into the room and stayed there for a long time.

'My husband got dressed again and ran outside . . .'

'Why?'

'In case the judge got the idea of throwing the body in the water . . . But he came back soon after . . .

'"It's low tide," he says. "You'd have to wade through mud up to your neck . . ."'

'The next day . . .'

Maigret was dumbfounded. He had seen some strange things in the course of his career, but these two elderly people, the retired customs officer and Didine, spying on the judge's house from their home, keeping the ladder up . . .

'The next day, the body was still there, in the same position.'

She looked at Maigret as if proclaiming: 'You see, we were right!'

'My husband watched the house all day. At two o'clock, the judge went for his usual walk with his daughter . . .'

'Ah! The judge has a daughter . . .'

'I'll tell you about her some other time! A whole other kettle of fish, that one! He also has a son . . . But it's too complicated to . . . When your man there behind us has stopped laughing, I may be able to continue . . .'

One in the eye for Méjat!

'Last night, high tide was at 9.26 in the evening . . . He still couldn't do anything, you see? . . . Up until midnight, there are always people around. After midnight, there wouldn't have been enough water any more. So my husband and I decided that, while he kept his eye on them, I'd come and see you. I took the nine o'clock bus. That gentleman told me you might not be coming today, but I realized he was trying to get rid of me. My husband said to me: "Tell the inspector that it's the customs officer from Concarneau, the one who has a little defect in his eye . . . And also tell him that I looked at the body through sailors' binoculars, and the man isn't someone from around here . . . There's a stain on the floor that must be blood . . ."'

'Excuse me,' Maigret interrupted. 'What time is the bus for L'Aiguillon?'

'It's already gone.'

'How many kilometres, Méjat?'

Méjat had a look on the wall map of the region.

'About thirty.'

'Phone for a taxi.'

He didn't care if Didine and her customs officer were crazy! He was prepared to pay the taxi fare out of his own pocket!

'If you don't mind stopping the cab just before the harbour, so that I can get out and they don't see me with you. It's better to act as if we don't know each other. People in L'Aiguillon are so suspicious . . . You'll be able to stay at the Hôtel du Port. It's the better of the two. That's where you'll see just about everybody after dinner. If you can get the room that looks out on the roof of the ballroom, you'll even be able to see the judge's house . . .'

'Inform my wife, Méjat.'

Night had fallen, and the world seemed to have turned to water. The old woman appreciated the comfort of the taxi, which had previously been a chauffeur-driven car. The crystal flower holder delighted her, as did the electric ceiling light.

'I say, the things they make! The rich are so lucky.'

The marshes . . . Vast flat expanses, crisscrossed by canals, with the occasional low farmhouse, known as cabins in the Vendée, and the piles of cow pats which, when caked, are used as fuel . . .

Something was stirring dimly in Maigret's soul, a kind of

hope. He didn't yet dare give in to it. Could it be that right here, deep in the Vendée, where he had been exiled, chance was going to bring him . . .

'I almost forgot. This evening, high tide is at 10.51 . . .'

Wasn't it staggering to hear this little old lady speaking with such precision?

'If he wants to get rid of the body, he'll take advantage of that. There's a bridge over the Lay that reaches to the harbour. From eleven o'clock, my husband will be on the bridge. If you want to talk to him . . .'

She knocked on the glass.

'Drop me here. I'll walk the rest of the way.'

And she plunged into the liquid darkness, her umbrella swelling like a balloon. Soon afterwards, Maigret got out of the taxi outside the Hôtel du Port.

'Want me to wait?'

'No, you might as well go back to Luçon.'

Men in blue, some of them fishermen, others mussel farmers, and bottles of white and rosé wine on long tables of varnished pitch pine. Then a kitchen. Then a ballroom that was only used on Sundays. It all smelled new. White walls. A ceiling of white pine. A staircase as flimsy as a toy and a room that was also white, an iron bedstead covered in gloss paint, cretonne curtains.

'Is that the judge's house I can see?' he asked the maid.

There was light at a dormer window which probably lit the stairs. They tried to persuade him to use the dining room, which was reserved for summer guests, but he preferred the main room. He was served oysters, mussels, shrimp, fish and a leg of lamb, while the men talked among themselves, in a strong accent, about things to do with the sea, especially concerning mussels. Maigret understood none of it.

'Have you had any visitors lately?'

'Not for a week . . . Or rather, the day before yesterday . . . No, it was the day before that . . . Someone got off the bus. He dropped in to tell us he'd be coming for dinner, but we didn't see him again . . .'

Maigret kept bumping into things: rails, baskets, steel ropes, crates, oyster shells. The whole seashore was crammed with the sheds where the mussel farmers kept their equipment. A kind of wooden village without inhabitants. A wailing every two minutes: the foghorn from the Baleines headland on the Ile de Ré, so he had been told, on the other side of the straits.

There were also vague intermittent lights in the sky: the beams from two or three lighthouses disappearing into the mist.

The murmur of water in motion. The waves pushing back the current from the little river, swelling it, and soon – at 10.51, the old woman had said – the tide would be high. In spite of the rain, two lovers stood right up against one of the sheds, lips together, not speaking, not moving.

He looked for the bridge, an interminable wooden bridge, barely wide enough to let a car pass. He made out masts, boats bobbing on the waves. Turning, he could see the lights of the hotel he had just left, then two other lights, a hundred metres further on, those of the judge's house.

'Is that you, inspector?'

He gave a start. He had almost bumped into a man, whose eyes he now saw squinting at him from close quarters.

'Justin Hulot. My wife told me . . . I've already been here for an hour, in case he took it into his head to . . .'

The rain was cold. Icy air rose from the water of the harbour. Pulleys squeaked, invisible things lived their nocturnal lives.

'Let me bring you up to date. When I went up the ladder at three o'clock, the body was still there. At four o'clock, I decided I'd like to see it once again before nightfall . . . Well, it wasn't there any more. *He* must have taken it down. I suppose he's keeping it ready behind the door so as to save time when the moment comes . . . I wonder how he's going to carry it. The judge is shorter and thinner than me. About the same height and weight as my wife . . . The other man, though . . . Shhh! . . .'

Someone passed in the darkness. The planks of the bridge shook one after the other. When the danger was over, Hulot resumed:

'On the other side of the bridge is La Faute. Not even a hamlet. Mostly small villas for people who come here in the summer. You'll be able to see it when it's light . . . I found out something that may be of interest. On the night of the card game, Albert went to see his father . . . Careful! . . .'

It was the lovers this time, who had climbed on to the bridge and were now leaning on the parapet and watching the river flow by in the darkness. Maigret's feet were cold. Water had seeped into his shoes. He noticed that Hulot was wearing rubber boots.

'It's a 108 tide. At six in the morning, you'll see them all going to the mussel fields . . .'

He was speaking in a low voice, as if in church. It was at once unnerving and a little grotesque. From time to time, Maigret wondered if he wouldn't have been better off in Luçon, playing cards at the Café Français with the owner, Dr Jamet, Bourdeuille the ironmonger, and senile old Memimot, who always sat behind them and shook his head at every hand.

'My wife is watching the back of the house . . .'

So the old lady was still involved, was she?

'You never know. In case he might have got the car out and had the idea of taking the body further away . . .'

The body! The body! . . . Was there really a body in all this?

Three pipes . . . Four pipes . . . From time to time the door of the hotel opened and closed, and footsteps could be heard moving away, voices. Then the lights went out. A rowing boat passed beneath the bridge.

'That's old Bariteau on his way to laying his eel nets. He won't be back for another two hours.'

How could old Bariteau see his way in all this blackness? God knows. You sensed the presence of the sea, very close, just at the end of the narrows. You could breathe it in. It was swelling, irresistibly invading the straits.

Maigret's mind wandered, he couldn't have said why. He thought of the recent merger of the Police Judiciaire and the Sûreté Générale and of certain points of friction that . . . Luçon! He had been sent to Luçon, where . . .

'Look . . .'

Hulot gripped his arm nervously.

No, it really was unbelievable! The idea that these two old people . . . That ladder held by Didine . . . The naval binoculars . . . And those calculations of tides! . . .

'The lights have been switched off.'

What was so extraordinary, at this hour, about seeing all the lights go out in the judge's house?

'Come. We can't see well enough . . .'

All the same, Maigret found himself walking on tiptoe in order not to shake the planks of the bridge. That siren lowing like a hoarse cow . . .

The water had almost reached the wooden sheds. A foot struck a broken basket.

'Shhh!'

And then they saw the door of the judge's house open.

A short, sprightly man appeared in the doorway, looked left and right and went back into the passage. A moment later, the improbable happened. The little man reappeared, bent over, gripping a long object that he started dragging through the mud.

It must have been heavy. After four metres, he stopped to catch his breath. The front door of the house had been left open. The sea was still twenty or thirty metres away.

'Oof . . .'

They sensed that 'oof', sensed the physical effort he must be making. The rain was still falling. Hulot's hand trembled convulsively on Maigret's thick sleeve.

'You see!'

Oh, yes! It had happened just as the old woman had said, just as the former customs officer had predicted. That little man was clearly Judge Forlacroix. And what he was dragging in the mud was definitely the lifeless body of a man!

2. 'Hold on a Minute . . . '

What gave the scene a somewhat ghostly character was that the judge didn't know. He thought he was alone in the emptiness of the night. From time to time, the halo of the lighthouse brushed over him, and they were able to make out an old gabardine, a felt hat. Maigret even noticed that he had kept a cigarette between his lips, although the rain must have extinguished it by now.

There were now only four metres between them. Maigret and Hulot were standing near a kind of sentry box. They didn't even think of hiding. The only reason the judge didn't see them was quite simply because he didn't turn his head in their direction. He was having a lot of difficulty. The burden he was dragging had come up against a rope stretched across the embankment, some twenty centimetres above the ground, and had to be carried across. He went about it clumsily, obviously unused to manual labour. It was clear, too, that he was hot, because he wiped his forehead with his hand.

It was then that Maigret, without choosing his moment, without thinking exactly what he had to do, simply said:

'Hold on a minute . . .'

The judge turned his head and saw the two men: Maigret enormous, the customs officer tiny. It was too dark to make out any particular expression on his face. A few seconds went by, seeming quite long. Then a voice – a little shaky, perhaps? – was heard:

'I'm sorry! Who are you?'

'Detective Chief Inspector Maigret.'

He had stepped forwards, but still couldn't see much of the

face. His feet almost touched the body, which seemed to be wrapped in sacks. At such a moment, why did the judge react by saying in a tone of surprise tinged with respect:

'Maigret from the Police Judiciaire?'

People were asleep in the surrounding houses. Old Bariteau, somewhere in the rustling darkness, was looking for holes in the seabed to place his eel nets.

'Maybe it's for the best.'

It was the judge speaking again.

'Would you like to come inside?'

He took a few steps, as if forgetting his package. There was such an oppressive calm around them that they had the impression they were living in slow motion.

'Perhaps it would be more convenient to take the body back indoors?' the judge suggested, reluctantly.

And he bent down. Maigret helped him. They did not close the door behind them. Hulot stood there in the doorway, and Forlacroix, who had not recognized him, was wondering if he was going to make his mind up to come in.

'Thanks a lot, Hulot!' Maigret said. 'I'll see you tomorrow morning. In the meantime, I'd prefer it if you didn't say anything. Do you have a telephone, Monsieur Forlacroix?'

'Yes, but we aren't connected after nine o'clock in the evening.'

'One moment, Hulot. Can you go and find someone at the post office? Ask to be put through to number 23, in Luçon. It's a hotel. Ask to speak to Inspector Méjat and tell him to come and join me as soon as possible.'

There! Now it was just the two of them, face to face in the passage, and the judge had switched on the light. He took off his hat, which was dripping with water, and his raincoat. The mysteries of the night had faded. What appeared in the light was a short, thin man with regular features, his face haloed by fine long blond and grey hair that looked like a wig.

He looked at his dirty hands, then at his burden. Maigret now noticed that the body had been wrapped in two coal sacks, one for the head and chest, the other for the legs. The two sacks had been clumsily tied together with string.

'Do you want to see him straight away?'

'Who is he?' Maigret asked.

'I have no idea. Take your coat off and come this way, please . . .'

He wiped his hands with his handkerchief, opened a door, switched on another light, and they found themselves on the threshold of a vast room, at the far end of which logs crackled in a fireplace.

At that moment, nothing could have been a greater surprise to Maigret than the pleasant warmth of this room, its brightness, its harmonious layout. Oak beams gave the impression that the ceiling was very low. They even had to descend two steps to enter. The floor was made up of white flagstones, over which two or three rugs had been thrown. And the white walls were lined with nothing but bookshelves, containing thousands of books.

'Please sit down, inspector . . . I seem to recall that you like heat . . .'

More books on an antique table. Two armchairs by the fire. Hard to believe that behind the door, sewn into two coal sacks . . .

'It's really lucky for me that I'm dealing with a man like you. I'm a little puzzled, though. I thought you were in Paris and . . .'

'I've been transferred to Luçon.'

'All the better for me. I'm sure it would have been hard to make myself understood by an ordinary police officer . . . Do you mind if I . . . ?'

From a Renaissance chest, he took a silver tray, a bottle and some crystal glasses, and these objects, artfully lit, glittered magnificently. There was an atmosphere of refinement and comfort about it all . . .

'Please have a glass of armagnac. By the way – it's only just occurred to me – how did that ugly, one-eyed old customs officer come to be involved in . . .'

It was only now, at this precise moment, that Maigret became fully aware of the situation. He literally saw himself, sitting comfortably in his armchair, his legs stretched towards the fire, warming his glass of armagnac in the hollow of his hand. He realized that it wasn't he who was talking, asking questions, but this short, thin, calm man, the same man who, only a few minutes earlier, had been dragging a dead body to the sea.

'Forgive me, Monsieur Forlacroix, but perhaps I could take the opportunity to ask you a few questions.'

The judge turned to him with a mixture of surprise and reproach, his eyes blue as forget-me-nots. He seemed to be saying:

'Why? I thought you were a different kind of person . . . Well, as you wish . . .'

But he said nothing. He bent his head slightly, politely, the better to listen. It was a gesture he made often, and which indicated that he was a little hard of hearing.

'You told me earlier that you don't know that . . . that man . . .'

My God, how hard it was! How difficult the simplest things became when you had let yourself sink into such a state of bliss!

'I don't know him from Adam, I assure you.'

'In that case, why . . .'

Come on! It had to be done! Maigret all but closed his eyes, as if swallowing a bitter pill.

'Why did you kill him?'

He looked. And saw again the same surprised, reproving expression on the judge's face.

'But I didn't kill him, inspector! Come now! Why would I

have killed someone I don't know, someone I never saw alive? I know it may be difficult to accept, but I'm sure a man like you will believe me.'

The most remarkable thing was that Maigret already believed him! It was as if he were under a spell in this silent house where nothing could be heard but the crackling of the logs and where, during the silences, you were aware of the distant murmur of the sea.

'If you so wish, I'll tell you exactly what happened. A little more armagnac? An old friend of mine, who used to be public prosecutor in Versailles, sends it to me from his chateau in the Gers.'

'You lived in Versailles too, didn't you?'

'Almost my whole life. A charming town. The people there still seem to be living in the court of Louis XIV, and I think it would be difficult to find elsewhere a society that was more polite in the old sense of the term. We formed a little group that . . .'

A gesture of the hand, as if to chase away pointless memories.

'That's of little importance . . . It was . . . Let's see now, it was Tuesday . . .'

'Tuesday the 10th,' Maigret said. 'You had friends over, if I'm not mistaken . . .'

The judge smiled slightly. 'I see you're well informed. You were with Hulot earlier. It wouldn't surprise me if you'd seen Didine. She knows what happens in my house better than I do . . .'

A thought suddenly struck Maigret. He looked around, sensing that something was missing in this house.

'Don't you have a maid?' he said, surprised.

'Not a live-in one. An old woman and her daughter who live here in L'Aiguillon come every morning and leave again immediately after dinner . . . Anyway, on Tuesday, my friends came as they do every two weeks. Dr Brénéol, who lives one kilometre from here, his wife and Françoise . . .'

'Françoise is Madame Brénéol's daughter?'

'That's correct. From her first marriage. That's of no importance, except for Brénéol . . .'

And a slight smile hovered again over his lips.

'The Marsacs, who live in Saint-Michel-en-l'Hermitage, arrived a little later . . . We played bridge.'

'Was your daughter with you?'

A moment's hesitation. A touch more gravity in his gaze.

'No, she was in bed.'

'And tonight?'

'She's in bed . . .'

'Didn't she hear anything?'

'No. I took care to make as little noise as possible . . . Anyway, on Tuesday, we finished about midnight.'

'And you had another visitor,' Maigret said, turning towards the fireplace. 'Your son.'

'Albert, yes. He only stayed a few minutes.'

'Doesn't your son live with you?'

'He lives near the town hall. We don't exactly have the same tastes. My son is a mussel farmer . . . As I'm sure you've already been told, that's the main activity around here.'

'Would it be indiscreet of me to ask why your son paid you a visit in the middle of the night?'

The judge stared at his glass, was silent for a moment, then finally said:

'Yes!'

And he waited.

'Did your son go upstairs?'

'That's where he was when I saw him . . .'

'I assume he went to say hello to his sister?'

'No. He didn't see her.'

'How do you know?

'Because, I might as well tell you straight away, given that you'll hear it from other people, I'm in the habit of locking my daughter in her room at night . . . Let's just say she's a sleepwalker . . .'

'Why did your son go upstairs?'

'To wait for me, because I had friends downstairs. He was sitting on the top step. We had a short conversation . . .'

'On the stairs?'

The judge nodded. Weren't they starting to get into the realms of the implausible? Maigret swallowed the contents of his glass in one go, and Forlacroix refilled it.

'I went downstairs to put the chain on the door. Then I went to bed, read a few pages and fell asleep almost immediately. The following morning, I went to the fruitery to get . . . To be honest, I find it hard to remember what I went there for. It's a room we call the fruitery because it's where we keep the fruit, but there's actually a bit of everything there. A junk room, if you prefer . . . There was a man lying dead on the floor, a man I'd never seen before. His skull had been smashed in with what you people call a blunt instrument. I searched in his pockets . . . In a while, I'll show you the objects I found there . . . But no wallet. Not a single paper that could identify him.'

'What I don't understand . . .' Maigret began.

'I know! That's going to be the hardest thing to explain! I didn't call the police. I kept the body in the house for three days. I was waiting for the tide to be favourable so that I could get rid of it at night, in secret, like a murderer . . . And yet, I'm telling you the honest truth, I didn't kill the man. I had no reason to do so. I have absolutely no idea why he was in my house. I don't know if he broke in while he was alive or if someone brought him here when he was already dead.'

Silence fell. Again the distant moan of the foghorn could be heard. There were boats out at sea. Fishermen were lifting nets heaving with fish up on deck. Had Hulot managed to make his phone call? If he had, the unbearable Méjat, with his brilliantined hair, must be getting hastily dressed right now. Did he have yet another conquest in his bed, as he liked to boast?

'Well,' Maigret sighed, drowsy from the heat, 'I don't think this is going to be an easy matter!'

'That's what I'm afraid of, too. Given the situation, I mean since the man was dead, it would have been preferable . . .'

He didn't finish his sentence, but looked towards the windows. The ebb tide would have carried him away, and nobody would have been any the wiser! Maigret started to move, shifted one leg, then the other, until at last he was able to get out of the excessively deep armchair; it looked as if his head might touch the beams.

'Shall we go and have a look at him anyway?'

He couldn't help admiring this low room, where it was so pleasant to spend time, where everything was so precisely in its place. He looked up at the ceiling: who was this girl who was locked up for the night?

'We could take him into the laundry,' the judge suggested. 'It's at the end of the passage.'

Now they were both trying to avoid getting themselves dirty. They were no longer out in the wet night. They had become civilized men again.

The laundry was vast, covered in red tiles. There was still linen drying on iron wires.

'Do you have a pair of scissors?' Maigret grunted, touching the two sacks. Coal-black water oozed out.

The judge couldn't find any scissors but came back with a kitchen knife. The fire was out. It was cold. Their wet fingers were turning red.

The most extraordinary thing about all this was that it wasn't tragic. The judge showed no horror at the prospect of seeing again the face of the man he had sewn into the sacks. Maigret was wearing his stubbornest, grouchiest expression, but the truth was that he was basking almost voluptuously in this investigation that had fallen into his lap, right here in Luçon, where he had been exiled. He was like a seal that had been juggling in circuses and now found itself back in the icy seas of the North!

How long had it been since he had last entered a house, as he had done earlier, and sniffed about, come and gone, heavily, patiently, until the souls of both people and things no longer held any secrets for him?

And that Didine with her Hulot! And that son waiting for his father, at midnight, sitting on the stairs!

Now for the other man! The victim! What would emerge from these filthy sacks?

For a moment, it was almost comical. You expect all kinds of things, but what real life throws up is always more bizarre. So it was that now, when the upper sack was removed, the face they uncovered was completely black. Because of the coal, of course!

It was only natural, but for a moment the two men looked at each other, and both had the same idea; for a split second, they had the absurd impression that they were in the presence of a negro.

'Do you have a towel and a little water?'

The tap made a racket. When the noise ceased, Maigret listened out. Another noise could be heard outside, that of a car engine. A door slammed. A bell rang loudly in the passage. Méjat didn't do things quietly!

'Where's the detective chief inspector?'

He saw him standing there. Méjat had a red nose and a lock of hair hanging askew.

'Did I get here fast enough? Shall I keep the taxi, chief? Is there really a body? Where's the crazy old lady?'

He had brought with him, on his person and in the folds of his clothes, some of the cold damp air from outside and also a crudity that altered the quality of the atmosphere. Now it was less muted, less muffled. Méjat, with his strong Toulouse accent, wasn't sensitive to nuances.

'Have you identified him, chief?'

'Not at all!'

Maigret was surprised at his own words, words that belonged to the past, words he had often repeated in the old days when he was floundering in a complicated case, and fools like Méjat . . .

'He received quite a blow to the head!'

The judge looked at Maigret, Maigret looked at him, and both were thinking the same thing, regretting the almost intimate peace of a little earlier. As for Méjat, he was looking through the dead man's pockets and, of course, finding nothing.

'How old do you think he is, chief? I'd say about forty . . . Are there any labels on his clothes? . . . Do you want me to strip him?'

'Go ahead! Strip him!'

Maigret filled a pipe and started to walk up and down the laundry, talking to himself in a low voice.

'I'll have to phone the public prosecutor in La Roche-sur-Yon . . . I wonder what he'll decide.'

And the judge, standing there in front of him, uttered gravely, not realizing how comical he sounded:

'It would be a *disaster* if they put me in prison.'

'Come now, Judge Forlacroix,' Maigret burst out, unable to stop himself. 'Don't you think it's a *disaster* for this man to have lost his life and to be lying here on these tiles? Don't you think it's a *disaster* for a wife, children perhaps, to be wondering what's become of him? And that it would have been even more of a *disaster* never to find out, because someone else preferred not to complicate his life?'

He wasn't even grateful! He had been given a wonderful armagnac, a log fire as penetrating as balm, an hour of gentle bliss, and here he was turning against his host, becoming once again the implacable Maigret of Quai des Orfèvres.

The mild Monsieur Forlacroix's only response was a reproachful look.

'There's a label in the jacket!' Méjat cried triumphantly. 'Let's see now . . . Pa . . . Pa . . . Pana . . .'

'Panama!' Maigret grunted, snatching the garment from his hands. 'That's going to make things easier for us, isn't it? A man who wears clothes made in the Republic of Panama! Why not China?'

The uppers of the shoes had to be cut in order to take them off. It was again Méjat who saw to this, and this young man who dressed so sharply, and was so happy to play the ladykiller, performed his task as naturally as he would have written a report, with the names circled, as he was in the habit of doing.

'The shoes are from Paris, Boulevard des Capucines. The heels are already a bit scuffed. In my opinion, they've been worn for at least a month. What do you think he could have been, chief? A Frenchman? . . . I think he was a Frenchman. A fairly well-to-do sort, who didn't work with his hands . . . Look at his hands.'

Neither of them gave a thought to the taxi waiting outside, or to the driver pacing up and down to warm himself. Abruptly, the door flew open. A man appeared at the end of the passage, as tall and broad as Maigret, wearing thigh-length rubber boots. On his head he had a sailor's sou'wester. His upper body was encased in an oilskin jacket beneath which he was obviously wearing a few thick sweaters.

He advanced, heavy and suspicious. He looked first Maigret, then Méjat up and down, bent over the body and finally stared at the judge.

'What's going on?' he snapped, almost threateningly.

Forlacroix turned to Maigret.

'My son . . .' he said. 'I'd be grateful if you'd explain to him . . .'

And with that, he quickly left the laundry with little mouse-like steps and went back to the low room where he had first received the inspector.

'What's going on?' the young man repeated, this time addressing Maigret. 'Who is this? Who killed him? You're police, aren't you? When I saw a car outside the house . . .'

It was already five o'clock in the morning! Albert Forlacroix had been on his way to the mussel fields when he had spotted the taxi.

'The driver told me he'd brought an inspector from Luçon.'

And suddenly, with a frown:

'My sister . . . What has he done to my sister?'

He was so anxious that Maigret had a kind of shock. Could it be that . . . While he and Forlacroix had sat there in soft armchairs, in front of the crackling logs . . .

'I'd like to see your sister, as it happens,' he said in a changed voice. 'Do you have a key to her room?'

The other man merely shrugged his massive shoulders.

'Méjat . . . Wait down here.'

Their steps made a noise on the stairs, then in the long corridor, which turned several corners.

'It's here . . . Could you stand back?'

And Albert Forlacroix lunged at the door.

3. The Airaud Trail

It was an extraordinary moment, and Maigret would never forget the taste of it. First the late-night weariness, and that smell of wet wool. That unknown corridor that seemed to go on for ever. Again they heard the foghorn. Just as Albert Forlacroix launched himself at the door, Maigret looked towards the stairs and saw the judge, who had walked up without making a noise. Behind him, still in the stairwell, Méjat's face . . .

The door yielded, and his impetus carried Albert right into the middle of the room.

It was unexpected. It was like nothing that might have been foreseen.

The room was lit by a bedside lamp with a finely gathered pink silk shade. A young girl lay on a Louis XVI bed. She was in an almost seated position, because she had lifted herself on one elbow, and, in the movement she had made to look towards the door, a swollen, heavy breast had escaped from her nightdress.

Maigret could not have said if she was beautiful. Was the face too broad perhaps, the forehead too low, the nose childish? But her lips were as full as a ripe fruit, and her eyes were huge.

Had she switched the lamp on when she had heard noises in the corridor? Had she been asleep? It was impossible to know. She didn't seem very surprised. And yet she could see the great bulk of Maigret in the doorway and her brother standing in his rubber boots in the middle of the room.

All she did was murmur in a calm voice:

'What's the matter, Albert?

Her father had not come in, but he had approached the door

and had heard. Maigret was embarrassed, unable to take his eyes off that breast, and Albert had noticed. Not that he paid any attention. He looked suspiciously about the room then went and opened a door.

Was it intuition? Maigret felt sure this door led to the famous fruitery, and he stepped forwards.

'What are you looking for?' he asked.

No reply, just a nasty look. Then suddenly Albert Forlacroix bent down. On the floor, both in the bedroom and in the fruitery, there were footprints. A man's shoes had left thin rings of mud, and the mud wasn't completely dry.

'Who is it?'

Albert walked to the window of the fruitery. It was half-open, letting cold air filter in.

Maigret returned to the bedroom to find the girl in the same position, her breast still bare. So there had been a man in this room, in this bed, during the night, perhaps when Maigret was already in the house . . .

Albert strode across the room. Maigret followed him. The judge, waiting in the corridor, murmured:

'I won't be able to lock the door again . . .'

His son shrugged and, ignoring everyone, started down the stairs, with Maigret at his heels.

'Méjat!'

'Yes, chief . . .'

'Keep an eye on the house . . . From the outside.'

He took his coat off the hook and grabbed his hat. It wasn't light yet, but the harbour was bustling, and voices and various noises could be heard from all sides.

'You didn't answer me just now. Do you know who the man is?'

Pretending not to see Hulot, who had been waiting for him, Maigret walked right past him, leaving the former customs officer quite crestfallen.

As for Albert, he was in no hurry to speak. A strange young man!

'Can I go and harvest my mussels? Or do you intend to arrest me?'

'You can harvest your mussels. Unless you have something to tell me. Like the name of the man whose prints you found in your sister's room.'

Suddenly Albert stopped and put his hand on Maigret's shoulder. They had reached the edge of the water. The land fell away rapidly, uncovering an expanse of brownish, swollen mud. Men, women in trousers, all of them in rubber boots, were loading empty baskets into flat boats that were then pushed out with the help of poles.

'The man? Let's see . . . It's him over there . . .'

A young man almost as tall and strong as Albert, dressed just like him, was helping an old woman into his boat and then immediately cast off from the shore.

'His name's Airaud . . . Marcel Airaud.'

With that, Albert opened the door of one of the sheds and came out again with a pile of baskets.

The maid at the Hôtel du Port was already up and was washing down the tiled floor when Maigret returned.

'Where have you been?' she said, surprised. 'Didn't you sleep in your bed?'

He sat down by the stove and asked for coffee, bread, sausage and cheese. Only then, comfortably wedged into his wall seat, did he ask as he chewed:

'Do you know a man named Airaud?'

'Marcel?' she replied, so quickly that Maigret looked at her with rather more attention.

'Marcel Airaud, yes.'

'He's a local lad. Why do you ask me about him?'

It would have been difficult for her to pretend that this particular young man was of no interest to her.

'Is he a mussel farmer? Married?'

'Not at all!'

'Is he engaged?'

'Why do you ask me that?'

'No reason. I got the impression he's been hanging around the judge's daughter . . .'

'First of all, it's not true!' she cried through clenched teeth. 'Others, maybe! And they don't need to hang around, or stand on ceremony, because if you really want to know, that girl's a . . . a . . .'

She looked for the worst swear word she could find, but in the end it was quite an innocuous expression that fell from her lips:

'. . . a good-for-nothing! Everybody knows that. If her brother had had to keep beating up the men who visit her in her room . . .'

'Are there many of them?'

'Almost all! And the time she ran away to Poitiers, where they found her in a real state! . . . If anyone's been trying to convince you that she and Marcel . . .'

'Could I have a little more coffee, please? One more question: the man who came by bus on Tuesday . . . What time did he arrive?'

'It was the four-thirty bus.'

'Did he leave straight away?'

'He said he'd be back for dinner. He set off in the direction of the bridge, I think. It was already dark.'

'Would you recognize him if you were shown his photograph?'

'Maybe . . .'

'All right! I'm going to bed.'

She looked at him in astonishment.

'Let's see, now. It's six o'clock. Wake me up at eight, with some very strong coffee. Can I rely on you, young lady? You're not angry at me because of Marcel?'

'Why should I care about that?'

★

He slept soundly. It was a great gift of his, being able to sleep anywhere, at any time, and forget his worries from one second to the next.

And when the maid, whose name was Thérèse, woke him with piping-hot coffee, a pleasant surprise awaited him. Everything had changed. Sunlight was coming in through the window. The hubbub of life filled the room, a commotion made up of a thousand noises from all sides.

'Would you be so kind as to bring me up some soap, my dear? If they sell safety razors locally, buy me one, and a shaving brush.'

As he waited, he leaned out of the window and drank in the cold air, as delicious as spring water. So this was the harbour that had seemed so dark and clammy last night? That was the judge's house? And the sheds on the shore . . .

Everything gave him a delighted sense of astonishment. The sheds, for example, were brightly painted, in white, blue and green. The judge's house was all white, covered in delicate pink tiles.

It was a very old house, which must have undergone a lot of changes over the centuries. It was a surprise, for example, to discover, next to the window of the fruitery, quite a vast terrace surrounded by a balustrade with an enormous green porcelain pot at each corner.

Below, beyond the garden, another house, also white, no upper floor, probably just two rooms, with a little garden and a fence, a ladder propped against an apple tree. Wasn't that Didine, in her white bonnet, standing in the doorway, her hands on her belly, looking in Maigret's direction?

The mussel farmers were already coming back. Twenty boats, thirty boats, strange flat craft called acons, had moored at the dock, and baskets and baskets of blueish mussels were being hoisted into big lorries with spluttering engines.

'I could only find a cheap throwaway razor for three francs fifty, but the shopkeeper says . . .'

The throwaway razor would have to do! Maigret wasn't sleepy

any more. He was as fresh as if he had spent all night in his bed. A little glass of white wine downstairs before he went out? Why not?

'Would you like me to polish your shoes?'

Of course! No more mud! Everything clean! He couldn't help smiling when he spotted Inspector Méjat in the distance, looking like a wet cockerel drying its feathers in the sun.

'Nothing new, my friend?'

'Nothing, chief. Two women arrived, an old one and a young one. The maids, I assume . . . Look.'

The three ground-floor windows were open. They were the windows of the library, where Maigret and the judge had spent part of the night by the fire. An old woman in a white bonnet was shaking the rugs, and a fine golden dust rose into the sun.

'What about the judge?'

'No sign of him. Or the girl . . . Oh, God, there's that oddball who's been bending my ear all morning.'

Maigret looked in the direction indicated and saw Hulot, squinting even more in the sunlight than at night. He was hoping they would call him over. He was only waiting for the signal and he would come running.

'Stay here until I get back. I won't be long.'

'Do I have time to get a cup of coffee?'

Permission granted! Maigret was in a good mood at this stage. Soon afterwards, he walked into the police station and introduced himself to the sergeant.

'First of all, I need to use your telephone. Could you call the prosecutor's office in La Roche-sur-Yon for me?'

The prosecutor hadn't arrived yet. His deputy listened to the verbal report and approved it. Then Luçon. Then two or three more phone calls.

Yes, Maigret would manage to get things moving eventually. Of course, he felt nostalgic. In Paris, he would have had his whole team around him, fellows who knew his methods, to whom he would barely need to speak: Lucas, who had been promoted, Janvier, Torrence, the men in Criminal Records . . .

Here, he had to wait until midday for the photographer to arrive, and the gendarme on guard near the judge's house was looking at the passers-by so fiercely that they were starting to suspect something at the café on the corner.

Maigret rang the bell. The old woman opened the door.

'I'll go and see if Monsieur can . . .'

'Let him in, Élisa.'

He was standing in the library, where perfect order reigned, and the sun came in through the three windows.

'I've come to photograph the body. You left it in the laundry, I hope?'

'I'll give you the key. I locked it, to stop the maids from . . .'

'Do they know?'

'Not yet. I preferred . . .'

'Is your daughter up?'

What a question! Couldn't Maigret hear her playing the piano on the first floor?

'I assume she doesn't know either?'

'She knows absolutely nothing . . .'

Maigret had perhaps never before encountered such unflappability.

Here was a man with refined manners, a quiet, cultivated man who, at the end of a bridge party, finds his giant of a son sitting on the stairs and regards it as quite natural!

The following morning, he opens a door and discovers the body of a murdered man, a man he doesn't know.

He takes even that in his stride, doesn't mention it to anybody and goes for his usual walk with his daughter.

He waits for a favourable tide. He sews the corpse into some sacks. He . . .

The police are in his home. His son appears, in an excitable mood. The door to his daughter's room is broken down. It's clear that a man has spent part of the night there.

He remains calm. The maids arrive as usual, and the house is cleaned without any fuss. The young girl with the naked breast plays the piano. The father merely locks the door of the laundry where the corpse is . . .

The photographer got down to work, and the judge watched him as if it were the most natural thing in the world to sit a dead man up and try to give him the appearance of life.

'I must inform you,' Maigret grunted, 'that the prosecutor will be here at about three in the afternoon. Until then, I don't want you to leave the house. The same goes for Mademoiselle Forlacroix . . .'

Why did it feel strange to say 'Mademoiselle Forlacroix'? Because he had seen her in her bed, one breast outside her nightdress? Because a man had left muddy footprints in her room?

'May I ask you if my son has spoken to you, inspector? You will have a glass of port, won't you?'

'Thank you. Your son simply pointed out a young man named Marcel Airaud. Do you know him?'

The judge blinked, and his nostrils became a little pinched.

'You also think it was this Marcel who was in your daughter's . . .'

A very low voice, a mere breath. 'I don't know . . .'

The door to the library was open. Logs were burning.

'Come in a moment, would you?'

It was a plea. He left the photographer at the door.

'I assume you've realized?'

Maigret said neither yes nor no. It was an embarrassing situation, especially dealing with a father.

'It's because of her that I left Versailles and moved here . . . This house has belonged to my family for a long time, and we'd sometimes spend a month here in the summer . . .'

'How old was she?'

'Sixteen. The doctors warned me that the episodes would be more and more frequent . . . At other times, she's completely normal . . .'

He turned his head away. Then, shrugging his shoulders:

'I didn't tell you about it straight away. I'm not too sure what I was hoping . . . You do understand now why it would have been better if the sea had carried the body away? They'll say . . . God knows what people's imagination will dream up! Not to mention that fool Albert . . .'

'What was he doing here that night?'

Too late. Already the judge's dismay had faded. For a few seconds, it had been possible to believe that he was melting, that he was going to open up.

Was it because Maigret had asked too specific a question? He looked at the inspector with his cold eyes, the pupils almost colourless in the sunlight.

'No, it wasn't about that! . . . It doesn't matter . . . Are you sure you wouldn't like some port? . . . I have a Portuguese friend who . . .'

One friend sent him armagnac, another port. Didn't he seem preoccupied with giving his life all the refinement he possibly could?

Through the gap in the curtains, he suddenly noticed the gendarme pacing up and down outside and gave a nervous little laugh.

'Is he here for me?'

'You know I have no choice . . .'

The judge sighed and said something unexpected: 'This is all very regrettable, inspector!'

Overhead, the piano was still being played, and Chopin's chords harmonized perfectly with the atmosphere of this grand house where life should have been so sweet.

'See you later!' Maigret said abruptly, like a man resisting temptation.

The men who had returned from the mussel fields were filling the main room of the Hôtel du Port. Who had spoken? Whoever it might have been, everyone watched Maigret as he sat down at a table with Méjat and ordered lunch.

Their blue clothes had been washed clean by the rain and the seawater into sumptuous shades. Thérèse, the little maid, was in an emotional state and, following the direction of her gaze, Maigret recognized Marcel Airaud, sitting among a group of men, drinking rosé wine.

A sturdy young man of about twenty-five, as heavy as the rest of them, especially in their boots, with a calm gaze and slow gestures.

The conversations, which had been noisy earlier, had ceased. The men turned towards Maigret. Then they took a slug of their drinks, wiped their mouths, looked for something to say, anything, just to break the embarrassing silence.

One of the older men left, then another.

'Off for my grub! The wife must be starting to bellyache . . .'

Marcel was one of the last to remain, one elbow on the table, a cheek resting on his open hand. Thérèse came and asked Maigret:

'Would you like the mouclade?'

'What's that?'

'Mussels in cream. A local dish.'

'I can't stand cream,' Méjat declared.

When she walked away, Marcel stood up to take her place. He pulled over a straw-bottomed chair, sat down astride it and touched the brim of his cap.

'Can I talk to you for a minute, detective chief inspector?'

No humility. No bravado either. He was at ease.

'How do you know I'm a detective chief inspector?'

Marcel shrugged. 'People talk. Since we got back from the mussel fields, they've been talking . . .'

There were only two men left, both fishermen, listening from a corner. A clatter of plates came from the kitchen.

'Is it true that a man was murdered in the judge's house?'

Beneath the table, Méjat's knee touched Maigret's. The inspector, his mouth full, raised his head and looked calmly at Marcel, who did not lower his eyes.

'Yes, it is.'

'In the fruitery?'

This time there was a touch of dew-like moisture on his upper lip.

'You know the fruitery?'

Marcel didn't reply, but threw a glance at Thérèse, who was just then bringing the steaming mouclade. 'What day did it happen?'

'I'd like to ask you a question first. What time did you get home last night? You live with your mother, don't you?'

'Did Albert say something?'

'I'm asking the question.'

'It was just after midnight . . .'

'Do you usually leave the judge's house so early?'

Another glance, this time towards the kitchen, into which Thérèse had just disappeared.

'It depends . . .'

A pity this was happening just as the mouclade had arrived, because it was a masterpiece. In spite of himself, Maigret was trying to identify a taste of . . . what could it be? . . . a slight hint . . . barely an aroma . . .

'What about Tuesday?' he asked.

'I didn't go there on Tuesday . . .'

Maigret frowned, sat motionless for a moment, staring into space, then suddenly cried triumphantly:

'Curry! I'd bet anything you like there's curry in this . . .'

'Don't you believe me?'

'About Tuesday? I have no idea, my friend. How could I possibly know that yet? . . .'

'I'm ready to swear . . .'

Of course it would have been nice to believe him!

Just as it would have been nice to believe the judge! Just as you instinctively believed Albert!

All the same, the corpse hadn't got there by itself!

4. Under the Eyes of La République

All in all, Maigret had no cause for complaint. It all went well, very well even, and at the end Monsieur Bourdeille-Jaminet deigned to utter a few feeble words which must have been meant as congratulations.

It was Maigret who had chosen the town hall, because the police station was really too dark and smelled of old leather, cabbage soup and unwashed brats. The town hall had a spacious reception room, with dazzling whitewashed walls. There was a flag in a corner, a bust of *La République* on the mantelpiece and a pile of family record books on the green baize table.

The gentlemen arrived in two cars: first the prosecutor, Monsieur Bourdeille-Jaminet, so tall that his gaze seemed not to reach the ground, with his deputy, then an examining magistrate whose name Maigret did not catch, a clerk, the pathologist and a lieutenant of gendarmes.

Other gendarmes had arrived from Luçon and seen fit to set up what amounted to a roadblock in the street, which meant that people would have gathered even if they hadn't known anything was happening.

The body was already there, in the courtyard. The pathologist had asked permission to work in the open air. The trestle tables used for banquets had been brought out. Dr Brénéol had finally arrived, looking quite nervous. He was distantly related to the prosecutor. They exchanged polite remarks and talked about the will of some cousin by marriage.

Everyone was smoking. Beyond the glass door was the ballroom, still hung with paper chains from the most recent dance, the benches lined up against the walls for the mothers.

'Excuse me, gentlemen . . . My dear colleague, may I ask you to . . .'

The doctors in the courtyard. The legal people in the reception room, the clerk sitting behind a pile of papers. As for the mayor, he was waiting in the doorway with a self-important air, chatting with a police sergeant.

After a while, Maigret began wondering if anyone would talk about the case at all, so remote did everyone seem from the drama. The judge was telling a story about a duck hunt he had attended the previous winter on the headland near L'Aiguillon.

'Shall we both begin?' Maigret said to the clerk.

He dictated in a low voice, a very low voice in order not to upset the others. Had they learned anything new since morning? Nothing really, apart from the fact that Thérèse had identified the traveller who had got off the bus on Tuesday. The bus driver had also identified him immediately, but couldn't remember if the man had got on at Luçon or Triaize.

Photographs had gone out in all directions. All the gendarmes would be provided with them. They would be shown to innkeepers and hoteliers. The following morning's newspapers would publish the photograph. In other words, the usual routine.

'You're going to wrap this up nicely, aren't you, inspector?' the magistrate asked pleasantly, as if awarding Maigret a good mark.

The doctors returned, unfazed, and washed their hands at the drinking fountain behind the mayor's office . . . A blunt instrument, as expected . . . The blow had been a violent one . . . The cranium had been shattered . . . The stomach contents would be examined later . . .

A strong, healthy fellow . . . The liver a little enlarged . . . He must have liked his food . . .

'I'm sure, my dear prosecutor, that my friend Forlacroix, with whom I played bridge that night, had nothing to do with this . . .'

'Shall we go, gentlemen?'

In a procession, on foot, because it wasn't worth getting in the cars. With the populace following on! And that cheerful sun up above . . .

'After you, prosecutor . . .'

The door opened without their having to ring the bell. Old Élisa showed everybody in. Judge Forlacroix was standing self-effacingly in a corner of the library. It was embarrassing: they wondered if they should say hello to him, shake his hand . . .

'I put keys in all the doors, gentlemen . . .'

His daughter, Lise, sat in an armchair, watching them with large astonished eyes, and a ray of the setting sun set a lock of red hair ablaze. Well, well! The night before, Maigret hadn't noticed that she was a flaming redhead.

'If you'd like to show us the way, inspector,' the prosecutor sighed, a man of the world apologizing for intruding in someone else's house and anxious to get it over with as quickly as possible.

'This way . . . This is the girl's room. The judge's room is at the end of the corridor . . . The fruitery is here . . .'

Six men in coats and hats, looking around them, bending down, touching the odd object, nodding.

'There are tools in this cupboard. There's a hammer here that the killer could have used, but I haven't found any prints . . .'

'Gloves, do you think?' the prosecutor uttered from his great height, as if saying something very intelligent.

It was a little like a tour of a house where the contents were being auctioned off. Were they going to visit the judge's room? Maigret opened the door. The room was of average size, furnished soberly but with taste. That same mixture of almost peasant simplicity and refinement.

Inspector Méjat was outside. Maigret had entrusted him with the task of keeping an eye on the onlookers, observing the reactions of certain people, listening in on conversations. Didine was in the front row, shaking her head, outraged at being left with the crowd, since it was she, after all, who'd done everything.

The magistrate and the prosecutor talked in low voices in a corner. The prosecutor nodded. He walked up to Maigret.

'I'm told you want him to be left free provisionally, at least for two or three days? . . . It's delicate, isn't it, very delicate, because the one thing we've established is that he was in possession of the corpse . . . Well, if you're prepared to take the responsibility . . . Your reputation . . . We'll leave you an arrest warrant. Perhaps a blank warrant, too, what do you think? . . .'

Satisfied, he screwed up his eyes, which was his way of smiling.

'Well, gentlemen . . .'

They were leaving. It was over. Dr Brénéol apologized and said he would be staying in the house with his friend Forlacroix. It only remained for the others to get back in their cars. Raised hats. Handshakes.

A big sigh from Maigret.

Phew! Now he could begin his investigation!

There she stood before him, all thin, lips pursed.

'If you'd like to come and see me, I may have some things to tell you . . .'

'Of course, Madame Didine! Let's see, now . . . I'll drop by no later than this evening . . .'

She walked away, pulling her shawl tight across her chest. Groups were standing here and there. Everyone was watching Maigret. Children followed him, one of them imitating his heavy gait.

A little world was closing in on itself again. Now that the formalities were over and the magistrates had left, the village was going to resume its life, the only difference being that Maigret was now embedded in it, so to speak. Pointless to chase the kids away! They'd get used to him!

He saw the mayor standing in his doorway and went to say hello to him.

'It occurred to me, inspector . . . Obviously you'll need a place to work . . . If you'd like me to give you the key to the town hall . . .'

An excellent idea! That big white room was pleasant, and Maigret went there immediately, as if to accustom himself to the atmosphere and make himself at home. The stove on the right. He would have to light it every morning and keep stoking it. A place for his pipe and his tobacco. Beyond the window, a courtyard with a lime tree in the middle, then railings, and the street leading to the sea.

Who was that walking so quickly? Oh! It was only Méjat. He came in, out of breath.

'I think I have something new, chief . . . Marcel Airaud . . .'
'Well?'
'Something I heard, listening to people talking. Apparently when he left you earlier, he went straight to his boat . . . He has a motor-boat . . . People saw it moving off towards the end of the bay, over by Pont du Brault. There's no reason for him to go to that side. It isn't time to harvest the mussels.'

There was a telephone on the table. Maigret tried it.
'Hello, mademoiselle . . . Is there a telephone at Pont du Brault? . . . You say there's only one house . . . An inn? . . . Could you put me through? . . . Yes, Detective Chief Inspector Maigret . . . I'm at the town hall and I'll be disturbing you quite often . . .'

He looked at the electric lamp, which only gave out a yellowish light.

'Find me a forty candle-power bulb, Méjat . . . Hello? The inn at Pont du Brault? . . . I'd like to ask you for some information, madame . . . No, this isn't the brewery . . . Have you seen a little motor-boat this afternoon? . . . Yes, from L'Aiguillon . . . You say he's moored outside your place? . . . A bicycle? . . . Hello, are you still there? . . . He had a glass of wine? . . . You don't know where he went? . . . Towards Marans? . . . Thank you, madame . . . Yes . . . If he comes back . . . Call the town hall of L'Aiguillon immediately . . .'

He ran to the door. In the gathering dark, he had just spotted the lieutenant of gendarmes getting ready to go back to Luçon.

'Lieutenant! Will you come in for a moment? . . . I assume you know Pont du Brault? What's it like?'

'It's all the way over there in the marshes. A canal leads from the end of the bay to Marans, ten kilometres inland. You're lucky to come across a cabin every three kilometres.'

'Will you have your men search the region? I need to find a man named Marcel Airaud, a tall fellow, one metre eighty, a solid fisherman type, who's not exactly inconspicuous. He sailed from here in his boat and left it moored near the inn at Brault. He took a bicycle . . .'

'And you think . . .'

'It's too soon to think anything, lieutenant. Can I count on you?'

Would he go to see Didine before or after dinner? He went before. Night had fallen. Pulleys were starting to creak again, and the beams from two lighthouses crossed.

A twisted vine ran along the wall. The door and shutters were painted green.

'Come in, inspector. I was wondering if I'd done anything to you . . .'

The cat jumped off a wicker armchair. Hulot stood up from his corner and respectfully removed a long meerschaum pipe from his mouth.

'Please sit down, inspector. You will have a drink, won't you? Justin! Get the glasses from the cupboard.'

She wiped them. There was an oilcloth on the table and a very tall bed in a corner, covered in a huge red eiderdown.

'Give the inspector the armchair . . . No, I insist! With all that's been happening, I let my fire go out. You can keep your hat on.'

She was talking for the sake of talking, but it was obvious she was thinking about something and knew perfectly well where she was aiming. She didn't resume her seat. She didn't know what to do with her hands, which were constantly moving. And, since Maigret was doing nothing to help her, she had no choice but to ask, out of the blue:

'Did you find the child?'

What did she mean? Was there a child in this case?

'I didn't think anybody would mention him to you. People around here don't talk much, especially not to strangers. In a while, maybe, when they're used to you . . .'

'But as I said to Hulot, I'm on your side.'

'I saw you questioning Thérèse . . .'

How had she seen that? Was she spying on Maigret through the curtains? She was quite capable of that! She and her husband must be keeping track of the inspector and staying posted about everything he did.

'Old people like us, who have nothing to do, have time to think, you understand? Another glass? . . . I insist! It never did anybody any harm . . . Not you, Justin. You know perfectly well you can't take it.'

And she moved the bottle away from her husband.

'How old do you think Thérèse is? From the look of her, you'd think she's just a kid, but she must be about twenty-three. Even twenty-four wouldn't surprise me. Well, ever since the age of sixteen, she's been running after Marcel. Yes, I saw him talking to you as well! Built like he is, and with property, two houses that belong to him, and the mussel fields and everything, he has no trouble finding girls. Thérèse is quite common. In the summer, her mother sells mussels and oysters door to door around the villas on the other side of the estuary.

'All the same, she landed him! Everyone noticed, three years ago, how big she was getting.

'But these people have their pride. She left, supposedly to work in the city. When she came back a few months later, I swear she'd lost weight!

'And I know where she goes every month, when she has her two days off. She goes to Luçon, where she put her child in the care of a level-crossing keeper.

'What do you think of that?'

To be honest, he didn't think anything of it yet. Thérèse and Marcel . . . So Thérèse had a hold over him . . .

'I'm talking about three years ago, mind you! Since then Marcel has started spending his nights in the judge's house. I suppose you already know that. There have been others before him . . . Maybe even after him . . . Only, I'm going to tell you what I think. With him, it wasn't the same. The others took advantage of her. Men are like that . . .'

A sly little look at her husband, who squinted even more and assumed an innocent air.

'I'm sure Marcel was in love with her, and I bet that, if he'd been able, he would have married her, in spite of the fact that she's not like other girls . . .

'Now suppose Thérèse brought someone she knew from Luçon, a man capable of avenging her. It's easy enough to get into the judge's house. Look out here. It's dark, but you can see the white of the terrace. Any man could climb up there. From there, you can get over the stone rim and into the fruitery. The window's almost always half open. He may lock his daughter in, but it's as if I was trying to keep water in my hand.'

Maigret gave a start on becoming aware, suddenly, of the course of his own thoughts. For a few moments now, as he listened to the old woman's voice droning on, hadn't he started indulging in some absurd images, images that were still vague, of course, but which, if he wasn't careful, might take on shape and form?

' . . . It's easy enough to get into the judge's house . . .'

He again saw old Didine in his office in Luçon, he heard her clear voice, the almost staggering precision with which she had described the drama even though she hadn't even seen it!

Her faultless reasoning . . . Her meticulous calculation of the tides . . . Work a professional policeman would have been proud of . . . And the two of them keeping an eye on the house, one watching the back, the other the front . . . Even down to the naval binoculars! . . .

All the same, it was incredible. These ideas had to be dismissed; you only had to look at this room, a poor peasant room, with its bed, its eiderdown, the thick glasses on the oilcloth, Didine's white bonnet . . .

'So you didn't know the judge when he moved here?'

Something clicked. He was sure of it. A barely perceptible shock, a quivering of the muscles just under the skin.

'It depends what you mean by that. I knew him when I was very small. I was born in the house opposite the town hall. The judge used to spend his holidays here with his cousin. When his cousin died, he inherited the house.'

'Did he keep coming here after he was married?'

'Not every year!' she replied, suddenly laconic.

'Did you meet his wife?'

'I saw her, like everybody. A fine-looking woman!'

'Unless I'm mistaken, you're about the same age as Forlacroix, aren't you?'

'I must be a year younger than him.'

'You went to live in Concarneau with your husband, and he settled in Versailles. When you came back to L'Aiguillon, he was in the house and was already a widower.'

'He isn't a widower,' she said.

This made Maigret sit up in his wicker armchair, which creaked as he did so.

'His wife left him, but he isn't a widower.'

'Are you sure?'

'I'm sure he wasn't a widower a month ago, because I saw her with my own eyes, as clear as I'm seeing you now. She got out of a car and knocked at his door. They stood there for a while in the passage, and then she left.'

He half expected her to tell him the registration number of the car. That would have been too good!

'It's your fault if you didn't know all this before. Instead of running around all over the place without coming to see me and without saying a word to my husband. I can admit this now. He was quite discouraged. Isn't that so, Justin? You can tell the inspector. He knows what it is to speak his mind, and that it's those who have nothing to be ashamed of who are never at a loss for words . . . Have your drink, inspector. What else would you like to know? It isn't that I've finished. The things I could tell you, we'd be here until tomorrow. But I have to wait for them to come back to me . . .'

It was enough! Too much, even! This little old woman was as calculating as a devil!

'It's like the doctor. I don't know if this is of any interest to you, but he's the judge's best friend. Have you seen his wife? A tall woman, a brunette, always heavily made-up, always with extravagant clothes. She has a daughter from her first marriage. You'll see her. Not much to look at. And yet Dr Brénéol is crazy about her and is constantly driving her around without his wife. They go as far away as possible. Even so, someone from here, whose name I could tell you, saw them coming out of a hotel in La Rochelle.'

Maigret was on his feet now, as exhausted as if he had been for a long walk.

'I'm sure I'll be back. Thank you.'

She must have thought there was now a conspiratorial closeness between them, because she held out her hand and signalled to her husband to do the same.

'Don't hesitate to come again. And above all, you can be sure I'm telling you nothing but the truth . . .'

There was a lighted window in the judge's house, the window of Lise's room. Was she already in bed? He walked around the outside of the house. By now, the maids had left. Just the two of them within those walls . . .

He entered the already familiar main room of the Hôtel du Port and was struck by the glance that Thérèse threw him. She was clearly anxious! Wasn't she trying to see from his face if there had been any new developments?

Méjat was leaning on the counter, having an aperitif with the hotelier.

'Tell me, Thérèse, did you know that Marcel had to go to Marans?'

'Marans?' she repeated like someone on her guard, anxious not to betray herself.

'Since you're so close, I thought he might have told you . . .'

'He has no reason to tell me what he's doing . . .'

'What's for dinner?'

'Soup, plaice and, if you like, a pork chop with cabbage . . .'

'Let's eat, Méjat!'

The inspector had news for him. The victim, whose photograph had been shown to all the hoteliers in Luçon, hadn't slept in that town. They would have to wait. Especially for the newspapers . . .

'Aren't you tired, chief?'

'I'm going to bed as soon as I've eaten and I don't plan to get up before eight o'clock tomorrow morning.'

He was hungry. He managed to clear his mind of too many thoughts as he watched Thérèse come and go. She was fairly nondescript, and not in especially good health. The kind of little hotel maid you don't usually notice, with her black dress, her black stockings, her white apron. The place was empty. The men were at home, having their dinner, and wouldn't come back and spend an hour here until after they'd finished.

The telephone rang. It was under the stairs. Thérèse answered.

'Hello? . . . Yes . . . What do you . . .'

'Is it for me?' Maigret asked.

She listened.

'Yes . . . Yes . . . I don't know . . . Nobody mentioned it . . .'

'What is it?' the hotelier asked, from the kitchen.

Thérèse hurriedly put the receiver down. 'Nothing . . . It was for me . . .'

Maigret was already on the phone.

'Hello? . . . Detective Chief Inspector Maigret, mademoiselle . . . Can you tell me where the call you just put through was from? . . . What? . . . Marans? . . . Ask for the exact number, yes . . . Call me back . . .'

He went back to his table. Thérèse, looking quite pale, served him without saying a word. After a while, the phone rang again.

'From a café? . . . The Café Arthur? . . . Put me through to the police station in Marans, mademoiselle . . . Hello? . . . Are you the sergeant? . . . Detective Chief Inspector Maigret . . . Go straight to the Café Arthur . . . Do you know it? . . . That's good . . . A man has just made a phone call from there . . . Someone named Marcel Airaud . . . Take him to the station and inform me immediately . . .'

A heavy silence. The pork chops. The cabbage. Thérèse coming and going without looking Maigret in the face.

Half an hour passed. The phone.

'Hello? . . . Yes? . . . Ah! . . . No . . . Wait for instructions . . . That's right . . .'

A pause. Thérèse still didn't dare turn towards Maigret, whose big back could be seen under the stairs. The inspector made a move with his hand, as if hanging up, but continued talking:

'He's wounded? . . . Take him to the prison in Luçon anyway . . . Thank you . . . Goodnight, sergeant . . .'

He returned heavily to his seat, sighed, wondered if he should have some cheese, winked at Méjat, then, taking advantage of the fact that Thérèse was in the kitchen, whispered:

'The rascal vanished immediately after his phone call . . . I wonder what he could have said to her . . .'

5. Someone Wants to Go to Prison

Was it really cruel? Thérèse hated him, of course. Every now and again, she would throw him such a black look that Maigret was forced to smile, and then she no longer knew what to do: rush at him and scratch his face or smile in her turn.

For more than an hour, he kept her dangling like a fish at the end of a line. Whatever she did – go in and out of the kitchen, try to eat at a corner of the table, respond when customers called her – she couldn't escape Maigret's tranquil gaze.

Perhaps, when it came down to it, that gaze attracted her? Wasn't this big, placid man, smoking his pipe and staring into space, more of a friend than an enemy?

She kept going from one extreme to the other, from excessive nervousness to anger to a degree of kindness. Having cleared the table, she came and asked:

'What will you have?'

But, after serving the calvados, she was obliged to rush into the corridor. When she came back, her eyes were red, and she was blowing her nose.

Men were playing cards, and she broke a glass as she served them. In the kitchen, she got up from the table without having eaten a thing.

Finally, she spoke to the hotelier's wife. From a distance, you couldn't hear the voices, but you could guess from the way they held themselves. Thérèse looked as if she was ill and kept glancing up at the ceiling. The hotelier's wife shrugged.

'Go on, my girl!'

Thérèse took off her apron and came to see if anything

remained to be cleared, throwing Maigret an insistent look as she did so.

'Before you go to bed, Méjat, make sure there's one gendarme keeping guard in front of the judge's house and one behind . . . Another watching young Forlacroix's house . . .'

He stood up and climbed the stairs, touching both the banisters and the wall. This whole part of the building was new. The wood was too bright, the walls rough, and you ended up with white on your clothes.

Maigret went into his room and left his door open. After a few minutes, he gave a start of surprise, became almost irritated, then glanced into the corridor and smiled.

The others below would still be there for an hour or two. Too bad if Méjat got ideas, hearing the chief inspector's voice in the maid's room! He went in. She was standing there, waiting for him. She had loosened the bun on the back of her neck and the dark mass of hair now framing her face made her features thinner and her nose more pointed, but also made her gaze less candid.

Sitting on the edge of the iron bedstead, Maigret examined her at his leisure, and it was she who had to speak first. 'I can tell you you're wrong to hound Marcel . . . I know him better than anyone . . .'

She was searching for the right tone, like an actor, but couldn't find it.

'The proof of that is that we were supposed to be getting married this summer . . .'

'Because of the child?'

She didn't show any surprise. 'Because of the child and everything. Because we love each other. Is that so strange?'

'What's strange is that the child is now three years old, and you're only now thinking of making it official . . . Look at me, Thérèse. I can assure you there's no point in lying. What did Marcel ask you on the phone?'

She looked at him for a long time, then heaved a sigh. 'Too

bad if I'm making a big mistake . . . He wanted to know if they'd found a paper in his pockets . . .'

'Whose pockets?'

'The dead man's, I suppose!'

'And that's the question you answered no to?'

'I think if they'd found something important I'd have heard about it . . . Just because Marcel asked me that doesn't mean he killed . . . As I said before, we were supposed to be getting married . . .'

'And yet he's been seeing Lise Forlacroix in her room almost every night . . .'

'He's never loved her!'

'An unusual way not to love someone!'

'You know how men are. It isn't love, it's something else. He's often talked about it. It's a kind of vice, and he swore to me he'll get over it . . .'

'That's not true!'

With a sudden shudder, she turned hard and vulgar.

'What gives you the right to say it isn't true? Were you there? Is it also not true that I saw him coming out of the judge's house, not through the window, but by the front door? And that the judge was being nice to him? And that he knew about everything . . . Who's the decent one in all this? . . . I had a child, that's true. But I don't lure men to my room . . .'

'Hold on a moment! When was it that you saw Marcel with the judge?'

'Maybe a month ago . . . Wait . . . It was just before Christmas.'

'And you say they looked as if they were getting along? What did Marcel say when you asked him to explain?'

She was going to lie again. It could be seen from the way her nose quivered.

'He told me not to worry. That everything was fine. That in four or five months we'd be married and that we'd get a house on the other side of the straits, over towards Charron, so that we never have to see these people again . . . He loves me, do you hear? He had no reason to kill a man he didn't even know . . .'

Steps on the stairs, in the corridor. A door. It was Méjat coming back and whistling as he undressed.

'Is that all you have to tell me, Thérèse? Think carefully. Half of what you've told me so far has been the truth and half has been lies. Because of the lies, it'll be hard for me to take the truths into account . . .'

He had stood up. He was too tall and too broad for the room. Suddenly, just when he was least expecting it, Thérèse threw herself on his chest and began sobbing desperately.

'There, there . . .' he said, as if calming a child. 'It's all right. Tell me what's on your mind . . .'

She sobbed so loudly that Méjat, who was opposite, opened his door.

'Calm down, my dear. You're going to wake the whole house. Don't you want to talk about it now? . . .'

She shook her head, still hiding her face in Maigret's chest.

'I think you're wrong. But there it is! Go to bed. Would you like me to give you something to help you sleep?'

Still like a child, she nodded. He put a sleeping pill in the tooth mug and ran some water.

'It'll be better tomorrow morning . . .'

She drank, her eyes and cheeks wet, and as she did so he backed out of the room.

He heaved a sigh of relief as he at last got into his bed, which, like Thérèse's room, was too small for him.

The following morning was sunny and very cold. Thérèse, as she served him his breakfast, looked more stubborn than ever. Méjat had got hold of some brilliantine from the barber's in L'Aiguillon and stank of it.

Maigret, his hands in his pockets, went for his little walk, watching the mussel farmers returning, the baskets of mussels, the greenish-blue sea in the distance, the bridge he had never been all the way across and beyond which were the beginnings of a seaside resort, a few holiday villas for people of modest means nestling among the pines.

A gendarme was stamping his feet in front of the judge's house. The shutters were open. All this constituted a delightful little world which was starting to become familiar to him. Some people said hello to him, others watched him suspiciously. He ran into the mayor, who was loading mussels on to a lorry.

'There are already some telegrams for you. I put them on your table in the town hall . . . I think the lieutenant is waiting for you . . .'

It was late. Maigret had slept in. Now he was calmly on his way to his office, just as in the old days, during slack periods, he would walk to Quai des Orfèvres through the Saint-Antoine district and across the Ile Saint-Louis.

The plaster bust of *La République* was in its place. The stove was purring. It must have been the mayor who had had the tactful idea of placing a sealed bottle of white wine and some glasses on the desk.

The lieutenant had come in with Maigret. The latter took off his hat and coat, and was about to ask a question when he was pleasantly surprised by a veritable explosion of children's cries. Right there, beneath his windows, in the sun, the whole school was having its break. Children went sliding across the frozen puddles, each time with a dull thud of clogs. There were red and blue and green scarves, pea jackets, shawls.

'Well, lieutenant, any news of Marcel Airaud?'

'No sign of him yet. The marshes are enormous. The cabins have to be searched one by one. At this time of year, some paths are barely passable. There are isolated cabins that can only be reached by boat.'

'And the judge?'

'All quiet. Nobody's been in or out of the house, except for the two maids this morning.'

'What about Albert Forlacroix?'

'He went out to the mussel fields as usual this morning. One of my men has his eye on him. Especially as they say he's a violent lad who loses his temper over nothing.'

Was it an affectation of his to warm himself with his back to the stove and slowly light his pipe when there were telegrams waiting for him on the table? Or was it rather a concern not to confuse things, to do everything in its own time, to have done with L'Aiguillon first before finding out what had happened elsewhere?

The first telegram, as if ironically, was from Madame Maigret.

Have put suitcase with linen and change of clothes on bus. Await news. Love.

'What time does the coach arrive?'

'A few minutes from now.'

'Would you be so kind as to collect a suitcase in my name and have it taken to the Hôtel du Port . . .'

Another telegram, a longer one, from Nantes.

Flying Squad Nantes to Detective Chief Inspector Maigret.
    Stranger discovered L'Aiguillon identified. Stop. Dr Janin, 35, living Rue des Églises, Nantes. Stop. Left home Tuesday 10 January without luggage. Stop. Inquiries continuing. Stop. Phone for further details.

The lieutenant had just returned. Maigret handed him the telegram and casually remarked:

'He looked older than he was.'

Then he turned the crank of the telephone, bade the postmistress a pleasant good morning and asked her to get him the flying squad in Nantes.

This was all good old traditional work. Let's see now! A third telegram, from Versailles, in response to a telegram from Maigret.

> According to latest information, Madame Forlacroix, née Valentine Constantinesco, lives Villa des Roches-Grises, Rue Commandant-Marchand, Nice.

'Hello? . . . The flying squad in Nantes? Maigret . . . Put me through to him . . . Guillaume? That's right, old chap . . . Yes, fine . . . You've been quick . . . I'm listening, yes . . .'

Maigret never took notes. If he had a propelling pencil in his hand and a paper in front of him, it was only to make doodles that had no connection with the case.

' . . . Émile Janin . . . Faculty of Medicine in Montpellier . . . Very humble family from the Roussillon . . . One interesting detail: two years as an intern at Sainte-Anne . . . So, he's good at psychiatry . . . Ah-ha! . . . Quite independent-minded . . . Enlists as a naval doctor . . . What ship? . . . The *Vengeur* . . . The *Vengeur* went around the world three or four years earlier . . . That explains the clothes bought in Panama . . . Still too independent . . . Not a very good record . . . Returns to civilian life . . . Settles in Nantes where he specializes in psychoanalysis . . .

'Hello, mademoiselle? . . . One more call, if you don't mind . . . Could you put me through as a matter of priority to the Sûreté in Nice, Alpes-Maritimes? . . . I'm most grateful . . . Yes, I know you're doing what you can and, before leaving, I'll bring you some chocolates . . . You prefer marrons glacés? . . . Duly noted . . .'

And, addressing the lieutenant:

'I wonder if I'm not going to have to use my blank warrant . . .'

Was it intuition? He hadn't finished when the phone rang insistently. The children had gone back to class. It wasn't Nice yet, of course.

'Detective Chief Inspector Maigret? . . . One moment . . . Chief Prosecutor Bourdeille-Jaminet on the line . . .'

The voice was still distant, as if detached from material things:

'I gather he's been identified? . . . In these circumstances, I wonder . . . I've taken on a great responsibility . . . Do you still have your arrest warrant? . . . Well, inspector, in agreement with the examining magistrate, I think it would be prudent to . . .'

Méjat had come in and sat down quietly in a corner, from where he squinted at the friendly bottle of white wine.

'Nice!'

'Thank you . . . Sûreté Nationale? . . .'

He gave his instructions, in just a few words, and when he had finished he looked mechanically at the paper lying on his desk and saw that what he had drawn was nothing other than a full mouth, the kind of well-defined, sensual lips you see in the paintings of Renoir.

He tore the sheet of paper into little pieces and threw them in the fire.

'I think . . .' he began.

Someone was crossing the courtyard: old Élisa's daughter, who worked with her mother in the judge's house.

'Show her in, Méjat.'

'It's a letter for Monsieur Maigret.'

He took it, dismissed the girl and slowly tore open the envelope.

It was the first time he had seen the judge's handwriting, handwriting that was neat, small and careful, elegant but perhaps too refined. Not one line higher than the other. A paper that was plain, but of rare quality and in an unusual format.

Detective Chief Inspector,

Forgive me for writing you this note instead of visiting you in your office at the town hall or in your hotel. But, as

I am sure you will realize, it is painful for me to leave my daughter unattended.

I have thought a great deal since our last conversation and have come to the conclusion that I need to make certain declarations.

I am perfectly willing to come and see you wherever and whenever you wish. I admit, however, even though this request may not be very proper, that I would prefer it if you could do me the honour of another visit.

Needless to say, I am at home all day, and whatever time you choose I will make mine.

Thanking you in advance for whatever you decide to do, inspector.

Respectfully yours.

Maigret stuffed the letter into his pocket without showing it to the lieutenant or to Méjat, both of whom were finding it hard to conceal their curiosity.

'How long ago were the newspapers delivered?' he asked.

'We should have copies any minute now. The bus that brings them in with the post arrived while you were on the phone.'

'Could you go and get me one, Méjat? And can you check once again that the judge didn't have any visitors this morning apart from his maids?'

He was less cheerful than he had been earlier. His gaze was becoming heavier. He kept moving objects around for no reason as he paced up and down the room. Then he stared at the telephone and finally turned the crank.

'It's me again, mademoiselle . . . I'll have to double the quantity of marrons glacés . . . Have you finished sorting the mail? . . . They haven't started delivering it yet? . . . No letter for Judge Forlacroix? . . . Tell me . . . Has he made or received any phone calls? . . . No? . . . No telegram either? . . . Thank you . . . Yes, I'm still waiting for an urgent call from Nice . . .'

Méjat returned, accompanied by three people, whom he left in the courtyard. As he came in, he announced:

'Reporters.'

'I see!'

'One from Luçon and two from Nantes. Here are the regional papers.'

Although they all published the photograph of the corpse, none of them, obviously, announced yet that the dead man had been identified.

'What shall I tell them?'

'Nothing.'

'They're going to be furious. You'll see them at lunch, they're all staying at the Hôtel du Port.'

Maigret shrugged and put some coal in the stove, then looked at the time, because he could already see the children coming out of school. What did they care, those people in Nice, in that sun that was like a metal disc?

One little detail was nagging at him, one point he couldn't clarify. Why had the judge written him this letter just when the body had been identified? Did he know? And if he did, how had he found out?

The telephone . . . Still not Nice . . . Marans informing him that there was still no trace of Marcel Airaud and that the search was continuing throughout the marshes . . .

Good! Nice, at the same moment . . . Three voices on the line . . .

'Hang up, Marans . . . Hang up, for heaven's sake . . . Hello, Nice? . . . Yes, Maigret . . . You say this person hasn't left Nice in the last three weeks? . . . You're sure of that? . . . No telegram yesterday or this morning? . . . What? . . . I didn't quite catch the name . . . Luchet . . . Van Uchet? . . . Could you spell it? . . . V for Victor . . . Van Usschen . . . Yes, I'm listening . . . A Dutchman . . . Cocoa . . . Yes, send me everything you can! . . . If I'm not here, leave a message with my inspector . . .'

He said in a low voice, more to himself than to the others:

'The judge's wife has been living for several years in Nice with a man named Horace Van Usschen, a wealthy Dutchman who made his fortune in cocoa . . .'

Then he opened the bottle of white wine and drank a glass, two glasses, looking at Méjat as if not seeing him.

'Don't move from here until I get back.'

The three reporters tried to follow him, but he had assumed his most stubborn air. It was aperitif hour at the Hôtel du Port, and men came to the doorway to see where he was going. He raised his hand in a brief greeting to the gendarme who was keeping guard outside the judge's house and rang the bell.

'This way . . .' Élisa said. 'The judge is waiting for you . . .'

In the library, so peaceful and so comfortable! Maigret noticed that the judge kept wringing his hands, from which the blood had drained.

'Sit down, inspector. Take off your coat, this may take a while and the room is very warm. I won't offer you any port, since I'm sure you're going to refuse it.'

A hint of bitterness in his voice.

'Not at all!'

'And what if, after what I'm about to tell you, you regret drinking with me?'

Maigret sat down in the same armchair as the other night, stretched his legs and filled his pipe.

'Do you know a Dr Janin?'

The judge really did search in his memory. It wasn't pretence.

'Janin? . . . Let me see . . . No . . . I don't think so . . .'

'He's the man you tried to throw into the sea . . .'

A strange gesture, as if to say: 'That's not what this is about. It's of no importance.'

He poured the port.

'Cheers, then!' he said. 'I haven't been trying to trick you. Before anything else, I'd like to ask you a question . . .'

He turned solemn. His face lit up beneath his light grey hair, which was still as dishevelled as a woman's.

'If anything happens and I'm not able to look after my daughter for a while, could you promise me, man to man, that no harm will come to her?'

'I assume that if . . . if what you fear does indeed come about, your daughter would be entrusted to her mother, wouldn't she?'

'When you've heard what I have to say, you'll know she can't be entrusted to her mother . . . So . . .'

'Provided it stays within the law, I'll make sure she's treated as well as possible.'

'I'm very grateful.'

He slowly finished his glass of port and walked to a drawer to look for cigarettes.

'You only smoke a pipe, don't you? Please . . .'

Finally, exhaling the first puff of smoke, he murmured:

'In these circumstances, I think, after mature reflection, that it's preferable for me to spend some time in prison . . .'

It was unexpected. At that moment, the piano could be heard above their heads. He looked up at the ceiling. When he spoke again, his voice was thick with emotion, as if he were holding back the tears.

'I killed a man, inspector . . .'

Outside, the gendarme's hobnailed shoes could be heard striking the hard stones of the pavement.

'Do you still want to finish your port?'

He took an old gold watch from his pocket and snapped open the lid.

'Midday. Not that it matters to me. But if you prefer to go and have lunch first . . . I don't dare invite you to eat here.'

He poured himself another drink, then came and sat down facing Maigret, beside the crackling fire.

6. The Two Englishwomen of Versailles

At about one o'clock, the gendarme standing guard outside the judge's house started to get nervous, and every time he passed the windows he would go closer and try to see inside.

At 1.30, he stuck his face against the window, and it took him a moment to discover two men sitting in armchairs on either side of the fireplace, their heads emerging strangely from a cloud of smoke.

At about the same hour, the clatter of forks and the murmur of women's voices could be heard from an adjoining room, and Maigret assumed it was Lise Forlacroix having lunch.

Every now and again, he would cross his legs. Some time later, he would uncross them to tap the bowl of his pipe on his heel. There were already lots of ashes on the tiled floor. What did it matter now? The judge, out of habit, stubbed out his cigarette ends in a green porcelain ashtray, and all these little white and brown ends spoke for themselves.

They talked calmly. Maigret would ask a question, raise an objection. Forlacroix would reply in a voice that was as clear and, in a way, as meticulous as his handwriting.

The ringing of the telephone at 2.15 startled them, as if they had both forgotten the outside world. Forlacroix looked inquisitively at Maigret. Was it all right if he picked up the receiver? Maigret nodded.

'Hello? . . . Yes . . . Just a moment . . . It's for you, inspector . . .'

'Hello, chief . . . Sorry to bother you . . . I don't know if I did the right thing, but I've been getting worried! . . . Nothing's happened, has it?'

The judge had sat down again and was playing with his hands and looking at the logs.

'Get me a taxi . . . Straight away, yes . . . It should be here in half an hour . . . No, nothing special . . .'

And he in his turn sat down again.

When the taxi drew up outside the front door and Méjat rang the bell, Maigret was alone in the library, walking up and down and devouring a pâté sandwich. On the table stood an almost empty bottle of old Burgundy. They had smoked so much, the air was almost unbreathable.

Méjat stood watching his chief, with a completely stupid look on his face.

'Are you arresting him? Is it over? Am I going with you?'

'You're staying here.'

'What do you want me to do?'

'Take a piece of paper. Write this down . . . Thérèse, the maid from the hotel . . . The two Hulots, Didine and her customs officer . . . Albert Forlacroix . . . We have to find Marcel Airaud whatever happens . . .'

'The others you've mentioned, shall I keep an eye on them?'

Footsteps on the stairs.

'You can go . . .'

Méjat reluctantly withdrew. The judge appeared in his hat and overcoat, looking very proper, very much the meticulous bourgeois.

'Do you mind if I phone Dr Brénéol about the convalescent home?'

Lise Forlacroix was coming and going in the room above them, along with the two maids.

'Is that you, Brénéol? . . . No, nothing serious . . . I'd just like you to tell me if there's a good convalescent home in the vicinity of La Roche-sur-Yon . . . Yes . . . The Villa Albert-Premier? . . . Just before you get to the town? . . . Thank you . . . Goodbye for now . . .'

Old Élisa came down first with two suitcases, which she carried out to the car. Then her daughter with some smaller items of luggage. Finally Lise, almost sunk inside a soft fur coat with the collar up.

It was all very quick. Lise and her father got in the back. Maigret took his seat next to the driver. From the corner of the street, Didine watched the scene. People were stopping. They had to drive all the way down the main street, past the hotel, the post office, the town hall. Curtains stirred. Children started running after the car.

In the rear-view mirror, Maigret could see Lise and her father, and he had the impression they held hands throughout the ride. Night was falling by the time they approached La Roche-sur-Yon. They had to ask several times for the address of the Villa Albert-Premier. Then to wait for the director, visit the rooms.

Everything was white, too white, like the nurses' uniforms, and the doctor's coat.

'Room 7 . . . Very well.'

Five people had gone in: Lise, a nurse, Maigret, the judge and the director.

Three of them came back out into the corridor. Lise had remained on the other side of the door with the nurse. She hadn't wept. Father and daughter hadn't kissed each other.

'In an hour's time, an inspector will come and stand guard in this corridor . . .'

Three more kilometres: the town, the gates of the prison, the register, a few formalities. By chance, no doubt, the judge and Maigret didn't have time to say goodbye to each other.

A brasserie. A fat woman at the cash desk. The railway timetable. A nice cold glass of beer.

'I'd like something to write with and a ham sandwich . . . And another glass of beer!'

He wrote an unofficial report for the prosecutor, then a few more telegrams, and caught his train just in time. From midnight until two in the morning, he had to wait at the station in Saint-Pierre.

Gare d'Orsay. At eight o'clock in the morning, freshly shaved, he left his apartment on Boulevard Richard-Lenoir. The sun was rising over Paris.

He changed buses not far from Police Headquarters and could even see the windows of his old office in the distance.

At nine o'clock, still in the sour January sunlight, he got off in Versailles and slowly, his pipe between his teeth, walked down Avenue de Paris.

From that moment, he really had the impression of being double, of living on two different planes. He was still Maigret, a detective chief inspector more or less in disgrace, exiled to Luçon. He had his hands in the pockets of Maigret's coat and he was smoking Maigret's pipe.

The setting was still Versailles that morning, and not a number of years earlier.

The avenue was calm, especially towards the end, where vast gates and high walls hide the most delightful little mansions in the world from the passer-by.

But it was a little like the reality of a film. A documentary film, for example. Images unreel on the screen. At the same time, the voice of an off-screen narrator comments on them . . .

The voice was the flat little voice of Judge Forlacroix, and it was impossible not to superimpose on the image of Versailles the image of the library in L'Aiguillon, the logs, the pipe ash on the tiled floor, the cigarette ends in the green porcelain bowl.

'We've been in Versailles for three generations. My father was a lawyer and lived all his life in the mansion on Avenue de Paris that he had inherited from his father. A white wall. A carriage entrance flanked by stone bollards. The gilded sign. Our name on a brass plate . . .'

Here it was. Maigret had located the house, but the sign was no longer there, nor the brass plate. The door was open. A manservant in a striped waistcoat had come out to beat rugs on the pavement.

'Once you get through the gate, a not very large main courtyard, with those little round cobbles you find in the great courtyard at Versailles and which are called king's stones. Grass between the cobbles. A glass canopy. High windows with small panes. Light everywhere. Across the hall, in the middle of which there's a bronze fountain, you can see a garden in the Trianon style, with its lawns and its roses. I was born there, just as my father was. I spent years there without bothering about anything except art and literature, a bit of good living, good food. I had no ambitions, and was content to become a justice of the peace . . .'

Wasn't it easier to understand him here than in the solitude of L'Aiguillon?

'A few good friends. Trips to Italy and Greece. A sufficient fortune. Some fine pieces of furniture and good books. When my father died, I was thirty-five and a bachelor . . .'

Weren't there others like Forlacroix in the surrounding houses, people who wanted nothing more than a pleasant life?

The manservant was starting to look askance at this man in his thick overcoat looking with such interest at his masters' house.

But wasn't it too early for the visit that Maigret had to pay?

Slowly, he walked back up part of the avenue, turned right, then left, looking at the names of the streets and finally stopping in front of a larger building, four storeys high, probably divided into several apartments.

'Does Mademoiselle Dochet still live here?' he asked the concierge.

'She's just now going upstairs with her shopping . . .'

He caught up with her on the first floor just as she was turning a brass door knob. She was as antiquated as the house.

'Excuse me, mademoiselle. You are the owner of this building, aren't you? I'm looking for someone who used to live here, about twenty-five years ago . . .'

She was seventy.

'Come in. Wait while I turn off the gas in the kitchen. I don't want my milk to get burned . . .'

Stained glass panes in the windows. Crimson rugs.

'This person was a musician. A great virtuoso named Constantinesco.'

'I remember him! He lived in the apartment just above mine . . .'

So it was true. And now it was the judge's voice again that superimposed itself on the scene:

'A bohemian, who may have been almost a genius. He'd been quite successful at the beginning of his career. He'd given recitals in America and all over. He'd got married somewhere, had had a daughter, had taken her away without worrying about the mother. He'd ended up in Versailles, in an old-fashioned apartment where he gave violin lessons. Some friends brought him over one evening when we needed a viola for a chamber music session . . .'

The judge had almost blushed, looking at his white hands and adding:

'I play the piano a little.'

The old woman now declared:

'He was half mad. He'd fly into terrible tempers. You'd hear him running down the stairs yelling.'

'And his daughter?'

The woman stiffened. 'Now she's married. And well married from what I hear! To a judge, isn't it? There are those who succeed and they aren't always the most . . .'

The most what? Maigret would never know, because she had fallen silent.

There was nothing more to learn here. He knew. The judge's voice did not lie.

Valentine Constantinesco. A girl of eighteen, with an already full figure and huge eyes, who set off for Paris every morning, carrying her scores, to attend classes at the Conservatoire. She was studying the piano. At the same time, her father was teaching her the violin . . .

And here was a little judge, unmarried and Epicurean, who watched for her at the corner of the street, followed her at a distance, got on the electric train behind her.

Avenue de Paris . . . Ah! The manservant had gone back inside and closed the door behind him, that door which Valentine had crossed a few months later, in her white wedding dress . . .

Wonderful years. The birth of a boy, then a girl. Sometimes, in the summer, they would go and spend a few weeks in the old family house in L'Aiguillon . . .

'I assure you, inspector, that I'm no innocent. I'm not the kind of person who's so happy that he doesn't see what's in front of him. Many's the time I looked at her anxiously. But when you see her eyes, which can't have changed, you'll understand. As pure and clear as you could imagine. A voice like music. With her sea-green or pale blue dresses, always very light in colour, very neutral, she seemed to be straight out of a pastel.

'I didn't dare be surprised to find I'd fathered a sturdy boy with lots of hair, as coarse as a peasant. My daughter looked like her mother.

'I found out later that old Constantinesco, who was constantly hanging around the house, knew all about it.

'Wait . . . At the time I'm going to tell you about, Albert was twelve, Lise eight.

'I was supposed to go to a concert at four in the afternoon with a friend who's written several books about the history of music. He was in bed with a bout of bronchitis. I returned home.

'Maybe you'll see the house? There's a little door in the big carriage entrance. I had the key to it. Instead of coming in through the hall, I took the staircase on the right leading to the first floor where the bedrooms are. I wanted to suggest to my wife that she come with me.'

Maigret pulled on the brass button, and a big bell rang, as low-pitched as in a convent. Footsteps. The manservant, looking surprised.

'I'd like to speak to the occupants of this house, please.'

'Which of the ladies in particular?'

'Whichever you like.'

At that moment, through a ground-floor window, he saw two women, both wearing dressing gowns in glaring colours. One was smoking a cigarette at the end of a long holder, the other a tiny pipe that made Maigret smile.

'What is it, Jean?'

A strong English accent. The women were both between forty and fifty. The room, which must once have been the Forlacroix family's large drawing room and had now been turned into a studio, was filled with easels, highly modernistic canvases, glasses, bottles, Negro and Chinese objects, a very Montparnasse-style clutter.

Maigret presented his card.

'Come in, detective chief inspector. We haven't done anything wrong, have we? My friend, Mrs Perkins. I'm Angelina Dodds. Which of us are you here to see?'

A lot of confidence, a touch of humour.

'Do you mind my asking how long you've lived here?'

'Seven years. Before us, there was an old senator who died. And before him, there was a judge, so we've been told.'

A pity that the old senator was dead! He couldn't have changed very much in this house, where Forlacroix had left him the furniture and some of the knick-knacks. Now a red and gold Chinese divan strewn with dragons stood incongruously in front of the most delicate imaginable Louis XVI pier glass.

Anyway! Two Englishwomen, eccentric obviously, crazy about painting, attracted by the prestigious setting of Versailles.

'Do you have a gardener?'

'Of course! Why?'

'Can I ask you to take me or have me taken to the garden?'

Intrigued, they both came with him. A period garden, too, trying hard to imitate the gardens of Trianon on a smaller scale.

'I tended to my rose bushes myself,' the judge had said. 'That explains why I thought of the well.'

Three wells, in the places indicated. The one in the middle, which was disused, must have contained geraniums or other flowers in summer.

'Would you mind, ladies, if I had this well pickaxed? There's bound to be some damage. I'm afraid I don't have a warrant with me, so I can't force you to agree . . .'

'Is there a treasure?' one of the two Englishwomen exclaimed with a laugh. 'Urbain! Come here with a pickaxe . . .'

In L'Aiguillon, the judge had spoken calmly, in an even voice, as if not talking about himself.

'You know what it means to catch someone in flagrante, don't you? You've seen it in hotel rooms, in more or less seedy apartments. There are cases . . . I think it all came from the fact that the man had a common face and was looking at me defiantly . . . And yet he was ridiculous, loathsome, half naked, his hair dishevelled, his left cheek streaked with lipstick . . . I killed him . . .'

'Did you carry a revolver with you?'

'No, but there was one in a chest of drawers in our bedroom. The drawer was within reach . . . I did it coldly, I admit. I was calmer than I am now. I was thinking of the children, who were due back from school . . . I found out later that he was a café singer. He wasn't handsome. He had thick greasy hair that formed a roll on the back of his neck.'

Maigret went straight up to the gardener.

'Remove the compost first. I assume it's only about twenty centimetres deep . . . And underneath . . .'

'Stones and cement.' Urbain declared.

'It's those stones and cement you need to pickaxe.'

Here the calm voice had become hallucinatory:

'I thought of the well . . . I carried the man there, his clothes, everything I found on him . . . The well wasn't very wide and, even cramming him in, I was only able to put the body in a crouching position . . . I covered it with large stones. I poured in several sacks of cement. But that's not what matters . . .'

It was about then that the gendarme had stuck his face against the window and the judge had shrugged.

'In the blink of an eye, my wife had turned into a kind of fury . . . In less than thirty minutes, inspector, I learned everything from her own mouth, the affairs she'd had before our marriage, the ruses she'd employed, her father's complicity . . . Then her many lovers, the places where she saw them . . .

'She was unrecognizable. She was literally foaming at the mouth.

'"And I really loved this one, do you hear, I loved him!" she screamed, without any concern for the children, who'd just come home and might have heard her.

'I should have called the police and told them the truth, shouldn't I? I would have been acquitted. But my son, and above all my daughter, would have spent their whole lives knowing that their mother . . .

'I did think about it, believe me, briefly. It's incredible how clearly things appear to us at such moments . . .

'I waited for night to fall. It was June. I had to wait until it was very late . . . I'm stronger than I look . . . Well, I was then . . .'

Eleven o'clock. The earth, frozen in the course of the night, was turning warm and damp in the rays of the sun.

'Well?' Maigret asked.

'See for yourself.'

The inspector leaned over. Something whitish, which the pickaxe had broken. A skull . . .

'I beg your pardon, ladies, for all this disturbance. Rest assured that you won't be bothered about it. This was a crime that took place a long time ago. I'll pay you myself until the official search has been done.'

The judge hadn't lied. He had killed a man. And for nearly fifteen years, nobody had known anything about it, except his wife, who lived on the Côte d'Azur, at the Villa des Roches-Grises in Nice, with Horace Van Usschen, a Dutch cocoa merchant.

'You will have a whisky, won't you, inspector?'

He hated whisky! Even more than talking about this case!

'I have to see the legal authorities in Versailles before midday.'

'You will come back?'

No, he wouldn't! It wasn't this crime he was dealing with, but the death, in a house in L'Aiguillon, of a certain Dr Janin. It was as if gold dust had been sprinkled over Avenue de Paris, so fine and penetrating was the sun. But now he had to be quick. A taxi was passing.

'To the Palais de Justice.'

'It's not far . . .'

'What difference does that make?'

To be announced. To see people looking at him with a mixture of scepticism and boredom. Such an old case! Was it really necessary to . . .

He had lunch alone, a sauerkraut, at the Brasserie Suisse. He read the newspaper without reading it.

'Waiter! Can you get me number 41 at La Roche-sur-Yon . . . Priority, police . . . One moment . . . Can you also get me the prison . . .'

The beer was good, the choucroute acceptable, very acceptable, and he asked for a second pair of sausages. It wasn't very Louis XIV, but too bad!

'Hello? . . . Yes . . . She's been quiet? . . . That's excellent . . . What's that? . . . She asked for a piano? . . . Then hire her one . . . But of course! . . . I'll vouch for it . . . The father will pay anything that's needed . . . Only, if you ever leave the corridor or if she gets out through the window . . .'

At the prison, nothing to report. At eleven o'clock, Judge Forlacroix had had a visit from his lawyer, and they had conversed calmly for half an hour.

7. 'Ask the Inspector . . .'

It was a joy, at eight in the morning, to walk down the overly narrow stairs, whose pitch-pine banisters shone in the sunlight, and find the main room of the hotel empty, then go and take your seat at your usual table, which was already laid with a heavy porcelain bowl, homemade sausage and shrimps caught that morning.

'Thérèse!' he called as he sat down. 'My coffee . . .'

It was the hotelier's wife who brought it.

'Thérèse has gone to the butcher's.'

'Tell me, madame. I don't see anybody in the harbour, even though the tide is low. Are people here scared of the cold?'

'It's the neap tide,' she replied.

'What's that?'

'They can't go to the mussel fields when there's a neap tide.'

'In other words, the mussel farmers only work half of the time?'

'Oh, no! Most of them have land, marshes, livestock . . .'

Even Méjat received a warm welcome, in spite of his brilliantine and his ridiculously garish green scarf.

'Sit down. Eat. And tell me what you discovered when you visited that poor old woman.'

He was referring to Marcel's mother. To be honest, Maigret had been happy to offload this mission on to Méjat.

'An old rustic house, I suppose? Old furniture that smells of times gone by. A grandfather clock with a brass pendulum that moves slowly . . .'

'Nothing like that, chief. The house is repainted every year. The old door has been replaced by a modern door covered in imitation wrought iron. The furniture comes from a department store on Boulevard Barbès.'

'She started by offering you a drink . . .'

'Yes.'

'And you simply couldn't refuse . . .'

Poor Méjat wondered what sin he had committed by accepting a glass of the local plum brandy.

'Don't blush. I was thinking of someone else.'

Maybe of himself, when he'd drunk in the judge's house?

'There are people who are able to refuse and others who aren't. You went to see that old lady in order to find out something that could be used against her son, and the first thing you did was drink her plum brandy . . . I think the judge is a man capable of refusing. Refusing anything! Even himself! . . . Don't try to understand . . . Did she cry?'

'You know, she's almost as tall and as strong as her son. She blustered at first, then got indignant. She said that if this went on she'd go and see a lawyer. I asked her if her son had been away recently. I got the impression she hesitated.

'"I think he went to Niort on business."

'"Are you sure it was Niort? Did he spend the night there?"

'"I can't remember."

'"How is it possible you can't remember, when you live alone together in the same house? Would you agree to showing me the bedrooms? I haven't brought a warrant, but if you refuse . . ."

'We went up to the first floor. Up there, the house was old, with old furniture, like you said before, huge wardrobes and sideboards, and photographic enlargements.

'"What suit does your son wear when he goes to town?"

'She took it out. A blue serge suit. I searched the pockets. I found this bill from a hotel in Nantes. Look at the date.

'It's the 5th of January, a few days before Dr Janin arrived in L'Aiguillon.'

'So you didn't regret the glass of plum brandy?' Maigret asked, standing up to greet the telegraph boy.

He came back to the table with several telegrams, which he

put down in front of him, although, as usual, he was in no hurry to open them.

'By the way, do you know why old Didine and her husband hate the judge so much? I looked for a complicated reason, and yet the truth is quite simple, as simple as this village, as simple as that lighthouse you can see over there in the sun . . . When the Hulots retired and saw the judge had settled in L'Aiguillon, Didine went to see him and reminded him that they'd known each other as children. She offered him their services, herself as cook, her husband as gardener. Forlacroix, who must have known what she was like, refused. That's all . . .'

He tore the strip from a telegram, read it, and handed it to Méjat.

Naval volunteer Marcel Airaud served his term on board destroyer *Vengeur*.

'But seeing as how the judge has confessed . . . !' Méjat exclaimed.

'Oh, has he confessed?'

'It's in all the newspapers.'

'And you still believe what the newspapers say, do you?'

He was patient enough to wait for ten o'clock, doing virtually nothing, wandering among the moored boats, looking at the house, and the only reason he twice went back to the hotel to have a quick drink was because it was really cold.

He smiled when he saw the two cars arrive one behind the other, because this respect for form was touching, even comical. The two men arriving from La Roche-sur-Yon so early in the morning were old friends, who had known each other since school days. It would have been more pleasant for them to have made the journey in a single car. But one was the examining magistrate dealing with the case in L'Aiguillon, the other the lawyer chosen by Judge Forlacroix. In such circumstances, they had debated for a long time, the previous day, the question of whether or not it was appropriate . . .

They both shook Maigret's hand. The lawyer, Maître Courtieux, was a middle-aged man who was considered the best lawyer in the region.

'My client told me he's given you all the keys.'

Maigret jangled them in his pocket, and all three headed for the house, which was still guarded by a gendarme. The examining magistrate remarked casually, although clearly concerned to show that nothing escaped him:

'Strictly speaking, the seals should have been put on . . . Anyway! Since it's Monsieur Forlacroix himself who gave the inspector the keys and asked him to . . .'

The surprising thing was seeing Maigret go in and make himself at home, hang his coat on the stand, knowing exactly where it was, and walk into the library.

'As we're going to be a while, I think I'll light the fire . . .'

It wasn't without a certain emotion that he saw again the two armchairs by the fire, the pipe ash that hadn't been swept away, the cigarette ends.

'Please make yourselves comfortable, gentlemen.'

'My client told me,' the lawyer began, a little upset: "Ask the inspector . . ."

'So it's you, inspector, who will tell us what he did after killing that man and walling him up, so to speak, in his well . . .'

'You go first, your honour,' Maigret said to the examining magistrate, as if he were the master of the house. 'Please note that I'm not hoping to find anything remarkable. The reason I've asked for this search is rather to help me reconstruct the life of Judge Forlacroix over the last few years . . .

'See with what sure taste all this furniture has been chosen and how each item, each knick-knack, too, is in its place.'

Forlacroix hadn't left Versailles immediately. He had written his wife quite a large cheque and thrown her out, simply, coldly.

Maigret could imagine him very well: small, thin, icy, with

his halo of hair and his precise, nervous fingers. He wasn't, as the inspector had said that morning, the kind of person who accepts anything he doesn't want to accept. Didine knew about that: despite the years that had passed, she hadn't forgotten how calmly and coldly her proposition had been rejected. Not even rejected – ignored!

'She didn't try to stay with you and her children?' Maigret had insisted when they were both sitting by the fire.

Of course she had! There had been ugly scenes! She had grovelled to him. Then, for months, she had written. She had begged, threatened.

'I never replied. One day, I found out she was living on the Côte d'Azur with a Dutchman.'

He had sold the house in Versailles. He had moved to L'Aiguillon. And then . . .

'Can you feel the atmosphere of this house, where everything exudes comfort and easy living?' Maigret sighed. 'For years, a man spent his days here, watching his two children and wondering if they were his . . . For his part, the boy, as he grew up, tried to understand the mystery surrounding him, asked questions about his mother, about his birth . . .'

He had just opened the door of a room, where toys of all kinds were still in their place, with, in a corner, a pupil's desk in light-coloured oak.

Further on, there was Albert's old room, still with clothes in the wardrobe. Elsewhere, a cupboard was full of Lise Forlacroix's dolls.

'At the age of seventeen or eighteen,' Maigret went on, 'Albert started, God knows why, to hate his father. He couldn't understand why his father kept his sister locked up. That was when Lise had just had her first attack.

'It was about this time also that Albert discovered one of his mother's old letters, a letter written soon after the drama . . . Here . . . It must be in this writing desk . . . I have the key . . .'

It wasn't only the key to the Louis XIV desk that he seemed to have, but the key to all these characters who had clashed with each other throughout the years. He was smoking his pipe. The magistrate and the lawyer followed him. To touch certain things, to tackle certain subjects, he drew on the kind of tact that might not have been expected from this big man with his thick hands.

'You can add it to the file,' he said without reading it. 'I know what it says. She threatens her husband with prison. Albert demanded to know what had happened. Forlacroix refused to tell him. From that point on, they lived like strangers. After his military service, Albert wanted to live as he pleased, but a strange kind of curiosity kept him in L'Aiguillon, and he settled down here as a mussel farmer. You've seen him. Despite his physique, he's a restless, violent man, who could easily become a rebel. As for the girl . . .'

The doorbell rang. Maigret went to open it. It was Méjat with a telegram; he would have liked to come in, but his chief didn't even suggest it. When Maigret came back upstairs, he announced:

'She's replied to my telegram. She's coming.'

'Who?'

'Madame Forlacroix. She left Nice at midday yesterday by car.'

It was impressive to observe Maigret. In fact, a curious phenomenon was taking place. As he came and went in this house that wasn't his, as he evoked lives he hadn't lived, he was no longer entirely the heavy, placid, rough-hewn Maigret. Without his realizing it, there was a little of Forlacroix in the way he moved, the way he spoke. The two men could not have been more dissimilar and yet, at certain moments, it was so striking that the lawyer was quite bothered by it.

'When I visited the house the first time, Lise was in bed . . . Look. This bedside lamp was on . . . Forlacroix loved his daughter. He loved her, and that made him suffer because, in spite of everything, he still had his doubts. What proved that she was his child and not the child of some passing lover like the singer with the greasy hair?

'He also loved her because she wasn't like anyone else, because she needed him, because she was a tender and impulsive young animal.

'Outside her attacks, I imagine she was like a six-year-old, her whims, her charms . . .

'Her father consulted specialists from all over. I can tell you this, gentlemen: young girls like Lise don't usually live beyond the age of sixteen or seventeen. When they survive, the attacks become more frequent, leaving them depressed and distrustful.

'The locals may have exaggerated, but we can be sure that several men, two at least, took advantage of her before Marcel Airaud.

'When Marcel came along . . .'

'Excuse me!' the examining magistrate said. 'I haven't yet questioned the prisoner. Is he claiming that he knew nothing about Marcel Airaud's nocturnal visits to his daughter?'

Maigret looked for a moment through the window, then turned.

'No.'

An embarrassed silence.

'So he . . .' the magistrate resumed.

And the lawyer was wondering already how he would present such a monstrous thing to a jury in La Roche-sur-Yon.

'He knew . . .' Maigret retorted. 'The doctors he'd consulted were all of the same opinion: "Marry her off! It's the only chance to . . ."'

'Between marrying her off and allowing an individual like Airaud . . .'

'Do you think, your honour, that a girl suffering from such a condition is easy to marry off? Forlacroix preferred to turn a blind eye. He made inquiries about Airaud. He was able to discover that he was quite a decent young man, in spite of his affair with Thérèse . . . I'll tell you about that another time . . . I'll tell you then that he also had his doubts as to whether

Thérèse's child was his. Since then she's been plaguing him. Airaud was really in love with Lise. So in love that he was ready to marry her in spite of everything . . .'

He paused, tapped the bowl of his pipe against his heel and announced in a soft voice:

'They were due to be married soon . . .'

'What did you say?'

'That Marcel and Lise were due to be married in two months' time . . . If you knew Forlacroix better, you'd understand. A man who has the patience to live for years and years as he has lived. He watched Marcel for a long time. One day, as Airaud was passing the house, the door opened . . .

'Forlacroix stood in the doorway and said to the scared young man: "Wouldn't you like to come in for a moment?"'

Mechanically, Maigret proceeded to rewind a clock that had stopped.

'I know that's what happened because I've also sat next to him by the fire. He must have spoken very calmly. He poured the port carefully into the crystal glasses and said . . . He said what he needed to say . . . The truth about Lise . . .

'Airaud was flabbergasted and didn't know what to reply. He asked for a few days to think it over. It was yes, without any doubt. Do you know any simple, solid people like him, your honour? Have you ever watched them at the fair? Have you heard them negotiating a deal?

'What I think is that Airaud remembered the former doctor on the *Vengeur*, with whom he may once have been friendly . . . He went to Nantes . . .'

A car horn. Long, unexpected sounds. Through the window, they saw a luxury car, driven by a liveried chauffeur, who got out and went to open the rear door.

Maigret and his companions were in a room which was something like Lise's boudoir, the room where the piano was. All three followed the scene through the window.

'Horace Van Usschen!' Maigret announced, pointing to an old man who was the first passenger to get out, with abrupt, automatic movements, as if his joints had not been oiled.

Some villagers had gathered at the corner of the street. Van Usschen was indeed a sight for sore eyes, with his light flannel suit, his white shoes, his vast check overcoat and his white cloth cap. Dressed like that, he would have caused no surprise on the Côte d'Azur, but was a somewhat unusual sight in L'Aiguillon, where the only tourists you saw during the summer months were people on very modest incomes.

He was as thin and wrinkled as Rockefeller, whom he somewhat resembled. He reached his hand inside the car. And it was then that a huge woman appeared, clad in furs, who looked the house up and down. She spoke to the chauffeur, who came and rang the doorbell.

'If you agree with me, gentlemen, we'll leave the Dutchman outside. At least for the moment . . .'

He went to open the door and saw at first glance that the judge had not lied, that Valentine Forlacroix, née Constantinesco, had been beautiful, that she still had wonderful eyes and sensual lips which, in spite of the sagging at the corners, recalled Lise's.

'Well, I'm here,' she announced. 'Come, Horace.'

'I'm sorry, madame, but for the moment I'd like you to come in on your own. That may be best for you, too, don't you think?'

Irritably, Horace got back in the car, wrapped himself in a blanket and sat there motionless, ignoring the children staring at him through the windows.

'You know the house. If you like, we can go in the library. There's a fire there . . .'

'I wonder in what way that man's crime is any concern of mine!' she protested as she entered the room. 'He may be my husband, but we haven't lived together for many years, and what he gets up to these days doesn't interest me.'

The magistrate and the lawyer had now also come downstairs.

'The examining magistrate here will tell you that we're not concerned about what he gets up to these days, but what you both got up to when you were still living together . . .'

A strong perfume gradually permeated the room. With a heavily ringed hand, the nails blood red, Valentine Forlacroix opened a cigarette box that was on the table and looked for matches.

Maigret reached an already lighted one to her.

The examining magistrate thought it time to intervene and play his role.

'I am sure you are not unaware, madame, that the law may pursue as an accessory not just a person who has participated in a crime, but also one who has witnessed a crime without reporting it to the authorities . . .'

She was strong! Forlacroix hadn't lied! She took the time to puff at her cigarette. Her mink coat open over a black silk dress adorned with a diamond brooch, she walked up and down the vast room, stopped by the fire, bent down, seized the tongs and straightened one of the logs.

When she turned, she was no longer playacting. She was ready for a fight. Her eyes had lost their brightness but had gained in sharpness. Her lips were tense.

'Very well!' she said, sitting down on a chair and placing one elbow on the table. 'I'm ready to listen to you . . . As for you, inspector, I shan't congratulate you on the trap you set me.'

'What trap?' the examining magistrate said in surprise, turning to Maigret.

'It wasn't a trap,' Maigret grunted, putting his pipe out with his thumb. 'I telegraphed Madame and asked her to come here and explain the visit she paid her husband about a month ago . . . In fact, your honour, that's the question I'd like you to ask first, if you don't mind . . .'

'Did you hear that, madame? I must inform you that in the absence of my clerk, this interview is not official and that Maître Courtieux here is your husband's lawyer.'

She blew out smoke with a scornful air and shrugged. 'I came to ask him for a divorce!' she said.

'Why now and not before?'

The phenomenon that Forlacroix had talked of now came about. In an instant, this diamond-bedecked woman became embarrassingly vulgar.

'Because Van Usschen is seventy-eight, don't you see?' she admitted crudely.

'And you'd like to get married?'

'He's been wanting to for the past six months, ever since his nephew came to scrounge money from him after losing hundreds of thousands of francs at roulette . . .'

'So you came here. Did your husband receive you?'

'In the passage.'

'What did he say?'

'That he didn't know me and so there was no reason to get a divorce.'

Maigret would gladly have clapped, so typical of Forlacroix was that answer. He wrote a few words in pencil on a piece of paper, which he passed to the magistrate, because from now on he had to step aside in favour of the latter.

'What did you do after that?'

'I went back to Nice.'

'Just a moment! Didn't you see anyone else in L'Aiguillon?'

'Who do you mean?'

'Your son, for example.'

A hate-filled look at Maigret.

'I see the man just can't keep his mouth shut . . . I did meet my son, as it happens.'

'How did you meet him?'

'I went to his house.'

'Did he recognize you after so many years?'

She shrugged.

'What does it matter? I told him he wasn't Forlacroix's son.'

'Are you sure of that?'

'Can you ever be sure? I told him I wanted to get a divorce, that my husband was refusing, that he was a cruel man, that he had a lot on his conscience and that if he, Albert, could get him to agree to a divorce . . . '

'In other words, you got your son on your side. Did you offer him money?'

'He didn't want any.'

'Did he promise to help you?'

She nodded.

'Did you tell him about the old crime?'

'No. I just told him that, if I wanted, Forlacroix would go to prison for a long time.'

'Did you write to him after that?'

'To ask him if he'd got anywhere.'

'Have you ever heard of a Dr Janin?'

'No, never!'

The magistrate looked inquisitively at Maigret, who murmured:

'If Madame is tired, maybe we could let her go and have lunch? I have the impression that Monsieur Van Usschen is getting bored in the car.'

'Am I under arrest?'

'Not yet,' the magistrate declared. 'I simply ask you to remain at the disposal of the authorities. If you'd like to give me an address in La Roche-sur-Yon, for example.'

'Very well! Hôtel des Deux Cerfs. I think it's the best one there.'

They all stood up. As she went out, she smiled at both the magistrate and the lawyer but had to restrain herself from sticking her tongue out or making a face at Maigret, who joyfully relit his pipe.

8. The Potato Eaters

'*Tierce* . . . That's trumps . . .'

'Not worth anything, my friend . . . Fifty . . .'

'Let me see! In case your fifty's full of holes . . .'

What time was it? The cheap clock on the wall had stopped. The lights had been on for some time now . . . It was hot. The little glasses had been filled three or four times and a smell of marc mingled with the smell of the pipes.

'Too bad! I'm playing trumps!' Maigret said, laying down a card.

'That's the best thing you can do, Inspector. Even if you have a nine after it . . .'

It was their fourth or fifth game. Maigret was smoking, tipped back slightly on his chair. His partner was the hotelier, and the other two were fishermen, including old Bariteau, the eel fisher.

Inspector Méjat sat astride a chair, following the game.

'I knew perfectly well you had a nine . . .'

'Tell me, Méjat. Do you remember the name of the pathologist?'

'I wrote it down.'

'I want you to phone him. Ask him if he can determine roughly how long before his death the man ate for the last time. And if it was a full meal. Do you understand?'

'Who was it who had a fifty? . . . And thirty-six . . .'

The owner was counting. Maigret seemed buried up to his neck in a kind of warm, mundane state of bliss, and if anyone had suddenly asked him what he was thinking about, he would have been surprised himself.

An old memory! From the time of the Bonnot case, when he

was thin and wore a long pointed moustache and a little beard, false stiff collars ten centimetres high and top hats.

'You know, my dear Maigret,' his chief at the time – Detective Chief Inspector Xavier Guichard, later to become commissioner of the Police Judiciaire – had said to him, 'all these stories about intuition' (the newspapers had been talking about his infallible intuition) 'are fine for entertaining the public. In a criminal case, what matters before anything else is to store away the fact, or the two or three facts, you're absolutely certain about, because, whatever happens, they'll stay solid, and you can use them as a foundation.

'After that, all you have to do is push ahead, slowly and surely, the way you'd push a wheelbarrow. It's a question of expertise, and what people call intuition is nothing but chance . . .'

As strange as it might seem, it was because of that memory that he had agreed to play cards, much to Méjat's astonishment.

After Valentine Forlacroix and the Dutchman had driven off in their car, the other two cars had left, those of the examining magistrate and the lawyer. Maigret had stood alone for a moment, seemingly helpless, in the middle of the street. Forlacroix was in prison. His daughter Lise was in a clinic. Before leaving, the examining magistrate had placed seals on the house.

He had left satisfied, as if carrying off his booty. All this belonged to him now! It was he, in his office at the Palais de Justice in La Roche-sur-Yon, who was going to proceed with the interviews, with bringing the witnesses face to face . . .

'Let's go!' Maigret had muttered as he walked back into the hotel.

Why was he so queasy? Wasn't it always like this? And wasn't this feeling, a feeling that resembled jealousy, quite ridiculous?

'What do we do now, chief?'

'Where's the list I dictated to you?'

    . . . Didine and her husband . . . Marcel Airaud . . . Thérèse . . . Albert Forlacroix . . .

'Who shall we start with?'

He had started with a game of cards.

'Can I play a lower card here?'

'Only in trumps . . . What about in Paris?'

'It depends . . . Anyway, here's my eight . . .'

After a while, leaving his partner to count the points, he had taken a pencil and a notebook from his pocket, even though he never took notes, and had written, pressing down so hard that he had broken the lead:

Doctor Janin arrived in L'Aiguillon on Tuesday at between four fifteen and four thirty.

That was the first sure-fire element, as Xavier Guichard would have said. And after that? He almost added that the very same Janin had been killed in the judge's house that night. But that was no longer certain. After three days, the pathologist had only been able to pinpoint the time of death to within a few hours. And nothing proved . . .

On Wednesday morning, Janin's body is lying on the floor in the fruitery of the judge's house.

'Hearts are trumps . . . Are you playing?' someone asked him, surprised to see him staring into space.

'Hearts are fine! . . . Whose turn is it?'

The hotelier respectfully refrained from saying the traditional: 'The idiot who's asking . . .'

Since then, Maigret had glanced from time to time at those two little sentences that constituted the only sure-fire elements of the case.

Méjat could be heard telephoning under the stairs, and, whenever he spoke on the telephone, he assumed a horrible head voice.

'Well?'

'The doctor had to reread his report. According to the contents of the stomach, a normal meal. There were quite strong traces of alcohol . . .'

Méjat couldn't understand why Maigret looked so pleased. The inspector sat so far back in his chair that he almost lost his balance and had to hold on to the table.

'Well, well,' he said after examining his cards, 'so the rascal had something to eat!'

It might not be much. And yet . . . Janin hadn't had dinner at the Hôtel du Port, nor at the inn opposite, and there was nowhere else to eat in L'Aiguillon.

'*Tierce* . . .'

'How high?'

'Kings . . . By the way, doesn't young Forlacroix have a lorry?'

'Yes, he does, but it's been under repair for the last two weeks.'

No motorist had reported driving Janin anywhere by car. So if he had eaten . . .

'Méjat . . . Run to the butcher.' He turned to the hotelier. 'Tell me . . . There is only one butcher here, isn't there?'

'And he only slaughters once a week.'

'Ask him if that Tuesday, between four and seven, anyone came in for a good cut of meat.'

'Who?'

'Anyone.'

Méjat put on his overcoat and left with a sigh. As the door opened and closed again, it let in cold air, which you could feel gliding between your legs. Thérèse was sitting by the stove, knitting. No sooner had the door closed than it opened again. It was Méjat, making signals at the inspector.

'What do you want?'

'Can I have a word, chief?'

'One moment . . . Trumps! . . . Clubs! . . . And you won't take this ace of diamonds away from me . . . You've lost, gentlemen!'

Then, to Méjat:

'What is it?'

'Didine's outside. She's asking for you to come straight away. Apparently it's urgent.'

'Give me my hat and coat, Thérèse . . . You, take my place for a moment . . .'

He lit his pipe before going out. The night was pitch black. It was freezing cold. Only a few lights could be seen in the street, and in the window of the grocery, covered in transparent advertisements. Didine's little figure somehow hitched itself to Maigret.

'Come with me. Let's not walk together. You just have to follow me, so that they don't know I'm leading you.'

She was carrying a half-filled sack and in her other hand she held a pruning knife, like those old ladies who go out to cut grass for their rabbits. After a while, they passed Albert Forlacroix's house, and a figure moved in the shadows; the gendarme on guard gave a military salute.

Every now and again, Didine turned to make sure that Maigret was following her. Suddenly, she disappeared, as if sucked into the black void that formed a gap between two houses. He turned into this gap. An icy hand touched his.

'Careful! There's barbed wire.'

By day, the place was probably ordinary enough. In the darkness, led on by this strange little witch with her sack and her sickle, Maigret was finding it hard to perceive the layout of the place. He caught his feet on oyster shells, then a strong smell of dustbins struck his nostrils.

'Step over. There's a little fence.'

Frozen cabbages. They were in a vegetable garden behind the houses. There were other, similar gardens, separated by old trellises. Something living stirred: rabbits in a hutch.

'I'd come to get some grass for my rabbits,' she said, still walking.

The village, in fact, had only one row of houses all along the street. Behind these houses were the vegetable gardens, then there was a ditch, filled with seawater at high tide, and finally the marshes, stretching to infinity.

'Don't make any noise. Don't say a word. Careful where you put your feet.'

She didn't let go of his hand. A few moments later, she was walking alongside a whitewashed wall.

He made out a figure near a dimly lit window. He recognized Justin Hulot, who placed a finger over his lips.

He would have been hard put to say what he was expecting. In any case, not the spectacle he had before his eyes a moment later, as peaceful and calm as a scene in one of those chromos that stay on the walls of rustic houses for generations.

Hulot had withdrawn to make room for him at the window. The latter being a little low for him, he had to bend down. Through the glass, he could see a stable lantern standing on a barrel, giving out a yellowish light.

Maigret had already calculated that they must be just behind Albert Forlacroix's house. What they discovered was the interior of a shed at the end of the backyard, which served as a storehouse, the kind you find in all country areas: empty barrels, saucepans, rusty old tools, sacks, crates, bottles . . .

In the fireplace, where the food for the animals was probably cooked, and a pig roasted at Christmas, a few logs were burning.

Two men were sitting by the fire, one on a crate, the other on an upended basket. They both wore high rubber boots pulled down at the knee, which always reminded Maigret of the Three Musketeers.

They were both tall, strong and young. Two strangely dressed giants. Of course they were merely wearing the traditional costume of the mussel farmer, but in this light, the two men were rather reminiscent of figures out of some painting in a museum.

One of them took a cigarette from his pocket and held it out to his companion, who grabbed a brand from the fire.

They were speaking. You could see their lips moving, but unfortunately it was impossible to hear a sound.

One of the two men, the one who had taken out the cigarette and who now took another for himself, was Albert Forlacroix. The second, sitting right up against the fire, was Marcel Airaud, barely recognizable because of a growth of blond beard already several centimetres thick.

Didine's thin body brushed against Maigret and she whispered:

'They were already there an hour ago when I looked in for the first time. It was just starting to get dark. Young Forlacroix left for a moment to go and look for potatoes . . .'

He didn't understand what potatoes had to do with anything, and the remark struck him as ridiculous.

'I didn't want to go into the hotel. I knocked lightly at the window, but you were playing cards and didn't even notice.'

What a strange little mouse! So she had trotted home and sent her husband to keep guard!

Was it only chance that had led her to take a look inside Albert Forlacroix's property while out cutting grass for her rabbits? If not, what other train of thought could have brought her to this place? That wasn't the least troubling aspect of the matter. Her husband had moved two or three metres away and was waiting.

'I suspected he would come back . . .' she resumed.

'And that he'd see Albert Forlacroix?'

'Shhh . . .'

Maigret wasn't good at keeping his voice low, so it was best for him not to say anything.

'Are you going to arrest the two of them?' Didine whispered.

He didn't reply. He didn't move. Behind them, the Baleines lighthouse turned in the sky at a regular pace, and occasionally a cow mooed out on the marshes. The game must still be going on at the Hôtel du Port, and presumably Thérèse was getting worried by Maigret's absence.

As for the two men . . . Maigret hadn't noticed before how similar they were physically. In both cases, their line of work, the salt water, the spindrift, the sea air, had turned their skin deep pink and bleached their hair . . .

They were both heavy, with the heaviness of people who are constantly struggling with the patient forces of nature.

They were smoking. They were talking slowly. Their eyes were fixed on the fire, and after a while Marcel stirred something in the ashes with the end of a piece of iron, his face expressing a simple joy.

He said something to Albert, who rose and went to the low door, bending to walk through it. When he returned after a short time, he was holding two big glasses, which he went and filled straight from a barrel in the corner.

White wine! Never before in his life had Maigret had such a yearning for white wine, so delicious did this one seem. As for the potatoes . . . Because, sure enough, there were potatoes . . .

It brought back childhood memories, the kind of engravings you find in books by Fenimore Cooper or Jules Verne. They were in France, in the very heart of a French village. And at the same time, they were a long way away. The two men could have been trappers, or castaways on a desert island. Their work clothes were of no particular period. Marcel's thick, shapeless beard added to the illusion.

And it was large, hot, blackened potatoes he was removing from the ashes with his piece of iron, potatoes whose charred skin he cracked between his big fingers. The white steaming flesh appeared, and he bit into it greedily.

Then his companion stood up, almost touching the ceiling with his head. He took a knife from his pocket and cut two sausages from the string of them drying above the fireplace.

'What are they doing?' Didine whispered.

He didn't reply. He would have given a lot to share that improvised meal, those potatoes cooked under ash, those sausages browned by time, that wine that appeared so refreshing!

The most troubling thing was the ease, the calm of those two strong men, who were far from suspecting that their gestures and lip movements were being spied upon.

What could they be saying to each other? There they were, confident in themselves, confident in one another. Almost crouching, they ate, each with a knife he had pulled from his pocket, in the style of peasants and sailors. They talked unhurriedly. From time to time, they would utter a few words, then let silence fall again.

'Aren't you arresting them?'

Maigret gave a start, because something had just brushed against his leg. It was only a dog, a little hunting dog, not much more than a puppy, which must belong to one of the neighbours and was silently rubbing up against him.

'Justin!' Didine called.

She pointed to the dog, which might bark at any moment. Hulot took the animal by the scruff of its neck and walked away with it.

There was no gaiety, though, on the other side of the window. No gaiety, but no anxiety either. A kind of ponderous tranquillity. Albert got up to get some more sausages, and for a moment, as he turned in his direction, Maigret thought that he had seen him through the glass. But he hadn't.

Finally, they wiped their lips and lit more cigarettes. Airaud yawned. How long was it, hunted as he was by the police, since he had last slept in peace? He scraped his teeth with the point of his knife and rested his head against the wall.

Once again, young Forlacroix disappeared. This time he was absent for longer, and Maigret started to get worried. At last he opened the door with his foot. He was heavily laden. He had a mattress folded in two on his head and some blankets and a pillow under his arm. Marcel helped him. They even displayed an unexpected concern for cleanliness. Before laying the mattress on the ground, Airaud went to fetch an old stable broom from a corner and gave the beaten-earth floor a bit of a sweep.

Hulot had got rid of the dog and come back to his post, where he was waiting patiently.

'Aren't you arresting them?' Didine whispered again, shivering.

Airaud took off his oilskin jacket and sat down on the floor to remove his boots. You could see him get rid of his socks and rub his swollen feet for a long time, with a strange kind of solicitude. Albert asked him a question. Was he offering him hot water to bathe his feet? Maigret would have sworn he was. Marcel stretched one more time and finally lay down full-length on the mattress with such a loud sigh you had the impression you could hear it from outside.

Albert Forlacroix took the stable lantern, glanced around him and frowned as he looked at the window. Had he forgotten about it? No, he was making sure! He knew it looked out on nothing but the marshes.

A curious gesture . . . A pat on his companion's shock of hair . . . Huge and heavy, carrying his lantern at arm's length, he walked away and closed the door behind him . . .

'Can we get out this way?' Maigret asked Didine after drawing her aside. She pointed to a low wall dividing Forlacroix's yard.

Leaving Hulot on guard, he again waded through oyster shells, dustbins and shards of broken glass, abandoned Didine in the street and walked to the police station.

When he had dispatched a gendarme to take Hulot's place, he went out into the street once again. Didine was still there, with her sack half full of grass and her sickle. He had the feeling she was looking at him with a sardonic air.

'So what do you think? It seems to me that without old Didine . . . How many of your gendarmes did you send off to track him down? . . . Gendarmes! . . .' She laughed scornfully. 'But me! Nobody bothers to come and see me, even though I could . . .'

'Go home!' he advised her. 'Tonight. Or tomorrow.'

'Or on Trinity Sunday!' she said, without any illusions. 'Come, Justin. I bet they'll still find a way not to put them in prison . . .'

The gendarme outside Albert Forlacroix's house was no longer in his patch of shadow, but in the middle of the street.

'Has he come out?' Maigret asked.

'There . . . You see that figure after the third street lamp? . . . That's him . . . He's just going into the hotel . . .'

Maigret followed him in a few minutes later. The game of cards was still going on. Méjat, as was to be expected, was discussing all the hands.

'I tell you that as long as you make an indirect call . . . At last, inspector . . . If I play hearts when . . .'

Albert Forlacroix was sitting all alone at a long table where there was enough room for ten people. He was following the game from a distance. Thérèse had placed a bottle of white wine in front of him, but he was in no hurry to drink it.

'Damn!' Maigret grunted, remembering the wine drawn from the barrel, the potatoes, the sausages.

'Do you want your seat back, chief?'

'Not now . . . Carry on . . .'

He hadn't taken his overcoat off. He was in two minds as he watched Albert, who sat there with his big legs stretched in front of him.

Did he feel up to it? Did he have the will for it? If he started, he'd have to see it through, come what may. The wall clock hadn't advanced. He looked at his watch. It was seven o'clock. Thérèse was laying the table.

Should he eat first? Or should he . . .

'Give me a half-bottle of white wine, Thérèse!' he ordered.

He was sure, though, that it was nothing like the white wine the others had drunk!

Albert Forlacroix was watching him pensively.

'Tell me, Méjat . . .'

'Yes, chief . . . Sorry . . . I forgot to call my *tierce*.'

'It's fine!'

'Did you see the butcher?'

'He's just been in. I asked him the question. He doesn't remember. He claims he'd remember if anyone had asked for a good cut of meat at that hour.'

He was going round in circles. He was still in two minds. He went down the two steps that separated him from the kitchen and lifted the lids of the saucepans.

'What have you made us for dinner?' he asked the hotelier's wife.

'Calves' liver à la bourgeoise. I hope you like it? I didn't think of asking you.'

That made up his mind for him. He hated calves' liver in all its forms.

'Méjat, when you've finished, come over to the town hall . . . Is the fire on?'

'It was earlier.'

At last, he went and stood in front of Albert Forlacroix. 'How about you and me having a little chat? Not here. In my office. I hope you've had dinner?'

Albert stood up without a word.

'Let's go, then.'

And the two of them set off into the night.

9. The 'Singing Session'

Someone from Quai des Orfèvres, a Lucas or a Janvier, wouldn't have needed to watch Maigret for a long time to understand. Even his back spoke volumes! Had it grown rounder? Were his shoulders sagging? Whatever the case, if they had seen that back looming in the long corridor of the Police Judiciaire, and if Maigret had shown a man into his office without a word, the inspectors would have looked at each other.

'Hmm! There's a witness who knows when he goes in . . .'

And they wouldn't have been surprised if, two or three hours later, they had seen a waiter from the Brasserie Dauphine bringing sandwiches and beer.

Here, there was nobody to watch Maigret and his companion as they walked in the darkness of the street.

'Would you mind waiting a second?'

Maigret walked into the little grocery, which was full of strange smells, and bought some shag and matches.

'Give me a packet of blue cigarettes, too . . . Two packets! . . .'

He could see the sweets he had liked most when he was a child, all stuck together in a jar, but he didn't dare buy any. As they walked, Albert Forlacroix remained silent, visibly trying to look as detached as possible.

The gate, the courtyard of the town hall, then, in the office, a blast of warm air, the stove glowing red in the dark.

'Come in, Forlacroix. Make yourself at home.'

Maigret switched on the lights, took off his hat and coat, refilled the stove, walked around the room two or three times, and as he did so, a kind of glimmer of anxiety could be seen passing over his face. He came and went, glanced here and there, moved objects about, smoked and muttered, as if expecting something that hadn't yet come.

And that something was the feeling of being at ease in his own skin, as he usually put it, glad to avoid the word 'inspiration'.

'Sit down. You can smoke.'

He waited for Forlacroix to do what many country people do: take a cigarette directly from an open packet in his jacket pocket. He lit it for him, then, before sitting down in his turn, remembered the window of that shed; he glanced at the window here in the town hall, thought of closing the shutter but couldn't get the pane open, and finally contented himself with lowering the dusty blind.

'Well, now!' he sighed, sitting down with evident satisfaction. 'What do you have to say for yourself, Forlacroix?'

The 'singing session', as they called it at Quai des Orfèvres, was about to begin. Albert was suspicious. His body tilted backwards a little because his legs were too long for his chair. He looked at Maigret with no attempt to hide his resentment.

'Was it you who sent for my mother?' he asked after a moment's silence.

So he had seen her, either when she had got out of the car or when she had got back in. He had also seen the Dutchman, Horace Van Usschen.

'Your mother's testimony was indispensable,' Maigret replied. 'She's in La Roche-sur-Yon right now. I assume she'll be staying there for a few days. Maybe you'll go and see her?'

As he looked at the young man, he was thinking:

'Your hatred for your father, or the man who passes for your father, is only equalled by your irrational adoration for your mother.'

Then suddenly, without transition:

'The last time you spoke to her, she confirmed to you that Forlacroix wasn't your father, didn't she?'

'I already knew!' Albert muttered, staring at his boots.

'For quite a long time, I bet . . . Let's see! How old were you when you made that discovery? It must have been painful for you, wasn't it?'

'On the contrary!'

'Did you already hate Judge Forlacroix before you knew?'

'I certainly didn't love him!'

He was being cautious, weighing his words, like a peasant at the fair, and, whatever his feelings, he was avoiding flying off the handle, perhaps because he knew his own temper.

'How old were you when . . . ?'

'About sixteen. I was at high school in Luçon. I was taken out for several days. My father, I mean Forlacroix, had brought a famous doctor from Paris. I thought at first it was for my sister, but it was for me too.'

'Was your sister already . . . different?'

'She wasn't quite like anybody else.'

'And you?'

Albert gave a shudder and looked Maigret in the eyes. 'Nobody ever told me I was abnormal. At school I was an excellent pupil. The doctor examined me for hours, took samples, did tests. The judge stood over him all the time, anxious and overexcited, talking about things I didn't understand. Or rather, he talked about blood types, A, B. For several days, he waited impatiently for the test results, and when the paper arrived, with a letterhead from a laboratory in Paris, he looked at me coldly, with a kind of frozen smile, as if at last freed of a great weight . . .'

Albert was speaking slowly, still weighing his words.

'I questioned the older boys at school. I found out that a child always has the same blood type as its parents, and that in some countries this is admitted in court as evidence of paternity. Well, my blood wasn't the same type as my father's . . .'

He said this almost triumphantly.

'I thought of running away, but I didn't have any money. I'd have liked to join my mother, but I didn't have her address, and the judge clammed up whenever she was mentioned. I finished school. I did my military service. When I was discharged, I decided to live like the people around here . . .'

'Your temperament was more suited to strong physical activity, wasn't it? But tell me, why stay in the same village as the judge?'

'Because of my sister. I rented a house and started to work at the mussel fields. I went to see the judge and asked him to give me my sister . . .'

'And of course he refused!'

'Why do you say "of course"?'

Again, there was suspicion in his eyes.

'Because the judge seems to love his daughter!'

'Or hate her!' Albert muttered between his teeth.

'Do you think so?'

'In any case, he hated me.'

He suddenly stood up.

'What does all this have to do with your case? You've been trying to make me talk, haven't you?'

He searched in his pocket but couldn't find a cigarette. Maigret held out the packet he had bought specially.

'Sit down, Forlacroix.'

'Has the judge confessed?'

'Confessed what?'

'You know perfectly well what I'm talking about.'

'He confessed to an old crime . . . He caught your mother with a man, back in Versailles, and killed the man . . .'

'Oh!'

'Tell me, Forlacroix . . .'

A silence. A heavy look from Maigret.

'Were you friends with Marcel Airaud?'

Silence again. As usual, the mayor had left some bottles of wine on the table, and Maigret now poured himself a glass.

'What difference does that make?'

'No difference. Not a big one, anyway. You're about the same age. He's a mussel farmer, like you. You must have met at the mussel fields, at dances, whatever. I'm talking about the time when he wasn't yet climbing in through the window to see your sister.'

'We were friends, yes.'

'You live alone, don't you? It's quite unusual, at your age, such a liking for solitude. Your house is quite big.'

'A woman comes in every day to do the cleaning.'

'I know. And what about your meals? Don't tell me you do your own cooking?'

Sombre-eyed, Albert Forlacroix was wondering what Maigret was getting at.

'Sometimes. I'm not a big eater. A slice of ham, eggs. Some oysters before the meal. Occasionally I eat at the Hôtel du Port.'

'Strange . . .'

'What's strange?'

'Nothing! . . . You! . . . Basically, you live in L'Aiguillon the same way you'd live if you were in the middle of nowhere. Haven't you ever thought of getting married?'

'No.'

'And your friend Airaud?'

'He isn't my friend.'

'He isn't your friend any more, that's true . . . Did the two of you fall out when rumours started circulating that he sometimes spent the night with your sister?'

Now Forlacroix's unease was becoming visible. At first, despite his mistrust, he hadn't attached too much importance to Maigret's questions. Now it suddenly seemed to him as if a fine net was closing in around him. Where was the inspector going with all this? Maigret poured him a drink and pushed the packet of cigarettes in his direction.

'Drink. Smoke. Make yourself at home . . . We may be here for some time.'

Then Forlacroix swore to himself – and the thought could be read on his face:

'I won't say anything more! I won't answer any more of his questions!'

Maigret took a little walk around the room and stood for a while gazing at the bust of *La République*.

'Aren't you hungry?'

'No!'

'Maybe you've already had dinner? But I'm starving, and I wish I'd thought of bringing a few potatoes . . .'

Oh, yes! Oh, yes! That startled you, didn't it? Although, of course, you're a cool customer, we know that.

'Anyway, Airaud and you, built as you both are, are rather like the two village roosters. All the girls must be after you.'

'I'm not interested in girls.'

'But Airaud is! He even gets them pregnant sometimes! When you found out he was your sister's lover, you must have been indignant. I'm surprised there wasn't more damage.'

'We did fight . . .'

'Several times, I assume? Because he just carried on. It's quite puzzling. I don't know him very well. You know him much better than me. Do you think Marcel was genuinely in love with your sister?'

'I have no idea.'

'At any rate, that's what some people say. They say he intended to marry her and that he'd come to an agreement with the judge. If that had happened, you could have made it up between you, couldn't you? He'd have been your brother-in-law. It's a pity he ran away, because that doesn't exactly strengthen his case.

You might as well know, I have a summons out for him. If he wasn't guilty, what reason could he have had to vanish like that and go to ground in the marshes?'

Cigarette followed cigarette. Every now and again, heavy footsteps could be heard on the path, people on their way to play cards at the Hôtel du Port.

And the 'singing session' went on. At times, Maigret turned to the wall, and an expression of discouragement crossed his face. There had been many others who had stood up to his questions for hours, sly, cunning, giving as good as they got.

The most famous of these interrogations, at Quai des Orfèvres, had lasted twenty-seven hours, and three officers had taken turns, not leaving the man a minute's respite.

But never before, perhaps, had he had such an inert mass to shift as Albert Forlacroix.

'Marcel's an only child, isn't he? And his mother's a widow, I think? Does she own any property? I ask that because, if he's found guilty, the life of that poor woman . . .'

'Don't worry about her. She's richer than most of the people in L'Aiguillon.'

'Good for her! Because the more I think about it . . . Look, do you want me to tell you, just between ourselves, how things happened? . . . One moment, I have to make a phone call. I almost forgot, and that might have been serious . . . Hello, mademoiselle . . . It's me, yes . . . I owe you a lot of chocolates . . . No, that's true, you prefer marrons glacés . . . Anyway, my debt keeps getting bigger and bigger . . . The office is closed, I know . . . All the same, do you think you could get me Nantes? . . . The flying squad, yes . . . Thank you, mademoiselle . . .'

Come on! He mustn't slacken. He had to keep Forlacroix on tenterhooks.

'At first, he only wanted to have a bit of fun, which is quite understandable at his age. He didn't really care that your sister wasn't exactly like anyone else. Then he fell in love with her. He envisaged the possibility of marrying her. Didn't he talk to you about it at that point?'

'We didn't talk!'

'I forgot! Though since he went to see your father, he could have gone to see you, too, to tell you that it wasn't the way you thought, that his intentions were honourable. But if you tell me he didn't . . . Hello? . . . Yes! . . . Maigret here . . . Look, I'd like you to do me a favour . . . Do you have the address of Dr Janin's maid? . . . Good! Listen . . . It's a bit irregular . . . She must agree of her own free will, otherwise I'll have to wait until tomorrow to have her summoned by the examining magistrate . . . I'd like you to bring her here . . . Tonight, yes . . . It's no more than twenty kilometres . . . Where? . . . I'll probably be at the town hall . . . No, don't tell her anything! . . . Thank you!'

He hung up and assumed his most cordial air.

'I hope you didn't mind. A formality I'd forgotten . . . Suppose the gendarmes get their hands on Airaud . . . They'll have to find him eventually, dammit! The marshes aren't a desert . . . Now this is what I think. Marcel envisages getting married. His mother probably dissuades him from marrying a girl who isn't quite normal. Even though he loves her, he's a bit worried himself . . .'

It was hot, of course, and the stove was purring. But was it the heat that caused beads of sweat to appear on Forlacroix's forehead?

'Then he remembers that a former shipmate of his, from the days when he was a sailor on the *Vengeur*, is now working as a doctor in Nantes. He goes to see him. He asks for his advice. Janin can't say anything without first seeing the girl. They both decide that he'll come here and examine her . . .'

Albert stubbed out his cigarette beneath his heel and lit another.

'You must admit it holds together, psychologically speaking.

I don't know your former friend Airaud as well as you do. Before anything else, he's a peasant. That means he's cautious by nature. He wants to get married, but all the same he'd like to make sure his future wife isn't completely mad . . . What do you think?'

'I don't know!' Albert said curtly.

'Have your drink. Are you sure you're not hungry? . . . In my opinion . . . and I may be mistaken . . . in my opinion, Marcel doesn't dare tell your father. To be blunt about it, your father is giving him his daughter, but giving her as she is. Plus, if she was healthy and normal, it's unlikely he'd marry her off to a mussel farmer . . .'

And here Maigret turned vulgar, laughing heartily like a travelling salesman telling crude stories.

'You can just see our Airaud telling his future father-in-law: "All right! You're very kind. I'll take your daughter, but I'd like an expert opinion first . . ."'

A look from Albert, a look full of hatred. Maigret pretended not to see it.

'So he has to have the girl examined without the judge knowing. Which is why I think he chose a Tuesday. That evening, Forlacroix is shut up for hours in the library on the ground floor with his friends. They're talking loudly. Drinking. Laughing. Nobody will have any inkling of what's going on upstairs . . . There's only one thing that bothers me, Albert . . . Do you mind if I call you that? . . . Yes, one detail bothers me. I know Janin is a bit unorthodox, even something of a hothead. All the same, there are rules the medical profession tends to follow to the letter . . .

'Just see how events pan out and then tell me if there isn't something not quite right . . .'

He, too, was hot and he mopped his brow and filled his pipe. At times like these, he realized what an effort a variety performer, for example, had to make to carry his audience with him, to keep a crowd of people in suspense for minutes on end, come what may . . .

He had only one man in front of him. But what a bad audience! The kind that declares in advance: 'This is stupid! I won't go along with it!'

'Listen, my dear Forlacroix. Janin gets off the bus. Airaud must have arranged to meet him outside, not far from the Hôtel du Port. He doesn't want anybody to know about this visit.

'Why does Janin feel the need to go into the hotel and order his dinner for that evening?

'Whatever the reason, he comes out. He meets Marcel. It isn't quite time to go to the Forlacroix house. The judge's guests haven't arrived yet. There's no way to see the girl on her own before nine in the evening.

'What do you think the two men could have done all that time? It was raining. I can't see them walking in the dark for hours on end. It's also curious that nobody in L'Aiguillon ran into them . . .

'Plus, they had something to eat! At least, we have evidence that Janin did . . . I don't mind telling you this, even though it's meant to be confidential . . . When they did the post mortem, they found the remains of a fairly copious meal in his stomach.

'Where could they have gone to eat, do you think?'

And Maigret, who had been walking, stopped for a moment and gave Forlacroix a firm slap on the shoulder.

'That's not all, my friend! The guests have arrived. Brénéol and his wife and daughter, followed by the Marsacs. Now's the time. They still have to get up to your sister Lise's bedroom, which is on the first floor. Marcel is in the habit of climbing along the wall . . .

'What I wonder is whether Doctor Janin, however unorthodox he may have been, also proceeded to clamber up the front of the house.

'It's the only possible hypothesis.

'Is Airaud with him?

'Whatever the case, it's quite possible the drama had taken place by midnight. You gave us the proof of that.'

'I did?'

'Oh, yes! Have you forgotten your own statements? Statements the judge has confirmed in detail . . . When he came up to the first floor after his guests had left, in other words around midnight, he found you sitting at the top of the stairs.'

Silence. Another pipe. More coal in the stove.

'By the way, if you'd fallen out with the judge, why did you keep a key to the house?'

'To see my sister.'

'Did you see her that night?'

'No!'

'And you didn't hear any noise, did you, either in the room or in the fruitery, even though you were sitting almost directly in front of the door? That's what makes me think it was all over by then . . .'

He gulped down a whole glass of wine and wiped his lips.

'That would seem to put Judge Forlacroix in the clear, but not a bit of it . . . How long were you in the house before the guests left? Not long, I suppose, since you knew the time they usually left?'

'Five or ten minutes.'

'Five or ten minutes . . . They were playing bridge . . . In bridge, there's always a dummy. In the course of the evening, Forlacroix may have taken advantage of the fact that he was a dummy to pop upstairs and make sure everything was all right. He sees a man he doesn't know. There's a hammer within arm's reach. He strikes him . . .'

'What are you getting at?' Albert Forlacroix asked.

'Nothing. We're just chatting. I've been wanting to talk to you about all these things for a long time now. One question occurs to me. Did Marcel Airaud enter the house at the same time as the doctor?'

'Why do you ask me?'

'No, obviously, you couldn't know, could you? He might have come in with him and been present at the examination. He could also simply have announced the visitor to your sister Lise, who was fairly reasonable when she wasn't having one of her attacks . . . You see, my friend, all hypotheses are allowed . . .

'If Airaud did go in, it's possible he quarrelled with Janin . . . If Janin tells him, for example: "You can't marry this girl . . ."

'He loves her! He asked the man for advice. But who knows if, when all is revealed to him . . .

'Last but not least, your sister herself could have . . .'

'You think my sister would have been capable . . .'

'Calm down! Like I said, we're just chatting! We're considering all the possibilities. Janin examines her, asks her the kind of specific, even indiscreet, questions a doctor feels permitted to ask . . .

'She has an attack . . . Or she is just afraid he'll stop Marcel from marrying her . . .'

Phew! His cheeks were red, and his eyes shining.

'That's why it would be interesting to know if Airaud was in the house or waiting outside . . . It's obvious that his running away doesn't make him look good. People don't usually hide if they have nothing to feel guilty about. Unless . . .'

He seemed to think this over carefully and then once again slapped Albert on the shoulder.

'Oh, yes! He does have an answer for us when we arrest him . . . Let's say he stayed outside. He waits. He doesn't see his friend come back. Late that night, he climbs the wall, gets into the fruitery and discovers the doctor's body. He tells himself it was Lise who killed him.

'The investigation begins. He's afraid they'll suspect her. He loves her. So to divert suspicion from his fiancée, he pretends to run away.

'Is it a way of gaining time, of maybe getting the case dropped? What do you think?'

'I don't think anything!'

'Obviously, you haven't the slightest idea where Airaud is hiding. Don't answer yet. You were his friend. He was going to become your brother-in-law. It's perfectly understandable that you wouldn't want to give him up to the law . . . I say it's perfectly understandable, on a human level, that is, but not from the legal point of view. Do you get my meaning? . . . Let's suppose you've seen Airaud since he ran away and didn't say anything. It's only a supposition. He may still be wandering around the countryside. It'd be hard not to draw certain conclusions.'

'What conclusions?' Albert asked in a slow voice, uncrossing his legs and crossing them in the other direction, letting the ash from his cigarette fall on his jacket.

'It may be thought, for example, that you, too, want to save your sister . . . You were on the landing for five or ten minutes, but we have no proof of that . . . You didn't set foot in the hotel that evening, did you?'

'Not after nine o'clock.'

'You must have had a key to your sister's room. You admitted as much yourself when you said you'd kept a key to the front door so that you could visit her. That key would have been useless if, once inside . . . But I guess you lost that second key, because on a particular night I saw you knock the door in with your shoulder . . . Maybe you were just in an emotional state, or were you trying to pull the wool over our eyes?'

Silence. Albert was staring pensively at the dusty floor. By the time he raised his eyes, he had made his mind up.

'Is this an interrogation?'

'It's whatever you want it to be.'

'And am I obliged to answer?'

'No!'

'In that case, I have nothing to say.'

And he stubbed out his cigarette with his boot.

Maigret walked around the room two or three more times, made sure there was no more wine in the bottle, and turned the crank of the telephone.

'Oh, good, you aren't in bed yet, mademoiselle. Could you put me through to the Hôtel du Port? Thank you! . . . Hello? Is that you Thérèse? . . . Call Inspector Méjat for me, my dear . . . Méjat? . . . Look, old chap, can you go to Albert Forlacroix's house? . . . Go across the back yard . . . At the end of it, you'll find a kind of shed . . . A man is in there, sleeping on a straw mattress . . . No, I don't think he's dangerous! . . . Be careful all the same . . . Yes, put the handcuffs on him, it's safer . . . And bring him to me . . . That's right . . . Forlacroix? . . . No, he won't protest . . . He's here. He's agreed to it.'

Maigret hung up with a smile.

'Inspector Méjat was afraid you'd lodge a complaint for forcible entry. Strictly speaking, it's not allowed without a warrant, especially in the middle of the night . . . Cigarette? . . . Really? . . . If I'd been there myself, I don't think I'd have resisted the temptation to take down one of those succulent sausages hanging above the fireplace.'

Then, in a softer voice:

'When exactly did you slaughter the pig?'

10. Didine's Little Dishes

During the minutes that followed, Maigret seemed to have forgotten his companion; he began by taking his watch from his pocket; he slowly rewound it, with exaggerated care, took it off its chain and put it down on the table as if, from now on, the passage of time was going to be important.

Then he waited. Albert Forlacroix didn't move, didn't even heave a sigh. He must have been ill at ease on his rickety chair. He must have wanted to shift, maybe to scratch his cheek, or his nose, to cross and uncross his legs. But, precisely because Maigret was keeping quite still, he forced himself with grim determination to do the same.

From where he was, he couldn't see Maigret's face as he pretended to be absorbed in staring at the stove. Otherwise, he would no doubt have caught a slight, almost playful smile.

It was just a professional ploy, of course, the kind of little trick designed to disconcert a man!

Footsteps outside. Maigret walked calmly to the door and opened it. Marcel Airaud was there in front of him, with handcuffs on his wrists, and Inspector Méjat, swollen with his own importance, was holding on to the handcuffs. A gendarme was behind them in the shadows.

Marcel didn't seem upset and only blinked because he was startled by the light. He stood there while Forlacroix remained on his chair.

'Can you take that one next door?' Maigret said to the inspector, pointing to Albert.

Next door was the ballroom, with its white walls, its paper

chains hanging from the ceiling, its benches all around for the mothers. Between the two rooms, a glass door.

'Sit down, Airaud. I'll be with you in a moment.'

But Marcel preferred to remain standing. Maigret gave his instructions, posted the gendarme to keep an eye on Forlacroix and sent Méjat off to fetch sandwiches and bottles of beer.

It was all happening as if in slow motion. Forlacroix and Airaud must be observing Maigret's behaviour with astonishment. And yet they had been caught up in the mechanism for some time now.

Was Marcel Airaud capable of humour? It was quite possible. He didn't seem thrown in any way by Maigret's overwhelming composure. He watched him as he came and went and simply stood there with a vague smile hovering over his lips.

On the other side of the glass door, Forlacroix had sat down on the bench, his back to the wall, his legs stretched out, and the gendarme, who was taking his role seriously, had sat down facing him with his eyes fixed on him.

'Have you been hiding at your friend Albert's house for a long time?' Maigret suddenly asked, looking elsewhere.

As soon as he heard his own voice, he had the feeling it was pointless. He waited a moment, then turned to his prisoner.

'Am I under arrest?' Marcel asked, glancing at his handcuffs.

'I have here a warrant signed by the examining magistrate.'

'In that case, I'll only answer the magistrate, and in the presence of my lawyer.'

Maigret looked him up and down, without surprise.

'Come in!' he cried to Méjat, who had knocked.

Méjat came in, his arms laden with little packets, and placed everything on the table: pâté, ham, bread, bottles of beer. He tried to whisper in Maigret's ear.

'Speak up!' Maigret grunted.

'I said, Thérèse is in the courtyard. She seems to suspect

something. She immediately asked me if he had been arrested.'

Maigret shrugged, made himself a sandwich, poured himself a drink and again looked Marcel Airaud up and down. There was no point in insisting, he was sure.

'Take him next door, Méjat. Tell the gendarme to stop them talking to each other. As for you, come back here.'

He walked. He ate. He muttered to himself. He shrugged. Every time he passed the door, he could see them on the bench, there in the big white room, the gendarme watching them with knitted brows.

'Is everything all right, chief?' Méjat asked, coming back into the room.

He fell silent, because one look from the inspector had sufficed. He wasn't yet used to it. He didn't know how to act. And Maigret was still eating, stuffing over-large pieces in his mouth and, still chewing, going over to the door and gazing in at his two captured animals through the glass.

Suddenly, he turned.

'Go and fetch Didine.'

'There's no need to go far. When I came in, she was standing guard just ten metres from here.'

'Bring her in.'

'What about Thérèse?'

'Did I mention Thérèse?'

Soon afterwards, Didine came into the ballroom and stopped in front of the two men with a satisfied look on her face, especially pleased to see the shiny handcuffs on Marcel Airaud's wrists.

'Come in, Didine. I need you.'

'So you got him after all!'

'Sit down, Didine. I won't offer you a beer . . . Or should I?'

'I don't like it . . . So you arrested him in the end.'

'Listen to me, Didine. Take your time answering. This is very important . . . You, Méjat, either sit down or go for a walk, but don't just stand there looking at me like an idiot . . . Now then, my good lady. Let's suppose that one afternoon, you're suddenly told that someone is coming to have dinner at your house. Someone from the town. What would you do?'

She might have been expected to react with surprise at the unexpectedness of the question, but that would have been not to know Didine well. Her features became sharper as she considered the question. It was pointless to advise her to think it over carefully. She was taking her time.

'What kind of person?' she asked.

'A respectable person.'

'And I'd only be told about it in the afternoon? At what time?'

'Let's say four thirty or five.'

The three men on the other side of the glass, Airaud, Forlacroix and the gendarme, were looking into the room, but they were in the position that Maigret had been in that afternoon: they could see lips moving but heard only a vague murmur.

'I don't know if you've quite understood me. You know what's available in L'Aiguillon, the local habits. You know what can be found at any hour when it comes to food and drink.'

'It'd be too late to kill a chicken,' she said as if to herself. 'It wouldn't be tender. Not to mention that it'd take too long to pluck and gut . . . What day of the week are you talking about, inspector?'

Méjat was stunned. As for Maigret, he wasn't smiling at all.

'A Tuesday.'

'I'm starting to understand. It's that Tuesday you mean, isn't it? It's as if it was meant to be. I said to my husband . . . That man, I said to him, must have eaten somewhere. He certainly didn't eat at the restaurant. He didn't eat at the judge's house either.'

'Answer my question, Didine. What would you have served him on a Tuesday?'

'Not meat. They do the slaughtering on a Monday here. On Tuesday, the meat's too fresh. It would have been tough . . . Wait! How was the tide that Tuesday? High tide was about eight in the evening, wasn't it? That means Polyte was at home. In that case, I'd have gone to Polyte's. He always goes out trawling with the morning tide. So he must have come back at about midday. If he had a good piece . . .'

'Where does Polyte live?'

'You won't find him at home. He's in the café. Not at the Hôtel du Port, the one opposite . . .'

'Do you hear that, Méjat?'

Méjat went out without needing to be asked twice.

'When Polyte has a nice pair of soles, or a nice dory . . .' Didine continued. 'That's the beginnings of a decent meal. As long as there's ham in the house. But . . . Wait, inspector! . . . There isn't only Polyte . . . It depends whether or not you like lapwings. Because then, it's worth going to see old Rouillon, who goes out hunting every morning.'

The three men were still there, beyond the glass. Forlacroix's gaze was sombre. Marcel Airaud, despite his handcuffs, was smoking a cigarette and squinting because of the smoke.

'Only, to prepare lapwings, you need . . .'

Méjat crossed the ballroom in the company of a thin fisherman with a pointed nose and a brick-red complexion, who stopped in surprise in front of Marcel.

'You here? D'you give yourself up?'

'Come in!' Maigret called. 'Are you the one they call Polyte?'

He peered anxiously at Didine. What could she have told them about him for them to call him in?

'Now then, Polyte. You remember last Tuesday . . .'

'Tuesday . . .' he repeated, like a man who wasn't quite all there.

'The day of the fair at Saint-Michel!' Didine said. 'The day when the tide was 108 . . .'

'Let's see . . . What was I doing that day?'

'Getting drunk like every other day!' Didine said, again feeling the need to butt in.

'Where were you during the afternoon?'

And Didine once more, tirelessly:

'In the bistro, of course! If he could, he'd sleep there. Isn't that right, Polyte?'

'What I'd like to know is if anyone came to see you that afternoon and asked you for a nice piece of fish.'

Forlacroix's sombre gaze, in the other room. Polyte thought it over, turning to Didine as if to ask her for advice.

'The day when the tide was 108 . . . Don't you remember?' he asked, with disarming candour.

And suddenly he turned towards the glass door and slapped his own forehead, while a triumphant smile lit up Didine's face.

'It's Albert who came,' he declared. 'I remember, because he was in a great hurry. I was playing cards with Deveaud and Fraigne. Wait just a minute, I told him. Then, as he was getting impatient, I told him to go and get some soles from my boat.'

'How many?'

'I don't know how many he took. I told him to help himself. We still haven't settled up . . .'

'That's all I wanted to know. You can go. By the way, Didine, where does Albert Forlacroix's housekeeper live?'

'Actually, she's his daughter.'

'Polyte's?'

'Yes. But she doesn't live with her father. If you want to see her, you'd better hurry, because she goes to bed early. Especially as, just for a change, she's expecting. One every year! Some girls are anybody's.'

'Méjat! Can you go and fetch her? And don't upset her, eh?'

He was starting to get excited. In the doorway, Polyte was still waiting for permission to go. At last he walked off with Méjat, pointing him in the direction of his daughter's house.

'God knows how come the men aren't disgusted by her. You'll see her. Maybe she'll clean herself up before she comes! If I had to eat what she's touched . . .'

She was surprised to see Maigret standing motionless in the middle of the room, listening to nothing, looking at nothing. An idea had just struck him. Suddenly, he rushed to the telephone.

'I hope you weren't in bed, mademoiselle? Get me the Albert-Premier nursing home in La Roche-sur-Yon . . . Number 41 . . . Ring until someone answers . . . There's at least one nurse on duty . . . Yes, I'm very grateful . . .'

He had forgotten Didine, who now asked calmly:

'Do you think it's Marcel? If you want my advice, knowing both of them . . .'

'Be quiet!' he cried, like a man in a temper.

He couldn't take his eyes off the telephone. For hours, for days now, he'd been searching . . .

'Hello? . . . . The Albert-Premier? . . . Who am I speaking to? . . . Tell me, mademoiselle, is the doctor still there? . . . What's that, he's at home? . . . Can you put me through to his apartment? . . .'

His cheeks were flushed and he was biting the stem of his pipe, looking mechanically at Didine as if he didn't recognize her.

'Hello? . . . Is that you, doctor? . . . You were just eating? . . . I'm so sorry . . . Detective Chief Inspector Maigret, yes . . . I wanted to ask you . . . Of course, you've examined her . . . What? . . . More serious than we thought? . . . That's not what I called you about . . . I'd like to ask you if you discovered anything unexpected . . . Yes . . . What? . . . What's that you say? . . . Are you certain? . . . Three months? . . . Thank you, doctor . . . Yes, of course, you'll make an official report . . . Has she calmed down? . . . Thank you . . . Once again, I'm sorry to have disturbed you . . .'

He was on edge. When he discovered the old woman still sitting there on her chair, he said:

'Now run along, my dear Didine. You've been very kind, but I don't need you any more for the moment.'

She stood up reluctantly, but didn't go yet.

'I bet I can guess what he told you . . .'

'Good for you. Now just run along! Wait next door if you want, but . . .'

'She's pregnant, isn't she?'

He couldn't believe his ears. He was almost starting to be afraid of her!

'I don't have time to answer you. Just go! And above all, keep your mouth shut . . .'

He opened the door. He was about to close it again when Méjat arrived, accompanied by a girl with dirty hair falling down the back of her neck.

'She didn't want to come with me because she was about to go to bed . . .'

At that moment, a little event occurred. At the sight of his maid, Forlacroix had stood up, as if wanting to intervene. The gendarme no doubt made a mistake in touching his arm, which had the effect of restoring his composure, and he sat down again.

'Good! Come in for a moment. I only have a couple of questions to ask you. What time do you finish work at Albert Forlacroix's house?'

'Sometimes at three, sometimes at four.'

'Don't you make his dinner?'

'I never make any of his meals. He does all his own cooking. He likes it!'

She said these last words with what might have been irony or contempt.

'I assume you do the washing up?'

'Yes, I get the dirty work. And there's plenty of that in the house! Men, when you see them outside, are all spruced up. But when you have to clean up after them . . .'

'How often does he have guests?'

'Who?'

'Your employer.'

'Never! Who'd he have as a guest?'

'Don't you ever find several dirty plates in the morning?'

'It happened last week.'

'Wednesday morning, wasn't it?'

'It might have been Wednesday . . . And ashes everywhere. They'd been smoking cigars.'

'Do you know who his visitor was?'

She turned towards the glass door and replied guilelessly, holding her belly in both hands with a mechanical gesture:

'Why don't you ask him?'

'Thank you for your help. You can go to bed now.'

'Is he the one who did it?'

It didn't surprise her. It didn't scare her. It wasn't much more than curiosity on her part. Sure enough, she added:

'I'm only asking so as to know if I need to go there tomorrow . . .'

Voices could be heard out in the street, beyond the gates of the town hall. People had had wind of something. A little group had formed. They stood looking at the cream curtains, behind which they could sometimes see shadows passing, especially the thick silhouette of Maigret, whose pipe occasionally, when he was at a certain angle, appeared immense, almost as large as his head.

'I think they've arrested both of them!' Polyte's daughter announced when she had been allowed to leave and the onlookers questioned her.

She was so sleepy that she didn't linger, and the noise of her clogs could be heard as she walked away over the frost-hardened cobbles. The door opened. It was Méjat, trying to recognize the faces in the darkness.

'Is Thérèse still there?' he asked.

From a shadowy area over to the side, a form emerged. 'What do you want with me?'

'Come inside! The inspector wants to talk to you.'

As she passed Marcel, she looked him in the eyes, but didn't open her mouth.

'Come in, Thérèse. Don't be afraid. I'd like to ask you a simple question . . . Did you know that Lise Forlacroix was pregnant?'

Hearing this, she turned towards the glass door, and it looked as if she might rush at Airaud, who couldn't have had any idea what was going on.

'It isn't true!' she said, thinking better of it. 'You're trying to trick me.'

'I assure you, Thérèse, Lise Forlacroix is three months' pregnant . . .'

'That's why!' she said in a low voice, as if to herself.

'That's why what?'

'He wanted to marry her.'

'So you admit he wanted to marry her? But he didn't tell you the reason? Well, now you know the reason. You know that . . .'

'What about me, don't I have a child? Aren't I just as good as the judge's daughter? Did he marry me?'

It must have been strange to watch her through the glass, because it was obvious she was angry, but hard to guess why.

'You know, even that night . . .'

'Yes, what did you say to him that night?'

'I told him that if he married her, I'd be at the church with his son and that I'd make a scene . . .'

'Hold on a moment . . . You spoke to him on Tuesday night? Where?'

She hesitated for a moment, then shrugged. 'In the street . . .'

'What time was it?'

'Maybe just before midnight.'

'Whereabouts in the street?'

She turned again with a vicious look towards the glass. 'All right, I'll tell you . . . Too bad! . . . At about ten, just as I was going to bed, I saw a light in Lise's window . . .'

'The window of her bedroom or the window of the fruitery?'

'Her bedroom.'

'Are you sure you didn't mix them up?'

She gave an ironic laugh. 'Of course I'm sure! I've spied on the two of them often enough! I tried to sleep but I couldn't. I got up again and decided to go and wait for him outside.'

'Intending to do what?'

'The usual thing,' she admitted wearily.

'You didn't threaten him with anything else except making a scene in church?'

'I told him I'd kill myself in his house . . .'

'Would you have done it?'

'I have no idea. I crept outside. It was raining. I'd even put my coat over my head. I wondered if he'd be staying late. Maybe, if he'd stayed too long, I'd have decided to climb up.'

'And what happened?'

'I was walking along, talking to myself, as I often do. I wasn't looking in front of me, because there was nobody in the streets . . . Suddenly, I bumped into someone. It was him. I was so surprised that I cried out.'

'Where was he?'

'Near the wall, behind the judge's house.'

'What was he doing? Coming out?'

'No! He wasn't doing anything. He seemed to be waiting. I asked him what he was waiting for.'

'What did he reply?'

'Nothing! He twisted my wrists. He was furious. "If I catch you spying on me again," he growled, "I don't know what I'll do . . ."'

'What time was it?'

'Not far off midnight, as I said . . . Maybe a little later . . .'

'Was there still a light on in the bedroom?'

'I don't know. You can't see it from there, because of the wall. "Go to bed, you bitch!" he yelled at me. "Do you understand? And if ever . . ." I'd never seen him so angry with me.'

Another glance at the other side of the glass. There, in the ballroom, Airaud was as calm as ever. The gendarme must have given him another cigarette, which he was holding askew because of the handcuffs.

'Do you mind waiting next door, Thérèse? I may need you again.'

When the door had closed again, a voice – Méjat's – said:

'Well, well, chief. I think . . .'

'You think what?'

'I think that . . . that . . .'

Poor man! He had tried to be nice, to congratulate Maigret on the results obtained. But the only response was a glare.

'Well? What do you think? Answer me. You're going to find the evidence, are you? Go and fetch me some beer! . . . Or rather, no . . . Bring me some real hooch . . . Calvados, rum, whatever . . . What time is it?'

It was midnight, and there was nobody left outside but three onlookers who stood there stamping their feet, hoping to finally hear something.

11. The Doctor's Maid

The hum of an engine, the noise of brakes, the slamming of car doors. A moment later, two inspectors entered the ballroom in the company of a woman in her thirties, who looked dazed.

'Sorry, sir. We had a flat tyre on the way here. The jack wouldn't work. We . . .'

'Is this her?' Maigret asked, examining the young woman, who was quite lost, her eyes darting all over in such a way that she saw nothing.

'She didn't want to come, because of her sister-in-law who's ill. We had to promise to take her back tonight.'

Suddenly, the woman noticed the handcuffs and gave a muffled cry.

'Do you recognize him?' Maigret asked. 'Take a good look at him. Tell me if he recently paid your employer a visit.'

'I recognize them,' she replied, recovering her composure.

'You . . . what did you say? . . . You recognize *them*?'

'Well, yes! I recognize both of them, because they came together.'

'And they both saw the doctor in his office?'

'Both of them. Not immediately, because the doctor wasn't there. I advised them to come back the following day, but they preferred to sit in the waiting room for more than two hours.'

'That's it!' Maigret muttered. 'I don't need you any more.'

'Shall we take her back?' the two inspectors asked, somewhat annoyed.

'If you like . . . Wait . . . Here's Méjat bringing something to drink . . . Only, I don't know if there are enough glasses.'

Then Didine again rose and touched the inspector's arm.

'In the cupboard,' she whispered.

'What's in the cupboard?'

'Glasses. There are always some, for council meetings. Would you like me to wipe them?'

She knew everything! She had seen and heard everything!

The policemen drank. As the doctor's maid was feeling cold, she, too, was given a little alcohol, but it only made her cough desperately.

The blood had gone to Maigret's head. He seemed so tense that Méjat was watching him with a certain anxiety. Suddenly, he opened the door. The inspectors had left. The car was setting off again.

'Come here, you!' he called to Airaud with unexpected abruptness. 'Take off his handcuffs, Méjat. He looks stupid like that. Come in! Close the door, Méjat. And you, I advise you not to try and be clever, do you understand? I've had just about enough! That's right, I've had enough.'

It was so unexpected that Marcel lost his composure.

'I bet you think you're intelligent. You're pleased with yourself, aren't you? Oh, yes! . . . Look at yourself in the mirror. And please, don't keep shifting from one leg to the other like a bear . . . What did your father do?'

It was so surprising that, despite his determination not to answer, Airaud could not help murmuring:

'He was a mussel farmer.'

'And you're a mussel farmer! And you imagine that a judge's daughter is something extraordinary, don't you? And you don't realize that you're nothing but a young fool that people laugh at. How long ago was it that Forlacroix made it up with you?'

A hostile silence.

'All right, don't answer. That makes you look even better!'

This time, getting carried away, Maigret spoke so loudly that it was impossible for those on the other side of the door not to hear, if not all the words, at least enough to catch the drift of what he was saying.

Talking all the while, walking about, chewing the stem of his pipe, he poured himself a drink with such frenzy that Méjat was astounded.

'That's it, don't answer! You're too stupid anyway and wouldn't have much to say . . . Wasn't your affair with Thérèse enough for you? Because you almost married her, didn't you? Everybody knows that. Only, everybody also knew what you didn't know.'

'I did know . . .'

'What?'

'That she was seeing other men.'

'OK! And you didn't marry her. That's something at least. You realized you were being taken for a ride. Only, Thérèse is nothing but a hotel maid, the daughter of a woman who sells fish in the street. Whereas the other girl . . .'

Marcel's features had hardened, and Maigret, in spite of his apparent excitement, glanced at his big fists, which were clenched. Didn't he turn away for a moment to wipe away a smile that rose to his lips? Didn't he need to take a big swig of his drink in order to keep up the tone?

'Monsieur was quite proud of being the lover of a Forlacroix girl, the daughter of a judge, someone who played the piano . . .'

'Listen, inspector . . .'

'Shut up! You won't speak until there's a lawyer present. You told me that. Monsieur is in love. Monsieur is raring to go. And when old Forlacroix, who's been watching him from behind his door, lets him in, Monsieur is reduced to a stammering little boy . . .'

'"What! You love my daughter? That's no problem! She's yours! Take her. Marry her."

'That's it, isn't it? And this big lump who's strong enough to kill an ox can't see further than the end of his nose.

'"Yes, sir, I'll marry her! Yes, sir, I'm an honest man and my intentions are honourable . . ."

'He's so moved, so filled with happiness and pride that he can't hold it in and goes to see his enemy, young Forlacroix, who's vowed a hundred times to smash his face in.

'"You have the wrong idea about me. I want to marry your sister. Let's make it up between us."

On the other side of the glass, Forlacroix was craning his neck, trying to hear, and old Didine had moved to the very end of the bench.

'Well, my boy, there's something I can tell you for sure, which is that they both tricked you. You still don't understand, do you? You told yourself they'd recognized your merits and were opening their arms to you.

'Only your good old mother suspected something. And I'm sure you were angry with her when she advised you to be cautious, not to get carried away.

'"I assure you, Mother, Lise isn't as mad as people think. When she's happy and well looked after . . ."

'The same old story! You poor fool!'

Marcel was breathing heavily now. Maigret looked him up and down and winked at Méjat, who wasn't quite sure what that meant.

'I'm sure it was your mother who had the one little spark of common sense. What could the poor woman do to persuade a boy as stubborn and excitable as you?

'"At least have her examined by a doctor. What if she's completely mad?"

'That's when you think of your old shipmate Janin. You convince Albert that you only want what's best. If, after examining Lise, Janin decides that . . .

'What? That's not the way it happened? Don't answer! You're not saying anything without a lawyer present, isn't that right?

'Of course, Albert knows that his sister's pregnant . . .'

It was so sudden that Maigret didn't have time to move back.

Or maybe this was the reaction he was after. Marcel had grabbed him by his lapel and was about to shake him.

'What did you say? . . . What did you say? . . .'

'Do you want the doctor at the clinic to confirm it to you? Later. You just have to talk to him on the phone.'

'Lise is . . .'

'Pregnant. Oh, yes! It does happen! That's why the judge is suddenly so happy to let his daughter marry a big brute like you.

'And that's why Albert goes with you to Nantes. He doesn't trust you. He doesn't want his sister and himself to become the laughing stock of L'Aiguillon.

'There was one thing that bothered me. I wondered if Janin had really agreed to climb along the wall to go and see a patient.

'Of course not! There was no need! You can't have him come to your house because then your mother would know, and you prefer to keep her out of this.

'The three of you have dinner at Albert's house. I can even tell you that you ate sole.

'Then, when the guests have arrived at the judge's house, when the game of bridge has started and the way is clear, it's Albert who takes the doctor there. He has the key. It isn't difficult to get up to the first floor without making any noise . . . I became suspicious when he saw fit, in front of me, to knock the door in with his shoulder. If he had a key to the front door, it was more than likely . . . But that's no concern of yours . . . He lets Doctor Janin into his sister's room. He waits . . .

'And you're left pacing up and down outside, near the wall you're so used to climbing . . .'

Maigret turned to the door and saw Albert Forlacroix standing beyond it, looking menacing.

'You had a strange time waiting there, didn't you? Thérèse interfering and threatening you . . . You wonder why the two men haven't come down again . . . Well, I'm going to tell you.

After examining the girl, Dr Janin joined Albert in the fruitery. What he told him isn't hard to guess. The first thing he must have said was: "Your sister is expecting a baby."

'Then . . . Look at him . . . No, not the inspector . . . Turn to the door . . . Look at his face . . .'

Albert Forlacroix stood there, pale-faced, and you could see a strange dampness on his lips and a pinching of his nostrils.

'Come in, Forlacroix. You'll be able to hear better. I'm going to tell you what the doctor told you. He told you that your sister was incurable, that it would be dishonest to throw her into the arms of an honest man, that her place was in a clinic, and that his duty as a doctor was to . . .'

'It isn't true!' Albert uttered in a toneless voice.

'What isn't true?'

'I didn't kill him. It was my sister . . .'

He bent his head forward as if about to charge.

'That's the story you told Marcel when you came back down on your own. Unfortunately, if Lise had killed the doctor with a hammer from the fruitery, it would never have occurred to her to then wipe the handle. Has she ever even heard of fingerprints? No, my friend! The one who struck him was you, in a fit of anger, and you're going to have another one if you're not careful . . .

'The doctor told you that he wanted to tell his friend Airaud the truth.

'You insisted. You wanted the marriage to go ahead, come what may.

'Then you had one of your usual tempers.

'And do you know . . . Yes, I'd swear to it . . . Do you know what must have gone through Dr Janin's mind when he saw you coming at him like a maniac?

'He must have thought your sister wasn't the only mad one in the family and that . . .'

Albert Forlacroix charged, his features twisted, his eyes shining, his breathing hoarse. But before he could reach Maigret, Marcel had grabbed him by the shoulders, and both of them were rolling on the floor.

Unconcerned by what was happening, Maigret went to the table, poured himself a drink, relit his pipe and wiped his forehead.

'Put the handcuffs on him if you can, Méjat. It's safer.'

It wasn't an easy task, because the two fighters were of more or less equal strength. Forlacroix had managed to seize his opponent's thumb between his teeth and was biting savagely. Marcel was unable to hold back a scream. A handcuff clicked. Méjat couldn't get hold of the other hand and so, in a panic, he started clumsily hitting out like a deaf man, pounding his fists on Albert's face.

Didine's face was pressed to the glass, her nose spread, a gleam in her eyes, the beginnings of a smile of contentment on her thin lips.

'Well?'

'There, chief . . . That's it . . .'

The other wrist had at last been imprisoned in the steel ring.

Marcel Airaud got unsteadily to his feet, squeezing his bloodstained left thumb with his right hand. He, too, seized the bottle of alcohol from the table. But it wasn't to drink from it. It was to pour some on his wound. The bone was exposed.

The gendarme knocked at the door and half opened it.

'Do you need me?'

At that moment Maigret looked at all of them, one after the other, with a vacant eye. He looked at Didine, who was nodding smugly, Méjat with blood on his hands and an expression of disgust on his face, the startled gendarme, Airaud wrapping a check handkerchief around his thumb . . .

Albert Forlacroix got up painfully, or rather sat up on the floor, and remained there, dazed, his body still shaken with spasms.

The silence was such that you could hear distinctly the ticking of the watch on the table. Maigret put it back on the end of its chain. It showed ten minutes past two.

'He made me believe it was her,' Airaud murmured, looking stupidly at his thumb. 'To divert suspicion . . .'

'Will you take care of them, Méjat?'

He went out, lit his pipe and walked slowly to the harbour. He could hear scurrying footsteps behind him. The sea was becoming swollen. The beams of the lighthouses joined in the sky. The moon had just risen, and the judge's house emerged from the darkness, all white, a crude, livid, unreal white.

The footsteps had stopped. Two figures had come together on the corner of the street. Didine had rejoined her one-eyed customs officer, who had been waiting for her, and was talking to him in a low voice.

'I wonder if they'll cut his head off!' she said, pulling her shawl tight about her shoulders to keep warm.

Soon afterwards, a door creaked. They had returned home. They were going to climb up into the high bed with its feather eiderdown and would probably whisper in the darkness for quite some time to come.

Left alone, Maigret caught himself murmuring dreamily:

'And that's it!'

It was over. He might never return to L'Aiguillon. From now on, it would be like one of those distant landscapes, tiny but meticulously accurate, that you see in glass globes: a little world . . . People from far and wide . . . The judge sitting by the fire . . . Lise in her bed, her full lips, her gold-speckled pupils, her swollen breast . . . Constantinesco in the apartment in Versailles, and his daughter on her way to the Conservatoire . . . Old Horace Van Usschen in his excessively light trousers and white woollen cap . . . Thérèse who would get someone to marry her, come what may . . . The widow Airaud, who had been thinking she would be alone for ever in her house, and who would suddenly be reunited with her giant of a son . . .

A regular sound, coming from out of the darkness, made him jump. He remembered that it was old Bariteau, off to lay his eel nets.

Come to think of it, how high was the tide tonight?

PB
82-902
26/12/17